ISBN 9781797600550

TRAITORS, THIEVES AND LIARS

Traitors, Thieves and Liars edited by Sean Gerace
Whatever Happened to Commissioner Sarsuk? edited by Rick Griffin
Cover and illustrations by Rick Griffin
Printed through Amazon KDP

www.rickgriffinstudios.com

For Doug, whose enthusiasm for these silly worlds of mine is and always will be invaluable.

And for Gre7g, who after reading Ten Thousand Miles Up *spontaneously adopted the geroo and let me know there was more potential in this setting, and this story, than I had first considered.*

ANOTHER STORY: Whatever Happened to Commissioner Sarsuk?

Chapter 0: A Lost Hope

This...flagrant display of insubordination would normally meet with the standard company policy," the yellow-scaled Commissioner Sarsuk said, his sharp teeth flashing with each word as though he were baring them on purpose. "But I feel it necessary to lay out the precise depth of your violations. From the moment of your births, you are indebted to us. The company provides you your living space, with plenty of room to grow food, power for your little toys, and a simple method for recycling your waste so you don't continue to wallow in your own filth."

The moment the broadcast had begun, Captain Ateri of the *White Flower II* had been sitting sunken in his rarely used office adjoined to the bridge. Tall and broad-shouldered for a geroo, he normally towered over the other geroo under his command, but at that moment, seeing Sarsuk's smug face on the small screen in front of him, he might as well have been a dust mite. His near-black fur stood on end—he'd been expecting this transmission for a long time.

His mate, Commander Jakari, had been sitting across from him, as they both worked on dry ship business together. They'd been fudging manifest numbers again, quietly shunting company materials to clandestine projects they'd worked on for decades. On hearing Sarsuk's voice, Jakari stood and hurried around the desk to watch the krakun's face onscreen. She wrapped her arms protectively across her broad-shouldered mate. The air turned heavy from their fear-musk. Her long, thick tail had curled around his leg, and his around hers.

Sarsuk inhaled sharply, as if to think about his words, even though he'd clearly scripted this out hours beforehand. "I've made this exact speech far too many times before. None of you were alive when I originally took the post as your commissioner, and so I must make this speech again, and again, and again—" his tone grew angrier with each repetition, "—and again, and *again, and again...*"

He stopped himself, as if to restrain a tremendous outburst of anger. Even half a galaxy away with his face projected onto the display screens throughout the *White Flower II*, Sarsuk, much like every krakun, was huge, Sarsuk himself over five times the height of any geroo—and that was only the vertical. Krakun, being quadrupeds, had horizontal length to contend with as well, adding to how massive they could appear sitting upright on their haunches.

But the geroo were used to Sarsuk's size. No, he terrified the geroo because he could crush them all at a whim; it would, in the end, only require a few minutes of paperwork on his part.

Sarsuk continued after his pause. "And just when I think, maybe, this time, it has sunk into your tiny, primitive brains that you could stand to be genuinely grateful, it comes to my attention you have violated that trust. We allow you pursuits in the sciences to sate your ravenous curiosity and keep those primitive brains as sharp as is necessary for the complex responsibilities entailed in your jobs. And what do I find you doing? Perverting that responsibility by outright hijacking Trinity power to steal the home that the company so graciously provides."

Ateri wasn't certain what Sarsuk was on about—had he discovered the real drive behind the trinity research project? Ateri clutched his chest in a panic. Had someone told Sarsuk about the Exit Plan? Half the ships in the fleet had exit plans, but none had ever succeeded.

The slate that laid immediately before Ateri on the desk, at that moment, carried in it treasonous material. That amounted to *volumes* of data on ways to overcome the trinity—the manner by which they were locked in this life as eternal "employees" of Planetary Acquisitions, Incorporated. Ateri's own Exit Plan was nowhere near freedom yet, as overcoming the trick of the trinity required ages of focused research, and they'd only recently discovered how it even worked, let alone how to modify it! That the company limited each ship to a population of ten thousand meant their own talent pools were small, but enough to make escape under their own power a tantalizing possibility.

And it newly terrified Ateri that he may have spent his whole life taking the bait.

"I dread to think what would have happened if you'd gotten to a stationary gate," Sarsuk continued. "Your presumptuous, naive ideas of freedom would get your whole crew killed by the first enemy who crossed your trajectory, all hands and property lost… You are fortunate this has come to my attention so I can save you from your foolish ambitions. Unfortunately, I cannot deliver your punishment in person, as I am tied up with equally serious business. I figured, however, this would be an excellent time for you to repay your company for its loyalty to you. So, crew of the *Silver Mint III*—"

Ateri exhaled a held breath with a shudder, though it ended with a whimper. Despite how he felt, he'd known Sarsuk hadn't meant *him* or the *White Flower II*. If Sarsuk had meant this ship, he would have *found* time to crush Ateri in person. Ateri's missing eye testified to that.

But knowing Sarsuk's true focus didn't soothe Ateri's nerves even a little. He knew the crew from the *Silver Mint III*. He was friends with its captain, Chinik, though they'd only spoken by correspondence a few dozen times. But he had no idea they'd gotten so far in their trinity research—or even if it was truly the case. More likely they were, like everyone, nowhere near discovering a flaw in the trinity. If Sarsuk so chose, he could invent a reason to punish anyone on the ship, especially on his bad days.

" — the company will simply have to bear the loss of a fleet ship if you are so eager to take it. But you may not take the company's power with you. In three hours, we will shut off the gate, severing the trinity, and you will be free to drift aimless in space until your power fades, your air turns stale, and the last one of you dies in the cold and filth to which you wish to return."

And then, Sarsuk flashed a grin that chilled Ateri to the core.

"However," he said, "because I'm so compassionate, and I understand that it is unlikely that those responsible involved the entire crew, should they have known of this plot at all, I am offering you a lifeline—an opportunity to redeem yourselves, reaffirm your loyalty, and return to my good graces. If you would like to avoid slowly freezing to death, in one hour you will receive a ship. Its crew is under orders to board and wait one more hour. You will stack the pelts of two hundred officers at their paws. They will count them. They will verify with the register that each pelt came from an officer. Only then will you return to the company's good graces, absolved of this misadventure."

Ateri panted hard, on the verge of hyperventilation. Two hundred officers! He had no way to contact Chinik—and even if he could, what would he say? He couldn't intervene, not when they were nearly six hundred light-years apart!

Despite his position in the ship, highest ranked of any individual he'd ever touched paws with—save for Jakari's father, the previous captain—Ateri had always, truly been powerless.

"To ensure this never happens again," Sarsuk concluded, "there will be no more Trinity research. You will have to get by on engineering standards so far as it concerns maintenance—all because you could not manage the simple faith we placed in you. You are not to shelve it. It is all to be deleted. I will verify on my next inspection of each of your vessels."

Ateri had stopped listening by that point.

"Ateri?" Jakari asked quietly when he seemed catatonic.

"Ancestors…" Ateri said, just above a whisper. "We need to call a general meeting. Now."

* * *

Reports of what happened on the *Silver Mint III* poured in before the meeting could gather. Ateri could not bear to look at them—a minimum two hundred officers dead left the entire officer corps of that ship with a few dozen remaining. They received no list yet detailing which officers the panicked crew descended upon like maddened beasts, and which, if any, they spared.

One long report stood out, an audio log. It contained only scattered bits of geroo speaking coherently; the majority was cold, random, and noisy. A loud banging on a door. Incoherent shouts. The flurry of knives plucked from ship kitchens. The heavy swing of unidentifiable blunt tools. The company forbade weapons aboard their gate ships, but that did not render the geroo entirely harmless, especially when pushed to panic.

Ateri leaned on a viewscreen window that lined the left-side wall of the meeting room, his ears lowered as he listened to the recordings. He winced as one scream punctuated the air, female, sounding alarmingly like Jakari's voice under stress.

"No, you can't!"

"Get out of my way!"

"This is wrong! This is—" The voice cut out with a heavy crack and the resonating whine of a metal bar, followed by the sound of retching, and vomit splashing against a wall and floor.

Wet tearing noises punctuated the silence. "That's three… Call Tessi and—what do you mean they're here already? Tell her to stall them!"

"Ancestors damn us…"

The other eleven officers in the room—all ranked subcommander or higher—surrounded the long conference table in various positions of standing, sitting, and leaning. Some engaged in open smoking and drinking; all were listening.

Crack. Gurgle. The sounds of spitting up blood. Ateri, strong as he was, imposing as he appeared, could not handle that sound. Not when it reminded him so pointedly of what happened to Sur'an thirteen years ago. He wiped his eye—his remaining eye, as he only had one left from Judgment Day, when Sarsuk himself had punished Ateri directly for this very sort of thing.

This very thing.

"Gods and ancestors," Ateri croaked, too choked to speak properly. "Turn it off! Father's sake, turn it off!"

Subcommander Tu-ana tapped the button on the slate in the middle of the table, muting the sound.

"Captain, are you alright?" Engineering Chief Otekka asked. The rotund geroo never seemed shaken, even now. He'd seen so much, he'd accepted it as the whims of fate.

Ateri shuddered, sighed, and gathered himself so he could turn to face them all. "In light of these events," he said, trying to sound formal, even with his voice cracking, "I am ordering the Exit Plan canceled."

"What!" The entire meeting erupted into protests. Commander Jakari held her paws up, placing herself between the officers and the captain. They soon quieted and nervously held their tongues.

"The company has decided that Trinity research runs too great a risk of insubordination," Ateri said, turning his head to the side and wiping his only eye to clear it. "And that continuing to pursue it will be at our own peril."

A'hee stood. The fiery red geroo four years Ateri's elder stepped past Jakari into Ateri's personal space, nearly touching nose-to-nose. "We've sacrificed too much already," he stated.

"That doesn't matter, does it?" Ateri countered, exasperated. "We don't have any leverage anymore. What little we had, it's gone! I had been operating this conspiracy under the assumption that the sheer audacity of escape was enough to keep us safe… But that was not the case with the *Silver Mint III*, was it?"

"Are you scared of the crew turning on us if they find out the truth?" A'hee asked, arms folded.

"Yes I'm scared," Ateri said, "but it's not just because I fear being torn limb from limb. What in the five hells do you think the general crew of the *Silver Mint III* are going through, being forced to choose between their own lives and this barbarism? Do you think they're *enjoying* committing these atrocities? That they'll even be able to cope with what they've done? *Do you think it can't happen here?* Would our people forgive us for the same crimes?"

"That doesn't mean we can't hold out hope," A'hee said. "We've always accepted the risk."

"Without the trinity research, we have no Exit Plan. We have no way to bring this ship under our own power. The cloaking device? Useless! Those defensive measures we've been researching? Pointless! Without the aid of the entire fleet science academy, all our progress will come to a standstill. Our only hope is to wait for a savior from the stars! We might as well pray to the gods who went deaf four centuries ago!"

A'hee sat, averting his eyes from the captain.

Ateri sighed. "There is no point in continuing except to risk a ship-wide purge. You are to inform every relevant subordinate that all matters related to the Exit Plan are hereby suspended, permanently, and to not expect their reinstatement again. All data relating to the Exit Plan is to be deleted, and all materials are to be dismantled and fed into the recycler. Dismissed."

The officers left quietly, their heads lowered in defeat, uneasy, some even openly sorrowful.

The last window had closed. They could never leave their employment.

Ateri remained at the head of the empty meeting room with his head in his paws. Jakari grasped his side in a firm embrace. The room was too large with everyone gone, the table too long and too empty, the monitors black and silent. When the subtle ringing of a once-full room had finally left them for the somber electrical hum of the ship, Ateri spoke again.

"I hate myself."

"You're making the best decision you can," Jakari said.

"It's not the best decision. It's a bad decision in place of a worse one! We've worked on this all our lives, and they've beaten us simply by shifting their priorities ever so slightly. We've never had a chance."

The conference room door opened again. Ateri looked up, expecting to see one of the subcommanders returning to fetch something they had left—but it wasn't. The young geroo, half albino-white with mixed-in patches of pigment over the other half of his coat, was Lieutenant Gert, promoted over junior officer not but a month out of the academy.

Ateri forced himself to regain his composure and stood. While Ateri stood taller than most of the crew, that was not true in the case of Gert, who'd reached his full height within the last year. Gert could have easily matched the captain's imposing stature, and his charisma alongside...if he didn't have the demeanor of a huge, lumbering rag doll.

"Captain, I'm sorry to interrupt," he said, as though he'd not just heard the horrible news. "I saw everyone leaving, so I thought it would be a good time to mention a few ideas I had about preserving our research data so that Sarsuk will never find it."

"Gert..." Ateri sighed, trying to mask the sadness in his voice with his usual gruff demeanor.

"We could keep a physical library," Gert said, paying no attention to Ateri's tone. "We can hide it in the spaces between the decks where the commissioner never checks. Looking up information will be much slower than keeping it electronically, but the krakun won't be able to scan our records!"

"Gert, that's impractical," Ateri said.

"Huh?" The smile did not falter from Gert's ears. "Well, I don't mean it'd all go on paper—we could have a dedicated computer system separate from the main network. It'll take time to set up a new system, but—"

"Gert," Jakari said, stepping around and laying her paws on the lieutenant's shoulders. "The captain's made a decision you need to hear," Jakari said.

"What is it?" Gert asked, turning to Ateri, with his ears up and attentive.

And without realizing, Ateri found himself at a loss for words.

Despite his studiousness, Gert had a child-like demeanor he should have grown out of, having just turned eighteen. Despite his peers looking down on him for his strange appearance, he never stopped wanting to help. Even then he was smiling, just for being in the same room as the captain—much like his mother, Sur'an.

Ateri hated himself for what he'd done, to keep the crew of the ship safe. But most of all, he hated himself for betraying Sur'an, who died on that day, deemed Judgment Day, to protect much of this critical information he now ordered destroyed.

Gert's ears slowly wilted as he waited for Ateri to respond.

Ateri saw Sur'an in his eyes. This clumsy, charming, brave patchwork geroo. Ateri had given him so much in penance. Paying for his upper-deck education. Keeping his grandmother who finished raising him in a nice apartment above deck ten. Inviting the little Gert along on lavish officer-only dinner parties. Helping out the lanky teenager learn to live by himself after his grandmother turned sixty. Could Ateri tell him now that his mother had died in vain?

No. That was sacrilege.

"We're scaling things back," Ateri said.

"Sir?" Gert asked.

"What?" Jakari asked, just as confused.

"I had to tell the whole senior staff that the Exit Plan is…not to continue. At least not in its current form. We can't risk having hundreds of officers in on the conspiracy any longer, not when Sarsuk has showed what he will do to us all. So, officially, the Exit Plan is off. Unofficially, we will still work on it together, by ourselves."

Jakari tilted her ears at Ateri strangely, as though he'd lost his mind.

Gert asked, "Then how many of us will stay?"

"Just us," Ateri said, quieter, trying to hide how uncertain he felt about all of this.

"Just three?"

"At the moment. After what's happened on the *Silver Mint III,* we have little in the way of recourse anymore. Right now, it's just a dream. It's doubtful we will get anywhere. But we need to keep it alive, together."

Gert nodded and saluted. "I understand, sir. I'll do my best—eep!"

Ateri pulled him and Jakari in for a firm embrace. He held onto the both of them, though Jakari whispered into Ateri's ear, "Are you sure you want this?"

"I need this," Ateri said. "Sarsuk can kill us if he wants, but we can't let him stamp out our last bit of hope, no matter how small."

FINAL DAYS OF THE WHITE FLOWER II
Book I

TRAITORS
THIEVES
AND LIARS

By Rick Griffin

Chapter 1: There If You Look For It

TEN YEARS LATER

Top Side smelled so nice, with a whiff of dirt and fresh green grass speckled with flowers. Today, the holographic recordings refrained from projecting the normal blue sky, instead opting to just play "birdsong"—small, music-like repetitions that some animals on Gerootec used to make.

An interrupting internal voice, Ateri's voice, repeated the conversation from a year before.

Gert, I want you to succeed me as Captain.

Sir... are you sure? This is me *you're talking about.*

Gert, the future of this vessel is of the utmost importance. You do want the captain's seat, don't you?

Well, yes sir, I do, it would be a great honor.

Gert found Top Side a nice respite from the ever-present ambient noise of the ship. He listened to the eclectic notes and the rushing water of the artificial brook. He ran the soles of his paws along the tips of the long grass just within reach of the sitting bench. He stroked Hiani's soft fur between her ears.

"Gert, can you please pay attention?"

"Huh?" Gert perked his ears and turned back to Hiani, the lovely geroo at his side. He'd been staring up at the orb in the dome—the planet C-18-3, split among the panels of the glass roof, still thousands of kilometers away, with the ship approaching for a final orbital pattern. It wasn't the first planet he'd seen with his own eyes—this one was a dead yellow-brown with fragments of white ice, bearing the scars of ancient oceans and rivers over its surface.

"Daydreaming again…" Hiani scoffed, then buried herself into his side. "I need you here, not somewhere in the stars."

"I'm trying!" Gert said, though the honest fact was he'd been thinking about his role in everything. The captain wasn't long for this galaxy. Soon it would just be Captain Gert and Commander Jakari, and soon after that, just Gert.

He didn't want to think about how lonely he would be, with no captain to support him.

"You're doing it again," Hiani said.

"Sorry," Gert said. "Just wistful, I guess."

"What are you wisting?"

Gert didn't want to spoil the mood with talk about the captain's imminent Going Away, so he brought up something else from recent memory. "Oh, well, you know how nobody's heard from the commissioner in at least…what is it now, six months?"

Hiani tilted her ears in a grin. "I thought you weren't supposed to talk about that."

"It's obvious, isn't it?"

Every day it became more difficult to hide Sarsuk's disappearance. Planetary Acquisitions had said nothing; they only spoke of internal matters on a need-to-know basis, and gate ships were the lowest need.

"I was thinking, if he's gone for good, things might improve around here. No krakun breathing on our heads. Maybe they'll forget about us. We could go off our own way." It was the closest he could honestly come to speaking about the Exit Plan with her. Not that the Exit Plan had gained much ground in the last ten years, either. Maybe Ateri was right, and it all was a pipe dream.

"Yeah, and maybe Krakuntec will explode in an armageddon of candy," Hiani said.

"Hey! I'm serious!"

"So am I." Hiani yarped a giggle. "I could go for some candy right now!"

The scarf she wore around her neck, a deep crimson, looked lovely on her. It made her well-featured face stand out all the more—what with those creamy patches of fur around her cheeks to frame the brown and tan atop the bridge of her muzzle and around her head and ears. She had such dark eyes, both in iris and around the lids, such that the whites appeared like the shimmer of distant lights across a smooth glass.

"Now you're just staring!" she said with a smirk splayed over her ears.

Gert pulled her close and kissed her. She seemed eager to kiss back, though he had to pull away. "I'll be busy today, what with the planet approach and all." He checked his strand. "Uh-oh… I should be going now."

"We are still on for lunch, right?" she asked, her ears turned down in a frown.

"What do you mean? Of course," Gert said, stroking the fur on her cheeks gently with his thumbs. "What's wrong?"

"You've canceled our lunches every day for the last three weeks!"

"I have?" The guilt struck like a punch to the gut.

"Think about it! When was the last time we even ate breakfast together?"

"Two days a… No, that was an officer meeting. Um…last week?"

"You canceled that too."

"Ancestors, I'm so sorry!"

"You've been off working even when you don't have to."

"You know I'm going to be Captain soon," Gert said, his tone getting more defensive than he intended. "There's a lot of responsibilities that go with—"

"Oh, hang the captain!" Hiani declared.

Gert stared at her, shocked with the callousness of her tongue.

"Well..." Hiani started, folding her arms, "I don't know if you really want to be Captain, to be honest."

"Of course I want to be Captain," Gert said. "It's what Ateri wants."

"And you do literally everything for that old cahuan," she said, referring to an extinct animal from Gerootec. "I just wish you'd sit up and notice he's got you by the balls."

"He practically raised me," Gert huffed. "Hiani, you're not acting very fair here. You told me you were okay with my rank."

Hiani planted her paws firmly on her hips. "Yeah, but not when it's getting in the way of you and me."

Gert spread his ears in a smile at her. Hiani wasn't herself interested in becoming an officer, and Gert couldn't fault her for that. In fact, he envied it. It was the biggest reason he enjoyed her company in the first place. When he was with her, he could stop thinking about command all the time and just have some fun!

If only that was a luxury he could afford.

"I'm sorry," Gert said as he rose to leave. "This'll all calm down soon, I promise—"

"Gert..." Hiani held onto his arm

"What is it?" Gert asked, remaining patient.

"Do you take us seriously?"

The question took Gert by surprise. Unknowingly, he pawed at the silver bead on his necklace. It was just one, but it was important to him, especially since he committed a social faux pas to get it. He'd taken it off the necklace of his mother, Sur'an, instead of leaving it where it was in the shrine case.

For the last *month* he'd considered offering it to Hiani. It wasn't a super official thing, but couples who were serious would exchange necklace beads. But he wasn't certain, and not because he didn't like Hiani—he did, he loved her.

But he didn't know what his life was going to look like in two and a half weeks. When the captain was gone…

Hiani's eyes, of course, flitted toward his gesture. She was waiting for him to pop the question, no doubt.

"Of course I do," Gert said. He wanted to add, *I want to spend the rest of my life with you,* but it wasn't the right time. Not when he was in a hurry to get to work.

"Do you want me, or do you want to be Captain?"

"I can have both!" Gert insisted. "Honest."

"Then promise me lunch together today. No canceling."

Gert had to refrain from openly sighing that she didn't herself ask him to become mates just yet.

"I will throw myself prostrate before the captain if I need to," Gert said, crossing his paw over his chest in a salute, which doubled as a sign of one's oath. "Regardless of how much I still need to train for the seat, you are important to me." He turned and sprinted toward the gravity wells. "Top Side Bistro, we can watch the planet up close!"

She gave him a significant look. "I'll hold you to that!" she called after him.

* * *

"Good of you to join us, Gert," Subcommander To'onai said, standing in front of the bridge entrance. The subcommander was a plain brown, gaunt and rugged for a geroo, and wore a permanently cross look about his eyes and ears. It was difficult to look at him and not feel like the object of his gaze had done something wrong.

"I'm on time, aren't I?" Gert asked.

"For your usual shift, yes, but if you'll recall—"

Gert slapped a paw against his forehead. "Dammit, how many training hours do I have left?"

"A hundred and twenty, by my reckoning," To'onai said. "Tesko technically has more hours than you in the captain's chair."

"That's what you get for putting off the training until the very last moment," the red-furred Subcommander Drelis said from the front of the bridge. "You need to be in that chair from shift start to end until the captain's no longer with us."

Gert's shoulders sank. He didn't like hearing them talk about Ateri's Going Away like that—it was utterly unfair that the company required them to *die* on their sixtieth birthday. And every single one of them was going to be subject to that rule.

To'onai's ears spread in a smirk, seeming to take pleasure in Ateri's favorite being taken down a peg. "Oh, don't worry," he said, patting Gert on the elbow. "I won't tattle."

Gert felt flush; he had to get over himself one of these days, he knew it. But To'onai was *deliberately* treating him like a cub.

"Nesti's taking your usual spot on com," To'onai said, pushing at Gert's back.

Nesti waved from the mirror console just behind Drelis, who sat at navigation. The whole bridge was arranged into three rows of consoles with a shallow downward slope toward the room's front, with more consoles along the right-side wall. It would accommodate up to twenty officers at once, though Gert had never witnessed anywhere near that many on the bridge simultaneously and especially not for establishing routine orbit.

The planet C-18-3 and its distant moon drifted across the main viewscreen, taking up the entire front wall. The particular camera facing also caught part of the gate, with a thick glowing band around the edge creating an arc on the screen's left side. Krakuntec would normally be visible from a straight-on view through the gate, but here it was not, just a starfield fifteen hundred light-years away that was nearly indistinguishable from the one behind C-18-3.

"This won't run past lunch, will it?" Gert asked Subcommander Tesko, who stood at the science station. She was glancing over sensor data across a half dozen screens. Tesko was the shortest full-grown geroo Gert knew, and he towered over her. She also wore a pair of large spectacles, her eyes not being conducive to medical correction.

"Orbit, or planetary scans?" Tesko asked.

"Uh, both I guess." Gert shrugged. "I mean if we can knock out the latter, that'd be good too."

"Orbit should only take an hour at most. Scans will take twenty-four hours at least." Tesko pointed to the dry technical data aside the picture readouts on the monitors. "Basalt crust, evidence of molten core, axial tilt, and rotational period within tolerance—seems like we'll be staying."

Gert blinked. "You think it's viable?" he asked, forgetting he wanted off the bridge as soon as he could; he was just as big of a science geek as the science officer herself. If this *was* a viable planet, that would be something remarkable!

Tesko lazily rolled her head and stared at him.

"What?" Gert asked.

"The odds of that are—"

"Nearly six million to one, I know," Gert replied. The entire geroo fleet had found and tested the planets of twenty thousand stellar systems since its inception, so just going by the odds, they still were nowhere near due for a strike. "But you sounded like it—"

"Has the absolute minimums for further testing," Tesko said. "I still say we'll be out of here tomorrow morning."

"How are you certain?" Gert asked.

"Because," Tesko started, like she was repeating herself to her own son, "the odds are—"

"I know, but I've been in here all of thirty seconds and even *I* could see your expression fall the moment the closeup pictures appeared on screen."

Tesko paused and glanced back at the acting captain. She smiled wanly with her ears. "You're right," Tesko said. "My hunch is…it's too yellow."

Gert looked at the picture of the yellow planet right at the end of his muzzle. "I… I thought sulfur *was* yellow." Their krakun masters breathed sulfur, so it only stood to reason they'd want a planet with lots of it.

"Lots of things are yellow," Tesko said. "But I've looked at the before-and-afters of every world the krakun have terraformed, and this is *too* yellow. But we must wait on the full spectrometer readings to know if my hunch is accurate or not."

"And that's disappointing? We still have more or less the same jobs to do regardless."

"I guess…" Tesko started, "but I was reading up on terraformation procedures. We've never had to implement them, but apparently there is a rule, the *Chiauo Gi* rule, that states once we begin the terraformation process, nobody aboard is allowed to die. From execution or Going Away or *anything*. And the process takes at least ten years."

Gert blinked. "Really? Where's *that* in the manual?"

"Section two hundred nineteen, subsection five," Tesko said. "It's buried deep. I'm not sure how serious it is, honestly."

"Then what do they do about suicides?"

"I don't know. I guess there's nothing they can do. It was just a thought anyway. It's about a year too late for it to matter to me…"

Gert nodded. Tesko had lost her own mate the year before. Although the geroo was only fifty, a serious incident had led to ten years being sentenced off his life. Still, the subcommander made Gert curious about *Chiauo Gi,* and wondered if it *really did* mean no executions, but it was at this point only idle speculation. There would be no point to getting his hopes up for a one-in-six-million shot.

Gert approached the seat at the top of the rows of consoles. It was a practical seat—one didn't sit in it like a king of ancient times. It had consoles alongside each arm, because even the captain was expected to work for a living.

Still, Gert touched the armrest reverently. He turned to sit, sliding his tail into the gap underneath the back rest. It was almost too much—his heart pounded in his chest, and he couldn't help but think as he sat there, *I'm not ready*.

But it was his duty to take it on. He closed his eyes and took a deep breath.

"Subcommander Drelis," Gert said, "take us into orbit!"

"Already ahead of you," the red-furred Drelis said from the bottom of the rows of consoles.

"Drelis!" Gert exclaimed, snapping his eyes open. "You're not supposed to do that until I order it!"

Drelis paused, her paws raised over her console. "Uh…" she said. Even her filler utterances twinged with that upper-class accent. "Apologies, sir. I was unaware we were doing this by the book today."

"I can hardly get experience if we don't do at least some things by the book."

"Understood, sir," Drelis folded her ears back in embarrassment. "We should have stability confirmation in fifteen minutes."

"Nesti," Gert told the acting coms officer, "relay our intentions to Krakuntec. Preliminary scans within boundaries of terraforming parameters. Request permission to maintain orbit for twenty-four hours for initial scanning phase."

"I know how it works, Gert," Nesti said from the coms unit just behind operations. She was big—not muscular, nor rotund. There was just a lot of her, especially in her hips. "I've been coms too."

"…That's 'aye aye'," Gert grumbled.

"Aye aye, Subcommander," Nesti said with a clear grin on her ears, putting the emphasis on their shared rank.

Gert sighed. He *should* have made the rank of commander by now. Ranking up wasn't strictly necessary; Ateri could name practically whoever he liked as his successor. Even then, Gert wasn't certain it would have done him much good. He well knew discipline on the ship was lax compared to his imaginings of a real command structure—listen to that, "real" command structure, like they were playing pretend.

In the sum totality of the universe, they *were*. This pageantry was solely for obscenely wealthy krakun far away who stood to become even more obscenely wealthy. Gert considered whether he was just being uptight. His only real knowledge of how a crew should respect a captain came through Ateri, and, well, he by far wasn't Ateri.

Maybe that was the problem.

Soon, Gert was back to wondering how he could have a future with Hiani when they could barely get their schedules to align on the best days. He constantly clung to guilt over working all the time, and even when he was working he felt guilty about not doing enough.

Gert was so lost in thought that it took several seconds before he noticed the light blinking on the console aside the captain's chair. Not unexpected—even with the lack of regular communications from Krakuntec, Gert presumed they'd send a curt affirmation to continue on with their orbit.

That was not what he received.

Once Gert tapped the message on his console, a video appeared. Gert's throat tightened—the krakun's face took up the entire screen, and for a moment, it reminded Gert of that day ten years ago when the *Silver Mint III* had its officers all purged.

He recognized the face, however—there was no mistaking the deep, shadowy black face and steel gray neckline of CEO Thrull.

"This message is for the captain and crew of the *White Flower II*," the krakun said. Suddenly, all around the bridge, geroo perked their ears. That was Krakunese they heard, and it bewildered them to say the least; they'd just gotten comfortable with never hearing a krakun voice again.

Gert tapped in the command to dump the contents of his monitor onto the main viewscreen. This was clearly a recording that the CEO left, though why he addressed the geroo directly... Well, normally he had commissioners to do that. The only reason Gert even recognized Thrull was from press releases and broadcasts meant for the company's real market on Krakuntec that was relevant to fleet operations. The officers on the bridge stopped and braced themselves for the inevitable bad news.

"Attention! This message will only play once. Your new commissioner has been selected. From now on, Pokokuro will assume Sarsuk's former commission. The *White Flower II*, being the first ship to reach a planetary destination since her appointment, will be first to host her. I expect all employees to treat her with the dignity and courtesy expected of her position. In one hour, she will—"

Everyone held their breath for a heartbeat, until it became clear the video had frozen. Gert tilted his head. "Uh," he started, "Nesti? Why did the video freeze?"

"I...don't know," Nesti said.

Gert rescinded the video message of Thrull from the main viewscreen, then tapped in commands at his console to see what Nesti was looking at. He checked the communication line for interruptions, but all of it was working.

"Ping the relay just outside the gate," Gert said. That was the last relay before messages bounced to Krakuntec.

"I can reach the gateside relay just fine," Nesti said. She turned to look at Gert. "I think the connection problem is on their end."

"That's impossible," To'onai said. "They have so many redundant relays on their side—"

Tesko adjusted her spectacles as she stared at the main screen, which now showed its original view. "Is something wrong with the gate?"

Gert turned to the screen with C-18-3 and the edge of the gate on the left side. It still seemed to be operating fine, with its glow still vivid and bright. "What makes you say that?" Gert asked.

"The hum changed," Tesko said. There was an omnipresent hum whenever the gate was running, though it was so low and constant most geroo had completely filtered it out of their perceptions, if they could even hear it at all.

Gert perked his ears. He wasn't sure if he heard the pitch-shift.

"I thought I heard that too," Nesti said. "I don't know, it's just…what if there was a weird power spike somewhere along the trinity?"

"Check up on the trinity right away," Gert said, pointing to Tesko.

"Aye aye, sir," Tesko said, as she at once put in a call to contact engineering.

Gert, meanwhile, brought up other monitoring cameras from the hull on his console, choosing one with a significantly better angle—and yet, when he looked through the gate to where Krakuntec should have been, there was nothing.

Seeing the empty spot was so eerie, Gert's neck fur stood up. The… The gate was still open, wasn't it?

"Tesko?" Gert turned to the science officer. "I'm not seeing Krakuntec."

Tesko paused, then turned. "What?"

Gert replaced the planetside view on the main screen with that of the head-on view of the gate.

"Uh, hmm…" Tesko was at a loss for words.

"Well," Drelis said from the bottom row of the bridge, "could the sisterside gate be moving?"

"I suppose it's possible," Tesko said. "But I'd have to guess that our gate was switched off."

"It must be," Gert said. "Shit. Maybe the rail broke, but the magnetic coil is still spinning." He was not looking forward to *that* spacewalk. Moving about on the outer hull of the ship, he'd done that before many times for maintenance and repairs. But the gate? That thing was five hundred meters in diameter. They couldn't afford to have it off for more than a few weeks, which could necessitate having dozens of geroo out in the vacuum of space for inspections. Geroo had died trying to repair that thing.

It was their only connection to the rest of the universe. Without the gate, they were dead. They couldn't even power the ship without the gate, due to krakun technowizardry known as "the trinity". It was a link between the gate, the drive, and the ship's recycler such that they all required running simultaneously. They still had enough fuel to power themselves for several weeks, but they wouldn't be able to go anywhere. Just starve and die.

Although it wasn't his field, and as the captain his job was to delegate, Gert checked the status of the trinity himself. He tilted his ears. Normally, if the gate had shut down, the whole Trinity would power down in moments. But the drive and the recycler were both online.

"Hey Tesko—" Gert started again.

"What is it?" she asked, focused intently on her screen.

"The Trinity's still—oh." Gert tilted his ears the other way. Now the drive and the recycler read as offline. "Guess I spoke too soon."

A delay in the trinity going offline… Stranger still. Something was deeply wrong. If the trinity went offline, the gate should stop at once. It could receive power, sure, but it was such a power draw it normally shut down automatically.

Suddenly, the entire ship violently lurched. Gert gasped and clutched at his chair fiercely. To'onai and Tesko had to grab hold on their consoles to keep from being tossed to the floor. Officers standing at the wall consoles stumbled and fell.

Even when deep space micrometeorites occasionally struck the shields, that was just a rumbling noise echoing in the hull. But no, this was full-on vibration, with everything rattling, as though the floor was about to lurch from underneath.

And then it stopped just as suddenly as it began, having barely lasted a full second. A warning siren sounded on the bridge.

"Ancestors save us!" Subcommander Drelis proclaimed, furiously inputting commands into her console. "Orbital engines are out of alignment!"

"Is it bad?" Gert asked, his voice faltering as he realized, even now in the middle of a crisis, he stated it in the dumbest way possible.

"Bad, yes," Drelis echoed, her hyperventilation slowing to long breaths. "Deadly, fortunately not. Probably related to the trinity going offline. Just…give me a few minutes to figure out how that threw us!"

The entire bridge crew recovered from various stages of staggering. The whole population of the ship must have felt it. Within moments, Nesti's console flooded with calls.

"Aw, dammit," she said. "Can someone take some of these? I've got fifty reports already…"

"Pass them to me," Gert said. "Let's get this cleared up."

"Someone should call the captain," To'onai said.

In a different situation, Gert would have felt bothered that To'onai didn't think Gert could handle this. But then again, Gert was only acting captain, and Ateri was going to need it explained this was definitely not Gert's fault, imminent Going Away or not.

"Then do it! Tell him we have things under control," Gert said. He shuffled through the flood of messages pouring onto his console.

"Most of these are going to medical bay," he said aloud, trying not to panic. It was the most unusual thing that'd happened in such a long time, and his chest tightened in response. Was Hiani okay? He couldn't let himself get distracted now when he had an entire ship to care for.

"I've counted at least a dozen reports of minor injuries already," Nesti said. "One runabout wreck on deck nine… Fire suppression has kicked in at various parts of decks five through seventeen. Recycler bay's sent ten reports in the last two minutes alone."

"We won't have enough medical. Send those reports to security," To'onai said as he punched in a call on his personal strand. "Uh, Captain, sorry to wake you…"

"What the five hells was that, Subcommander?" Ateri sounded tinny over the strand. "We're fortunate we were lying down! Just tell me, did we run into the moon?"

Gert fussed about more with the messages, trying his best to clear them all as fast as he could parse them, but they just kept pouring in from Nesti's console. Then he stopped at one message in particular, between the columns thick with them.

Among all the unusual things that happened within the last ten minutes, this should have been the least among them. On its face it looked like a jumbled barrage of random characters. He should have dismissed it as a message that got corrupted somewhere along the line, but that itself was such a rare occurrence, he instead clicked on it to inspect.

No, the characters weren't random, despite being a bizarre mix of geroo and krakun letters. They were arranged in such distinct clusters that Gert could imagine them pronounced together.

Officers called out orders to one another: Subcommander Drelis frantically recalculating the orbital trajectory, To'onai juggling his strand and his own flood of messages to the rest of security, Tesko still trying to diagnose the issue…while Gert was toying with a weird puzzle.

He mentally slapped himself for it, and for this mind of his that got stuck on the most trivial things at the worst times. He kept passing the other messages he received over to To'onai before they noticed his mind was on something else.

The first several letters—krakun *aith*, geroo *be*, geroo *eh*, krakun *chog*, geroo *hee*, krakun number for sixteen pronounced *aru*…

"*Abechi-aru*…" Gert pronounced under his breath. He blinked. That was the ringel word for *attention*.

Gert jumped out of his seat and ran for Nesti's console.

"Nesti, pass those messages to Lieutenant Arvo," Gert said.

"But I finished—"

"I'll pass them back to you," Gert said. He opened a drawer beside Nesti's chair—Gert's usual chair—and he pulled out a pad of plastic scratch paper and a pen. It seemed like paper would be an obsolete technology out in space, when all messages could save to the computer. But the company relay command on Krakuntec monitored all transmissions, and so having a pad of paper nearby often proved handy when coded messages were involved.

"What are you doing?" Nesti asked.

"I don't know yet!" Gert rushed back to the captain's seat, though he didn't bother sitting down.

"*Abeichi-aru… sahg… sahlg?… Arahbe…*" *The captain*? Gert furiously scribbled down each of the word clusters together as best as he could figure.

"Gert?" To'onai asked, looking over at him. "What in the five hells are you doing?"

"*Abechi-aru sahlg arahbe Finan Dohuo Chyo*…" Gert pronounced his own words back to himself.

"What's that mean?" To'onai asked.

"Uh…" Gert muttered. If he had any more unwelcome surprises this morning, he expected his heart just might explode inside his chest. "I need to speak with the captain right away."

Chapter 2: Regrets

You made a terrible mistake.

You should never have canceled the Exit Plan. Protect your people, yes, but you let your fear get the best of you. You crushed everyone's hope so you could save them.

They never forgave you for it.

THOOM.

Ateri jumped from his bed and at once regretted it; his tail had developed a crick, and it was painful. He rubbed the sleep out of his one remaining eye—the other having a metal placeholder that always felt odd to the touch, even if it also crusted with sleep.

Jakari, next to him, stirred, though she'd taken the sudden rattling of the ship gracefully. Ateri had been too close to a heart attack too many times already, but the shaking lasted less than a second. It was less awful than the adrenaline coursing through his veins insisted it was.

Some seconds later, as he tried to decide if he should wake her, his strand on the bedside dock beeped at him.

"Uh, Captain?" To'onai's voice came in over his strand. "Sorry to wake you…"

"What in the five hells was that, Subcommander? We're fortunate we were lying down… Just tell me, did we run into the moon?"

"We are not sure yet, but I haven't seen evidence of a hull breach…"

"Is that the alarm I hear?" Ateri grumbled.

"Yes, sir. Minor medical emergencies. In fact, it's not that bad from the looks."

"Just scaring the ancestors out of their graves," Ateri said. "Is Gert doing alright?"

"He's doing fine, sir."

"Then let him handle it. I was hoping to sleep in today."

"Yes, sir. I'll leave you to that, sir."

Ateri ended up tossing the strand on the floor. It slid over the carpet and under a loose blanket on the floor where it muffle-beeped—likely someone else calling who didn't need a response. They could call the bridge.

The floor was a mess—it always had been. Boxes, cards, batteries, bottles, cans, polymer bags, trophies, knick-knacks, a tile game set, dishes, standalone computer slates Ateri hadn't yet returned, and a myriad other devices heaped around the edges of the room, waiting for a more opportune time to organize.

There was never enough time.

Ateri winced as he turned out of his bed, and the sharp pain in his spine forced him to gasp, and he groaned.

"Hon?" Jakari, from the position in bed next to Ateri, sat up on her elbows and yawned. She looked unsullied, her soft pale fur seeming to glow in the low light of the room. "Are you all right?"

"Think I threw my back out," Ateri muttered. "Or something's out of place."

"From that jostle?"

That was far more than a jostle. Jakari must have been sleeping a lot deeper than he had.

"No," Ateri said. "Just moving after it…"

"Want me to page the doctor?"

"They will be swamped for the next five hours. I can manage."

"No, you can't. Here, lie on your front."

Wincing, Ateri lay down on the mattress, burying his muzzle into the still-warm pillow. Jakari straddled his tail and shoved the flat of her paws deep into his back. She mostly missed the actual problem area, but it was always nice to have her strong, warm paws there. As much as Ateri hated growing older, besides the all-too-frequent pains and aches, the problems that developed didn't seem to stymie his strength.

What a waste to see it all gone because of the predetermined limit.

Jakari's ear twisted toward the muffled beeping. "Is that your strand?"

"It can wait a minute— Yeeeowch!" Ateri contorted as Jakari's palms shoved something inside him, which popped and cracked as the bones moved back in place. "...I need to lie here for that long. Thank you, Commander. Hopefully my legs don't go numb."

"Need something for the pain?" Jakari climbed off her mate and rubbed his back in shallow, clockwise circles.

"Just one pill."

Jakari rummaged through her bedside stand—full of empty and half-empty medicine bottles—for the proper container, double-checked the print on the front, and shook one of the small white pills into her paw. She pushed it with a finger between Ateri's teeth, and he chewed it and swallowed. He felt stupid about it, much like any time he had to rely on someone else, but it was a great comfort knowing Jakari was still there and would still be there for a while longer.

Without prompting, Jakari climbed off the bed and rummaged with her paws through the mess on the floor, looking for Ateri's strand. But the moment she answered, there would be no excuses for him to ignore what was in front of him, and he'd be off captaining and performing his captainly duties, despite his sixtieth quickly approaching. It was as close as anyone ever came to a vacation.

"I had an odd dream," Ateri said, to stall her.

"Odd of you to bring it up," Jakari said.

"It was of your father."

Jakari swiveled her ears and cocked her head at the captain. Ateri left out the part where a good part of his dreams were nightmares, as happened when one's old friends ended up dying in violent ways, because Jakari already knew all of that. She was often the only one allowed to see the captain in his weakness.

"I know what you'll say," Ateri said. "It's anxiety. Not one of us wants to die on our sixtieth, no matter how slowly it sneaks up on us. Well, Captain Idal was there reminding me I am going to die because everyone is mortal. But even on medieval Gerootec, even if the average age at death was forty, we often reached ninety, or a hundred years of age, and medicine unhampered by our limited resources could push it farther. Then he said that if I am so determined to die when I reach sixty, I might as well put my all into the Exit Plan."

"Hon…" Jakari frowned. "That's no longer in our paws. My father passed the duty onto you, and you will pass the duty onto Gert. That's how it has always gone."

"But we canceled the damn thing, and now I'm regretting it. We were so close I could taste the fresh air of a new world! Then, it's just us three."

"That was not your fault," Jakari said. "You made the right call."

"I know, but I disappointed everyone. Myself especially." Ateri sighed into the pillow. "I can't help but feel tempted. The only chance I have of seeing my sixty-first is if we uncanceled the Exit Plan and pushed things into motion *now*. Not in another century after which it may already be too late for all of us."

"It's only seventeen days until your birthday," Jakari said. "That's not enough time."

"I know, I…" Ateri sighed. "I know."

"Love…" Jakari lowered her voice. "Did you want me to arrange a fake death?"

Ateri snorted and chuckled to himself. "I appreciate the offer, but I'd rather go about this honorably."

"I'm just saying, we've pulled it off before, we could do it again."

"That wasn't even our doing. And it didn't mean trying to hide one of the most recognizable pelts in the fleet."

"Well, they have plastic surgeons on the *Golden Strand IV*. We could sneak a transfer over there, replace your eye, bleach your pelt—"

"Hon, I am not going into hiding just to live the rest of my days working for Planetary Acquisitions anyway!" Ateri hoped he didn't sound as angry as he figured the words sounded. "Even if the admiral approved—and he wouldn't—it's not that I want to survive. I want to *succeed*. If I died, but the plan succeeded…I'd be satisfied."

"You never know," Jakari said, turning back again to scrounge for the fallen strand. "Perhaps our commissioner's absence is a sign that the company will hand control of the fleet over to us!"

"Jakari, I love you, but don't make me laugh when I have back pain."

He rolled so he was facing his nightstand, and pressed a paw to his back—still sore, swollen but not painful. Jakari rejoined him on the bed, wrapping her arms around him from behind as she kissed him, and dropped his strand onto the mattress before him.

"Oh, you found it," Ateri said flatly.

"It's fine, it's not important," Jakari said, kissing him more on his neck. "We still have an hour to lie here, or do other things…"

"I like other things." Ateri leaned back as much as his loosening back would allow and nuzzled her. "Though speaking of, do you ever regret I passed on your father's birth token?"

He didn't say it out loud, but as Idal promised, Ateri regretted the decision not to take the former captain's birth token. There was always an edge of stoicism to everything Ateri did for the good of the crew, including taking his and Jakari's name off the lottery, and it would be silly to place it back on now. Jakari could still bear a child, but she was fifty-five herself, and those five years would have ensured that such a child would grow up without parents.

"Regret?" she asked. "No, not regret. As much as I'd have loved a cub of our own, I don't know if it's right to bring one up in this place."

"Maybe when we hypothetically fake my death, we could hypothetically have a cub off the record, too."

"While we're dreaming, let's go mountain climbing. I always wanted to stand on top of the world and look out and see nothing but open land for a thousand kilometers."

"That sounds amazing." Ateri yawned. "What was it anyhow?"

"Hmm?" Jakari hummed into his back.

"On my strand, who was paging me?"

"Oh, it was just Gert."

Ateri's ears involuntarily twitched. Though, just because Subcommander Gert wanted their attention didn't mean it was trouble. But he was still a hundred hours short for a promotion to commander himself, and that was five hundred hours in! He couldn't come to Ateri with every single problem he had; that would defeat the whole purpose of taking command.

"What'd he want?" Ateri asked.

"It's not important. Something about the running lights on the gate…"

Ateri snapped open his good eye. A chill ran down his back, and Jakari felt it from her position, since she pulled away.

Ateri yanked himself out of Jakari's arms and dressed, pulling his shoulder cuff over his arm and shoving the strand inside, grabbing his eyepatch from the nightstand and affixing it. He then pulled his boots on—not necessary, but always a fine addition when one didn't know where they would tread.

"Captain!" Jakari exclaimed, just as on edge as her mate. "That wasn't a code, was it?"

"We've been hailed. Top secret."

"An ark?"

"Pirates."

Jakari's eyes widened and her ears flattened.

"I know this ruins our morning plans, but we have a duty, Commander," Ateri reminded her.

"Yes, Captain."

She dressed much the same way as her mate, though Ateri kept the pocket with his strand on the opposite shoulder from tradition, for what were obvious reasons to anyone who thought about it long enough. But besides the tail ring and the crewman's boots, Jakari tied a sash around her midsection, with the knot above the base of her tail.

"Jakari…"

"If we are dying today, I want to look fashionable. It'll be the last chance I get."

Ateri kissed her. She seized him and kissed back with a show of force, clutching his shoulders in her paws, her tail perked up as she did so. Ateri let her and asserted himself in return, though there was no chance of a last-minute romp. They released one another, nodded in unison, and turned for the apartment door.

Ateri tapped his strand with his free paw, the other entwined with Jakari's. "Gert, we're coming."

There was only one section of apartments on the top deck, just underneath Top Side Command, though the building wasn't used for its intended purpose. Neither was the whole of Top Side. The enormous space used to be an observatory in its history, but had instead become something of a terrestrial dome. As the captain and his mate could live anywhere they wished, he'd chosen a block around Top Side's edge, even though the actual living space was small. But it was a reminder every time they stepped outside together how beautiful the limited greenery was, and how more beautiful still it would be if they could find an endless expanse to call their own.

A wedge of light shone between the dark sun panels that blocked the geodesic glass dome over the top of the ship— composed of triangular panels, not noticeable unless the solar shutters closed to block the light of a nearby star. The planet C-18-3 and its moon drifted across the clear side of the dome—a dead yellow-brown planet with fragments of white ice, bearing the scars of ancient oceans and rivers over its surface. The planet was not important to any of them, so far as their little limited lives were concerned, as it was just another stop in their endless journey across the galaxy.

"After you, Commander." Ateri opened the passenger door to the runabout.

"Thank you, Captain." Jakari bowed and moved in, threading her tail through the opening in the back of the seat.

He started up the electric engine and coasted across Top Side's expanse.

Chapter 3: The Situation

*A*ttention: Captain of the White Flower II. *We have disabled your ship's Trinity. We demand parlay at no later than 1000 hours. Any attempt at resistance will be disastrous, regardless of your unlikely chance at victory by arms. You are to come alone to the coordinates listed below. You will not be harmed, and shall be returned promptly should you cooperate.*

Ateri lowered the slate and laid it on the conference table. He, Jakari, and Gert were the only ones in the conference room offside the bridge. Gert folded his paws, looking away like he'd done something wrong.

Ateri didn't even know what to feel at this point; the situation seemed unreal, like it wasn't happening just yet. Outside this room, the ship was still in a state of minor panic, with the trinity down and injuries all over. His crew could handle that; he'd been confident enough of that to nearly roll over and go back to sleep. Mostly, all the officers needed to do was act like they knew what the hells was going on and were on their way to fixing it.

This was one complication too many. He wanted this shit to stop happening to his people.

"Is this a prank?" Jakari asked, her mouth hanging open in shock as she read the message off the slate.

"That seems unlikely," Ateri said. "Someone aboard just happens to know Ringelese, just happens to send this message to the bridge the moment that the trinity shuts down in unusual circumstances?"

"How could they have known we'd catch it?" Jakari asked.

"Interesting you should ask," Ateri said, tugging his strand out of his shoulder band. "You looked at my stand and said Gert had contacted me, but it was still blinking after To'onai had ended the call."

"Oh… That's right, there was another message on there, but it was from an unknown number. I figured it wasn't important."

Ateri looked at his messages list and tilted his head. "Hmm. It seems to have deleted itself."

"It wouldn't surprise me if they surreptitiously sent the message all over in places you'd likely see it," Gert said. "Prompt you to seek a code-breaker. I just noticed it first."

"How'd you even notice?" Ateri asked.

"It seemed straightforward," Gert said. "The moment I tried to pronounce the letters regardless of origin, it fell into place. They wanted you to break the code, but it had to look like gibberish otherwise. The only uncertainty left would be no one onboard knowing a word of Ringelese Standard."

Gert was not the only geroo onboard who knew Ringelese, but studying other languages was more a pastime than a necessity. Sure, they had to communicate with other species owned by the krakun from time to time and so having translators at paw were often helpful, since the krakun loathed the slave species dirtying Krakunese by speaking it so imperfectly.

Gert studied those languages for fun, and so relieved others of the burden of learning them. It seemed to pay off in this case—could the pirates have known who aboard could speak their language?

"Do the pirates know we saw the message?" Ateri asked.

Gert shrugged. "We have read receipts in the system, but I don't know how the pirates tapped in. The message didn't seem to have a valid origin I could trace."

Ateri sighed and tilted his head at the message. This wasn't the first time his ship was put at risk, but every other time it was at Sarsuk's own doing. Pirates were something altogether new, even if they also were not unheard of. They had secret codes for many unlikely scenarios. Ateri had met with pirates once before, a long time ago. It seemed impossible these were the same ones, ringel or not.

This kind of meeting was inevitable. The slave ships of Planetary Acquisitions were ripe for picking off by pirates. Their primary defense was that they were far, far out in unknown space, much farther away than any pirate would dare travel, but they had an enormous amount of proprietary krakun technology aboard. Ateri had a history of trading such secrets—his missing eye would attest to his commitment—but a krakun slave ship would be a tantalizing prize should any pirate ship find their way to one.

"We don't have many good options here," Jakari said. "Should we tell the rest of the officers?"

"I'm not certain," Ateri said. Whether to tell the crew in general, definitely not. Widespread panic would be the certain outcome of that, and the result of panic would be someone doing something stupid. No matter what they decided, it had to be a secret.

"How many geroo aboard speak Ringelese?" Ateri asked. "Estimate for me."

"Erm, it's not a super popular subject." Gert pulled out his strand and went through video and book download lists. "Most of my live classes were just me and a couple cubs trying for a language credit—I think there's maybe a dozen aboard who have a rough handle on the language, but they wouldn't have practiced much since primary school, at least not to the extent I have."

Jakari nodded. "Most geroo don't keep up with those studies unless it's relevant to their job."

"I might be the only *adult* who's downloaded the language materials in the last forty years," Gert concluded.

"And there's no sign of a ship sharing orbit with us?" Ateri asked, turning to his mate.

"Not that I saw," Jakari said. "But that means nothing if they're using a cloak."

"I figured as much," Ateri said. "At least that all means we *can* keep it a secret for the moment. However, they've not given us a wide window by which to act. We should decide whether to tell anyone else only after I've heard what they have to say."

"You can't go out there by yourself!" Gert said.

"I'm not. By their brazen actions, they've made it clear they wish to play a very dangerous game, and if I should do anything, it should demonstrate that I will not be their pawn to act as they command. So, I want you to come with me."

Gert lowered his ears. "Me?"

Ateri tilted his head. Gert never shirked his duty. Forget or have it slip his mind, yes, but never shirk.

"I'm not scared!" Gert said. "...okay, I'm scared. But...how long is this going to take?"

"Is that important?" Ateri asked. "We are talking about averting a potential pirate attack here."

"I...I had lunch plans with Hiani, and I promised her," Gert said. He lowered his head. "Yeah, it sounds stupid when I say it out loud. But it's not like I can tell her, hey, cancelling lunch again, pirates are happening."

"I could come instead," Jakari said. "Gert still needs to log time in the chair."

"Unfortunately, we may need you here in case Krakuntec calls back," Ateri said. Normally, it took seventeen hours to bring the trinity back online minimum, but this was clearly not a normal shutdown. Who knew when it might revert itself? "The next-highest-ranking officer should be here to deal with whatever's happening with the new commissioner. Besides, we may be fortunate and they may be looking to strike a deal, in which case, I need our next captain to listen in on the discussion."

Jakari nodded, but Gert still twisted uncomfortably.

"Gert?" Ateri asked. "Are you alright?"

"Yes, sir," Gert said. "Just, give me a minute to call Hiani."

* * *

For five minutes, Gert's finger hovered over the call button. He felt awful inside, like every part of him below his chest was crumbling into some black rot and falling out from underneath him. How should he even go about it? Did females like it when a male acted self-assured? Should he be contrite? It didn't matter. She would hate him for this.

After breathing calmly for another full minute, he tapped the button. Then was the long wait for her to pick up her own strand. He strummed his fingers on the conference table, pondering if he should open the electronic tile game on his strand just so he didn't have to be alone with his thoughts.

"Gert?" Hiani asked, her wonderful face appearing onscreen.

"Hey…" Gert said. "Are you alright? That was a nasty shake we had."

"Yes, I am," Hiani said, ears perked in a smile. "Fortunately the new manufacturing facility is well-secured. We've been looking around for damage and only found that a few things fell over, nothing major broken. I've been calling around and it seems everyone's okay, thank the ancestors!"

Gert tried his best to not wince. If she knew the ship was okay after that shock, the harder it would be to convince her that something was wrong.

"How are things up on the bridge?" she asked.

"Some things are…" Gert started, then swallowed. "Well, a few… There were a lot of minor incidents all over the ship, but there were also…major things I need to attend to, and—"

"You're canceling," Hiani said, her ears and eyes narrowing out.

"The captain needs me to handle this! We're spread thin at the moment—"

"You're the communications officer, Gert!" Hiani said. "Anything that could be wrong in your department, engineering would handle it better! Go back to the captain and tell him you deserve to have lunch today, ship-quake or no! We'll survive you having an hour off."

"He…" Gert averted his gaze. "He can't. It needs to be me."

"You didn't even argue with him!"

"I did!" Gert countered. "But I agree with him. Nobody else can do this job right now!"

"Is this about the captain's chair?" Hiani asked, her frustration growing. "I told you I didn't care about that!"

"What?" Gert stammered. "No! I mean, yeah, I still have a lot of hours to put in for the chair, but this has nothing to do with that. I swear, tomorrow we can do Top Side! What's wrong with lunch tomorrow? The restaurant will still be there. Hopefully."

Hiani sighed, her anger shifting over to hurt. "Right, whatever," she said with tears in her eyes. "That's the last time I date an academy boy…"

"Hiani—"

Her picture disappeared from the strand screen.

"Hiani, wait!" Gert said, far too late for her to hear. Gert smacked his strand against his forehead several times. "Ugh, mother…" he half-prayed, half moaned. "Why does it have to be like this?"

He considered calling her back right away, but the last thing he wanted to do was make himself look so desperate. She wouldn't listen to him unless he chose her over his duty! Or maybe she wanted him to keep trying… Though after her last comment, she clearly didn't want this anymore.

Who'd want me anyhow? I'm the most spineless geroo on this ship when it comes down to the important things…

He considered walking away from his duty, but that thought lasted only for a breath. No, he couldn't live with himself if he up and quit the moment the ship and his captain needed him the most. If he had to suffer heartbreak for the good of everyone, then so be it.

Gert stifled his tears, though he had to blow his nose and sniffle a few times before he was fit to return to work. Ateri wanted him down at airlock four, the area closest to where the pirates wanted to meet them. He put on brave ears before turning and leaving the conference room.

Chapter 4: Love in All The Wrong Places

Gert locked the helmet on, and it treated his ears to a loud, rushing hiss. At once the HUD inside the helmet flashed, reading, "Systems primed and ready."

"I don't feel ready," Gert said. The suit, like many of the environments suits, used the strands for radio contact. His mind was still on Hiani, thinking of a few ways to apologize to her, but he'd been through the song and dance enough times it made him empty inside.

He'd hoped Hiani would be the one, but...

"The suit knows what it's doing better than you," Ateri said. The golden anti-glare screen covered his face, save for the vaguest outline. "Unless you mean how the inner seal is riding up your backside. That's normal."

"Well, yeah, but that's not what I mean," Gert said, trying to scratch at the base of his tail, an impossible act between the bulky gloves and the thick outer suit.

He tried to push fear out of his thoughts. He knew what he was getting into when he signed up for the academy, and when Ateri asked him to be part of the Exit Plan conspiracy. It had gotten his mother executed. He wanted to do her *and* Ateri proud.

That was before he'd let himself think about the pirates.

He'd never even seen a ringel in person. Only his language studies had given him an idea of their demeanor—rude and crude. That characterization must have been unfair; he was sure nice ringel existed somewhere in known space—they were just stereotyped as aggressive, hypersexual thieves, right?

But he had to get over himself, and so did his duty, despite his fear. He tried his best not to hyperventilate.

The airlock pumps switched on and hummed as the air evacuated the tiny space. His HUD beeped at him, warning Gert that his heart rate was too high. He stared at the outer airlock door, waiting for it to crack open so he'd face the infinite, empty void of space with nothing but a thin shell of atmosphere keeping him alive.

The airlock door shifted and slid open. Gert took a deep breath and followed Ateri out.

The boots of the pressure suit stuck to the outer hull, their magnetic seal-and-release process allowing normal walking without letting both paws leave the hull at the same time. Nevertheless, the whole null-gravity process was disorienting. As they stepped over the edge of the airlock lip, they both turned ninety degrees, so the sheer drop became instead a rolling landscape of metal before them. Gert felt too slow and lightweight. His organs shifted around inside.

Ateri groaned over the strand.

"Captain, you doing all right?" Gert asked, a fine thing to do since he desired to throw up inside his helmet. He'd done the spacewalk enough to know how to handle himself in null gravity, but he still never considered he would become used to it.

"I'm fine, it's just been a while since my last spacewalk."

Looking back and forth across the vast hill that was the hull though, Gert saw nothing, and he looked up into the stars above, perhaps at first to glimpse a ringel ship he missed.

And it struck him—how many points of light there were in the whole sky, including the thick band where they clustered closer to the galaxy center. In the galaxy alone there were a hundred billion stars—*a hundred billion!* It would take fifty lifetimes to just visit every star for one second apiece, and there were a trillion more galaxies just like this one. He'd known it before; it had fascinated him since he was a child just how much bigger everything was than their tiny, isolated ship, moving from light to light at a rate of one star every decade. In the scope of things, the fears he had about his tiny, isolated dot in the middle of nowhere seemed almost—

"Watch your head," Ateri radioed.

"What?" Gert turned to the captain, and then THUNK. His helmet collided with a flat surface, starting up that awful ringing in his ears again.

The lack of gravity kept him from falling, but he flailed in place a few seconds, trying to return his other boot to the hull surface. He twisted his head around, still seeing nothing to run into. Ateri put his gloves up and pressed against…nothing.

"Right here, Subcommander," Ateri said.

Gert put his paws up, and a strange tingling sensation ran across his fingers, like static electricity only something else, as his fur didn't stand up in his gloves.

"Oh… Oh!" Gert said. "That's right, the cloaking devices…"

He hadn't considered their small shuttlecraft would itself use a cloak. He'd never seen one in operation, as the company expressly forbid the devices. So of course Ateri had done his best to acquire one, years ago. That whole incident led to…

Gert realized there were many things he should not think about, because they all led down the path of awful intrusive thoughts. His life wasn't a total wreck, for all the things he pretended were fine. His mother died so long ago, and it still hurt to think about it.

Still, it hadn't occurred to him that a cloak would be so perfect, especially for a tiny shuttle.

"Erm," Gert started, "how do we tell them we're out here?"

As if on cue, the nothing opened between them, folding out a small staircase that led into a much smaller airlock. It was eerie watching it through the absolute lack of sound.

The opening seemed to flicker in and out of existence, like a viewing monitor that had its receiver improperly hooked up.

"After you." Ateri held his paw out to the opening.

Gert looked into the small room floating in space, with no clear shape backing it from the other side.

"Captain, are you *sure* this is a good idea?" he asked.

"No, but that hasn't stopped me before."

Gert groaned and climbed up into the airlock. Ateri was in right behind, and they were far too close together. Even with the spacewalk suits between them, Gert had rarely stood so close to the captain, brushing tails, bumping shoulders, squeezing down into the too-small space. It puzzled Gert why the shuttle airlock was so small; even a single ringel in a pressure suit would have trouble fitting inside!

The hatch resealed behind them, wedging them together, but soon a loud hiss and a pinkish gas emitted from the conduits around the airlock.

"Gas!" Gert blurted out.

"Decontamination spray," Ateri said, his helmet wedged into Gert's shoulder. "Look, I told you—"

"Sorry, sorry… I'm jumpy."

The inner hatch opened and they both tumbled onto the empty cargo bay floor, Gert on top of Ateri. He scrambled to climb off.

"Sorry, Captain!" Gert grabbed his captain's glove and hoisted him up.

"And don't apologize so much," Ateri said. "We're dealing with ringel, they—"

"They play things tough, I know." Gert had done his homework long ago.

"That's cute," said a voice in the room, speaking their language. Her accent was thick, and also unplaceable.

Gert turned his head toward the door to the cockpit. Standing there was the first ringel he'd ever seen in person. His mouth hinged open, and he felt very fortunate she couldn't see the dumb expression on his ears.

Piercings littered her scruffy, masked face—five in each pointed ear, two on each eyebrow, one in her nose, one on the lip, one on each nipple, and possibly even more underneath. The brown longcoat she wore gave her apparent thickness, though the thing hung so loosely on her shoulders it exposed the true width of her body anyway—so much smaller than a geroo, except…

Gert had flashbacks of himself lying in bed, looking at his language course materials. Pictures of the ringel littered the columns, and other aliens with other languages. He was so embarrassed, he'd told no one he'd found them *attractive*. Even when krakun language course materials had the most bland and clinical descriptions of aliens possible, teenage Gert spent more time than he cared to admit making lewd doodles of alien species…

That was over a decade and a half ago. He was certain he'd grown out of it.

The course materials on the ringel didn't show their breasts like *that*. It was like she was far past the point of ready-to-nurse. Strange how the figure was so appealing. Even though she chomped down on a long cigar that dirtied her teeth, and her unkempt fur stuck out in little spots here and there, and her ringed tail was much too long and held too high…

"I thought we told you, the captain was to come alone," she said.

"Tell her you're the captain," Ateri whispered, so only Gert heard him through the strand.

"Huh?" Gert asked. "Why?"

"Figure out how long they take to call a bluff," Ateri said. "We can learn out how much they know about us. Besides, if they were just two weeks later, it'd be true anyhow. Practice for me."

"Yes, I am the—" Gert began, before remembering he had to press a button to allow his voice to carry through the helmet-mounted speaker, and repeating himself. "I'm the captain. I… You can't go around telling us what to do! It might be dangerous. I should at least have a bodyguard." Fortunately he was wearing several layers of the spacewalk suit at the moment, or he might even be more embarrassed.

"Warning," his HUD flashed at him, "blood pressure rising."

Ancestors, why of all people in the universe did he have to be attracted to *her?*

The ringel shrugged. "Eh, not my problem. Looks like you're not armed. But you better not go causing trouble anyhow. Ours is an armed and jumpy people."

"Is that a threat?" Gert asked.

"It's a warning," she said. "It'd be a shame if something happened to you."

That definitely sounded like a threat. Still, she held her paw out, and Gert lifted his to meet it.

She touched his paw, and Gert worried that she could tell he was shaking, even through the suit's thick glove. If she could, however, she kept her surprise concealed.

"The name's Inzari," the ringel said, "I will be your pilot for all of five minutes, and you had better not scuff up the inside of this shuttle or I will kick your tail from here planetside."

"That doesn't sound diplomatic," Ateri said through the strand.

"Uh-huh," Gert grunted in response.

"Because you're supposed to arrive in one piece, strap yourselves in. The gyro stabilizer has been on the fritz for the last few months and I don't have the parts to fix it, so there will be a hell of a lot of turbulence."

If Inzari thought something was amiss, she didn't act so. She instead grabbed Gert by a strap on the suit and yanked him toward the cockpit. "You, copilot seat. And you, other geroo, I didn't bring a seat for you. There are cargo straps on the walls; you'd better figure it out fast."

"Um, sir—" Gert said over the strand, worried.

"I'll be fine. Not the first rough ride of my life," Ateri said.

The door shut behind them, and Inzari shoved Gert into the hard seat on the right. She yanked the harness over him and fastened the belts, her ears unhappy, as if she was being forced to babysit. It stuck Gert in place, facing the forward viewscreen—not an actual clear dome, but a monitor that gave a panoramic view of the front of the ship, displaying more of the *White Flower II's* hull.

Gert writhed on the inside, being seated next to this ringel. Even as she sat in a huff and flipped switches in sequence, chewing on the end of that cigar like she were about to eat it, Gert had to admit to himself he'd never overcome his infatuation with aliens.

He'd always figured once young geroo males grew up, their preferences went one and only one way—females with charming personalities, and nice round hips he'd like to squeeze in the privacy of a bedroom. Not the weird, underfed look of a ringel who was so unhinged and abrasive as her.

"I can't see you through that helmet, but I know you're staring at me. Stop it," Inzari said. She took a long drag of the cigar before shoving the rest on a long spike that protruded from the console— blunt at the end and bent to be parallel with the dashboard, but a dangerous modification anyhow.

Gert turned and faced forward, though he still cast his eyes her direction. Ancestors, if something about her didn't get his heart going. Just something so…wild!

What's wrong with you? She's part of a pirate crew who is making bodily threats against you and everyone you know! That's not sexy, that's terrifying!

He tried to think about Hiani instead, but that only saddened him. Hiani was rightfully upset, and Gert already expected she wouldn't forgive him, much less ever consider getting back together—he'd strained their relationship too far, and it broke. And that kinda, sorta meant he was available again, right?

No, no, you're supposed to talk yourself out of liking the dangerous pirate, you idiot!

"Quiet, aren't you?" Inzari asked. "Anything rattling around in that brain of yours?"

"I was uh," Gert said, trying to even out his voice as he tapped the talk button on the helmet, "I was thinking…you seem tall for a ringel."

"Still not as big as you, tubby."

"I'm not tubby!" A beat later, he followed it with, "Did you ask me to share my thoughts just to insult me?"

Inzari just laughed—it was a sharp cackle that resembled a yarp with jagged timbre. She turned and yanked a release switch, and the whole ship swayed underneath and it rose off of their position. "You in back, strapped in? Good!" she said to the intercom without waiting for a token response. "Blastoff in five!"

"Erm, Inzari—" Gert started.

"Five!" She smashed the throttle and cackled, whether from her dumb joke or glee at forcing discomfort on her passengers, Gert couldn't tell. And he had more important things to focus on, like his face trying to reach the back of his head through his brain as the ship lurched forward.

Chapter 5: The Jet Black Sword

Everything quieted to a dull roar after a while, and Gert panted, wanting to remove his helmet because the suit was not cycling his air fast enough. The ship jerked around several more times as—from what Gert could make out—a landing bay opened in the middle of nothing like a huge mouth with long teeth made of stars. Once through, Inzari set the ship down with a heavy thud. The engines whined as everything powered down once again.

"Welcome aboard the *Jet Black Sword* mark two," Inzari said with her finger mashed on the intercom button. "Please return your internal organs to their full and upright position."

Gert groaned.

Inzari flomped over in her seat, draping herself in a way only someone with a loose spring for a spine could feel comfortable. Her bare paws dangled right near Gert's face. "It's about another five minutes for the bay to pressurize. So, this your first time on a ringel ship?"

"For me, yeah," Gert said. He knew he was playing the part of the captain, but he didn't figure Inzari would interrogate him—she didn't seem all that enthusiastic about the rendezvous.

"Are you all right?" She tilted her head. "Did I liquefy your brain or something?"

"No, I'm... I'm fine," Gert said, finger on his call button.

"I know little about your geroo slave ships, but lemme tell you, it's not as bad as you might think. There's an order to things—there has to be or you don't last for long in confined spaces. Backstabbing leads to a thin crew and worse recruits. You'll survive, stop being so nervous." She pressed her paw to the glass of Gert's helmet, shoving him playfully.

Gert hadn't given much thought to anything he was doing up to this point—going along for the ride was quite a test of endurance on its own. But if he would be the captain, there were things he needed to do, right? No matter how appealing this ringel was, he needed to be resolute. Right!

"I'll feel better the moment you tell your captain to re-establish the trinity on my ship," Gert said.

"Oh?" Inzari scoffed. "Worried over a little communications blackout, huh?"

"It's not the blackout that's the problem," Gert said. "The sooner I get in contact with your captain, the better!"

"If you have a problem, you can tell me!" She shoved at Gert's helmet with her underside paw, grasping at it with the flexible toe that worked like a thumb.

Gert grabbed her—gingerly, he hoped—by the ankle and brought her paw down. She didn't resist, instead grinning in the weird ringel manner with the teeth bared. Was she toying with him?

"And I'd tell a mere pilot, because…"

"Hmm…" Inzari tilted her ears and wiggled her toes with her heels rested on Gert's armrest. "Maybe I'm curious."

"I'm serious!" Gert said. "My people will get in deadly trouble with Planetary Acquisitions if you don't re-establish that link soon!"

It was rather hard to talk to Inzari in a serious tone when Gert could not keep his mind from going, *Huh, I wonder what her body would feel like pressed against mine*. It was a good thing Hiani broke up with him, or else this would be even harder to justify.

Inzari pouted. "I think you could survive a little reprimand. Maybe we don't want to risk you tattling."

"Can you be certain you're not going to put us into a worse position?" Gert asked. "I can assure you, only three people from my ship know you're here, and we have no intention on getting on your bad side *or* the bad side of the company."

Inzari huffed, then tapped a different switch on the intercom board. She spoke in Ringelese, though Gert had remembered enough of the language to pick out what she said. "Drygan, tell Sinon that we have Captain One-eye onboard, and he's demanding we re-establish the trinity on the gate ship. It's safe in my estimation; he's not going anywhere."

"Aye aye," the voice on the other end said.

"Captain One-eye?" Gert asked, habitually commenting rather than asking it seriously. He was playing the captain, yes, but he'd forgotten he was pretending to be Ateri specifically.

"What? On account of…" She stopped and looked at Gert. "You speak Ringelese?"

"A little," Gert lied.

She tilted her head. Standing up, she leaned in close to Gert, squinting with her paw over the visor to block the overhead light. "You're not the captain!"

"Uh…" Gert flushed. He tapped the intercom button. "Yes I am."

"You don't have an eyepatch!"

"And you know I should have an eyepatch…how?"

Inzari opened her mouth, then stopped. She sat back down in her seat. "Oh," she said, pointing. "I *like* you."

"Uhh…"

"You sneak!" Inzari rapped him on the helmet with the back of her knuckles. "Trying to pry information out of me. Oh, no you don't, not until Sinon's debriefed you! Anyhow, I better go check and make sure I didn't turn the real captain into chunky stew." She lifted herself out of the seat, without even touching her arms to hoist herself, and slipped through the narrow space to the cargo bay.

"So you are an officer then?" Gert asked to delay her departure. Her attitude was still rather acerbic, but he didn't want her to leave.

She stood up straight. "How did you know?"

"Drygan responded with an, '*aye aye*', like he was receiving an order," Gert said. "If you were a mere pilot, that would have only been a request."

Inzari turned and cocked an eyebrow, then peered at him. "Alright, genius. I am *Quartermaster* Inzari." She bowed.

Quartermaster: second-in-command of a ringel privateer vessel. Gert swallowed, going back over everything he'd said in his mind, in hopes he didn't ruin the diplomatic side of the negotiations.

"You would find out eventually," she continued, "but I enjoy the proactive manner in which you pry information; it makes you sound like a ringel. But watch that sly tongue of yours or someone might…" And closed her sentence by snapping her sharp teeth together. She slipped into the hold, the doors dilating open and closing behind.

Knowing she was an officer onboard the ringel ship made Gert *more* attracted. He rapped himself on his helmet. Was it the suit? Was the suit's inner seal too tight?

"Maybe I'm suffocating!" Gert said to himself. "The air mixture in the suit is reading wrong, I'm not getting enough oxygen! Ha! Ha ha!"

"Gert?" Ateri asked over the strand, "are you sure you're okay?"

Gert slapped his own helmet in a facepalm. "Yes, sir. I'm alright."

* * *

Ateri had been on a ringel pirate ship before, but nothing like this.

They took a lift out of what at first appeared to be a small bay, but the catwalk with glass panes overlooking the whole shuttle bay stretched on hundreds of meters. And it was not just shuttlecraft.

Ateri had studied enough foreign ship styles to recognize fighters when he saw them, at least a hundred, sometimes two to a chamber, with dozens of chambers that seemed to stretch on forever. The floor on the catwalk moved on its own, one in each direction, carrying them down the hall to see just how massive the pirate fleet was.

Inzari had parked at that end on purpose, Ateri was sure. The pirates needed to brag about how armed they were. None of this would stop a single krakun dreadnought—this army, this ship, they were puny in comparison, which was what called for such a clandestine approach to getting what they wanted.

Still, they must have gotten it all from somewhere.

The first place Quartermaster Inzari took them was a medical bay. They removed their suits inside a clean chamber, which was only a glass box with a plain white wall at one end bearing a low shelf.

"Everything removable comes off, and put it on the shelf," Inzari said through an intercom as she spoke for their shipboard doctor. "For decontamination."

"Is this necessary?" Gert asked, setting his helmet on the only shallow shelf. "We're a sterile generation ship unlikely to have crossover microbes as it is. And besides, we're *not* inoculated against anything you might have."

"First, because we don't want to take unnecessary chances, and second, that's not my problem."

She watched Gert through the glass. As per her instructions, Ateri had removed his eyepatch, and dislodged the glazed metal placeholder in the socket underneath—he hadn't taken that out in a month, but it was due for cleaning anyhow.

"*Arakshet ushu audei,*" the old ringel doctor said to Inzari, pointing toward Ateri as he had his back turned.

"Doc wants to know about the scarring," Inzari said.

Ateri had several faint whip-marks across his back that would have been impossible to notice if it weren't for the fact there were so many of them. They appeared even more distinct where they crossed—almost like the stars, if one squinted.

"There's a story to it," Ateri said, "but we don't have time for stories."

"He's asking if it's some kind of skin disease," Inzari said.

"No," Ateri said, stroking fingers down his back. "It's all physical."

"Necklaces too," Inzari stated. When the geroo glared at her in doubt, she reiterated, "Seriously, you do *not* want any metal on you during decon."

Gert paused before taking off his necklace. The necklaces rarely came off—the few times they did were when adding beads. He pawed the silver bead at the corner of his string, staring into space.

Ateri was about to say something—he didn't know what. Comfort him, perhaps, as Gert's silver bead was always a reminder of what happened to Sur'an. However, Gert shook his head, removed his necklace, and placed it on the shelf.

Once he did, the entire shelf folded in, dumping everything on it onto the other side of the white wall.

"Hey!" Gert shouted, turning to the glass to face Inzari, "*you had better give those back!*"

"Calm yourself!" Inzari said. "You'll get them back, once we've processed them."

"Undamaged?" Gert asked.

"Of course. You have my word." She looked Gert up and down, now that he was standing in front of her. "Also, gods of known space, you're huge, aren't you?"

Gert's indignance melted into a strange bashfulness. "Well uh, I am tall for a geroo, yes."

"I thought it was just the suits, but damn."

Gert shyly twisted his paw on the deck, which Ateri eyed. He let out a low hmm, and wondered if she wasn't trying to distract them to what they had really done. Their strands were on the shelf with the spacewalk suits, and Ateri considered how they might plant tracking bugs on their own devices. He might have to get a new one when they returned to the *White Flower II*, if the ringel allowed them back at all.

But true to her word, Inzari returned everything but the bulky suits right away, and that left them free to follow Inzari down the rest of the corridors to wherever she was leading them. This time, they saw the ringel close-up as they passed by. Though an average geroo was a solid forty centimeters taller than any ringel—not to mention broader and with a thicker tail—Ateri and Gert were another ten on top of that. Most of the pirates, despite looking as roughly furred as Inzari herself like they'd each just gotten out of a scuffle, seemed startled by the newcomers. They stood with backs flat to the walls as Ateri and Gert strode by, despite there being enough room in the main corridors for six geroo or ten ringel to stand shoulder-to-shoulder.

The interior of the ship was a solid gray, though a darker and slicker material than what composed the *White Flower II*. The place had an unusually new shine and smell to it—very unusual, given ringel were known for getting their scents, not to mention fluids, all over their public spaces. Whenever Inzari passed beneath the overhead lights, her softened image appeared in reflection against the floor. Gert tilted his ears at his own dim reflection in the walls. He was also rubbing his arms for warmth—it was a touch too cold for comfort.

Once out of the hall, Inzari led them up a grand central ramp. It could only have been the main hub of the ship, fitted more like a bazaar. A ring encircled two decks, the lower one they'd just left and the upper one they crossed over to. At the center in the base, there sat a small terrarium with greenery. Ringeltec and Gerootec were very similar planets, or at least were back when Gerootec still existed, but they had clear differences. The thin needle leaves of the plants in their little garden were far different than anything rescued from their home planet.

And around the ring on both levels were multiple wide open doorways, like little storefronts but without the signage, leading into a darkened lounge, or a dimly lit arcade or locker room. They were all on the other side of the ring, twenty meters away, and it was difficult enough to see with Ateri's vision and all the ringel crowding the floors.

It was strange because this wasn't *anything* like the other pirate ship he'd visited. That one was practical with its lounge spaces out of the way, not in the middle of traffic between the halves of the ship. This place, with unusually wide corridors for such a tiny species, seemed too opulent for a pirate ship.

The three of them entered the doors at the top of the ramp to find a rather comfortable—if still cold—room with lounging couches, a large monitor, and what appeared to be a wet bar with dozens and dozens of bottles stacked behind. Other entrances graced all four walls of the room—two more normal dilating doorways and an archway that led to a darkened staircase.

"Sinon will meet you here." Inzari turned in place and faced them. "He will be down in one minute."

"A common area? Seems a little public for such a discussion," Ateri said. "What with the big corridor outside."

Inzari snorted. "Oh, Captain, you're the last one onboard who doesn't know what's going on!"

"You tell your subordinates everything, then?"

"I will flag the room private," Inzari said. "You can rest easy knowing nobody will walk in on you to interrupt your, how did he put it, *parlay*."

"If the captain thinks it is private enough for him," Ateri said, "I suppose that's fair." He continued standing while Gert moved to sit down on a couch. Inzari grabbed Gert by the shoulder.

Ateri interceded, smacking her paw away. "Don't touch him."

"Yow, you're touchy yourself," Inzari said, waving her paw to shake out the pain. "Your little trick or no, this is not for his ears. The captain is particular about this discussion."

You mean, he wants as few ears as possible—keep himself at an advantage during negotiations.

"I don't mind if you touch me," Gert said.

"I brought him over as a bodyguard," Ateri said. "And besides, you knew ahead of time about my appearance, so you cannot be ignorant of my age. He is also my successor as captain, so his presence may be crucial should you need something from us within the next seventeen days."

"Oh right, the whole sixty year thing," Inzari said. "Sucks for you, I guess. But nah, Sinon knows. We discussed it. This is still for your ears only."

Ateri huffed. "What reassurance can you give that you won't take us hostage?" he asked. "And splitting us up is just a prelude to that?"

"Ugh, fine! Listen, if the krakun suspected, it would jeopardize the entire plan. Sinon will explain, but the *last thing* we want to happen is for your officers to disappear. Good enough?"

Ateri nodded to Gert. "Make sure she does nothing funny."

Gert nodded back. "All right." He turned to walk out with Inzari. "So…how do I address you anyhow? Quartermaster?" he asked.

"Inzari is fine."

"My name's Gert."

"I didn't ask, geroo."

The door sealed behind them.

Ateri, while waiting, swiped a fingerpad over the bar and looked at it. Spotless. Everyone figured pirates to be dirty wretches, but Ateri knew better—pirates were enterprising people, not too different from shrewd businessmen. They put a high priority on appearance because appearance gave one the slightest edge in any diplomatic power play.

"Captain!" said a new voice. Ateri turned to the archway with the staircase where Sinon descended, wearing a thick longcoat and boots. A long ringed tail swished behind him. His species bore dark patches over their faces, which also extended to various parts of their bodies. The stripes on Sinon peeked out from under his coat and pointed down his front at his navel. He also wore jewelry everywhere—along his ears, in his round black nose, and on his lips and fingers, sparkling in an array of colors from a dozen different alloys.

He also wore a belt around his midsection, with two plasma pistols holstered in either side, visible when Sinon pulled the coat away on a pretense of reaching to scratch his back.

Ateri tensed, but he supposed he had to trust they would not do anything to him. Too much preamble just to shoot the captain dead.

"You are may to call me Captain Sinon," the ringel said, gesturing towards his chest. "You are please to be honored."

"Your Geroonic is not fantastic," Ateri said.

"Not, but I also to expect your Ringelese just as worse."

"You have me there. Do we have any mutual languages? Can you speak Krakunese general dialect?"

"Ah, Krakunese," Sinon said, shifting to a different cadence along with the language, if still accented. "I did not think you would have been pleased to speak in your captor's tongue, na?"

"I'm not used to speaking it out loud," Ateri said, "but your krakun sounds far more fluent." Though Ateri practiced speaking it often enough so he could get himself used to the unfamiliar consonants, it was company policy that any meeting between geroo and krakun was to keep the geroo speaking Geroonic and the krakun speaking Krakunese, and they would have to know enough to understand each other. Knowing multiple languages was a trivial matter for most krakun, but they didn't wish to speak any other.

Nevertheless, the few times that Ateri managed to contact other species, Krakunese often served as a convenient intermediate tongue. The krakun probably knew and hated that fact.

"Good." Sinon nodded. "And since you are here, it follows that you received my message!"

"Your threat, yes."

"And the tone, good. Do not misunderstand, now that you are here, I want to ensure you are most comfortable."

"That should prove difficult," Ateri scoffed. "You've already jeopardized our ship."

"Oh, it is a misunderstanding is all," Sinon pleaded, his paws on his chest. "I needed to get your attention, but I did not know you would get in trouble with your superiors for what could be explained as a power hiccup."

"You should know how petty the krakun can be over matters out of our control." "They've massacred us for far less."

"In either case, the trinity on your ship should be restored by now, na?"

"I will take your word for it, on the assumption you are acting in good faith and don't want us dead just yet."

"Captain, your words are bitter! I believe you'll find our terms agreeable, and…" He swung a paw around in search of the right word, "…mutually beneficial."

"Is that the actual term you're looking for, or are you sweetening your words? I reiterate, you have jeopardized the lives of my crew."

"I went to great expense to come out this way, and I should not like to go back empty-pawed. This is to impress on you what kind of enterprise this is, and," he inhaled, and smiled to himself as if to savor the words, "who is holding all the cards."

They used tiles in traditional table games among the geroo, but he understood Sinon's intent.

"I thought you wished me to be comfortable," Ateri said. "That is difficult when I am not the one who is armed."

"Then here—" He removed one pistol from its holster and, holding it by the barrel, tossed it over to Ateri. He caught it in both paws. Ateri considered turning it and shooting Sinon, but that wouldn't help matters in the slightest. He couldn't commandeer an entire pirate ship on his own.

"Thank you," Ateri said. Weapons with a higher energy output than a kitchen knife were forbidden onboard a slave ship, but Ateri was intent on taking everything he could lay a paw on. Besides, a small high-energy plasma coil could be useful. He had no place to put it, so he laid it down on the bar.

"Come, sit," Sinon said, moving to the two central couches. He swept back the tail of his longcoat, sat at a couch, and gestured to the other one across a low-lying table. Ateri sat down.

"So," Sinon said, "what do you think? It took me many a year to acquire a ship of this scale."

"I noticed you practically have an armada."

"For what I plan on doing, I need an armada." Sinon swept his paws in a wide, encompassing gesture.

"What, threatening a defenseless slave ship?"

"Captain, I have nothing against you or the geroo if you will share in the profits with me."

"And just what is so profitable? A krakun generation ship?"

"I thought you were more clever than this!" Sinon exclaimed. "No, I don't want your ship! Think, please. Why do I contact you the same day you hover over an unknown planet, scanning it for your masters to find it suitable for krakun life?"

A chill ran up Ateri's spine. He understood, all too well.

"You want to steal a krakun terraforming device," Ateri said, his tone low.

"Now," Sinon said, gesturing to the space between them, "we understand each other."

Chapter 6: Commissioner Pokokuro

*P*okokuro: daughter of CEO Thrull of Planetary Acquisitions the entry read, and it said little else, even when most krakun biographies at least listed their major work history. Pokokuro seemed to have none.

The bridge calmed from the incident once the trinity had re-established itself. Jakari had been tight-lipped about where Ateri and Gert had gone, making vague implications it had to do with the trinity but saying nothing in particular. Once the system was back online, however, they would ask why the captain wasn't answering his strand. It would take all of five minutes for the questions to roll in, so she left a recorded response on her own strand—*far too busy, get back at about 1200 hours.*

Subcommander Tesko, standing at the console aside the bridge, stared at the reports sent to her from the engineering team. They'd run out of ideas what happened, and so it was up to the science officer to hypothesize. Jakari stood behind the short subcommander, arms folded behind her back as she waited for Tesko to say something.

"Well?" Jakari asked, once the surrounding noise had dipped to quiet.

"As far as I can tell," Tesko said, "it looks like some kind of interruption cascade, except instead of re-establishing the link within a few seconds, it held for over forty minutes."

"What does it mean, do you think?"

"I don't know! I'd have to test things out, but that would require us to take down the trinity to do it, and something tells me I will not get your permission for that task."

"That's a fair assessment," Jakari said. Taking down the trinity would mean a minimum downtime of seventeen hours; they were fortunate enough this interruption didn't knock it offline entirely. "What I'd like to know more is if you can stop it from happening again."

"That'd require knowing what in the hell of ignorance happened in the first place. I mean, even my most serious guess makes this seem like sabotage!"

Jakari's ears stood rigid. She would have liked to tell Tesko that they were under attack by pirates, but it would have helped nothing.

"Ugh, I don't know… I'll try running simulations, but I won't get anywhere."

Jakari's strand sounded, bypassing the silent mode she'd set it to. That only meant one thing, which she confirmed on looking at the screen.

INCOMING TRANSMISSION FROM PLANETARY ACQUISITIONS

Jakari cleared her throat and swallowed to remove the lump. She'd dealt with Sarsuk frequently whenever Ateri was indisposed, and had not found it too difficult—terrifying, perhaps, but they were, at their heart, businessmen, and refrained from purposeless cruelty. It was only when their cruelty became purposeful that she worried. Pokokuro should be no different.

"Tell me if something turns up," she said, patting Tesko on the shoulder.

Tesko sighed with her ears low. "Good luck, Commander."

She addressed the scrappy geroo seated at the security station, looking as tired as everyone else. "Subcommander To'onai, you have the bridge," Jakari said as she entered the conference room.

The large screen at the far end switched on the moment she entered, and Jakari halted in her tracks.

"Dead gods!" groaned Commissioner Pokokuro. "You took long enough, insolent mammal…"

The enormous, pale-and-pink krakun was not sitting at a formal desk as Jakari expected, but instead was in the middle of an enormous personal bath, ankle-deep in water, though splayed out on her backside in thralls of luxury. Water cascaded from the sides of the walls all over her body, sending billows of steam that would have obscured the camera if they had not equipped it to compensate. A dozen tiny attendants, dressed in heavy-duty environment suits, walked on her front side and scrubbed her scales down with long, hard-bristled brushes. She snorted as though insulted, and turned, dumping all of her attendants into the water, where they scrambled away, avoiding being crushed as she scooted herself into an upright sitting-slash-lying position.

"Apologies if I've interrupted anything, Madam Commissioner," Jakari said with a deep, sweeping bow. She knew how to make her voice sound pleasant and warm when necessary — it was the quality that often made the crew think of her as the ship mother. She also could bear a perpetual, honest smile on her ears.

"Quit your groveling," Pokokuro snapped. "I know perfectly well this is a scheduled…" She screwed up her long muzzle and peered at the screen. "You're not Captain Ateri."

Well, nice to know she had a better memory for geroo faces than Sarsuk ever did. Though, it had been less like Sarsuk couldn't remember geroo faces and more like he didn't care about individuals. Krakun had excellent memories when they wanted to use them.

"Commander and First Officer Jakari, madam. I regret to inform you that Captain Ateri is indisposed at the moment. We had an emergency with the trinity."

Pokokuro huffed. An enormous amount of pressure billowed from her nostrils, and the steam around her face blew out like a miniature explosion. "That…is not…protocol," she intoned, as though Jakari would miss her words.

Jakari paused. Sarsuk rarely cared if Jakari had met with him in place of Ateri, and occasionally even one of the subcommanders would substitute for the job. It was not in keeping with protocol, but it was their understanding that protocol was only a *guideline* for what the commissioner would expect of a gate ship.

At least, that was how Sarsuk took it.

"M-my apologies, Madam Commissioner," Jakari started.

"Apologies, regrets… Excellent first impression you've made!" Pokokuro snarled. "I didn't expect a snub on the first day! I do not wish to repeat myself to him later!"

Jakari kept her ears broad and smiling anyway, paws folded. "The captain is my mate. I assure you, Commissioner, that I won't keep anything from him."

"Oh, you'll repeat my message word-for-word, will you? That's an excellent workaround for the unnecessary *problem of an absent captain!*"

"I understand, Madam Commissioner," Jakari said, bowing. "This mistake will not happen again."

"And it had better not," Pokokuro said. "Remember that obedience yields life." Pokokuro spread out her claws in the water, and the slaves scrambled forward to scrub down her talons. "So, when you repeat my message to the captain word-for-word, inform him I will arrive at 1200 hours sharp for the survey inspection. If he is not there, I will execute every geroo I see until I see him. Understand?"

"Yes, Madam Commissioner," Jakari said, keeping her head down.

"And I noticed your gate closed at a most inopportune time," Pokokuro said. "And you managed to open it up again within the hour. I had to reschedule my flight! Can you explain this?"

"A result of the previously mentioned trinity issue. We do not have an explanation yet, Madam Commissioner."

"Then you will provide me one the moment I arrive."

Jakari made a mental note to have Tesko invent something. Pokokuro wouldn't look too deep, so long as it sounded plausible. At least, that was what Jakari hoped.

"And remember in your report to the captain," Pokokuro continued, "to mention that this is a fair warning to you; I am not so corrupt as Commissioner Sarsuk was. Planetary Acquisitions is a serious enterprise, and they will no longer tolerate corruption such as Sarsuk's."

Jakari swallowed, but kept smiling.

Sarsuk was, to Jakari and her people, the worst kind of monster, the one who killed and destroyed and made them say, "thank you for the favor". The only reason such a beast was at all manageable was because he needed the ship operational due to the enormous return on investment, and because he did not care about the ship's operations beyond the broadest strokes.

And Pokokuro thought he was corrupt? That worried Jakari, because *none of that* made Sarsuk contemptible to the krakun. In fact, so far as Jakari knew, Sarsuk was a paragon of virtue to the krakun. On the screen, Pokokuro flexed her talon and admired the filing job the three workers had done on it.

Jakari cleared her throat and tried not to think too hard about it. "Commissioner…"

"Don't tell me, I know what you're about to say," Pokokuro said. "You're curious, how precious. Well, the company did not see it fit to inform you of the details of Sarsuk's fate, and there is no particular reason I should give such details to the commander of an unimportant starship!" Pokokuro snapped, clutching her claw tight. Then she broke into a huge grin—a grin that Jakari had only seen on Sarsuk when he was about to do something awful.

Pokokuro laughed.

Jakari had never heard a krakun laugh like that. It made her feel cold under her fur.

"Believe me, I would enjoy nothing more than to expound on that wretch's failures, even if it is to a mammal like you. Unfortunately, there's still a gag order wrapped around the whole ordeal, so I cannot tell you any details about the trial."

"Trial?" Jakari gasped.

"Oh yes, that much I can say—and the outcome, seeing as that is a matter of public record."

"Which was?"

Pokokuro grinned again. Slowly, and with a large amount of gesticulation for a krakun, she raised her chin and slid a claw across her throat.

Jakari winced. Now she was even more curious. Government affairs and contracts composed a lot of Planetary Acquisitions's business, but they were not themselves the government. What could he have done to warrant a death sentence? Multiple murder? Treason? Insult the emperor?

"And so, you have me," Pokokuro said as she yanked her other claw out of the water, causing the suited creatures to fall over once more. "Someone with the integrity needed to fill the role, since all the other fleet commissioners are now…well, I shouldn't say. You never know who is listening."

All that meant to Jakari was that if Pokokuro were corrupt, she would be far more likely to get away with it. Jakari couldn't decide whether the new commissioner being corrupt or incorruptible—for a krakun, naturally—would be a worse fate for them all.

"One more thing," Pokokuro said. "Since the *White Flower II* is of primary focus at the moment, I will want constant updates on your scan. Initial reports are not promising, but we will be thorough. I want this to be quick and accurate without falling into sloppiness; that's how we ended up with accidents like the first attempt at Krakuntec IX."

Jakari inhaled sharply. The fur on the back of her neck stood up, and for the first time, her smile faltered. This should not have been so painful—it wasn't her memory, but it was impossible to not feel anger and pain when krakun so often used it for crude mockery, to wound the pride of the geroo.

"What?" Pokokuro asked, noticing right away the change in Jakari's posture.

"Forgive me, Commissioner, it was nothing—"

"No, something bothered you right then. What could that be—" She looked to the side, toward another monitor on a wall out of view. Then Pokokuro once again broke out into a grin and laughed so the water below her vibrated and the slaves dove away to avoid drowning in the surge. "Dead gods! How sweet. Tiny mammal, you must be so heartbroken. I had no idea that planet used to be Gerootec."

Jakari felt a sudden pinching somewhere in her face, and she ignored it.

"It was just called Omni Sector P-33-4 in all the file footage. I was just a whelp then, but oh I remember that so. Yes, it was a disaster of a mission. Captured my young imagination, it did! The evaporation of the oceans, the magma breaking through the ground... To see something like it is to witness the face of true power." She licked her lips and teeth with her long tongue, as though savoring a delicate flavor.

Jakari's fists clenched so hard behind her back, they turned cold and slick. Claws stabbed into her palms.

"Great for broadcasts, not so much for profits," Pokokuro said. "Ah well, it was not the company's fault your planet was not receptive to—" She noticed that Jakari was even less composed, and grinned again. "Oh I'm sorry, did I hurt your little feelings, Commander? Hah! You mammals and your mammalian emotions... Well, you are dismissed now, to go cry or whatever it is you feel like doing. Remember—because I'm certain I must remind you—twelve hundred hours, and I only want to see the captain when I arrive."

"Yes…Commissioner. He'll be there."

"He'd better. Transmission over."

The screen cut out. Jakari unclenched her paws and blood spilled out all over the floor. Sniffling, crying, she made her way to an emergency medical kit and cleaned up the gashes as best she could.

Not that she missed Gerootec, though it was a dream she'd considered for all her years. But the image was a constant reminder of everything wrong—how the system stole away her father too soon, how it would take her mate next, how it had kept her from ever having a cub… She didn't need yet another reminder. Now she failed to make a serious impression with the commissioner, but it was likely as serious as it would get anyhow—it was not as though krakun respected geroo officers. The worst Jakari did was reinforce the krakun's idea that the geroo were just the slightest step above kerrati. Perhaps it was better than appearing defiant.

She sealed off the wounds with medical foam and rubbed her paws together to sweep away the excess. She sighed and returned to the bridge, walking as upright as she could manage. The bridge crew shuffled about, the commotion that had taken place not but an hour beforehand forgotten. The time was just past 0900 hours; geroo all around talked less about their jobs and more about what they would have for lunch.

"Commander!" Subcommander To'onai said from the captain's seat at the top, standing and saluting as she walked out. "What's the news?"

Jakari approached the captain's chair and saluted To'onai. The subcommander, ignoring the formal gesture, grabbed her paw and looked at the four white markings on each.

"You did this to yourself," To'onai said.

"Let's say, the new boss is at least as bad as the old," Jakari breathed. "It's nothing to concern yourself with, Subcommander. Right now we need to prepare for the new commissioner."

"Commander," To'onai said. "I assume you'll be informing the captain, since I haven't been able to contact him for the last hour?"

"I will," Jakari said, biting her lip.

Ancestors help us, love of my life. You'd better come back in one piece, and soon.

Chapter 7: Drinking Game

I don't know," Gert squeaked. "I figured a tour would show me things other than just the bar."

The bar, lit by the blue overhead lamps and the wide-open archway into the main corridor, stunk of thick smoke. Ringel occupied nearly every seat in the room—at least half of who chomped on cigars like the one Inzari sucked on earlier. The room was spacious enough at least for standing room, including the gang toward the back who argued over the setup of an arcade game, on the verge of coming to blows.

"It's not a tour," Inzari said. She shooed away one occupant at the bar so Gert could have a seat next to her, the ringel glancing at Gert's large frame before scurrying off at the quartermaster's orders. "I brought you here because one, I don't trust you, and two, I'm not letting you interrupt my routine." The barkeeper slid a huge, clear, plastic mug of something blue into Inzari's paw. She downed half in a single swallow and wiped her lips of the foam.

"What's that game they're playing?" Gert asked, looking back at the arcade monitors obscured by the dark ringel silhouettes.

"It's Three-man Joust, and they're not playing, they're arguing," Inzari said. "When the game starts, you'll see the holographics on the floor there, in front of the emitters. It's a team strategy game; the skill and harmony of each player is crucial. Nozak there is likely upset because Onon won't let him substitute his regular player with one he wants when they're playing for money."

Inzari shrugged and downed the rest of the drink. "Dunno why they're so uptight; we're all going to be rich soon enough."

Gert tilted his ears at the remark. He was keeping his ears open in case Inzari spilled even a little of their purpose here, and she seemed almost casual mentioning it out loud right now. She did say everyone but him and Ateri knew what was going on…

"Say, did you want a drink or something?" Inzari asked. "You look like you're about to explode."

"I have nothing to pay with." Gert turned his paws out and shrugged. He figured they didn't accept credits from his strand.

"Nonsense, you're a guest. Shinzon!" she called out to the barkeep and continued in Ringelese. "One of these for the geroo here, my tab."

"I don't—" Gert started. The barkeep, thick for a ringel though still narrower than even an adolescent geroo, set down a mug in front of him, the blue inside fizzing to the top. Gert gave Inzari a look.

"What? It's not gonna hurt you," Inzari said, "You drink, right? All shipmen do."

"Yeah, but our physiology is different. What if it poisons me?"

"Yer a biped who breathes oxygen and can drink alcohol," Inzari said. "It's fine!"

Gert picked up the mug which was cold to the touch, and for a moment thoughts of a death sentence gripped him. He was certain this was gonna kill him, but the ringel were too concerned with their own machismo to care. He sniffed the beer. The foam smelled of disinfectant. And so, trembling just a little and pinching his eyes shut, he put the edge of the container to his lips and drank.

He opened his eyes. "Hmm!" he said as he drank down the rest—it tasted sweet and fruity enough to be a carbonated soda, but had a thick caramel flavor that lingered in the mouth, but didn't outstay its welcome.

Inzari seemed impressed. She leaned on her elbow and watched as Gert chugged the rest of the glass to satisfy her.

"Damn," she said, "look at you go."

"Was there any alcohol in that?" Gert asked, not getting the usual sensation of warmth in the tip of his toes following a drink.

"In a Barkwater? Not much—that's an on-duty drink. But most of the crew have to work their way up to that one."

"Really? That?" Gert knew he sounded incredulous.

Inzari could only laugh. "Yeah, damn. What do they serve on your ship, engine coolant?"

There must be some spice or bittering agent I'm unable to taste, Gert thought.

"You need something stronger than that," Inzari said. "Barkeep, two Half Gutbombs."

Gert swallowed. The barkeeper filled the small tumblers half-high with a fizzing liquid otherwise clear as water. All the fizz, though, fell to the bottom of the glass rather than rising. Gert held it up to inspect it, the glass warm between his fingers. Before he turned the glass to see how it sloshed, Inzari stopped his paw.

"Don't tip it; the top half is a dense gas. You're supposed to drink that part too."

"Does…this have alcohol?" Gert asked.

"Hell yeah," Inzari said, holding up her glass to him. "How about a toast?"

"What's a toast?" Gert asked, unfamiliar with the ringel word.

"Like a drink offering, only you drink it."

Gert blinked. "…What's a drink offering?"

"Just drink at the same time I do, dummy."

"Oh, okay." Gert picked up the glass and sniffed it. It did not smell as nice as the Barkwater, and instead fumed like strong detergent. He grit his teeth.

"To our daring enterprise," Inzari said.

"Whatever that is," Gert added.

Inzari downed the glass in one go. Gert took his much, much more carefully. And it burned—not from the temperature, but a chemical burn like when he'd breathed in krakun compromise air.

The invisible, liquidy top gas creeped down his throat, searing the entire way. Gert hacked and coughed, needing to belch, but it was too dense for him to force back up. So instead he did the only thing he could, steeled himself, and downed the rest of the glass to force it all in as fast as he could. It still burned, though not any more than at first since the stuff coated his throat. However, once he set the empty glass down, the burning sensation all but vanished. His stomach felt queasy after, but not painfully so, and his toes turned flush.

Gert wiped his eyes where tears were forming. "Yikes, that was something else."

Inzari whistled low.

"Now what did I do?" Gert coughed.

"The whole thing, huh?"

"I don't know!" Gert threw up his paws. "You're not explaining these drinks before you have me drink them!"

Inzari laughed. "That's half the fun! You're a better sport than I took you for!"

Gert's ears turned flush, probably from the alcohol. The more time he'd spent with Inzari, the less he uncontrollably thought how much he would have liked to touch those slim curves. But now she was complimenting him, and he would likely be drunk soon, and then what was he going to do? Embarrass himself in front of the entire bar when he was supposed to be representing his whole ship?

"Oh, stop it. You look like you're gonna explode," Inzari said.

"That's what worries me," Gert said. "What happens to the gas?"

"It condenses at body temperature. I've seen geroo drink these before; it's not gonna dissolve your esophagus or anything."

He appreciated the reassurance. "You've met other geroo?"

"Course I did. I learned to speak the language, didn't I?" Inzari said. "Kinda."

Gert's ears perked in curiosity. He wanted to hear more, but before he could ask, she interrupted.

"Hey, you know what would be fun?" Inzari leaned in.

"Oh, ancestors," Gert swore to himself in Geroonic.

"I've been wondering since we started out here, how well you shipboard geroo could hold your liquor. So we've both had the same drinks so far—"

"What, like a drinking game?" Gert asked.

"Oh, so you have those?"

"Sure, every imbibing culture does." Gert thought of his own experiences at the bar. The game geroo most liked to play with their drinking involved balancing. Contestants would stand on one paw and their tail, leaning farther and farther back with a long rod to ensure they were at the same angle. The geroo who refrained from falling over first won—usually more beer. There were a dozen variations to make it even more dangerous, like just using the tail and both paws, doing it atop tables or chairs, or a fan favorite: while already drunk. It was all a bit much, especially for a ship that prohibited alcohol.

"Excellent!" Inzari waved the barkeep over again—though he'd been standing there the entire time giving Gert strange looks—and spoke in Ringelese. "Hey, Shinzon—"

"Oh no," Shinzon said. "You're on duty, I don't care if you're the quartermaster. I'm not risking my tail on the captain finding out how much I served you."

"Hey!" Inzari snapped. "I am entertaining our guest, which is my job, and sometimes that job involves copious amounts of alcohol." She paused and considered her words. "Okay, it *usually* does. Do you want me to explain how you snubbed our guest to Sinon…in great detail?"

Shinzon snorted. "Fine, but I'm recording your statement on this. That's your tail, not mine."

"Good. Blood Fountain shots. Keep them coming, and don't stop until one of us hits the floor."

"What!" Gert exclaimed. "That's all? No skill? Just drink until someone passes out?"

"Hey, you must speak Ringelese decent to have caught all that," Inzari said. "You're a geroo of many talents."

It surprised Gert he could catch most of it once he heard Ringelese spoken. Namely the *hit the floor* part, an idiom which he understood in this context as being literal.

Shinzon placed two tiny glasses of an opaque red drink on the bar.

"Alright," Inzari said. "Rules are, we drink one at a time at the same time, and you gotta drink everything in the glass. It's a slick drink so it won't stick, but you turn it upside down on the bar when you're done and nothing can drizzle back out, otherwise you take another full shot as penalty. Last one upright wins."

"That's it? That's the game?"

"What'd you expect? You have different rules where you're from?"

"A bit," Gert said, trying not to let his nervousness make his words turn wheezy.

"Yeah, okay. You ready?"

"No, but I don't think that matters." Gert grit his teeth again.

"Go!"

Gert downed the drink, expecting it to burn like the last one. This one burned, but pleasantly—it was spicy. This one was, however, a kind of bitter he could taste, like a very strong beer he'd only recently become accustomed to. Tipping the glass all the way back, he tapped the glass on the table upside down, just after Inzari.

"Good?" Inzari asked.

"I wouldn't drink a whole glass," Gert said.

Two more glasses. Gert drank again, the spiciness building on itself. Another two. It concerned him because he could not taste the

alcohol in the drink, and had no way to gauge how much there was. Another two. Inzari eyed him.

"Bet you're feeling numb now!" Inzari said.

Gert presumed she meant from the spice. "A little," he said, "but I can still feel my tongue."

Another two. The other ringel in the bar took notice, gathering around. Another two.

"Who's that drinking with the quartermaster? I haven't seen him onboard before."

Another. Gert's sinuses flared, draining into his mouth. He wasn't sure if ringel culture preferred him to spit or swallow or blow it out, much less in the middle of a 'drinking game', so he tried to ignore it. Another.

"Sixteen on Inzari," said a ringel. "Where's the betting table? Who's got the odds?"

Another.

"Is he a geroo? Just put that on the board. Inzari five, geroo one. How many drinks will it end at?"

Another.

"I dunno, he has the mass for it. He is kinda pudgy."

"Gods, he's big, isn't he?"

Another.

"Is that a geroo? Are they all that big?"

"What are they up to? Eleven? Damn!"

Another. Gert asked Inzari, "So what is in this stuff, anyway?"

"Hell if I know." Inzari slurred her speech, which defaulted to Ringelese—odd, given that Gert wasn't *that* numb. Her movements had become exaggerated as she tried to ward it off. "Hey Shinzon, tell our guest what's in a Blood Fountain."

"Mako root juice and charsnap," Shinzon grunted at Gert, placing another two glasses. "The good stuff is fermented and distilled—this uses *shinkodi* to speed up the process."

Gert did not recognize that word. He downed the glass, turning it upside down on the bar next to the grouping of others.

"So…what's *shinkodi*?" he asked, trying out his Ringelese for the first time.

"That's where you mix the sugars with a strong acid to make the alcohol," Shinzon said.

"Oh, an ester catalyst!" He picked up the next glass set in front of him, then stopped. "Doesn't that produce glycerol, not ethyl glycol?"

"I didn't follow what you said. Um, maybe?" Shinzon shrugged. Gert had to ask with those words in Krakunese because he never learned how Ringelese named the alcohols—that was technical chemistry.

"Hey!" Inzari muttered, tapping her finger on the table. "Upside down!"

"Oh, sorry." Gert checked the glass, drank it, turned it upside down. He tested his mouth with his tongue, robbed of taste altogether from the spice. But he was sure, thinking back, that there was the barest hint of sweetness to the drink hidden under the other flavors.

And it was also an alcohol that had *absolutely no effect* on geroo physiology.

Three more glasses down. Inzari looked rough, staring into Gert's eyes, wondering why he wasn't moving. On the next glass, the ringel were all shouting, "Do it! Do it!" Gert drank his, set the glass on the table upside down.

Inzari slammed back her shot glass and held it up to cheers. However, it did not make it back to the bar. Inzari tried to slam the glass down again, and slipped off her seat.

The ringel cheers died as they all gaped at the quartermaster on the floor. A couple applauded for the geroo. Another complained, "Oh, come on, how do we know he drank it for real!" The betting manager said all bets were final.

"Damn, kid," Shinzon said, "You sure can take your drink, huh?"

"Yeah, I guess," Gert said, shyly turning his shoulders inward. He wanted to get out of the bar before the losers turned their ire toward him. But at the moment he was looking down at Inzari, and felt cold seeing her sprawled there with nobody moving to help her up. The rest of the ringel were busy changing money and snapping at one another, either as preamble to a fight or to stop one from breaking out.

Gert wasn't certain of the polite thing to do, but he knew the right thing to do, and he knelt down to help Inzari sit back up.

"You don't have to bother," Shinzon said, shaking his head. "The bouncer will be over soon to drag her out."

"I'd rather help her to her quarters," Gert said as he checked to make certain she was still breathing okay. "You know where those are?" He put his arm under her legs to lift her up.

"Hey!" Inzari muttered, her eyes coming back to alertness. "I can walk myself, thank you!"

"Er…okay," Gert said, pulling his paw back and helping her sit up. "But I should come with you anyway, seeing as how you're keeping an eye on me and all."

"And don't forget it!" Inzari toppled forward so her head landed on Gert's chest.

Gert sighed as he stood her up. Shinzon was about to clear the bar of the un-imbibed drinks, but Gert said, "I think I'll need this," took the glass in front of Inzari's stool, and downed it.

Chapter 8: The Exit Plan

The *White Flower II* had three missions. The first was to find planets suitable for krakun living conditions. If that was not the case, then second was to find living planets that the krakun could "liberate". And third, if possible, was to locate planets that were, living or dead, possible to bring to life and atmosphere suitable for the krakun.

Captain Ateri had never even *seen* a terraforming device. All his years as captain, and they'd never found a single planet worthy of terraforming for the krakun—none of the ships in the entire fleet had. Even the vast empire had only worked its way up to twelve homeworlds, though they had over a hundred colonies otherwise.

"You realize what treason is, don't you?" Ateri asked. "You are asking me to condemn ten thousand geroo to die a slow, agonizing death—and even more if this implicates any other ship in the fleet."

"We'll all be long gone before they could leverage any charges against you, Captain," Sinon said.

Ateri leaned back in the seat and folded his arms. "But you're not giving me a choice, are you?"

"I will not be so crude. I hope to be fair. You will receive your share of the bounty. Besides, I'm sure your people all would enjoy a taste of true freedom! It's rough going the first few years, but the profits will more than make up for it."

Ateri considered what Sinon might consider freedom; he had little working knowledge about the politics of Ringeltec, beyond the glib summaries taught by the krakun. They called the planet a "protectorate" of the empire, with issues of "minor terrorist cells" causing trouble. Assuming which side Sinon would have found himself, that life didn't sound much like freedom, and so Ateri could only assume Sinon meant *after* he took up piracy.

"Let's say I will entertain your proposal," Ateri said, despite the major obvious flaw in it. "I have more than a few questions."

"I am as the moon on a clear night, there for all to see," Sinon held his arms out wide. "Ask me anything."

"First. How would I know you won't sell us out to the krakun at first opportunity?"

"That would not be beneficial for anyone involved. We've been on this mission for over five years now. What profit is there chasing down a slave ship for that long only to sell information of betrayal to the krakun, then to travel back empty-pawed after they reclaim everything of value? The krakun do not pay well for information; they believe they have a monopoly. No, I have no interest in selling you out."

"Then satisfy my curiosity. If you're not krakun agents, how did you *find* us?"

"That is not much of a question," Sinon said. "I am here, aren't I?"

"The last time I ran into ringel pirates," Ateri said, "was at a planet called Missun-3, that had a hidden gate. In fact, everyone I've run into out here—the few there have been—was due to a nearby gate. The only other way to get in contact with us would be to follow us *from* a gate, for far longer than five years. Had you done so, you would have had no guarantee we'd run across a planet that even appeared viable without an enormous amount of foreknowledge that even the krakun do not possess. So either there is a gate here, and you've been waiting for someone to approach for five years—which again is not long enough—or you had another trick up your sleeve."

"What do you think, Captain? Where in this system could I find a gate?"

"I know what you want me to say," Ateri said. "That you've been hanging around in the high orbital space of Krakuntec Prime, and you hopped through *our* gate. I don't buy it, not even with this cloaking device—that's the most traveled area of space outside Liotec Prime. You can't just sit there."

"Oh, maybe a little, but we did not need to wait long there when we had our information." Sinon said, flourishing his paws as though to brush away the dismissive comment. "There's a little over thirty thousand gates in high orbit around Krakuntec Prime. That sounds like a lot, but that covers a huge area of space. Planetary Acquisitions has cloistered all their thousand-something sister-gates in their own reserved spot. And that means we can observe them all at once."

"So you've got a confederate on Krakuntec Prime?"

"The funny thing, I don't know. That's not my part in all of this."

"Who hired you?"

Sinon bit his lip for a moment. "They are enemies of the krakun empire."

"Who is it." It came out more as a command than a question.

"I cannot give you their name," Sinon said, "but I'm guessing you wish me to tell you they're…turek."

Ateri stood up. "Negotiations are over. I'm not handing you anything."

Sinon stood up as well. His demeanor was not pleading though, but serious. He'd expected this objection, and his counter was well-prepared. "Captain, before you make a rash decision, ask yourself what you know for a fact about the turek."

Ateri folded his arms. "Only what I am told. I've never had the misfortune of encountering them."

"Precisely."

"But they have told me a lot," Ateri said. "For instance, of the geroo fleet, *we* have lost five ships to turek raiders. That is five more than any other known power has taken from us. Now, the krakun may exaggerate that fact to keep us in perpetual fear of the turek, but why would they do that for the turek, and not the empire's worst enemy, the lio?"

"In part because it is true," Sinon said. "I do not dispute that the turek are far more proactive in their acquisitions, but they are not an unreasonable people. In fact, a good part of my dealings with them is based on our common ground that we both wish to harm the krakun. I ask you to keep an open mind here. They do not require you to meet them—only I do that."

Ateri glowered at Sinon. This was already more than he wanted to get involved, though in the back of his mind, he was holding out to hear the reward for this endeavor, turek or no.

Ateri understood nothing about the real politics of the turek. Hostility was not guaranteed. But the turek—beastly lizards who spoke the language of war like it were fine poetry—were just as mean and brutish as the krakun, so far as Ateri could tell.

Nearly everything Ateri learned about any species outside the krakun was through their onboard education—provided by the krakun. They had a tendency to exaggerate the evils of their enemies, so for all Ateri knew, the turek were fun-loving peaceniks out to make the galaxy a better place. But he doubted it.

"If not that, then I appeal to your wisdom," Sinon said. "Did your world produce a philosopher who said something like, '*the enemy of my enemy is my friend*'?"

"Perhaps." Ateri sat back down. "But don't take this as my acceptance just yet. Tell me the extent of your dealings with them."

"They're funding this enterprise."

"And they're not stealing the terraformer on their own?" Ateri asked. "So far as I understand, they don't place a great value on their own lives, so why would they care enough to pay a bounty to a species who does?"

Ateri could only say as much because the krakun were specific on at least one point about the turek: the krakun never captured them in battle for any reason. Turek commit suicide as a response to irreversible failure. One would think that would devastate to their population, but apparently not so.

"That's an oversimplification. The turek are a very…direct people. Even more so than ringel. They understand the value of subterfuge, but they lack talent for certain details."

"So the turek needed to hire you, and somehow provided you with information regarding our fleet movements," Ateri said. "You discover we're approaching a system observed beforehand with a Krakuntec-like planet, which takes only five years because you have over a thousand ships to choose from. So the only reason you are talking with me is coincidence."

"That is true," Sinon said. "You discovered the sequence of events—I marvel at your reasoning skills. I thought krakun slaves were not well-educated in such ways."

"It's different for gate ships than most." Ateri ignored the slight insult; Ringel rarely bothered with coyness in their speech. "We have a high demand for technical jobs, so our education access needs to be extensive. From what I understand, krakun tried to teach the basics only, but it never worked out as well as comprehensive education—as much as they hate it."

"All the better for you! But, you see how it works now, ne?

"Not quite. My second question. How do you plan on luring the krakun into sending a terraformer out here? There's no evidence yet that the planet is viable for a krakun settlement."

"That, my friend," Sinon smiled, "is what we in the business call a fib."

Ateri raised an eyebrow. "The data we send is verified. We've already begun the process of planetary scans."

"I brought a secret weapon for hacking," Sinon said. "Still, this weapon is not omnipotent—we will require your cooperation. For instance, if any evidence of data tampering turns up, smooth it over for the inspectors."

Ateri furrowed his ears. He didn't like that sound of that too much. "Let's say it works," Ateri said. "How do you then plan on stealing the terraformer? That's one of the most guarded secrets of the empire. Even if your fleet here is enough to overcome the defense force, they will scuttle it long before you could secure the thing intact."

Not to mention how simple it would be to damage the White Flower II *during battle and make off with your prize alone.*

"I have plans in place," Sinon said.

How vague. "I had a feeling you would avoid that question."

"But I already showed part of this plan to you, ne?"

"You did?" Ateri asked, ears sloped in confusion.

"By disabling your ship's Trinity."

Ateri tilted his head along with his ears. "How does that affect the terraformer?"

"Ah, the genius captain has not reasoned out that part, all right! This is top secret information. I cannot reveal to you what it is until I am certain you will play along with us. But you can trust me on this—I know what needs to be done."

"You could at least tell me something," Ateri responded.

"How about, the control mechanism of the terraformer is as rudimentary as they come. Even elementary."

"For a krakun device? That seems unusual."

"The krakun love things to work as intended, ne? They'll make everything ridiculously obtuse on the back end just for fun, using physics nobody understands, but it will be push-button start."

"I will buy that," Ateri said, knowing just how long the entire fleet had been working on the physics behind the trinity. Or at least, they used to.

Ateri felt a slight sinking in his chest as he recalled his decision to abandon the Exit Plan all those years ago. It was the cowardly thing to do, he was sure of it, yet what else could he have done? They were all under threat of execution for pursuing even the most basic matters in understanding the trinity. There was no other way out. He would die in space, and by his actions, leave his people robbed of hope that things would ever get better for them.

He looked up at Sinon, who was grinning.

Unless you make a deal with the devil.

"So," Ateri continued, "how long will this take?"

"Once the krakun affirm the viability of the planet, they on average take about three months to construct the terraforming device. Using it for their purpose takes several years, from what I have heard, but we will not need to stick around that long."

"So three months from now, somehow, we steal the terraformer while avoiding its destruction. Then what?"

"What…what?" Sinon asked.

"What do I get for my trouble? You said we share this prize. The big problem there is that the krakun would do one of two things—if they concede the loss of the terraformer, they shut down the sister-gate of the *White Flower II*, and it becomes impossible to start up the drive due to the trinity. Your ship here is impressive, but I doubt it'll hold ten thousand geroo for three years, were you even willing to host us. On the other paw, the krakun could not concede, which seems more likely, in which case the only way to stop them from coming back through the gate is to dismantle the trinity ourselves, leading to the same problem. Either way, we are stuck. This reduces the *White Flower II* to a useless aluminum can, and this enterprise is of no value to us."

Sinon's toothy grin spread wider, and he tapped his round black nose knowingly.

"What?" Ateri asked.

"I know what you want," Sinon rumbled in a sing-song tone, "but I cannot give it to you until you say yes."

Ateri's breath caught in his throat.

Is he implying…

"You can't… You can't know how to subvert the trinity!"

Sinon put his paws up. "I say nothing more until we reach an agreement."

"I can't agree to this!" Ateri said, once again showing his irritation with the proceedings by standing up, towering over the slumped figure of Sinon. "You've given no proof you hold the precise thing I've been looking for my whole life! I have no guarantee you will not wring all useful labor out of us, take the terraformer for yourselves, and leave us adrift!"

"Just tell me, Captain. Is it something you want?"

Ateri felt that tightening in his chest. He didn't want to show his weakness in front of the ringel, who seemed to already be feeding off of it. This plan would guarantee that Ateri would live to see it through. By the *Chiauo Gi* rule, the company would refuse him his Going Away on his sixtieth birthday should they believe terraformation was possible. That alone, having another *three months*, was so tantalizing a possibility that he couldn't make himself say no.

But he said nothing. Sinon grasped the meaning anyhow.

"You want my guarantee?" Sinon asked. "Fine. We are at the point you understand what is happening, so I will lay out the precise offerings before you. First, you were clever in knowing even this ship could not hang around the orbit of Krakuntec Prime for long. So, where do you think we were instead?"

Ateri blinked. "You were…where?"

"There are many gates in this galaxy. Not all of them have fixed origin and exit points. Do you understand? It is not so much the secret of the trinity as it is…let's call it a key to your gate. With this key, I can attune a gate to yours. It does not need to be your sister-gate. And you know so long as that gate is running, the trinity can operate. There is no rule that makes it need to be the sister-gate other than this key."

Ateri's mouth hung open. *Is it true?*

"And you want a better guarantee I am not trying to trick you? Here it is: my life and the lives of my officers."

Ateri blinked, shaken out of his thoughts. "Your—"

"You don't approve?" Sinon asked.

"How do you mean that?"

"Simply that you can hold us on your ship. I have about twenty officers under me. I know you don't have a brig on that ship, but you can lock us in an unused apartment for however many months it takes to get the terraformer out. For that time, my ship will be at minimal weapons capabilities. And understand that I and my officers do not wish to die."

"Yet you are offering me your lives for wealth," Ateri said.

"That is what you are risking too, is it not? You require even less than us to risk your lives. Such is the nature of your existence—I do not mean that as a slight, just a simple truth. So ask yourself, how much are you willing to risk for your freedom?"

Sinon held out a paw. Ateri stared at it with his only eye for a long, long moment.

What are you doing? He's given you your proof—his life is in your paws! Of course, you can never reveal you're holding a ringel onboard to anyone… The officers will all despise you for risking their necks for this again after you swore up and down the Exit Plan was off. Or if they discover and believe you did this to stave off your own death! And that's not even to think of what the commissioner would do to you!

But Ateri couldn't shake away the temptation.

We could be free.

And that one thought alone overpowered all the others, even his personal survival. For a moment—just a moment—he didn't care about any consequences. He closed his eye and believed right then he would do *anything* to be free of the krakun. Even *if* he died securing it.

He opened his eye again, looking Sinon in the face. With a moment of hesitation, which disappeared with his determination, Ateri touched his paw to Sinon's. A chill ran through him.

What are you doing!

"On the condition that your life and your ship is mine should you turn on me," Ateri said, ignoring his fur as it stood up on the back of his neck, "I accept."

"No need to be so formal about this!" Sinon let out a crackled ringel laugh and slapped Ateri on the shoulder. "Excellent! Excellent! Now that we are partners, it is time for you to meet the secret weapon."

He turned to the staircase, put his fingers to his lips, and whistled. Somewhere up the staircase echoed the soft whir of an opening door.

Sinon called up something in ringel. Ateri knew little of the language; the last time he'd used it was over two decades ago, and even then his knowledge had been rudimentary. He could only make it out as something like, "Come down and meet the captain."

Eye toward the staircase, Ateri expected to see yet another ringel descend, but the feet he saw were not long, broad, or even dark. They were a pale-orange color and tiny, as though walking on tip-toe, followed by slender but substantial legs and body. She wore just a bare amount of jewelry on her feline face—not as much as the captain or his quartermaster, but enough to show yes, she was a part of this crew despite not being ringel. She was a geordian.

Ateri shouldn't have bristled at the sight of their species, but he did.

She said something in Ringelese to Sinon, and Ateri picked out, "Are we doing this or not?"

"Captain," Sinon said, "let me introduce you to our chief hacker, and your second hostage, Moani."

Already Ateri was regretting this decision. He wasn't sure how in the five hells he could make himself work with a geordian...but he would not take back his word now.

Chapter 9: Private Quarters

Gert carried Inzari down the hallway, though she insisted on walking with her slumped over his shoulder. Ringel in the hallways gave him a strange look, carrying the quartermaster as he did, though Inzari was just conscious enough to wave them away, uttering a, "Mind your own business!" or two. It was strange not seeing anyone salute her, not that she was in any condition to salute back. Given she was the quartermaster, however, they gave her and Gert a wide berth.

Inzari directed Gert towards the officer's quarters of the barracks, and it surprised him to find she had a room to herself. However, he could only stare at the blank box aside the door lock. Was there a ringel equivalent to strands?

"Uh," he tried to ask, hoping Inzari was conscious.

"Fingerprint scanner," Inzari muttered, flailing her left paw at the plate.

Gert did not understand what she meant by "fingerprints", but he caught on enough to place her paw there for her. The door slid open. He dragged her inside and heaved her onto the bed, where she lay motionless, her longcoat flapping wide open.

Gert leaned on his knees and panted, trying not to stare at her. "Sorry about all that."

"Get me the bottle from the closet," Inzari mumbled—hard to tell at first what she said.

"It's not alcohol, is it?" Gert asked.

"No, stupid. It's antidote."

Antidote? Gert's throat clenched, wondering if there was some kind of poison in that drink she had not told him about. But that would have been *ridiculous*. Why would they serve that to their own crew? Then again, he didn't know much at all about the culture of ringel pirates.

Gert peeked in the first side door—bathroom—and the second, finding the closet packed to the brim with personal belongings. Stacks of data disks, a bandolier with dangerous plasma pistols just lying there, a case of jewelry, other odd technical gadgets, and strangely, behind her four identical longcoats, what looked to be a clear family portrait of ringel. Gert pressed the backlight button, and saw who must have been Inzari's parents, along with four cubs—four! That was an unthinkable luxury aboard the *White Flower II*, and Gert could only imagine what it would be like to grow up with three brothers.

He squinted at the portrait. No, all the cubs in the picture were male. The adult female didn't look like Inzari, the stripes were all wrong, though the cub he'd mistaken for Inzari had a V-mark on his chest similar to hers. Was he mistaken? What was this picture then if not a family portrait?

He learned, though, that ringel wore jewelry even as cubs, though none of them had as many piercings as the pirates did. They were also incredibly fuzzy as small cubs.

As he turned, his nose bumped into a satchel hanging from the overhead shelf, the neck of a bottle poking out from the open zipper. He removed the bottle and examined the front, which in those weird Ringelese letters read *alcohol antidote*.

"Is this it?" Gert asked, bringing it out to Inzari, but she had passed out where he dropped her. Gert shook her by her shoulder, hoping she wasn't too far gone.

She blinked. "Hmm?"

"The bottle." Gert shook it in front of her. "What is it?"

"Antidote."

"I've never heard of an antidote for alcohol," Gert said.

"'s simple." Inzari reached up and yanked it from Gert's paw. "It bonds to alcohol in yer system, 'n you piss it out."

"Huh. That's ingenious, but it must be horrible for your kidneys."

"Th' what?"

Gert wasn't certain if she meant, "What did you say?" or had implied that ringel didn't have kidneys, but it didn't matter. He'd been reckless to try alien liquor without knowing whether it would harm geroo—trying their antidote would be idiotic.

Inzari took a swig, then hacked and coughed. "Tastes like utter shit, though,"

The pungent aroma hit Gert's nose—even compared to the alcohols he tasted, it stood out. His eyes watered. "I can imagine," he said, teeth grit. Fortunately, that scent dissipated rather than filling the room.

"Ugh," she moaned, "as much as I drank, I need to down half this bottle… Make sure it gets into me, would ya? I still got a job to do and can't wait five hours for this to pass."

"Alright but, speaking of, can I use your toilet? I also drank way too much."

"Piss away." Inzari gestured toward the bathroom door, then slammed back another large swig of the bottle.

Gert hoped that what he urinated into for what seemed like several minutes wasn't the sink. The basics of this alien vessel seemed easy enough to puzzle out, but many of its smaller functions looked different from how he was accustomed. He pressed a nearby button and a quick, but loud vacuum cleared out the basin. He couldn't identify any soap, so he went out to ask Inzari.

Back in the bedroom, he found Inzari clutching the bottle to her chest and snoring.

Gert sighed as he wandered over beside her. This wasn't how a meeting with pirates was supposed to go, was it? He should have been more frightened. The pirates were intimidating—rowdy, unkempt, and more than a little vulgar. And Inzari was too, but she was also…appealing. She treated him like "one of the guys", despite him being about as dissimilar to a pirate as possible. She didn't even mind being vulnerable around him—alone, with a strange male, when she had had too much to drink. True, she would break his spine if he tried to take advantage of her, but the unexpected intimacy she showed him…

Not that he would. Gert couldn't abide the thought of taking advantage of anyone. He refused to be mean or awful, even if they were an enemy.

Nevertheless, he couldn't get his mind off of Inzari, and he wondered if this was a betrayal to Hiani. *She was clear how she felt about me.* But if things didn't work out with Inzari—

If things didn't work out with Inzari? Gert's reverie broke wide open. Why was he fantasizing about romancing a pirate, someone who was more apt to stab him in the neck than she ever was to respect him? He pushed her out of his mind. No matter how…infatuating he found her, there was no point in pretending she had any interest in him.

He pried the bottle from Inzari's fingers—trying not to touch her any more than necessary—and held it up to the light. She'd barely made it a quarter of the way through. He nudged her with his knee.

"Nng," Inzari muttered.

"Come on, gotta drink more," Gert said. Her scent was so strong here. She tried to hide it away with those cigars she smoked, but here in her bedroom, even their foul stink couldn't mask it; in fact, they enhanced it. It was a deep earthy odor like what emanated from the farming levels when the crops were at their peak, like a pleasant memory of one's appetite. That scent soaked into the pillow, the sheet, even her mattress.

"I'm swearing off drinking, Dad," Inzari said.

Gert held the bottle near her nose, and she jolted alert, coughing.

"Come on, a bit more," Gert said, pushing her to drink. Some of it dribbled out the side of her mouth, but she swallowed despite the odor. Gert could imagine that the ringel might have smoked so much simply to kill the taste buds.

He held the bottle up to the light again as Inzari slumped back on the bed. Nearly half. That ought to have been enough for it to work, he hoped, because he didn't want to force Inzari through any more of that. He set the bottle on a bedside table and looked on the back.

"Cuts inebriation to one-fifth potency." He wasn't sure of his translation work, but that likely meant that Inzari would have an hour to sleep it off rather than five. He left the bottle on the bed's nightstand.

Then he sniffed himself and noted that even only taking a half hour, the stink of the bar's cigars had penetrated his own fur. That would not do for when he got back to the ship, so he entered the bathroom once again and climbed into the tiny shower space.

The showerhead on the ceiling dropped a dollop of cold goop on him. "Gross," he grumbled, ears low in disgust. "Can I have soap and water, please?" The shower didn't answer. The goop at least smelled antiseptic, so making do with what he had, he scrubbed it into his fur and figured he'd find out how to rinse it off later.

He tried to clean as much of his body as he could with the limited amount of "scrub", but it all seemed to disappear with just the tiniest amount of lathering. So he focused on his face, arms, and chest, to hold him over until he could get a real shower when he got back home.

After about five minutes of careful working, Inzari burst into the bathroom, shouting, "Out of my way!"

Gert wasn't even in her way, but he froze up at her frantic scrambling. The shower door was translucent, but still he turned away to give her privacy. He wished again that a noisy spray flowed from the showerhead. But he stood in silence, listening awkwardly to the sound of her urine splashing against the steel bowl. It went on and on without an end. Gert felt so very conspicuous; he'd only ever had one girlfriend close enough they'd share a bathroom.

"I thought that would take you at least an hour," Gert said. Instantly, hot water blasted him from the ceiling. "Shove me in the recycler!" He swore.

"Oh, watch out for that," Inzari said. "The shower waits for you to lather before turning on, to save water. Now I need something for the headache…" Inzari giggled. She peeked her head inside the shower. Without her longcoat, her body was so much more slender. "Say, I know you're not ringel, but I gotta ask, are you shy?"

Gert stood there, dripping wet, looking down at her. He wiped the water from his eyes. "I am, but it seems to matter less and less around this place."

"You're catching on!" She shut the shower door again, and a gout of hot, dry air blasted up under Gert's tail. The things he swore would have made his mother cringe, rest her weary soul.

He stepped out of the shower, only a little damp under his crevasses, when Inzari grabbed him by the paw and yanked him toward the bed, tossing him on top, and then herself on top of him.

"Woah, what!" Gert exclaimed, trying to wrap his head around what he'd gotten himself into.

"I asked if you were shy!" Inzari said.

"Is that like asking for…"

"Sex, yes, you can say it. Great for headaches, y'know?" She sat up atop him and stretched.

Gert stared for a long while at her body, and he was all too aroused, which seemed off to him. She had her arms around his neck, and licked and nibbled up his cheek and ear, trapping him in a pleasing situation. But Gert was way, way too confused, and he pushed lightly at her shoulders.

"You need to explain things for once," Gert said. "Not that I'm not flattered."

"You're killing the mood!" Inzari said, scowling a bit at him.

"Yeah, and I don't know you!"

"You were aroused from the moment you laid eyes on me!" Inzari snapped, and folded her arms. "Don't think I didn't see. You were making it so obvious an anup priest would take notice!"

Gert felt flush. He'd hoped than an alien might not recognize the scent of geroo arousal—but then again, he'd been told, over and over and over by every girl he knew, that his thoughts about them were transparent. At least on the shuttle he'd been in the suit to cover up the most blatant indicator of his desire, but there was nothing but the cabin air between them now, and increasingly less of that as Inzari leaned into him.

"Still!" Gert said, "I'd like to know if…we have anything in common?" It was a weak excuse, but the only thing that came to mind—no female he'd been with intimately had ever acted anything like Inzari. He must have missed a step somewhere.

"Hmm." Inzari flopped over to his side on the bed and rubbed a spot on her temple. "So you are shy."

"What's that mean? You just…have sex because you're not shy?"

"Bashfulness is not a virtue among ringel," Inzari explained. "That's… That's when people are too afraid of each other to be honest, with their words or with their bodies."

"I think something's being lost in translation," Gert said.

"Perhaps it's the wrong word," Inzari said. "Maybe it's like…are you intimidated by me?"

"Yeah, I am," Gert said. "But that's not a deal-breaker."

"Whatever. The point is, I want sex because I like you."

"You do?"

"You're an awkward git, no doubt about it, but you're a sport, you outdrank me, and you helped me back to my quarters. That's not a small thing in my files."

"You like geroo?"

Inzari shrugged. "You got two eyes, two arms, two legs, and at least one penis, that's good enough for me. But if you're asking if I find you attractive, eh, I suppose? I kinda like big guys. Your fur pattern is cute. I like your broad noses, it's different. Could stand to be a little thinner, but…"

Gert bit his lip to stifle himself from blurting out something dumb, but he did anyway. "Oh, thank the ancestors, I thought I was the only one!"

Inzari side-eyed him. "What do you mean by that?"

"I mean, uh…" Gert sighed. He'd already begun, why stop, vulnerable as he was? Even with Inzari's snark, she seemed willing to entertain him, and he'd felt bottled up for so long.

So he confessed. "See…my first lessons in Ringelese were when I was an adolescent, you know, and the course materials had pictures of your kind, and uh…"

Inzari grinned, turning over to lie on her front and lean on her elbows. "Go on," she said, her face leaning in closer to Gert's.

"Oh ancestors, this is embarrassing," Gert covered his face with his paws.

"I won't tell anyone; be all embarrassing at me!"

Gert wasn't even certain if he could trust her on that, but he'd longed to tell someone, anyone, for so long, it all just came spilling out. He described the depths of perversion—dirty drawings he'd burned after finishing, fantasies about being roughly handled or held in place or locked in a made-up stasis field or in regular old manacles, including a long and extensive one about being kidnapped by aliens. Not specifically ringel, but it always felt more "plausible" with them since they breathed such similar air.

"And the one where we have space suits but they're somehow thin and you can…uh, in zero gravity, and…" Gert trailed off, expecting Inzari to have fallen asleep by then.

"Damn, that's some imagination you got!"

"I know, I'm weird and off-putting."

"Buddy, you haven't cracked the top hundred in weirdest sex fantasies I've heard of," Inzari said. "I was just thinking how it sounds quaint listening to you get flustered over nothing!"

Gert uncovered his eyes. "Nothing!"

"Listen," she said, "sex is weird. On any planet that's developed sexual reproduction, it's weird. Why? Who knows!"

"Probably because the logistics of pulling two different individuals together to procreate consistently millions of times requires evolution to hardwire certain sexual desires in without making them too specific, because creatures with too specific of desires are on top of the list to die out when circumstances change," Gert said in one breath.

"Okay, what I meant was, who cares? I remember how it was when I was growing up. Sorting out one's desires is not always an easy thing, even on Ringeltec. Much easier just to rent a couple pornos and try to piece it together from there."

"We got sex education onboard," Gert said. "Not that it matters much; we can't have cubs unless someone dies first. All the females onboard have nanomachine contraception for population control purposes."

"Sounds good to me," Inzari said. "I don't even like kits."

"It's kinda weird then," Gert said, "when intelligent direction takes over control of evolutionary forces and we have to deal with all these vestigial needs…"

"Like sex," Inzari added.

"…and it has nothing to do with its initial purpose. It's weird to think about it too much—and yeah, I guess I've been thinking about it too much."

"Is that a problem?" Inzari asked. "You gonna turn down a fancy seven-course dinner because it's more than evolution built you for? Or are you gonna enjoy letting someone press your buttons, whatever they are?" She walked her fingers up along Gert's chest. "You're not slave to evolution, or some remote gods or whatever, you're in this weird and confusing life *for you*."

"I suppose."

They lay there for a while, Gert looking up at the blank ceiling, Inzari stroking the fur on his chest.

"Geroo and ringel can't have cubs together anyway," he said.

"You're making it transparent what's on your mind," Inzari said.

"So, you're not gonna expect anything out of me?"

"It's just sex, there's no commitment involved."

"Then yeah," Gert said. "I'd like to have sex with you."

"Finally!" Inzari rolled back on top of Gert and straddled him. "Let's screw!"

Chapter 10: The Geordian

Moani held out a paw. She wriggled strangely, as her kind had very flexible spines and often seemed to pivot above the waist when gesturing. She also wore a backpack that was connected by wires to her arm, ending in a bracelet with a small computer attached to it. *Was that how she survived in this atmosphere?* Ateri stared at her paw, otherwise keeping the same rigid posture, paws behind his back and chest out.

As much as the krakun educational system always tried to frame the annexation of Gerootec as a positive, that they gave *life* and *meaning* to the geroo, it was impossible to sweeten the destruction of their home world. Geordians were a part of all that. Despite having never met, Ateri hated her on principle, much as how he hated all krakun, despite only ever being face-to-face with one.

"I won't bite," Moani said, ears out smiling. Her geroo was flawless.

"Apologies," Ateri said, reaching his own paw out to touch hers. "My life rule is to trust no one."

"Ah," Moani said, her ear swiveling toward Sinon. "Then you're like most captains."

"Hear hear!" Sinon said as he rummaged around the wet bar in the corner of the room. He pressed his paws, clutching the necks of two bottles, to his chest. "You're a geroo after my heart, Captain. You sure you don't want a drink?"

"Quite sure," Ateri said.

Moani turned her eyes up and studied Ateri's face. He realized he was holding his breath.

"Hard to tell with that eyepatch," Moani said, "since it adds to that stoic look. But you're stiff."

"Perhaps."

"Do you have a problem with me, Captain?" she asked, placing a paw on her chest, and at once, Ateri knew she didn't mean her, personally.

He resolved not to bring up the geroo-geordian issues. If she was instrumental to Sinon's plan, Ateri would learn to live with it. But that didn't mean that there weren't obstacles to this arrangement they needed to overcome.

"I still have many questions," Ateri said. Ever since he arrived, he only had questions. Being pulled into a conspiracy did that— Ateri had so much catching up to do. Moani being a geordian should have been beside the point, so far as it concerned the plan's logistics.

Ateri rubbed his forehead to ease the tension. "First, I agreed it would be suitable for you to give me hostages. Assuming we can smuggle you all back onboard the *White Flower II*, you are all going to be under house arrest not simply to ensure your cooperation, but also for your safety. If you are, as Sinon put it, his secret weapon, how will you perform your duties while locked in a small room?"

"Ah, she in particular will need more freedom of movement than the rest of us," Sinon said. "You can keep her under guard by some trusted security, can you not?"

Ateri huffed. Imposing this deal on the rest of the crew, even his own subcommanders, was already not going to be easy, and also not something he could demand that Sinon do himself.

"You have security you can trust, don't you?" Sinon asked.

"I'll need to put Gert on that detail," Ateri said.

"The one you came in with? Doubling up on his duties much, isn't he?"

"Who I can spare is beside the point," Ateri said. "The fact is, she is a *geordian*. Even if we avoid alerting the krakun, the crew would lynch her the moment they glimpsed her onboard!" That was a minor exaggeration. If they had a reason for one to be present, a geordian would only bewilder and confuse most, but Ateri never took it for granted that *someone* would escalate tensions. "How in the five hells are we supposed to hold a geordian hostage aboard a geroo spacecraft?"

"Oh, he didn't tell you!" Moani turned to Sinon. "You didn't tell him about the thing!"

Sinon shrugged. "He didn't ask. And I figured you'd enjoy telling him more."

"What thing?" Ateri asked.

"This thing I'm wearing," Moani said, gesturing to the backpack strapped to her shoulders with a cable running to the polyvinyl-and-metal bracer on her arm.

"I thought that was life support," Ateri said.

"No, I have a forty-eight-hour heart pump installed for that," she said, pointing to a medicine injection tube embedded in her skin, just under her clavicle—looking like an off-center feature of the silver necklace.

She returned her gestures to the bracer. "*This* is a camouflage unit—a personal cloak. It's like the cloak that hides the ship." With a button press, she glowed, and a young female geroo took her place, with shiny fur and red-and-gold beads on her necklace. The camouflage unit disappeared.

Ateri's mouth hung open, and he stepped forward to look the geroo in the eye.

She pointed to her cheek. "My eyes are down here, but the illusion is so complete it looks like I'm staring you right in the face. The device is silent, has no visual flaws to naked eye resolution, and matches the motions for anything I do to make it appear as if I am the correct size."

Ateri reached out to touch the geroo's cheek, only to find that his fingers, while they didn't scatter the illusion, passed right through and touched the edge of Moani's ear.

"Impressive, but it'll never work," Ateri said. "You don't smell a thing like a geroo."

"No, this device only tricks the eyes and a broad variety of scanners—it will trick infrared, ultraviolet, anything a krakun can see. As for smell, the krakun rarely pay attention to individual smells of us mammals."

"Yes, but it's the other geroo onboard I worry about."

"Yeah, that's why we're also bringing odor-masking solution," Moani said. "It's not absolute, but it will ensure I can pass without drawing attention."

"Okay, I've changed my mind," Ateri said, turning to Sinon.

"Oh?" Sinon looked worried—almost disappointed.

"I have a demand on top of my agreement. I want one of those."

Sinon laughed. "Certainly," he said, "I'm sure there's an extra lying around somewhere…"

When Ateri turned back, Moani had switched off the illusion. She undid the straps on those and hefted off the backpack of dense-weave cloth, which hit the table between the sofas with a loud thud.

"How heavy is that thing?" Ateri asked.

"I've had to practice carrying it." Moani huffed, as though she had to catch her second wind just for that. "Though your people are stockier, I imagine you could get used to these quick."

Ateri tested, lifting the bag by a loop on its top, and found the backpack was heavy even for him—ten or twelve kilograms. Not that it was difficult to lift, but imagining something that weight, on his back all day… Not with his back, anyway, though Gert would have no trouble.

While he sated his curiosity, Moani pulled out a tubular device from her other bag resting on her hip, and plugged it into the port below her neck. It glowed blue. She seemed satisfied enough to shove the indicator back into the bag, fetching no medicine.

"I suppose, with limited enough exposure, we could pull this off," Ateri said. "Assuming your skills are all you built them up to be."

Moani tilted her head up proudly. "I know everything about krakun ships, gate ships in particular, and everything I don't know, I can figure out."

"Even a terraforming device?" Ateri asked.

"That's the exception," Moani said. "Our understanding of what a terraformer even looks like is limited, much less how it works. But that's why you need me for this. I should be able to figure it out if I look at it long enough."

Sounds like Chendra, Ateri thought. Chendra was his own genius, one among the pawful of crewmembers he could call such. Ateri needed to curate the very intelligent and not waste them; among a crew of ten thousand, it would not do to let talent flounder when their lives depended on these complex machines.

Despite that, it was a boast. At least the pirates studied enough about the ships to disable the trinity... So Ateri only had one question for her.

"Are you the one who knows how to hack the gate and subvert the trinity?" Ateri asked her.

Moani's ears fell, and she turned toward Sinon.

"That's payment," Sinon reminded them. "Nothing about that until we conclude our business."

"Of course," Moani said.

"But at what point can I expect to receive the payment? The exchange will need to happen before we acquire the terraformer. I believe you have what you say, but not that you will deliver it. I expect you can assure me of that."

"That is simple," Sinon said, downing his glass. "In the final stage of the plan, when we're prepared to take the terraformer, we will disable the trinity for safety sake. At that point we will deliver the key to you, and you are free to test it for yourself. We cannot do it beforehand."

"But at that point, haven't you locked me into this plan regardless?" Ateri asked. "You shortchange me and I have no recourse."

"But you trust I have it?"

"There's no other way you could arrive here, so you must."

"In that case, make sure Moani or one of my other hackers survives, and you can torture the information out of her."

Moani flinched. "Sinon, that's not funny!"

Sinon laughed. "I know. You'd spill the secret before he touched you!"

Moani fumed. "Ateri, sir, believe me, we will put that information in your paws when the time is right, and there won't be any need to get physical."

Ateri tilted his head at the exchange, at Sinon making light of his subordinate getting abused. Ateri was himself aggressive, but such comments seemed wrong. If he was to fight someone, it would be a serious matter, not a joking one.

"So is that enough?" Moani asked, folding her arms. "Because we need to get started now."

"So quickly?" Ateri asked.

"How long ago did you start your scanning of C-18-3?"

"Right as you were disabling our ship," Ateri said. "They're likely already an hour in."

"I'll need to gain computer access, then access to your sensor array within the next four hours, or it will be too late to alter the readings. And then there's nothing we can do."

"I dislike being rushed,"

"She is right. However," Sinon said, "if the plan satisfies you—"

Ateri scoffed and flattened his ears. "It does not."

"Captain… We touched paws on it. Now, I understand your concerns still, but I have extended myself as far as I can go. I gave you my plan, I gave you my hacker, I gave you my officers, and I gave you confirmation I can pay. This is your last chance to affirm your agreement. And I should point out that if I must leave here empty-pawed, so be it; I will have to wait a year or two for the next ship to approach a planet and offer another captain the deal."

Ateri twitched. His immediate reaction was an internal but resounding *no!*

He knew it was still too good to be true, but he could feel himself drawing ever closer to his day of execution. The company allowed no geroo aboard a slave ship to live past sixty, not even the captain. And he'd wasted the last ten years making no progress on freeing his people.

Foolish or not, trick or not, this is my opportunity. No more hesitation. I'm going in on this.

Sinon grinned as he watched Ateri's expression change—he must have been perceptive to read geroo expressions, because other species often had trouble. "So you see, Captain. Once we start this snowball rolling, nothing will stop the avalanche."

What the hells is a snowball? Ateri wondered. He'd learned what snow was, but could not for the life of him solve the idiom except through context.

"One final thing," Ateri said. "I will need to speak with my first officer. And the sooner I can, the better. It will take time to arrange quarters for…how many officers total?"

"Twenty-one," Sinon said. "We carry our own rations; you won't need to worry about feeding us."

"Right. Even scouting out which deck will be most appropriate might be difficult—transport, circumventing landlords…"

"Then make your call," Sinon said.

"You can use the patch-in program I made," Moani said. "That was how I got in your message system. It should support a video call and it bypasses the server records. You need to do it from the hardware on this ship."

"Thank you," Ateri said, bowing just a little to Moani and Sinon. "I will let you know how things turn out. Gather your officers and supplies together for transport."

* * *

"You told them *what?*" Jakari sighed. Her backdrop was of the captain's office, so Ateri could be certain nobody was eavesdropping.

"You think this is because of my impending Going Away," Ateri said.

"I'm worried that's motivating your judgment, yes."

"Maybe it is. But suppose this happened a month from now. I would be dead, and barring Gert, this would be your decision. So, in your capacity as my first officer, what do you think?"

The line was silent for a long moment. Ateri hated having to put her on the spot like this, but he needed her opinion. He'd hate to think he was alone in all of this.

"I'd want to talk to them myself," Jakari said. "What did Gert think?"

"I haven't spoken with him about it yet," Ateri said. "Just tell me, would the possibility even be on the table for you?"

"I…" She hesitated, and rubbed a paw across her face. "Listen, regardless of what you've chosen, you need to come back right away. Even beyond the crew asking questions, the new commissioner isn't pleased. She'll be here at twelve hundred hours, and you need to be here or she'll execute crewmembers!"

Ateri winced, then paused, straightening his ears up. "She will?"

"That's what she said, and I have no reason to believe she meant otherwise! She's a krakun, and pissed off, and can do with us as she pleases!"

"But not when we're preparing for planetary scans, remember?"

Jakari paused, then tapped her chin. "Oh, that's right. That happens so infrequently I forgot about that rule. I didn't even know the company enforced it."

To Ateri's knowledge, the company did enforce the rule, but they didn't unfurl it upon a banner. He did not know much about company politics because Planetary Acquisitions did not bother to educate the geroo about them, but he had access to krakun news broadcasts, and he'd gleaned enough.

Whenever a fleet ship approached the remotest possibility of a viable planet, company shares went up. Ateri also didn't know much about how stocks worked, but he knew money, and the company liked money. If the planet was viable, then share prices skyrocketed.

As a result, the shareholders *hated* it when problems arose on the money-making side of the process. There was a ship once—Ateri believed it was in the geordian fleet, as it was named *Chiauo Gi*—that protested during one such terraformation opportunity when their commissioner executed several officers at once. The protest turned into a riot, which became so violent it ended up scuttling the ship. And it could take *hundreds* of years for the company to reroute a slave ship to the same sector, leaving them wide open for interception by foreign powers.

So, for this one occasion, the shareholders created the *Chiauo Gi* rule. During the planetary research phase, no company employee, geroo or otherwise, was to be removed from the ship's skill pool without a detailed risk analysis. This applied to anyone, geroo and krakun alike—despite most any reason, including crimes, or just because the commissioner wished them dead. Not even one's sixtieth birthday was an exception to the rule. On rare occasions, geroo had lived an additional month or even a *year* beyond their fixed date simply because the ship's operations in research or terraforming could not spare them.

Ateri needed to refresh himself on the rule once he returned to the ship, but he was certain he could make use of it. Yes, the geroo feared the commissioner, but the commissioner feared the company, and the company feared the shareholders.

"I think they will enforce it," Ateri said. "And once the pirates have falsified the planetary data…"

"They have to treat us nicely while terraformation is going on." Jakari's ears perked. It still turned into a frown a moment later. "But…we're still counting on the word of some pirates we can pull this off and escape…"

"We *could* escape though," Ateri said. "How could we say no to this opportunity?"

"By remembering we have to preserve the lives of our crew first," Jakari said. "Hon, the Exit Plan is a nice dream, it always has been. But we need to be practical."

"Then I'll leave it up to you—"

"Don't you dare." She leaned into the screen with her ears up stiff. "I will do as you will. I love you and trust you, regardless of misgivings I may have. If you have listened and considered what I've said, and you still want to do this, I am behind you all the way."

"I understand. It just feels like it's too big a step for even the captain to take, even if it's the right one."

"Do you believe it is the right one?" Jakari asked.

"For the immediate safety of our ship and crew, perhaps not," Ateri said. And he knew full well if the wrong people found out about this plan, they'd recycle him on the spot. There would be no stopping a mutiny. "But for the future of our species, I can't say no."

"We will pray to our ancestors it is not the wrong decision. Please come back. We'll see this through to the end."

Chapter 11: Code X

All crew, Code X. Calling to docking section B3: Boatswains Chur, Jorjin, Drygan; Sailmasters Syyra, Stix; Quartermaster Inzari…"

How am I even going to break this to the captain?

Gert sat in a laundry room, inspecting their spacewalk suits for damage. After that intercom announcement, he paid little attention to his surroundings the whole while. For the all-too-brief moments he was with Inzari in her bed, he seemed to still be there, his mind stuck on repeat.

Gert didn't like keeping secrets from Ateri, for reasons not the least of which he knew Ateri would find out. But more than that, he could not abide violating that trust the captain placed in him.

But it wasn't as though Ateri *ordered* him not to have sex with any of the pirates. The topic had never come up. Then again, it might have been so obvious he should have assumed it.

As Gert sat there, thinking, he heard the door open behind him. But he was so lost in his thoughts, he didn't react until Ateri sat down next to him.

"Captain!" Gert exclaimed, jumping from his spot.

"Are the suits intact?" Ateri asked.

"Er, so far as I can figure." Gert realized he'd only been looking at the seal around his suit's neck for the past five minutes.

Rick Griffin

"We won't need to wear them again," Ateri said. "The transport we're taking back can seal onto our airlocks. Apparently, they waited to use that one until they had my assurance of clearance."

"Erm… What is happening?" Gert asked, pulling his thoughts away. "The intercom said something about *Code X*… What is that?"

"We have little time before we return, so I need to give you the short version. I've agreed to make a deal with the pirates. We will fool the krakun into thinking C-18-3 is a viable planet, let them send over a terraformer. The pirates will steal it, and then we'll get the secret to keeping the gate open while keeping the trinity intact."

Gert blinked. "I… I have a few questions, sir—"

"As collateral, the captain offered me his life and the lives of all his seniormost officers. We'll be holding them on the *White Flower II*; Jakari is already making arrangements. But I need to know first if you are still willing to go through with this. I can't afford to spare you, but I would much rather you come into this willing and capable of carrying out everything I need of you if we hope to see this through to the end."

Gert wasn't certain what all could have snapped him out of his reverie, but he wasn't expecting that. He expected at the least the pirates may have wanted to trade something, but conspiring to steal *a terraformer*…

"I don't know, give me three seconds!" Gert said. "I… Ancestors, Captain! How am I supposed to handle all this when you're gone?"

"You won't have to worry about that. If things go according to plan, *Chiauo Gi* will be fully in force long before my sixtieth. I'll be able to stay and continue directing things."

"*Chiauo Gi*… I heard Tesko talking about it on the bridge this morning. That's real?"

"Yes it's real. They don't fill the manual with procedure and code just for a gag."

Gert could hardly express his relief, but it only loosened the anxiety in his chest the smallest amount. "Still! There's no walking this one back if we fail! How the hells do we expect to pull this off without the company executing us all?"

Ateri didn't respond. He was looking down at the floor as though he was ashamed for what he'd done.

"I mean," Gert said, "do you believe this will work?"

"It's not even a matter of believing it will work anymore," Ateri said. "I'm very old, and very tired, and this may be the most selfish thing I've ever done. I want to believe in this. Their captain has enough faith in this plan to put *his* life on the line! I feel as if I have no choice but to trust them." He put a paw on Gert's shoulder. "I need you because we can spare having you off the bridge for as long as it takes to hack our systems and send over the falsified data."

"What'll happen afterward, sir? Assuming this all works, and we're somehow not dead…"

Ateri sighed. "I hope we'll be free. We'd be able to connect the gate to somewhere else in the universe. There's a network of deep space stations out there. With the trinity intact, we could become a part of that. We could work for ourselves rather than the krakun. Maybe even help our people find a new Gerootec."

That was the end goal of the Exit Plan, but Gert had never given the reality of the situation any thought. It was a huge risk! If Krakuntec caught even the slightest whiff that they falsified the data… *Poof.* They were gone, and *Chiauo Gi* would not save them.

"Are we going to tell the other officers?" Gert asked.

"In time. We need to be careful about who we tell and when."

"I think we should tell Subcommander To'onai."

"Perhaps. Though To'onai will assume I've lost my mind."

"What if Jakari told him?" Gert asked. "They're cousins, right?"

"Jakari is cousins with half the ship," Ateri said. "She might get away with telling her niece, except Nuiska isn't an officer and so wouldn't be worth telling."

"But everyone will have to learn about it sometime."

Ateri was silent for a long moment.

"Sir?"

"It's brought to mind the *Silver Mint III* again." Ateri's ears slowly fell aside like they'd deflated. "That day, it upset some officers that I would give up so soon. It relieved many of the others. Well, guess how it split them. The ones who didn't want to give up, they were all the old ones, well into their fifties. Most were in on the plan since Captain Idal. The others still had lives ahead of them and weren't so willing to sacrifice another thirty years. They're the ones still around."

Ateri sat down on a bench, the thick spacesuit slumping over in his arms. "When Sinon explained it...I could feel it. Like I could just reach out with my fingers and take it. But make no mistake, it is a damned longshot. I'm placing my faith in the faithless and trusting that their greed will see this through. If I was a fool then for giving up to save everyone from a terrible fate, what kind of captain am I to throw them all back in the fire?"

"I don't know, sir," Gert said. "But whatever it is you and our people need, I will do whatever is necessary."

Ateri looked up at Gert with his only eye. "Gert, when you set your mind to it, you are the most capable officer on my ship. You can do what I ask. But for your sake, I worry it may be too much."

"How could it be too much? You've been training me to take your place. If I can't do it, then who could?"

* * *

Gert then had his new assignment: looking after the "hostages", though for the time being he was to escort their hacker wherever she needed to go. Time back on the ship was just before 1100 hours. Gert hoped the pirates wouldn't dally too long if the other things Ateri told him—especially about the new commissioner—were as dire as he made them.

When they arrived back at the hangar, the ringel officers milled about as ringel crew rolled crates of supplies aboard, and returned from the back of the transport with empty dolly carts. Every single officer in the line was smoking.

"Get your fill of vices now," said one, who Gert presumed to be Sinon by the manner he addressed the other ringel. "I want no one giving away our position with your noxious odors."

"Hey, geroo!" said one of the female officers. She was more svelte than Inzari. "We'd better be getting a large enough room once we're onboard; I ain't sharing my bed with any of these shits."

"I'm not in charge of your accommodations," Gert said. That job was Jakari's, who as first officer of the *White Flower II* had more clearance than even he did. "I'm not even sure what we can spare."

"Syyra, come on, please?" a short male pleaded with her, as he sucked on a long cigar like he was inhaling it. He had dyed his headfur vivid blue. "I said I was sorry! I meant nothing by the bet, you're one of the best aims I know. It's just you were drunk and all—"

"And I said I don't care," she told him. "Get someone else to wet your cock, I ain't touching yours."

"But it'd be three months! At least!"

"Have a heart, Syyra," said another male, who had a smoother voice and was the widest of the bunch, though that wasn't saying much; by geroo standards, a strong A/C unit could blow him over. "We signed on for the money, not to be ascetic monks."

"If it's so important to you, Drygan," Syyra said, "then you can suck off Stix."

"Why would you tell him to do that?" Stix, the blue-topped ringel, said as he wrung his long tail in his paws.

"Yeah!" Drygan said. "That's not a solution to this problem. I *already* suck him off all the time, so it wouldn't change anything."

Gert backed away to dislodge himself from the argument, regretting just how in-depth he had studied Ringelese. At least Ateri heard none of that. He was too busy looking over the crates being carted on the ship, checking them in case they thought to bring on contraband.

"I'm sorry I was not specific about what you could bring aboard," Ateri said, pulling out a long rifle from one crate, "but this is out of the question."

"We have to defend ourselves when the times comes, Captain," Sinon explained. "Seizure of the terraformer will not come without a fight, no matter how things pan out."

"I don't want weapons on my ship!"

"I gave you the one plasma pistol as a sign of good faith," Sinon retorted.

Ateri was silent for a moment. "Fair enough. I will allow your sidearm."

"There's twenty-one of us!"

"Then you can lend it to whoever needs it when they need it." He put the rifle back in the crate and shoved it down the ramp after a lanky pirate who scrambled to keep the dolly cart from plowing him down. "No other weapons!"

"You heard the captain," Sinon said, sighing. "Weapons stay aboard the Jet Black Sword."

"But—" Syyra started.

"We'll make do, Sailmaster," Sinon said. "Coats open for inspection, now!"

The officers opened their longcoats and about three dozen firearms of various sizes fell to the ground about them, to a lot of grumbling and consternation.

While the crew cleaned up their litter, Gert picked up one of the wrapped food bars from an open crate. The lettering announced it was a pre-processed ration bar with most essential nutrients for a ringel soldier. Inzari appeared, peeking around his shoulder, and made a face.

"Yech, I am not looking forward to eating these for three months," she said. "They stop you up hard. You need to drown yourself to keep regular."

"Oh, there you are," Gert said, feeling flush. "I'm sorry, maybe I could treat you to some shipboard food instead sometime."

"Well, we have sorta similar diets," Inzari said. She grinned at him. "I'll think about it."

Gert sniffed the bar, though with the foil wrapping it produced no odor. "So what do these taste like?"

"You're welcome to try; we have a million."

Gert started to open the bar with his gloved paws, and then thinking better, he placed it back in the slot he'd pulled it from. "I'll pass."

Inzari barked a laugh. "He can be taught!"

Gert stepped back from the crate as a ringel dragged it off, and he bumped into another of the officers standing there, almost knocking her over. Gert wheeled about to apologize—though paused when he saw it was…

A geordian.

Gert couldn't help but show surprise on his ears. Ateri had neglected to mention that part.

"Oh, Gert, this is our hacker," Inzari said. "Moani."

"Oh, hi," Gert said, forgetting his apology.

"Savior of Vala, kid," Moani said, "watch where you're going!"

Gert tilted his head at her, reaching a paw out to touch hers, though also leaning in to catch her scent. It wasn't striking, just unoffensive—but the orange geordian was appealing to the eyes. "I will be escorting you around the ship," he said. "With some kind of cloaking device, I heard?"

Moani screwed up her face as Gert lumbered right into her personal space. "Erm, right," she said, touching paws to Gert's.

"Don't your people need ammonia compounds to breathe?" Gert asked. "Georditec's atmosphere is—"

"Yes, that's what the pump is for," she said, tapping the notch near her necklace. "It's installed near my heart to disperse azane into the blood."

"Oh, neat! So you've been living with that for a while then?"

"Fifteen years so far." Her eyes brightened "It's for geordians to live in oxygen-nitrogen atmospheres, so they're common. I still sleep with a breather mask when I can, but otherwise it's about twenty-four to forty-eight hours of dosage at a time."

"Well, let me know the moment you need any help with it," Gert said, ears up in a smile. "I need to make sure you're well-taken care of!"

Moani gave him a weird look. "Okay, what's the deal? You seem cheery for a geroo."

"Are we not?" Gert asked. "I have to confess I know little about how we're perceived to the rest of the galaxy. I've kinda lived my entire life on a ship."

"I dunno, but I won't complain," Moani said. She grinned how the ringel did, with teeth bared. Maybe she had been living around them too long? "I was expecting my escort to be surly and uncooperative, like your captain."

"He's fine once you get to know him!"

"I somehow doubt getting to know him will sweeten the sour blood between us," Moani said. "I may have lived with ringel most of my life, but even I know geroo and geordians have never gotten along. I've already resigned myself to that fact, and am ready to hold my breath as I walk through this job."

"You can be assured," Gert said, "I won't hold my breath around you. You don't even smell all that much like ammonia!"

Moani's ears flattened and she narrowed her eyes. She glanced at Inzari and, deliberately switching to Ringelese, asked, "Does this idiot have to be my escort?"

"He's all they can spare," Inzari said, giggling and slapping Gert on the back.

"Hey, what!" Gert protested as the two passed him by to board the transport. "What did I say?"

Chapter 12: Taking The Backdoor

Each airlock had a ten-meter by thirty-meter bay which rose an additional deck, with the space above reserved for the operator's booth. The room served both as manual control, observation, and also the stopgap in case anything happened to the airlock itself; it could seal the entire chamber off from the rest of the ship.

Three crewmembers carted in a series of two-meter cube crates. Jakari shooed them away when they finished, then locked the door behind from the operator's booth.

"Is the airlock bay secure?" Ateri asked over the strand.

"Primed and ready, Captain," Jakari said.

The inner airlock door hissed as it opened, and Ateri stepped out, carrying his spacewalk suit rather than wearing it. Behind him, the outer airlock door led into the open cabin of the alien transport ship, with over a dozen ringel inside, strapped against the walls with the seats along the sides. Gert rose above the crowd, pulling his seatbelt off, and hurried in after Ateri.

Jakari saluted when Ateri approached, and Ateri returned the salute. Then he closed the distance between them and they embraced.

"Welcome back," Jakari said.

"Don't hate me for this, please," Ateri whispered.

"I won't. I will believe in you, my captain."

As they spoke, Ateri took her paws and noted the bandage plaster on her palms.

"Something hurt you," he said.

"It's nothing," Jakari said. "The new commissioner said a few things, and…well, it wasn't intentional. I clenched too hard."

"It must have been awful. Here…"

He kissed each of her paws, and then her nose. Then he kissed her on each cheek as he leaned in to wrap his paws around her tight.

"Damn, I've missed you," Ateri said.

"It's only been a couple hours," Jakari chided, though she didn't stop him from touching her.

"That's a couple hours more than we should have been apart."

"Ah, then perhaps I should have come with you." Jakari giggled. "And you could have left Gert in charge."

They turned to Gert, who was looking away. He clasped paws behind his back, hummed to himself, and rocked on and off his tailtip. When he felt the captain and commander's eyes on him, his ears turned flush, and he called to the ringel in their language.

"Okay, we'll make multiple trips to get you all to your apartment, which is on deck fourteen. It has no furnishings, but we'll try to get mattresses in there before twenty-one hundred hours tonight!"

"I hope it has plumbing," Stix complained. "Three months, gods damn me…"

"Does it have plumbing?" Gert asked Jakari.

"Yes," Jakari said. "It was a normal set of apartments, but they became caught in the middle of deck reorganization. They're now behind the new manufacturing quarter."

"Oh," Gert said, then paused. "Wait, that's the one everyone had complaints over, wasn't it? The big court case?"

"It's perfect!" Jakari said. "It's on an isolated hallway near the rim. It's been empty for the last year, and we're still not scheduled to replace them for at least another."

"What about Moani's quarters?" Gert asked. "I think she wanted something more private."

"Oh, right," Jakari said. "I figured she could bunk with you."

"What!" Moani exclaimed. She'd seemed almost like she'd blended in, as she was already wearing the camouflage that made her look like a rather flattering geroo. She also had her large bag of equipment hanging around her shoulder which the camouflage was kind enough to incorporate into the illusion rather than hide it.

Jakari raised up a new strand and snapped a picture of her. "There we go!" Jakari said, then tapped a few more things in on the screen. "Since you'll need to move about the ship, I got you a strand. You're in the system now, should anyone ask weird questions." She handed the strand over to Moani.

She pouted and took the strand, glancing at its screen. "Keeping my name Moani?"

"It's close enough to a geroo name it should work," Jakari said. "Keep things simple and all."

"And I'm a cadet in the officer academy?"

"If anyone asks where you should be," Ateri said, "you can excuse yourself as being on job training, and you can refer to the three of us if you're in trouble."

"Well…thank you," Moani said. "Though I should get my own apartment."

"We could get you a separate apartment on the deck nineteen block," Gert said, "but nineteen is kinda—"

"A dump."

Gert tilted his ears. "How did you know that?"

"That's how it always works on these ships," Moani said. "Recycler and all the garbage is at the bottom, all the nice clean rooms for high-grade manufacturing and research are at the top. Over time, the desirability of any deck becomes a rough gradient between those two. So, no thank you on deck nineteen." She pinched Gert's shoulder and tugged him along. "Come on, we need to get down to the main computer room before we run out of time."

"Ow!" Gert protested, "Ow, I'm following, okay!"

* * *

Lieutenant En-den-to, second in charge of computer operations, looked much older than he was. Besides his grayish mottled coat, a discoloration some geroo never even got in their old age, he sat hunched over a computer as he typed away, bags under his eyes like he hadn't slept in weeks. From what Gert understood, he might not have—but he still got all his work done on time.

"En-den-to, just the geroo I needed to see," Gert said, with Moani in her disguise following behind.

The moment he turned—and saw a beautiful female right behind the subcommander—he perked up, which shaved at least ten years off. "Oh?" he asked. "And who is this?"

"Moani is being added to the academy roster." Gert gestured toward the smiling female geroo at his side, holding her slate in both paws like an eager schoolgirl. "As a favor I'm giving her a head start on learning the system layout."

En-den-to's nose twinged in her direction, ears twisted in confusion over her lack of scent. "Oh, absolutely, Subcommander," En-den-to said without even looking at Gert.

The three of them were the only ones in the central server— every other computer operator had drifted off to lunch. It wasn't a terrible surprise En-den-to was still here, working, because that was all he ever seemed to do since his mate had her premature Going Away. Still, Gert would have preferred to see him rest once in awhile.

"In fact," En-den-to continued, "if the young female is pursuing computers, I'd be available as her tutor—"

"That won't be necessary," Gert said. "The captain's already given me that task. However—" he put a finger up to stop En-den-to's protests about how Gert always seemed to get special treatment. "—if you'd like to do her a favor, she's looking for an apartment of her own, and deck five would be preferable."

"I hear it's quiet up there," Moani added.

"Er, yes sir," En-den-to said. On top of this job, he was also landlord for the officer's apartment block on deck five. He had quite a few side-jobs—company policy required every adult aboard to work one eight-hour shift for critical or critical-adjacent jobs, both officers and un-enlisted crew. They could do whatever they liked on the sixteen hours off—sometimes even sleep!—and many took on additional jobs for the extra money. En-den-to seemed to take on jobs just so he'd have something to do.

"Though," he said, "I don't know if there's any room left. And the application needs to go through the finance committee, given the subsidy."

"Aren't you on the finance committee?" Gert asked.

"I'm not the only member," En-den-to said. "And they won't award an apartment to a cadet."

"I could speak with them," Gert said.

"The captain himself could speak with them, but he can't overrule the civil court's distribution of public funds. Even the captain is subject to those rules."

That's what he lets them think, anyhow, Gert thought, before realizing how sinister that made him sound. He frowned at himself. "Well, can you check first? Let's find an open apartment and then we'll iron things out."

"Subcommander, please!" En-den-to pleaded. "I am busy, you know!"

"It's for Moani here."

En-den-to looked at the cute geroo again, and his ears turned flush. "I… I'll go see what I have…" He muttered his apologies and excused himself from the room, the door snapping shut behind him.

The moment they were alone, Moani sat in front of the central mainframe in the center of the room—a large aluminum tower which extended deck to rafters. "Your ID will be handy here. I'll erase the logs after."

Gert activated the computer screen with his strand—as a subcommander, he had access near everywhere on the ship, though the commissioner could look up such information wherever he had gone. But, given they were in the room where they stored all such information, it was only a matter of Moani installing a backdoor into the system. She plugged her personal pad into a port and started up one of her many programs loaded on board.

"I was wondering," Gert said, looking back at the door to ensure nobody else entered, "how old is your information on these systems?"

"Fifteen to thirty years depending," Moani said. "But they've barely changed in six hundred years. Even when the company commissioned the geroo fleet, they only gave systems a firmware fix. If the krakun have a major weakness, it is that they prefer security through obscurity. They think none of us are smart or clever enough to get in without—"

A flashing alert popped up on the mainframe monitor. Then the alert popped up on all the mainframe monitors and every computer station situated around the central tower.

Exception in registry. Unauthorized access suspected, contact computer administrator at once.

"Shit," Moani said.

"What did you do!"

"I can fix this," Moani said, laying the pad aside and placing her paws on the computer interface. "They must have patched that hole. Give me a minute!"

Please enter access code to continue.

"Double shit," Moani said. "Do you have the code?"

"I don't even know where you are in the system!"

The door at the head of the room snapped open, and En-den-to rushed in again. "What's going on? I leave for all of a minute and get a security alert!"

Gert turned sheepish, but did his best to put on a commanding tone.

"My fault!" Gert said. "Moani was showing off and attempted a bite larger than her head—I think she mistyped something somewhere."

En-den-to glanced at his strand. "Registry access though? Thirty seconds after I left?"

"She was really showing off."

"Subcommander, I can't come rushing down here every time to fix the mistakes of a pre-cadet…"

En-den-to ushered Moani aside, then typed in the access code into the computer. The alerts disappeared off of the monitors. En-den-to pulled out his strand again and called everyone on computer security alert.

"False alarm, back to your posts," En-den-to said.

He grumbled and fell back into his chair. It allowed him no rest, however, because almost as soon as his rear end touched the seat, his strand flashed for an incoming call. "It's Nesti," he said.

Gert swallowed, then said, "I'll speak with her." He took En-den-to's strand and tapped the answer button. Subcommander Nesti's face popped into view, from a camera position on the table to she wouldn't touch her strand with stained fingers. Behind her were the distinct walls of one of the best places to eat onboard, Top Side Bistro. She had looped a napkin through her necklace, covering her chest, and she ate roasted meat dripping with a cream sauce with fancy silverware.

It reminded Gert that he was missing his lunch date with Hiani. Then he remembered they canceled anyhow. His ears wilted.

"Lieutenant, what's… Oh, Gert!" she said. "So that's where you've been all morning. What'd you to do my computer, huh?"

"Nesti!" Gert said as sweetly as possible. "This is a misunderstanding. I brought a student here who is joining the academy—she had an interesting program she wished to show me and I think it irked system security."

"On the mainframe?" Nesti asked.

Moani peeked over Gert's shoulder. "Hi! Pre-cadet Moani from deck twenty! It was a theoretical process, I needed to see if it would work in practice. Unfortunately I should have tested it out where security wasn't so touchy."

Nesti sighed. Gert well knew of her temperament—she preferred enjoying her off-hours to her work, but she took her work seriously. Else, how would she be able to afford all her expensive habits?

"Gert," she said, "what is your relation to this female?"

"She's a new friend of mine," Gert said.

"I thought you were dating what's-her-name, Hiani?"

Gert knew his ears burned, but everyone must have seen the red blush through the whites on his cheeks. "Ah, not... Not anymore, no."

"Well regardless, if she intends to pursue computer operations in the academy, she's already received a black mark. That's not a good start for her career."

"Aw..." Moani's voice sounded so genuinely hurt.

"Nesti—" Gert started.

"That is my prerogative," Nesti said, "Captain's friend or no. Still... When we meet in class, I'd like to see that code. Perhaps that could mitigate some of this issue."

"Oh, absolutely," Moani said. "Anything you need, Subcommander."

"Then don't interrupt me again. I will see you in our training program someday soon." She nodded. "Subcommander." The connection broke off.

En-den-to took back his strand and pocketed it again. He huffed. "Fine mess you got me into—"

"You?" Moani huffed. "She was chewing me out. I deserved at least that much."

"Either way, I should stay here and supervise."

"That won't be necessary," Moani said, tugging at Gert's shoulder again. "We were just leaving."

"Ow, Moani, that spot's getting tender," Gert complained.

"Already?" En-den-to asked, his ears perked.

"Yeah, I'm…gonna have to look over my code more in a less testy environment," Moani said.

Gert nodded with her. "Yes, I'm sorry, it was a mistake to move this fast. We'll be back when Nesti is here to observe. If you can, please, we'd still like an apartment for her."

"Moani, wait!" En-den-to started, stepping toward them as they were already most of the way out the door.

Moani turned. Gert stood just behind her, outside the open door.

"Is that true? Are you and Gert, erm…dating?"

Moani blinked. She cast eyes at Gert, who'd frozen up. "What? No! No no no. Of course not. Definitely not."

"Then if I haven't put you off, we could go out for a drink sometime?" He sounded hopeful.

Moani perked her ears in a smile. It was strange how well the camouflage could translate her facial expressions to that of a different species. If she'd intended the expression.

"Erm, Lieutenant…" Gert said, "I thought you were dating Subcommander Tesko."

En-den-to perked his ears. "I… I suppose I am," he said. "It's not serious, though. I can go for a drink with a cute female!"

"Not serious?" Gert asked.

"It's a little serious," En-den-to said, with a heavy sigh. "I don't know. We're not exclusive or anything. I'm not even sure I'm ready for that kind of commitment again."

"Don't you think it'd be better to know for sure, though? I mean, if you're serious, and you'd like Tesko to know you're serious…"

"I…" En-den-to lowered his ears. "You're absolutely right. I need to think about it…" He rushed a quick salute to the subcommander before the door snapped shut behind them.

Gert sighed in relief. In any normal circumstance he would not have cared because the Lieutenant was right—who he was dating was personal. While it was mission-critical to dissuade En-den-to and Nesti from looking in too much further, he wanted to tell them everything…but he knew better than to do that. Ateri was right when he said nobody could know about the plan just yet. They could not risk things being muddled up now because someone got the shakes and blabbed all their plans to the krakun, hoping to receive amnesty.

But the krakuns' mercy was only the slightest bit less awful than their punishments. They would all do their jobs better so long as they didn't know.

"Ugh, ancestors…" Gert wrung his paws around his neck to get the sweat off his pads. "Did you get the backdoor in the system already?"

"Once he bypassed the alert, my program installed the backdoor," Moani said. "I can get access from anywhere in the ship now, so long as it's hard-wired to the mainframe."

"Then we need to get to the scanning array next, right? I'll need to look that up; that's something engineering handles."

Moani was silent as Gert looked up directions on his strand. As he waited for the system to grant him access, he said, "Your geroo disguise might be too attractive."

"Oh, you think?" Moani asked, looking down at her geroo shape. "Maybe it was a mistake to rip this design from an actress I found on one of your videos. I thought it was rather average."

"Oh, no," Gert said, "most geroo males are into big hips and a tummy."

"Geroo hips are already huge!" she sighed. "Every time you think you've done enough research, something else pops up to throw a wrench into the works…"

Chapter 13: Safety Measures

Almost have it," Moani said.

Gert looked back at the outline of the doorway that led inside—not even a proper door, given the path to the spectrometer sensor array was more like a maintenance access tunnel. The difference being that the door was a wiring-and-tubing-dense passage that led into a dead-end before the outer baffle. It had no connection to the rest of the maintenance tunnels that snaked around the insides of the ship because this was one of those sensitive pieces of equipment. He and Moani jammed themselves into a small space they both had to duck and crawl through, the only light coming from Moani's slate. Nobody would bother coming up this way unless something were wrong with the spectrometer—and so far, it appeared Moani had managed it better than the mainframe. She plugged her slate into the computer controller that faced the array. The array itself had no console in the vicinity, but her slate could act as a makeshift one to get the readouts without them going through the mainframe first.

The slate emitted a tinny fanfare. Several more items popped up on its screen.

"Huh," Moani said.

"Good huh, or bad huh?" Gert asked. He shifted his posture to sit on the floor with Moani.

"I-need-to-double-check huh," Moani said, "because on one end this seems too easy."

"Don't tell me the numbers are suggesting we stumbled on a viable planet," Gert said.

"Radiation counter and gravometrics are both fine," Moani said. "Gravity is on the light side for krakun, but still within specifications. Background radiation under limits. If this planet could hold an atmosphere, it would deflect solar wind. We might not even need to do any tweaking to those systems."

"What about the spectrometer itself?" Gert asked.

"That's harder to—there we go! There's the problem I was waiting to crop up. So far the data suggests it is not viable for krakun life, but it's not all in yet."

"So what's the solution? Change the readings to say what we need?"

"That'd be nice, but the system sent a good chunk of it to the science station and they've already passed most to Krakuntec. It would look like something grafted the "good" data on. I had a few ways to make it look like the surface material was obscuring the readings of the underlying material, but that doesn't seem possible now."

"You can't wing something?"

"I'm a hacker. I don't know a damn thing about astrogeology, I'm just trying to match these numbers to other numbers. Jain knew all the astrogeology stuff."

"Partner? Mate?" Gert asked.

"Mentor. I'm by far the fastest at this thing. And I think none of them were all that keen on mingling with geroo."

Gert huffed.

"Hey, I'm just saying," Moani said. "In the grand scheme of things, you're all relative newcomers to this pan-galactic empire thing. Most of what we know about geroo is academic."

"So?"

"So…sometimes we make up stories about you. To fill in the gaps."

Gert folded his arms over his chest. "Like what?"

"I'd love to share, but we have a job to do here," Moani snipped. She sighed at the data, like one would at a menu with nothing appetizing. "I suppose I could send this data back to Jain and the others and see if they can come up with something. But the spectrometer is going to run all that time and it'll make the window to fix the data tighter and more implausible."

"Then we're not looking for an astrogeological solution," Gert said, "we need a hacking solution."

Moani perked her ears. "Now that you mention it…" She opened another window on the slate and had the machine do a few calculations. "Alright, I need you to call up whoever is in charge of maintenance here and tell them there's been a static charge building up behind the collector dish."

"Throw the data out?" Gert asked. "That would get us in trouble for sure! Krakun hate us wasting company time—"

"Not throw it out, but act as though the static charge has been responsible for a data bias. If we can get the numbers down here, then our good numbers won't look so suspicious when we add them in."

Gert pulled out his strand, but hesitated. He didn't like the fact he had to keep lying to everyone, but that was part of this job, wasn't it? He punched the button for the chief engineer.

"Aye—oh there you are, Gert!" the rotund Chief Engineer Otekka said, and sipped from a cup. "Everyone on the bridge was wondering where you'd run off to. Where are you, anyhow?"

"Yeah uh," Gert started, "is your team done putting out the small fires everywhere, from the trinity malfunction?"

"We haven't determined it was a malfunction yet," Otekka said. "I've been comparing notes with Tesko, and she thinks—"

"This is about something else!" Gert said. "The captain's having me do a visual audit of some sensitive systems, you know just in case, and I'm at the spectrometer array with an academy pre-cadet. She thinks there may be a static buildup that's affecting the collector dish."

Otekka tapped keystrokes into his computer out of Gert's view. "I...see nothing. Course that's indicative of nothing. I'll come up there and see if we can't find out what's the matter."

"Got it," Moani whispered. "That's all ready for him."

"It's a little cramped in here; you'll want to get someone on the small side," Gert said.

"Gert, come on," Otekka said. "Everyone's small compared to you."

Moani unplugged and tucked away her pad and followed Gert back out through the access tunnel. In fact she was right up on his tail-end the entire way out, and Gert felt flush having her there. He hadn't said it to her, but her geroo form was not just beautiful to Enden-to. With that cloak on, he didn't have to think of her as a geordian—she made a good geroo.

He had to fold himself around again to ensure he came out the exit boots first, relieved he could get his rear end out of her face. Not that she'd have been able to distinguish the scent he was giving off.

When Moani came back out of the duct after him, she was panting.

"Moani?" Gert asked. "What's wrong?"

"It's warm on this ship, you know," she said, leaning over on her knees. The gesture was difficult for the cloak to match, given that geroo legs were short. "Ugh, damn. Next time we're out, bring cold water."

"How's your ammonia count doing?" Gert asked. He reached into her bag, then she slapped him away.

"Hey! Do not touch my bag. I can't afford to misplace *anything* I have in there!"

"I'm sorry," Gert said, wringing his paws. "I just want to make sure you're okay."

"Oh," Moani said. Her cross expression softened. "Well...I'm okay, so stop worrying."

Right then, before Gert could reply, a ground vehicle rolled up with four engineers onboard, including Otekka, already wearing discharge gloves and carrying thick plastic bags filled with tools. They all piled out at once.

"Is this the one who found a potential static buildup?" Otekka asked, swinging his ample body out of the passenger side gap. Even for a geroo he was bulky and wide. The other three, cadets of varying years, already made their way into the short access panel leading into the small corridor.

"Yes, sir!" Moani relaxed, at least more so than Gert, gripping her slate in both paws. "I noticed there were some strange fluctuations in the data—the receiver's initial wiring is analog, and after checking the receivers—"

"Oh, is that all!" Otekka laughed. "That's nothing! The data interpretation is on the computer side of things, and hells if I know why it makes the choices it does. Still, it's good you noticed. You getting into the academy?"

"Oh, yes sir!" Moani said. "Computer operations is my specialty!"

"Maybe you should get some engineering in. I'd love to have someone careful on my team—just, a little more experienced perhaps." He smiled at her before turning back to the access panel and calling in. "Yessi, you see anything?"

"We have the cover off," Yessi called back, "Collector isn't picking up any widespread static, but..."

When she didn't speak for several beats, Otekka called after her. "But?"

"I smell ozone."

"Ozone?" Otekka lowered his ears in concern and scratched his head. "We might have an electrical overload in the coils. Jaki, take the system offline so we can—"

Then, a cracking, popping noise.

"Ow, shit!" one engineer shouted.

"Get out of there!" Otekka shouted. "We need to initiate shutdown at once, but clear the area first!"

Gert started forward at once. "Otekka," he said, climbing up into the small gap. "I'll grab one and then you yank me out when I have hold—"

Another crack, and a resounding explosion hit Gert in the chest, throwing him back hard enough to bowl Otekka over. Gert looked up in horror as smoke poured from the open access door.

He glanced over to Moani, her jaw dropped in shock.

Ancestors, no…

Gert scrambled back into the narrow conduit just as it started filling with fire-retardant foam. Behind him, he heard Otekka scramble for his strand and turn on the emergency beacon. "Medical emergency! Deck thirteen, Corridor J-34, need a team down here now!"

"Get up!" Gert shouted into the blackness beyond the open hatch door. "Get up! If the shock didn't kill you, the foam will!"

"Subcommander, Yessi's hurt!" came back one voice, muffled in the building foam.

"Get her to my paws, I'll pull her out!" Gert reached forward, still blind. Figures shuffled in the parts beyond his vision, the faintest outlines of a moving geroo. Then something furry brushed against his outstretched paw, and he seized hold.

Gert pulled. Jaki emerged, with Gert holding his ankle. He was about to protest—if Yessi was hurt, she was priority!

But pulling him out further, Jaki was holding tight onto Yessi's waist.

"Ow, damn, hells!" Yessi cried in pain. "Ancestors, help me!"

Gert shifted his slick grip to grab Jaki's midsection. "Otekka, grab and pull!" he shouted behind.

Otekka grabbed Gert's midsection, and they pulled again. Yessi emerged after Jaki, much of her upper body slicked over in red.

Jaki stumbled as he came out and held onto Yessi, lowering her to the floor. Foam spilled out after them. Yessi quaked in shock. The explosion had torn much of her left side chest open.

"Moani!" Gert shouted at her, "first aid kit in the vehicle—bandage foam, stimulus needle, stop the bleeding now!"

"I don't know anything about first aid!" Moani protested.

"*Then learn fast!*" Gert shouted, before climbing right back into the conduit door.

He slipped a few times on the path back—the foam itself was difficult to wade through, and now the blood on the deck and on his paws were adding to the difficulty navigating even a single narrow passage. It was also becoming hard to breathe—even with the space behind the walls, the foam kept the air from refilling the short tunnel.

Damn these krakun safety designs—they don't care half as much about saving the lives as they do salvaging the equipment.

Gert struggled to see in the dark gap before remembering he had a light on him. Wiping his blood-slick paw off on his chest, he reached into his pocket and pulled out his strand, and after two taps, its light turned on. He swept around, looking for the third member of the engineering team, finding only chest-high foam everywhere.

"Cadet!" Gert shouted, hating himself and feeling like he'd already left this one behind. The foam shifted, and a paw reach just out of the top. Gert shoved his strand back into his shoulder pocket and, taking as deep breath as he could without inhaling foam, dove under.

He groped around for several long moments before his paws found warmth where the cadet's body lay. Gert wrapped his arms around him and pulled, finding far more resistance than he expected. Feeling around with his paws again, he found a thin but firmly stuck aluminum bar wedging down one of the geroo's knees, which was itself torn open. Gert gripped the bar and pulled—it shifted, creaking with protest. Gert shook as he pulled harder, and the bar creaked as it bent. He slipped the cadet's knee out from underneath.

Taking hold on the cadet's midsection again, Gert had to swim through the foam in what he hoped was the right direction through the corridor, but he had no resistance to move himself—the floor was too slippery and the cadet too heavy. The foam had little density and he could find no purchase against it.

Feeling the panic rise in his lungs as they demanded air, Gert shifted positions—wrapping the cadet with his legs, then reaching out with both paws to grip the cords and bars on the side of the tunnel. He pulled himself through as though climbing a horizontal ladder, sliding along the blood-and-foam slicked floor.

As he burst from the exit, Gert gasped for air. Otekka and Jaki caught him before he fell, and placed their paws under the other geroo, lowering them both to the floor. Gert righted himself onto his knees and coughed, foam spreading out all around. Jaki pulled the other cadet away from the door panel as Otekka closed it off. Moani was off toward the side, leaning over Yessi, looking into an open eye for a response. Gert didn't bother correcting her—and despite Jaki's protests that Gert needed to catch his breath, he put an ear to the third cadet's chest, and heard no breathing.

He opened the geroo's mouth and seeing no foam, Gert sealed his lips to the geroo's muzzle and forced breath into his lungs.

After three tries, the cadet coughed and sputtered, opening his eyes.

"Shit, shit," he muttered, tears forming in his eyes.

"You okay? Feel cold?" Gert asked.

"What!" the cadet shouted.

Gert checked his ears for the foam, finding nothing. "Are you alright?"

"Subcommander, I can't hear you!" he shouted again.

Gert fell back into a sitting position. He heard the medical flatbed coming down the corridor, making its distinct whirring alarm, and with everyone at least breathing—if far worse for the experience—Gert sank.

Ancestors, let there be no sacrifices, he prayed.

Chapter 14: Sacrifices

The pressure burst Cadet Rotai's eardrums, including breaking the inner ear bones on both sides. He's in restorative surgery, and should get back eighty percent of his hearing. Other than that, some abrasions and minor laceration to the arm, a significant laceration to the left leg, and more damage to his back—as he was facing the other way when the blast occurred. Cadet Jaki, treated for abrasions, broken bones in the wrists and tail. She said Cadet Yessi was in front of her when the coil blew, so she avoided most of the force of the blast. Yessi, besides the gash along her axillary artery, had a punctured lung and several other abrasions all over her face and abdomen. With proper treatment her fur will grow back just fine, though she developed scarring such as iris damage to her left eye, which will leave it dilated unless we were to replace it."

En-den-to would not enjoy hearing this. Yessi was En-den-to's younger sister by about fifteen years, and she'd taken the worst of the blast. A pit sat in Gert's stomach.

"Thank you, Doctor," Gert said.

Moani, still wearing the camouflage, sat on a chair in the corner of the room, her head in her paws.

"Is she alright?" the doctor asked.

"She's fine, no injuries," Gert said.

"It would be good to do a look-over—"

"I'm sure you have many other patients to see today," Gert said, trying his best to usher the doctor toward the door without touching her. "Please, we could use the privacy."

"All right…" The doctor backed from the room. "Subcommander." The doctor bowed rather than a proper salute, given she was not an officer. The door snapped shut behind her.

"Oh thank the ancestors nobody died," Gert said, lying his flat head against the wall.

"Yeah," Moani said.

Gert looked over to her. "*Are* you doing alright? You haven't said a word since we got here."

"Camo's being uncomfortable. I uh…" She sighed, shifting her shoulders about with the weight on them. "I'm…"

"I know, Moani, you didn't mean to do it," Gert said. "But these things happen sometimes."

"You're being generous. At this point though, I don't even know if we succeeded. I… I may have taken too big a risk."

Now that was disappointing. Gert couldn't help but feel pity as he watched Moani's geroo form sink lower and lower, like she was about to retreat into herself.

"You did the best you could."

"You have no idea what I'm capable of."

"Okay, I don't," Gert admitted, "but I know people like you, and I'd still say the same to them. You shouldn't beat yourself up over a mistake."

There was a knock at the door. Gert turned to see Captain Ateri's dark face and distinct eyepatch. He entered without even so much as a perfunctory salutation.

"Captain!" Gert said, standing straight and saluting. "Uh, it's already past twelve hundred hours, aren't you supposed to be at the docking bay, for the new commissioner?"

Ateri didn't respond, he marched straight to Moani at the corner of the room. Moani stood to meet him. The moment Moani's legs were in range of Ateri's feet, he snapped his leg out, hooking Moani under her knee and yanking her off balance. Moani stumbled and fell onto her tail. She yelped in pain, but not as much as when Ateri jumped on top of her and planted both paws around her narrow throat.

"Captain!" Gert exclaimed, horrified.

"What did you do!" Ateri shouted in Moani's face. "In the name of all gods in known space, what did you do? You could have killed someone!"

"Gyk— I can't breathe…" Moani shook and wheezed on the floor. Her paws gripped Ateri's wrists, digging claws into him.

"Captain!" Gert shouted. Without even thinking, he was atop Ateri's scarred back, and had hooked his arms under Ateri's. He had no leverage from this position, given he and the captain were identical in height and weight. Yet somehow, planting a boot aside on the tile deck, he managed at least to crane Ateri back from his position atop Moani, though the captain kept his grip on her throat tight.

"Gert!" Ateri snarled, "Let go of me at once! *That is an order!*"

"*Sur'an's name, Captain! Stop hurting her!*" Gert bellowed.

Huffing, Ateri released his grip. Moani gasped deep for air.

Gert pulled Ateri back farther, twisting his grip and turning until the captain's back hit the floor. Gert's paw planted on Ateri's chest as if to hold him there. He put no weight into it, but Ateri didn't resist.

"That's unfair using your mother to call me out like that," Ateri said.

"It's the only way you'll listen sometimes!" Gert snapped. He hated it when his temper flared, but in this case, it was the only thing that gave him the strength to defy Ateri.

The door opened again, and an orderly peeked into the room to check what all the commotion was about—between Moani struggling to stand, and Gert bearing down on Ateri like he was about to punch him. Ateri snapped his head up to look at the orderly upside-down.

"You saw nothing," Ateri said.

"Uh," the orderly said, closing the door again on the scene. "Y-yes, Captain."

The moment they were alone, Gert climbed off of Ateri. The captain sat up, groaning as he put a paw to the base of his neck where he hit the ground first. Gert was about to say something, but Ateri went back to what he was doing.

"Moani," Ateri said, emphasizing every single world. "What. Did. You. Do."

"Started an overload." Moani rubbed at her throat as she explained. "…Captain, if they were coming to check for a static discharge, there needed to be some problem there for them to find… I didn't know what would happen! I'd never done it before!"

"You put the lives of three crewmembers in jeopardy, and you didn't think to tell me there might have been a risk?"

"I'm sorry!" Moani cried. "I didn't mean to hurt anyone!"

Ateri started after her like he wanted to pounce, but Gert stopped Ateri again, putting his thick arm in front of the captain's shoulders. Ateri huffed at Gert.

"Captain," Gert intoned, "stop."

"Let's get one thing straight," Ateri said, "*both of you.* I am in this to save the lives of every one of the geroo onboard this vessel. I am not above making necessary sacrifices, but you are *not* backing me into a corner where I must surrender innocent lives."

Ateri pushed the subcommander aside. Gert had jostled the captain far more than he'd intended. The captain was getting old and showing it, though even in this state, Gert would not underestimate his strength even for an instant.

"Three cadets," Ateri said, holding up three fingers to emphasize. "Three. I don't care if you are Sinon's golden hacker. If any of them had died because of this action, I would not hesitate in *sending your head back to him in a box.*"

"Ancestors, Ateri!" Gert said. "You don't have to scare her like that!"

"You will address me as 'Captain'," Ateri said, turning his eye toward Gert. "And don't think you're getting out of the blame, Subcommander. I trust you with my life, and you didn't even think to do risk assessment?"

"How in the five hells am I supposed to do risk assessment? We've never tried to hijack our own ship before, not like this! If you want this done, I have no choice *but* to trust Moani. And threatening her life will not get us what we want!"

"So you're suggesting we let her walk over us?"

"Captain!" Moani pleaded. "I swear, I will not walk over you!"

"You look like a geroo, Moani," Ateri said. "You even talk like one pretty well, but you are *not* a geroo. You do not and cannot understand what this job means to us, and your flippant disregard for our lives has made that clear."

"Do you feel that way about me, sir?" Gert asked. "Do you think I don't understand what's at stake here?"

Ateri turned his head to Gert.

"...I don't believe you do, Subcommander."

Gert's jaw dropped and his ears fell at the rebuke. "Captain, this was your plan. If you don't want me in charge, then fire me."

"I can't." Ateri's shoulders and ears both lowered in sync. After all this time, his voice softened. "And I wouldn't anyhow."

"Then what's the problem? I acknowledge this is dangerous, I acknowledge we screwed up—"

"Subcommander, do not take this the wrong way. I have been waiting for the past several years for you to outright fail at something, because I don't know how you handle failure. Yes, you climbed into that ventilation shaft and saved all three of the cadets, and for that I commend your bravery, and I would not wish for any other outcome of such a disaster. But I can't help but notice it's always worked out that way for you. You are too comfortable with risks *because* you've never failed. Do you understand?"

"No, sir," Gert said. "You say that like I wanted this to happen. I didn't."

"We don't get to decide what we *want* to happen," Ateri said. "We only manage. What would you do if those cadets had died?"

Gert's ears fell. He didn't understand what Ateri was driving at. "Sir, I *know* what it's like to experience loss." He meant his mother, if nothing else, but there were plenty of less devastating examples. "You *know* I've been carrying it most of my life by now. Is that not enough for you?"

"Gert..." Ateri started. He paused a moment, choosing his words carefully. "There's a *big* difference between loss and *losing*."

"Well, whatever it is," Gert said, "does it mean you don't think I'm ready to be Captain? Because I've been working as hard as I could to prove I am." Gert, frustrated, swiped his paw down the back of his nape. "Sir... what more do I need to *do*?"

Ateri's strand vibrated. Staring at Gert the whole time, he answered it.

"Commander," Ateri said.

"Where did you go?" Jakari asked. "The commissioner's shuttle is landing *right now*. You need to be at the docking bay five minutes ago!"

"I was checking up on the sensor malfunction," Ateri said, still not looking at the strand screen. "I figured the commissioner would ask."

"Well, she's another five minutes away from asking!"

"I'll get Otekka to give me a ride then. Commander." He saluted the screen and ended the call.

"It looks like whatever you did worked," Ateri said, directed to Moani. "The company will have noticed."

"If it was our only option," Moani said, still sitting on the floor, "then we had to do it."

"I agree with you," Ateri said as he left. "But we still must live with the things we have to do."

Chapter 15: The Ultimatum

Between himself and the rushing noise of the pumps, Ateri stood alone.

He waited the last thirty seconds outside the hangar bay, waiting for air to refill the space before entering. The worst part was it would not be the normal station air; it was a mixture of the air breathed by geroo and that breathed by the krakun, pumped with the whiff of a sulfuric compound present in Krakuntec air. It was by far not in the concentrations that krakun preferred—five or ten percent sulfuric gasses, which would kill any geroo that inhaled two full breaths, or even stood in it for a few seconds—but it was enough to notice, and suffer due to its presence. But to add insult to injury, Ateri had doubted for a long time that the krakun needed the air mixture themselves. The mixture was not enough for krakun to benefit from it. The krakun could exist in a geroo oxygen-nitrogen environment for at least a full twenty-four hours before suffering any major effects.

It was not practical. Just another method of punishment and control.

The all-clear light above the door switched on.

Once the opposite door opened, Ateri forced himself from wheezing, though he couldn't help how his eye watered at the odor. But much like their linguistic divide, they did not allow Ateri any help—they expected him to suffer anything asked of him, and he'd

done so for forty years. And so, wiping his uncovered eye and steeling himself, he marched right up the wide ramp toward the bay floor, where Pokokuro's ship laid waiting.

It was far different from the usual company shuttle; this one was smaller, but longer, with smooth streamlined sides and collapsible wings, perhaps for in-atmosphere maneuvering, and windows tinted to black. Instead of the utilitarian cobalt coloring, the hull was bright red with long, horizontal stripes of yellow across its face. And perhaps most strangely, it was devoid of any Planetary Acquisitions logo.

Almost as soon as Ateri crossed the threshold, the gull-wing door on the ship's side opened wide, revealing nothing but dark shadow. Ateri waited a moment, but the commissioner was not forthcoming. Ateri's heart pounded faster as he stepped forward to wait at the end of the ramp, but once he approached, he heard a voice call out in krakun.

"Captain— Oh good, you are the captain. Step inside, please."

Ateri hesitated. The air inside the cabin, even though it dissipated quickly once the door opened, would hover near-lethal levels. He smelled the heavier parts of the air pouring out from inside, threatening to burn his throat. But there was no way to refuse a commissioner's order—besides, being higher up might help. He climbed up the ramp and stood just inside the doorway. The deck just inside was ornately plush, and he had to raise his paws high just to wade into the carpet. He suppressed a cough, though he could tell at this point if he breathed in much more sulfur, his mouth would blister.

In the shadow beyond, he spied Pokokuro's outline, the enormous lizard shaped rather different from Sarsuk. The long, narrow neck, glistening bright scales, the tail curled around her taloned feet on the floor. She lay on a cushion and her body posture sank into it—she was not planning on getting up.

High up, near the ceiling of the cabin interior, her eyes caught the bay light and shone through the shadows.

"Dear Captain!" she said, her teeth flashing in the dark with every word. "Such an honor to finally meet you."

Ateri lowered his head. "I regret that ship matters kept me from speaking with you earlier," he said, speaking in geroo. "The first officer has conveyed your eminent presence, I fear, insufficiently — you are a sight to behold."

"Dead gods!" Pokokuro snorted a laugh. "You're much better at this than your mate—I might get to like you. Unfortunately, the time in which we may get used to one another grows short."

Ateri swallowed.

"So," Pokokuro said, "I want your report. First, the trinity outage that occurred this morning."

For that, Ateri didn't even need to look at his strand, which he'd hoped would score him more rapport with this commissioner. He recited the excuses Tesko provided him. "There was a power fluctuation in the main breaker of the drive. When the breaker tripped, the drive shut down and took the trinity along with it."

"How in the hell did you manage that?" Pokokuro asked, her tone somewhere between a sneer and genuine curiosity.

"On approach to C-18-3, when we switched the drive from maximum to minimum power, the third power channel relay became stuck in the on position, feeding power into a drive that wasn't accepting it."

"If there was a mechanical malfunction, the computer should have caught that at once," Pokokuro said.

"The sensor *did* trip. The switch moved about ninety-five percent of the way off, which was sufficient for the sensor, but still kept the power channel open."

"And nobody caught this in the engine room?" Pokokuro snipped. "Where did they think the extra power was going?"

"The engine room knew that the drive was powering down. However, given the usual leniency for time variations, they were not aware the drive was already supposed to be at minimum power draw for the twenty minutes it was not."

"Twenty minutes should have been far more than enough time to take notice," Pokokuro said.

"The incident happened right in the middle of morning shift rotation," Ateri said. "That is twenty minutes between at least two sets of eyes."

"How unfortunate. These things happen in space." Her voice was smooth and calm, and despite her overt reassurance, the fur on his neck stood up when she said it.

"Yes, Commissioner," he said, and bowed.

"And I will expect a complete incident report written up with recommendations on amendments to company policy to ensure such a mistake never happens again."

"Yes, Commissioner." Ateri felt fortunate that Tesko, despite her reluctance in falsifying the report, was good at it, making an unlikely scenario sound plausible without needing proof it could have happened that way.

Pokokuro strummed her fingers, one claw clacking against the metal lining that edged the carpet she laid on. "However, that does not explain this notice I received on my way out of the atmosphere. A…coil *explosion?*"

Ateri exhaled slowly, keeping his ears steady. He listened to Otekka's report on the incident, but had no time to craft a convincing lie.

"The report is being compiled as we speak," Ateri said. "We identified the problem before the overload took place, so the post-mortem will not take as long to investigate."

"How fortunate," Pokokuro said, as coldly as the last matter was its opposite. "But I understand the coil explosion happened right underneath the very important spectrometer array. You're in the middle of running your surface scan, and that happens to blow."

"The spectrometer is only run once every few years, Commissioner. Static buildup likely happened due to an unforeseen incident sometime between maintenance cycles—"

"Between maintenance cycles?" Pokokuro's voice crescendoed, and the force of her breath threatened to knock Ateri right over. "Captain, the entire purpose of maintenance cycles is to ensure these problems *don't* occur! Problems are only unforeseen if you do not have the foresight to pick them out. Why was this not detected sooner, rather than delay the outcome of this scanning mission by a full day!"

"Commissioner," Ateri started, "I—"

"The company has a schedule to keep, Captain!" she bellowed. Her head lowered, still not out of the shadows, but close enough Ateri's soft skin blistered at her breath. "Sarsuk's insubordination has clarified that we cannot afford to let these problems slide! I could almost—*almost*—let slide the trinity incident, but the spectrometer *on the same day*? When you knew you had a job to do on arrival at this planet?" She huffed. The floor rumbled as she strummed her talons against the carpet.

"What are your orders, Commissioner?" Ateri asked.

Pokokuro reached her claw out and snapped it down. Ateri fell onto his back hard against the carpet, the tip of her sharp talon digging at his chest. He panted, his heart pounding wildly, as she leaned forward again. This time her head poked through the light, the glistening pink scales covering her face in full view. Long, thin horns jutted from the back of her head, and her teeth drew close to his soft body.

"C-Commissioner," Ateri croaked, "I need to remind you of company policy. We're still in scanning phase—"

"As much as I *hate* the *Chiauo Gi* rule, I will abide by it," she intoned in a rumble like a shuddering, dying engine. "The board's eyes are watching this planet. Shareholders are expecting payouts. I *hate* that you know this, and are taking advantage to act sloppy. I hate that the board buckled to the pressure of your precious mammalian feelings. *But…*"

She spoke in a much quieter tone, rumbling from deep in the back of her throat. "I want you to know that geroo is best eaten fresh. See, what you do is you skin their pelt—" She dragged her talon down Ateri's belly, as though making an incision mark, though Ateri was certain she drew at least a little blood. "Rip it off, and while they're still gasping for their breath, throw them on the hot skillet in oil. A light snack you can have any time, day or night."

Her enormous tongue jutted out of her mouth and slid all the way up Ateri's body. Ateri shuddered. Her saliva didn't burn, but it was thick, and coated him over.

"You can eat them raw, but I find the fur gets stuck between my teeth," she said, each tooth half as tall as Ateri and razor-sharp, up close and personal. She said it so close to Ateri's head that any closer and she would have bitten it off. "Just a little tidbit I'm sure Sarsuk didn't make…explicit. He lacked class."

She sat up, and Ateri panted—glad to even be breathing the burning air that surrounding him. His heart pounded like it was about to explode.

"So if I were you, I would ensure that there are no further delays in the schedule," Pokokuro said. "Although, I will not be giving you the opportunity. Do not bother continuing your scans."

Ateri would have jolted up in protest, but he was unable to refill his lungs. Were they canceling the planetary scan? They wouldn't do that; this was the entire reason they were out here!

"Until such a time as I can determine your systems are up to par," Pokokuro continued, "I will run the scans independently. I've already begun negotiations, and expect to have a scanning ship here within the week."

Yes… It happened on occasion, but this threw a wrench into their already tenuous plans. Did Moani have a backup in place for when the ship doing the scanning was of unknown origin?

"Stop casting your eye aside, Captain," Pokokuro said. "I have not dismissed you. You have *humiliated* me on my first day. I want it well-known how displeased I am with you, the state of this ship, the state of this *gods-be-damned fleet*, and the *inborn disrespect* and *ignorance* of the geroo. However, I'm not going to bother with the paperwork.

"But," she said, leaning in closer, "the moment I prove that the planet down there is unviable for terraformation and you are once again underway…I will kill you."

Ateri froze up.

"And not just you," Pokokuro said. "*Every single officer* aboard this vessel will die. I get to begin fresh, and every ship in this fleet will know what respect I am due. Now, get the hell off my ship."

Before Ateri stumbled to his paws, she reached out two talons, and with a single flick, launched Ateri clear across the bay. Ateri slammed hard against the metal deck, just away from the ramp as it slid closed. Ateri huffed and righted himself. He stood weakly and hurried to the exit door before it locked and trapped him inside.

The moment he was clear, the airlock snapped shut behind him, centimeters away from clamping on the tip of his tail. He dragged himself back to the doorway where Jakari waited. Back in plain air, Ateri fell at her paws.

She gasped, and picked him up by his shoulders. Medical personnel already stood by, injecting him in the neck with the anti-toxin that could counteract sulfur poisoning.

"The hells did she do to you?" Jakari demanded.

"Jakari," Ateri creaked as the medics crowded him, strapping an oxygen hose to his muzzle and bandaging the wound on his gut. He wanted to tell her, this wasn't just about the Exit Plan anymore—

they were staring down another *Silver Mint III* incident. But he couldn't just blurt it out, not with so many ears listening in. They'd panic.

"I'm sorry… I…"

He felt so exhausted, right then, with the extra oxygen flowing into his nose and mouth, he could relax. He just…

Chapter 16: The Long Afternoon

Moani switched off the camouflage and shoved it into the bedroom closet. She'd been silent most of the way to Gert's apartment, though the disguise had concealed some of her displeasure. Even though Gert didn't know all that much about geordian physiology, the way her ears had sunk, her slit pupils narrowed, and the fur around her neck and shoulders stood told him she was upset.

"Moani, you don't have to take it personally," Gert said. "The captain can be passionate—"

"Gods of known space and the Savior of Vala!" Moani exploded—Gert had to presume it was a curse. "I got the message, I didn't need all *that*!"

"Well, you did almost kill three people," Gert said.

"I know! I'm still kicking myself over it! This was the *easy* part of the mission, one quick in-and-out and they send the terraformer over, and I *fucked it over!* Gods, what am I going to tell Sinon?" Moani sank and whimpered. She pulled the meter out of her bag and checked her ammonia levels. "Ugh, my heart's been racing for over an hour now… And Sinon has most my medicine. I'm gonna have to talk to him at some point."

"We could lie to him," Gert said. "We don't have to paint it as your fault—"

"It couldn't be anyone's fault but mine," Moani said. "I endeared myself to Sinon because I was a supergenius, the best hacker he'd ever seen that wasn't already working for some planetary power or another. I've been training for this moment for over a decade and what the hell do I do when the time comes? *I choke!*"

"We can still salvage this. The spectrometer needs repairing, so my guess is that we get that fixed and then you can alter the data at your own pace. The backdoor into the system will work that long, right?"

"It should, but I am sick and tired of sitting around and waiting. Ugh, gods… I don't want to go through another year of nothing."

There was a knock at Gert's apartment door. He perked his ears, swiveling them that direction. Moani did too.

"Uh, is that—" she started.

Gert tapped the porch camera on his strand, which brought up the view just outside his door. He tilted his ears when he recognized the geroo. "Uh, hmm. Go hide in the closet, please," Gert said. "I kinda need to take this."

"In your bedroom?"

"And don't come out until I say so."

Moani grabbed her bag and slunk behind Gert's bed. Gert lamented the fact he'd still had no time for a proper shower when he still smelled like smoke and fire-retardant foam, but he went to his front door anyway and answered it.

"Hi, Hiani," he squeaked.

"Hi, I heard what happened earlier," Hiani said. "And I asked Otekka about it and he said you were going back to your apartment… Can I come in?"

"I don't know about—"

"I brought lunch if you haven't eaten." She produced a bag from behind her back that had two food containers inside.

Gert's stomach rumbled. Against his better judgment, because his hunger-judgment was ruling on this case, he opened the door all the way and stepped aside so Hiani could walk in.

She set down the bag on the dining table, and without even being prompted, pulled two bottles from Gert's cooler. Gert stood at the doorway, not knowing what to do with his paws as she set out the food.

"Where'd you pick it up?" Gert asked.

"Ah, I wish I could have gotten it from Top Side Bistro, but they were busy," Hiani said. "So this is from a weird place down at Gateside. It's good meat, though. I like their sauce."

Gert wanted to protest more than he did, but he felt too grateful she showed up with food. He turned his ears toward his bedroom and the closet within, wondering what the food was like aboard the *Sword*, and if Moani missed having something fresh to eat.

"Gert?"

"Huh?" Gert snapped his gaze back to her, terrified she'd been reading his mind.

"I'm… I'm sorry about what I said this morning," Hiani said. She took his paw and eased him down to sit beside her at the bench around his table—which Gert did because he wasn't certain how to react. "I acted selfish. I understand you have a job to do, and it's important."

"Oh, um…" Gert started, feeling flush around his ears. "You had every right to be upset with me after I broke my promise."

She shook her head. "No, *that* was rude of me; I take the fact this ship stays intact for granted. It didn't even worry me when we had that quake earlier because I knew the crew could handle it, and you're part of that."

Gert's ears flattened out.

"I'll make a promise to you," Hiani said. "I'm willing to wait as long as I need until we have our schedules meet again. Okay?"

Gert blinked. He wasn't certain what to say; even responding in a general affirmative felt wrong. It had only been a few hours since their conversation, but Gert felt like at least a week had flown by.

And he'd *already* slept with someone else.

"Hiani," Gert started. "Is…it okay if I think about this?"

Hiani perked her ears. "What do you mean?"

"I mean I would like nothing more than to stay with you, but—"

There was a knock at the door.

Gert turned his head with his ears perked up, and Hiani did too.

"Who's that?" she asked, as Gert pulled out his strand and checked the camera again. It was a female geroo Gert hadn't seen before, holding a box under her arms.

"I don't know…" Gert said, as he excused himself and got up to answer.

He opened the door. "Uh, you might have the wrong apartment," he said.

"Oh I have the right apartment," she said with a strange, thick accent.

Gert's eyes widened. "Inzari?"

She didn't wait for him to stand aside, she burst in with the box under her arm and tossed it down on the first table she saw. "Hah, weren't expecting to see this face, were you?" She laughed.

"Inzari, I have company right now!" Gert mumbled through his teeth. "Also, where did you get that disguise?"

"This is the extra one your captain wanted," Inzari said. "Looks good, doesn't it? Look at me, I got huge hips!" She swung them around like they were hers. "Your captain could look like this too, if he wanted."

"Please stop doing that," Gert said, averting his eyes.

"So where'd Moani slink off to, anyway? I need her to give a report to Sinon."

"That's not who I meant when I said I had company!"

Hiani approached from the kitchen door with the most perplexed look on her ears. "Uh…Gert, who's this?"

"Hiani!" Gert stepped in front of the disguised ringel, just in case Hiani approached to touch her. "This is Inz—" No, that wouldn't do; the consonant cluster wasn't great for geroo names. "In…dari. Indari."

"Indari?" Inzari exclaimed.

"Yes, Indari," Gert said. "Which is a name that means *charming* in Old Geroonic."

"Yes, but that's a *masculine* name in—"

Gert clamped his paw over Inzari's muzzle. He paused and blinked. His arm shifted positions from where he threw it—it appeared to clamp over the geroo illusion's muzzle rather than the middle of her throat where her actual muzzle was. "Dang, that's good," he said.

"What's good?" Hiani asked.

"Anyway, yes," Gert said to Hiani, ignoring her question. "Indari. She's uh…helping us with some stuff. I wasn't expecting her!"

Inzari pulled her muzzle free of Gert's paw. "Oh, I also got lunch in case you were hungry," she said, yanking a bag out of the box on the table. "I figured with you running around with Moani all morning you might be starving. No idea what this food is, but it smells okay."

"Would you stop!" Gert said through his teeth.

"I could come back later," Hiani said, her ears flattened out.

"Ancestors, please stay!" Gert said. "She doesn't bite!"

"Oh, I might," Inzari said, snapping her teeth.

Gert grunted in his breath at her, "Indari, Hiani is my—" he paused, right there, because he didn't know what to call Hiani at this point.

"I'm Subcommander Gert's girlfriend," Hiani said, approaching Inzari and reaching a paw out.

Inzari glanced at her paw, then made a sly aside glance at Gert, her ears spreading out in a vicious grin. Gert swallowed, and his ears twitched in sync with the discovery of this brand new ordeal. Inzari touched paws with Hiani briskly, so as not to give away the real texture of her pads. Hiani nevertheless glanced at her own paw, as though something were amiss.

"So, uh," Hiani said, "you aren't an officer, are you?"

"Naw, naw," Inzari said, waving her paws about. "I'm just running errands."

"Okay, I was about to say, I've never heard your way of speaking from anyone on the ship before."

"She's from deck twenty-two," Gert said. "Uh, from the personnel transfer last year. Her accent is an offshoot of the…South Greenlay families."

"Whatever he said," Inzari added.

"We had a personnel transfer for a lack of errand-runners?" Hiani asked.

"Oh no, she has a very important job on this ship," Gert said.

"Which is?"

"Which… Is…" Gert glanced toward Inzari, who didn't bother to conceal her shrug. "That…she reports…to me."

"Even though she's not an officer?"

"Right," Gert said. "Ship management side of things and all."

"Specifically, ship communications," Hiani said. "Because you're a comms officer."

"Yes."

"Huh!" Hiani's ears perked up in a smile, sold on the last minute-and-a-half of conversation. "Well if you're a friend of Gert's, I'd love to exchange contact info with you," she said, pulling out her own strand from her red shoulder band. "Maybe we could have lunch sometime and gab about Gert's dirty secrets."

"As much as I would love to do that," Inzari said in a tone that suggested she was not even exaggerating, "my strand is on the fritz at the moment, so I'm gonna have to put the kibosh on that until it's repaired."

Gert perked an ear. *Oh, the strand she's wearing is just part of the illusion.* The commander only provided a strand for Moani; she would not issue one to any of the other pirates without more negotiations.

"Oh?" Hiani asked. "I work strand manufacturing—that's where Gert and I first met! Maybe I could see what's wrong for you." She held a paw out.

"It's some kinda software glitch!" Inzari added. "Not hardware."

"I'm familiar with the software too! Gert and I consulted a lot about that thing—you could call that our first date."

"Gee," Inzari glared at Gert, "it sure would have been nice if you mentioned that at some point."

"This conversation left my control a while ago, and I gave up on salvaging it."

There was another knock at the door.

"Oh, do come in!" Gert cried, far more loud than necessary. "We're apparently having a party! Hope you brought cake!" He checked the front door camera again, then sighed in relief. "It's Commander Jakari." She looked worried; even with the high angle on the camera it caught her flattened-out ears.

"Aw cripes," Inzari said. "She's not supposed to know I'm out of my room."

Gert slapped a paw to his face. "Go hide in the bedroom closet do *not* make a sound."

"Ooh, kinky," Inzari said. She swished past Hiani without touching her and retreated to the back room.

"Huh?" Hiani asked, looking at Inzari and then back to Gert. "Is she in trouble or something?"

"No, no!" Gert said. "It's fine. We're fine. It's all fine here. I'll talk to the commander."

Gert opened the front door.

"I need to talk to Moani right away," Jakari said without bothering with an introduction, and stepping inside. Gert protested, but Jakari continued. "Thanks to her stunt, the commissioner is taking us off of scanning duties and is bringing in a third party ship, so—"

"I have company!" Gert blurted out.

Jakari turned to see Hiani standing just beyond her initial view, near the door to the dining room.

"Uh, Commander," she said, her paws doing the awkward flail where she wasn't sure whether to salute. She settled on rubbing the back of her neck. "Do you need privacy?"

"If you please, Hiani," Jakari said, with a nice smile on her ears.

"I'll be in the bedroom," Hiani pointed her way to where Moani was.

"Don't go into the bedroom!" Gert blurted out.

"Why not?" Hiani asked. "You said—"

"Jakari and I will go into the bedroom, you stay here!"

Hiani tilted her ears. "Wouldn't it be better the other way around?"

Gert didn't answer her, instead taking Jakari by the wrist and leading her past the dining room into the bedroom at the back. He shut the door and turned to Jakari. She opened her mouth to speak, but stopped when Gert marched past her to the closet door and poked his head in.

"Moani?" Gert asked, peeking his head in.

Moani was putting her camouflage back on. Inzari had already taken up space in a corner by a series of boxes, one of which was open, already going through Gert's things. He would have protested, but he poked around Inzari's closet. Would it seem hypocritical?

Before Moani responded, Inzari held up a frame. "Hey, who's this pretty lady?" she asked. "Some other crush of yours, loverboy?"

"That's…my mom," Gert said, his ears burning hot.

"Really?" She turned it back around. "I'm not up on geroo ages, but she still looks young in this."

"Well she died when I was a cub, so thank you for dredging that up, Inzari," Gert said.

"Oh…" Inzari's ears flattened out. "I meant nothing by it."

"Then stop going through my things!"

"Inzari?" Jakari poked her head over Gert's shoulder, trying to process who the geroo in front of her was. "Wait, one of the pirates? What are you doing in Gert's bedroom?"

"Hi, Commander." Inzari waved. "Funny story…"

"Do you need me for anything?" Moani asked, turning on her camouflage so she appeared as a geroo. "Or are you all just going to keep yelling at each other?"

Jakari pushed past Gert, reached into the closet to grab Moani's wrist, and yanked her out. She jabbed a finger at Inzari. "We will speak about this next."

"Yes, mother dearest," Inzari said.

"Ow, ow!" Moani intoned as Jakari dragged her to the foot of the bed. "I know, I did an awful job with the array, you don't need to beat me up over it a third time!"

"Sorry," Jakari said, releasing Moani's wrist. "But the fact of the matter is this: you destroying the array prompted the commissioner to bring in a third-party scanning ship."

Moani's ears perked up. "What! When?"

Inzari also popped out of the closet, geroo ears at attention.

"Don't know yet, could take up to a week," Jakari said.

"What build? What kind of array specifications? Are we going to need environment suits for it?"

"I don't know yet!" Jakari said. "Do you not have a contingency for this? It's not a unique occurrence!"

"I'd like to know this too," Inzari said. "Especially since Sinon is gonna rope me into piloting—"

"Yes, we have a contingency for it," Moani nodded, her voice pitching to a frantic tone. "That's the problem! We have six thousand contingency plans, and I don't have time to prepare for all of them!"

Jakari frowned and thought on this for a moment. "Then you might have to improvise."

Moani slapped a palm to her muzzle. *"That's what started this goddamn mess in the first place!"*

There was a knock at Gert's bedroom door.

"Oh hells," Gert said, rushing to stop anyone from entering, but the door opened a crack and Hiani peeked in before he could reach it.

"Gert, your landlord stopped by," Hiani said. "En-den-to? He said to tell you he has no housing for a Moa—" Her eyes fixed on the new geroo in the room with a perplexed look. "—ni?"

"Uh, hi," Moani said. "Hiani, right?"

Gert froze in place. Hiani looked back to the door, then back into the bedroom, and cast her eyes between the three other females in the room. "I saw no one else come in…"

"She was here already," Gert said, burying his face into his paw.

"Okay…" Hiani said. "Why didn't you tell me?"

"Because as I was trying to say before all the interruptions, if you showed up and it appeared like I already had found another girlfriend, then you'd hate me even more than you did this morning!"

Gert only realized just how loud he was shouting when the entire apartment went quiet, with Hiani, Jakari, and Moani all staring at Gert in shocked silence. Inzari, in the other paw, clasped her paws over her muzzle, barely containing her laughter.

"…*Is* she a new girlfriend?" Hiani asked.

"NO!" Gert blurted out, his voice cracking.

"Well then there isn't any reason to be paranoid, is there?"

"I don't know anymore!"

Inzari burst out laughing, sounding only barely like a yarp-fit.

"Are you okay?" Moani asked.

From the space behind Hiani, there was another knock coming from the front door.

"Ancestors spare me, whoever it is, just tell them to go away!" Gert said, fumbling for his strand.

Jakari peeked over his shoulder at the front door camera. "Oh, it's the delivery."

"What delivery?" Gert asked.

"I figured with you running around this morning, you mustn't have picked up any lunch for yourself."

Gert blinked. He pulled off his armband and set it and the strand down on the desk across from his bed, kicked off his tail ring, and then stepped into the open bathroom. The sound of the shower faucet at full blast filled the bedroom.

"I think he's not hungry," Moani said.

"Is anyone else hungry?" Jakari asked. "It'd be a shame for it to go to waste."

Chapter 17: The Date

On the grounds that Inzari would do nothing to jeopardize the mission, Jakari allowed her out and about on the ship only if Gert was escorting her. Otherwise, she expected Inzari to stay with the pirates or in Gert's apartment. Since Moani was reporting to Sinon, and Gert's actual official shift was ending soon, Inzari made it her full intent to hang out around him because she could. The bridge was near empty at the moment. The orbital process had been a success, but now with the whole ship waiting for Pokokuro's scanner ship, other business took precedence, such as catching up on a vast backlog of maintenance issues that never grew shorter.

Gert's mind, however, lingered on the second bit of news Jakari brought to him in the apartment—that Ateri was in the medical ward. Gert wished she'd led with that news, but every bit of that news was such high priority it would have been impossible to know which came first.

Oh, and that third bit of news, which Jakari could only report once everyone else had left—if the planet proved non-viable for terraformation, *every single officer aboard this vessel would die.*

Gert wished Jakari hadn't told him that. Not that there was much chance of walking this mission back if it failed, but now even that remote possibility vanished. This whole mission wasn't some fanciful whim to get them a grand prize of freedom anymore; it was survival.

Putting all of his concentration into this was difficult because Inzari was standing over his shoulder, wearing her geroo disguise and swishing her tail about dangerously.

"Inzari, would you knock it off?" Gert glowered at the fake geroo. "What are you even doing out of your hideout anyway?"

"Touchy." Inzari sniffed. "What's got you so worked up?"

Gert looked on at her incredulously. "My responsibilities? The end of my existence as I know it?"

"Mortality hangs over everyone's heads."

"Well, I can do something about it. I have to do something about it. If I fail at doing something about it, everyone is going to die!"

"Everyone's gonna die anyway."

"That's not helping!"

"Gert..." Inzari pulled Gert's muzzle toward her own and kissed him. "Relax."

Gert huffed, though inside he was grinning. Inzari just made him giddy in a way he couldn't reconcile with wanting to have a nice life with Hiani. It was as though Hiani was a fruit whose sweetness he craved, and Inzari had come along and offered him pure crystal sugar.

"How can I relax now?" Gert said. "You're kissing me, and I'm supposed to be dating Hiani—"

Inzari tilted her head. "I thought you were worried about dying."

"I can worry about two things! In fact, I worry about a lot more than just two things." Gert attempted to return his attention to the console before him, but his concentration had been shot. His paws hovered over the screen like he was about to resume his work despite having completely forgotten what it was he was doing.

Inzari marched around from behind Gert to the opposite side of his console, and she draped herself across the top—not blocking his view of the screen, but it hardly mattered as Gert didn't take his eyes off hers.

"What's the deal with Hiani, anyway?" Inzari asked. "Do you really like her?"

Gert didn't answer. He attempted to get back to his work again, but nothing he was reading on the screen managed to congeal into a complete sentence.

"I'm just saying, you seem to be having trouble with this relationship, and—"

"She's my last shot, okay?" Gert finally said.

Inzari's short geroo ears perked. "Last shot at what?"

Gert tried to ignore this line of questioning, given how personal it all was, but he relented with a sigh and a slump of his shoulders. "Before her, I hadn't had a girlfriend for three years."

Inzari lifted herself off the console with an exclamation of, "What!" She easily swung herself so she was sitting atop the console. She appeared far too heavy to be sitting on a delicate piece of equipment, though it could easily handle her true, light ringel frame.

Gert folded his arms defensively. "What do you mean, 'what'?"

"You're a hunk that any gal should be falling over themselves to get at. If you were a ringel, you'd..." Inzari paused, scratching a finger along her chin. "Er, you'd be a ringel. I don't think I need to explain further."

"Well, it didn't happen," Gert huffed. "I've had three girlfriends total. First girlfriend, Bomi... broke up because her friends all thought the cubs would look like freaks. Second girlfriend, Tete, said my uh..." Gert pointedly looked down at his own sheath, with Inzari following his eyes. Gert snapped his head away, his ears turning red. "...Er... was too big."

"Hey now, if *I* could fit it—" Inzari started.

"You didn't, not the whole thing."

"Then she just didn't want it enough!"

"That's the problem!" Gert threw his paws out to the sides, exasperated. "I don't seem to be offering *anything* that females want enough."

"And Hiani is the only eligible mate who truly understands you?"

Gert winced. This was the part of the conversation he hadn't wanted to get to. "She... She doesn't really want me to become Captain."

"That seems like a big obstacle."

"Like I said, this is my last shot. What else am I supposed to do?"

Inzari looked back and forth, as if to check and see if anyone had entered the bridge in the time they'd taken to speak with one another. She leaned forward. "I want you..." she said softly, "to think about what Hiani would be like as a captain's mate. Would she be complaining that you're always busy and never have enough time for her? Or would she be sitting here talking you through all the problems of being in the big seat and willing to suck you off afterwards?"

Gert's ears flushed. Inzari was making a very clear remark as to her intentions—despite having promised no commitment, it sure sounded like she was intent on staying attached to Gert's hip. At the same time, Inzari wasn't exactly *wrong*. Hiani's disdain for the whole captaincy had been a thorn in their relationship from the start, no matter her promises that she'd learn to adjust.

Was it really what he wanted? It seemed a juvenile thing to do, to continue going behind Hiani's back. But Gert couldn't help but feel like she'd forced him into the situation in the first place. He couldn't bring himself to be *mean* to Hiani; he still loved her! But what did that matter if Hiani didn't respect him?

Gert cast his eyes up at Inzari again, as if to read her intentions. But Inzari, or at least her disguise, did nothing but spread a warm smile over her ears.

Gert groaned. "Fine! I'll give you one week."

"Yes!" Inzari pumped her fist in the air.

"But only because we're probably all going to die in a week anyway. Ancestors forgive me, but... dammit, I need to know if I'm just being a fool. I don't think I've met any geroo like you, Inzari."

"That's probably because I'm not a geroo." Inzari grinned. "So you're breaking up with Hiani?"

Gert shrank. "N-no, because, well, I might be wrong. If I break up with her now just to try out another lifestyle for a while, she'd *never* want to get back together with me."

"Oh right, last shot." Inzari shrugged. "Well, it's fine by me if you want to play the dangerous game... Okay stud, where are you taking me for our first date?"

Gert couldn't recall promising Inzari a date in the conversation, but he'd been idling on the idea for a while. He needed to get his thoughts off their imminent demise, anyway. "Can you eat the food we have aboard?"

"Seems like! Nothing's stood out as poisonous, least as long as it's simple stuff like carbs, fat, and salt. Three food groups, you know."

"Actually," Gert said, perking his ears, "I think I know a perfect place to go."

* * *

Moani stood nervously with her paws clasped behind her back. She didn't like reporting bad news to Sinon in person—preferably, Jain would handle that, but Jain was back on the ship. This was her responsibility now.

Sinon clicked his tongue as he took in the news. Despite the modest accommodations, the ringel had constructed a sizable lounge for themselves in the walled-off apartment block. Sinon sat on a makeshift couch made of some scraps of cushioning foam Jakari had found for him, with his paws kicked up on one crate they'd brought along. Other officers were still in the back room, arguing over the insufficient number of mattresses and who had to sleep where.

Sinon had forgone wearing his usual longcoat, instead sitting around uncovered like the rest of the geroo, and like Moani did. She'd never had a longcoat because she'd never become an officer under Sinon's command. There was just no way the other ringel would listen or take orders from her—which was just fine, because she hated giving orders to actual people anyhow. Computers were far more obedient.

"The question is," Sinon said, "can you salvage the operation? Because the moment it seems like it's lost—"

"Absolutely," Moani said, though the truth was she didn't know. She had to put on a front of being certain because that was the only way to get through this. She was positive. "I...I need time to prepare the contingency."

"And there won't be another mishap this time?" Sinon's face had turned graver the more he considered her words.

"The only reason there was a problem was because of a tight schedule. So long as we can get aboard the scanner ship, there shouldn't be any problem."

"That's not as reassuring as you might think it sounds."

Sinon stood and walked over to Moani. She didn't move, instead putting on the stoic ears she often did when she was alone with the captain. He took her chin in his paws, his claws digging into her in a way that was almost teasing if it he weren't squeezing so hard.

"I don't want another mishap," Sinon said. "I want to be rolling around in my ill-gotten lucre. Do we understand each other?"

"Yes, sir," Moani squeaked.

"Good," Sinon said, releasing the tension in his paw. "It would be a damn shame if we have to start all over the moment we dealt out the cards."

"I know, Sinon," she whimpered, her ears flattening out. "I want this to be over as much as you do."

Even more so, seeing as I'm doing ninety-nine percent of the work here...

Sinon smiled, and it was always strange how he could flow from intense to warm in the flash of an eye. Moani didn't get that sense from the geroo captain; even when Ateri was civil, he wore his intent for all to see and did not try to hide it—a fact he demonstrated by attacking her in the hospital room.

It wasn't as though Sinon had never done something so harsh before. She was used to this being her life. Which made it even more difficult to resist when the tone of the situation changed to something so much easier.

"You're all too eager to never have to see my face again, aren't you?" he crooned.

She whimpered. She hated what he was doing—softening like that make her ache somewhere inside, like she was missing something only he could provide.

"Captain, I—" she started. Oh gods, his eyes were so warm, how the hell did he do it? He placed his paws on her side and rear and kissed her. She didn't resist, she couldn't. She wrapped her arms around him and kissed back. He pulled her back to the makeshift sofa and pulled her down along with him.

Still, somewhere in the back of her head, a voice not quite silenced experienced an even more intense relief she was sleeping elsewhere on the ship tonight.

* * *

By the time Gert and Inzari made their way down to the Screening Room, the video *Tentacle Monster From Margus X* was already fifteen minutes in, but it did not matter because that was when the good part started. Geroo crowded the entrance, which had a large, scrolling marquee over the front that detailed that night and the following night's shows, running from mid-afternoon to midnight. Gert stood between Inzari and the crowd—not because he found them seedy and needed to protect her, though that was a good idea—but just to guard anyone from bumping into her disguise.

Having no proper wait staff, they collected their food from an automat just before the titular screening room, then shuffled between the long rows of bar tables before finding a decent spot in the middle where other geroo didn't flank them. Inzari let her invisible backpack drop to the floor with a loud thump nobody noticed. Their respective sandwiches were dripping with grease, enough to turn the napkins transparent. The dry, crunchy root chips sopped up most of it.

Inzari tested her juice and made a face. "You all like stuff sweet?" she whispered to mask her accent. She needn't have bothered, because what kind of geroo paid attention to what the rest of the audience was saying during a show?

"You knew it was fruit juice when you bought it," Gert said. Well, when she had *him* buy it.

"There are a lot of different fruits!" Inzari said. "It wasn't that specific."

"You don't like it?" Gert's ears frowned. "We could get something else."

"Aw no, it's fine. I guess it's decent for ship food. But you ever had food from planetside?"

"No, I've lived here my whole life."

"That's sad. Tell you what, when all this is over, there's a place on a free planet, Anizel—they grow all their own food on this thousand-hectare lot and serve it straight into their restaurant. It's damn amazing. I should take you."

"What? Food like, from the ground?" Gert asked. "Regular, untreated soil?"

"Sure, that's where most of it comes from."

"Doesn't that make it…dirty?"

She slugged him in the shoulder. "They wash it, genius!"

Gert rubbed where she struck and pouted.

As they watched geroo actors get unconvincingly tossed around by even more unconvincing animated tentacles, and as the food on their respective plates dwindled, Inzari's tail rose and wrapped around Gert's middle. The geroo tail visible only swung in his direction, but her real tail, far more prehensile, he could feel envelop him. It was thick and soft, and he blushed and wanted to stroke its fur, though at the moment grease still covered his paws. Instead he looked over bashfully toward Inzari, but the movie invested her. She leaned on her elbows and watched with her mouth hanging open.

For the last several hours, Gert had been translating that false geroo face into her real ringel face in his head, but she wore the thicker muzzle well—even the disguise she wore was intriguing. For a moment, he could imagine that she wasn't a ringel who'd had to hide her true features, but a for-real date. He entertained a brief fantasy, envisioning himself and Inzari just spending several long nights together in an apartment in the officer's block, and later on, little cubs running around…

Cubs? Well, it was a fantasy. Even if geroo and ringel were compatible—which they weren't—she admitted to being barren, and what kind of female was Inzari to want offspring anyhow?

Inzari took a big swig of her drink, despite what she'd said. "When I said I wanted something crunchy and salty…"

"Well, they were crispier before they soaked up the grease," Gert said.

What would a cross between a geroo and a ringel look like? Some geroo had faint shades of rings on their tails, but that was where comparisons stopped.

"So they really made this video onboard one of these ships?" She gestured at the screen. "I mean, they're actors, it's obvious, but that's damn good set design. I like how the planet made of tentacles recedes into the background, makes you forget they're standing in at most a twenty-by-thirty room."

"Mm-hmm," Gert said, still staring.

Inzari glanced at him. "You're not even watching!"

"I've already seen this one," Gert said.

"You dirty scamp." Inzari smirked. "It's almost like you didn't care about the movie at all!" She pulled him off his stool and tugged him closer until he was close enough to feel the grease still staining her lips. That didn't matter much as the food had killed off most of Gert's sense of taste, and when they kissed, it mattered even less.

She squeezed his hips with her knees, tightening the curl of her tail all the while. Gert, quaking, knew he was showing at that point, but it was dark in the room and kissing sessions were not uncommon. He gripped her midsection in thick arms, running fingers up and down her back. Even though she wore that scent-blocking spray, this close he could still smell that lingering musk of cigar smoke that clung to her.

Then she touched him down there—she'd cleaned off her paws, but still—Gert turned flush with embarrassment at once. He was enjoying it, but that wasn't the only factor!

One thing Gert knew about ringel, even though he wasn't certain it was true, was the casual way they treated sex. It was one thing when she'd taken him into her bedroom, but this?

Gert's ears flopped into a stupid grin. "Inzari," he said, his voice wavering as her strangely textured fingers touched his sensitive bare flesh, "geroo aren't...accustomed to..."

"I know," she said, her voice barely audible. "I've been behaving for you. But if you be quiet, and lean in, and nobody has to know."

Gert nodded, trying to suppress himself as he pulled Inzari closer, turning to cover both their crotches with the table. She was so amazing with her paws, though she kept her touches to long, gentle teasing alone.

The video was an hour long, as most geroo videos ran, and the double feature started up after — *Lost in Love Space*. Inzari considered it, smashing Gert into her bosom and leaning her head atop his. Ten minutes after, Inzari said, "Yeech, I can't stand the way they babble baby talk at each other. How in known space is that supposed to be romantic?"

"Beats me, sweetie-boo," Gert giggled into her shoulder.

Inzari pinched his ear and twisted, which was good, because she was leading him out of the restaurant, and he'd needed something to cure him of his sustained erection before they emerged in the light.

* * *

"I should get back," Moani said. "So I don't have to wake up Gert."

"Come on, stay a little longer," Sinon said. He reached into a box beside the couch and pulled out a smaller box with a fancy label on it. "At least smoke a cigar with me."

"Ateri was adamant no smoking while onboard."

"I match his rank, so he doesn't get to order me around." Sinon laughed. "Come on, we don't have to finish it."

After Sinon took a short puff, he held the tip out for Moani, and she sucked on the end. She was so used to the action it didn't register in her mind until she'd done it, when she felt that strange wash over her ears. It made her body tingle. Not as fiercely as it did when she first tried it, but the effect was palpable all the same when she hadn't touched it for at least a week.

She breathed the smoke out, and it hung in the air. Sinon nibbled on her ears, and he took another inhale of the cigar and passed it back, and Moani did too. Oh gods, it was like she floated in a pool of warm water. Before she knew it, she'd finished the cigar down to a stub. Sinon pulled her close, even after she and her less-robust geordian physiology lost energy for sex.

Though even with the captain's ringel stamina, he fell asleep, three centimeters of the cigar still pinched in his fingers. The room was dark, and the other officers had gone to sleep—or a variation thereof—in the other room, with only small glimmers of light. Moani pulled herself away, still swimming in that fuzzy feeling. Ignoring the desire to throw herself on top of Sinon and kiss him all over again, she stumbled toward the door, just remembering to grab the camouflage device before she did.

Ugh, how do ringel stand those things without becoming woozy?

As she tried not to trip over her own tail, Moani wobbled along the dim corridors and followed the path of light, until she came to the gravity wells. High population ships like the *White Flower II* had elevators for cargo, but the crew preferred the wells' speed and convenience. The low-gravity chambers certainly required less effort than stairs or ladders. She giggled to herself, having not experienced one of these since her childhood. All her fur stood up when she stepped into the upwell, and her body became lighter. She barely even noticed that she'd flipped around, upside down—but the memory came back just the same, and she moved with the turn.

With a single leap, Moani could jump down the ledge and clear an entire deck. She couldn't help but let out an excited, "Eee!" as she did, almost stumbling and falling down another floor as she landed with a gentle bounce, laughing to herself.

Oh where was I going… Deck five, right.

She'd overshot it by two floors, but leaping upward—or, well, downwards—was not too hard. Moani weighed only a few kilograms in the well, even with the camouflage pack on her back. She could make a leap all in one go, grabbing the edge of the platform and hoisting herself up, losing no momentum.

When Moani righted herself in normal gravity, she took a full minute to read the station directory on the wall and wander her way again toward the familiar hall with Gert's apartment somewhere on it.

She knocked at the door.

Gert answered, and in shock, pulled her inside.

"What? What!"

"Moani, your camouflage is off!" Gert said.

"It is?" Moani asked. "Shit, I thought… Dammit…"

"Did anyone see you?"

"I saw nobody," Moani said. "What time is it?"

"It's just about zero hours," Gert said. "Dammit, Moani, what were you doing?"

"Ugh, I…" Moani sighed. "Yeah okay, I was an idiot. I was in the officer's chambers for too long. I should have just stayed there…"

Inzari, wearing no camouflage, turned up out of nowhere, making Moani jump. Gert's apartment was also dark, even if the two of them didn't look the least bit bleary-eyed like they'd been sleeping. Inzari sniffed her. "Dammit, did Sinon get you to smoke something again?"

"I thought it'd be fine," Moani said. "He's the captain and all."

"I'm gonna have to talk to him about that…"

"What's wrong with the cigars?" Gert asked. "Besides the odor, I mean."

"It causes mild euphoria," Inzari said, "and it's a magnitude stronger in geordians, and she's a lightweight to boot. Moani, how much did he make you smoke?"

"I don't know," Moani said. "Like, we had a cigar together…"

"Can you even feel anything?"

"Is she overdosed?" Gert asked in a panic.

"I didn't… No, it's not an overdose," Moani said. "I needed to…walk around."

Despite her instructions to herself, she stood there as Gert and Inzari watched her. Then, all at once, she walked into Inzari and held onto her tight, and flopped her head into Inzari's neck.

Inzari, flush, held onto Moani. "Uh, okay," Inzari said. "We'll just play this by ear, so long as you're breathing okay."

"I'm fine. Refilled my ammonia pump before I left…"

"I mean if your lungs are working," Inzari said. "You remember what happened when—"

"I'm not a kit," Moani insisted. "I'm twenty-five…"

"Are you sure?" Gert asked, his tail curved around his ankle with worry. "I kept the captain from killing her earlier, and—"

"Uh," Inzari said to him, "you don't mind if the bed's crowded, do you?"

A minute later, Moani lay down between Gert and Inzari, and felt at least for the moment, tiny and warm. It was nice there—she knew it was the drug talking her into thinking this way, but it was sweet the way Gert acted concerned, and the way Inzari held her.

She knew that no one cared if she lived or died. She thought, as she drifted to sleep, they needed her, and that's why they worried and treated her kindly. It was the only reason she could think of why anyone would care.

But here in the dark and silence, cuddled up close to the two like family or lovers, she could pretend. She could pretend that the ringel she clung to were a true family and not merely a clan of convenience. She could pretend the geroo didn't purposefully hate her, that the big one was more than merely polite. She could pretend her life was…

Something else, whatever that would be.

Chapter 18: Never Prepared Enough

ONE WEEK LATER

I think it makes you unique," Gert said. "Mismatched eyes are rather cute."

Yessi shrunk with her ears flattened out, looking down at her food tray and folding her arms. The accident left her with a dilated left eye—perhaps fixable on another world, but they had limits to how much effort they could spend repairing something as fine as an iris muscle. "It makes me look weird," she said.

"Weird is cute too!" Gert insisted. "They call that eclectic."

The six—Gert, Inzari, Moani, and the three young engineers discharged from med bay—sat at the same table at the Gateside Bazaar. Gert had told Hiani that his current officer duty was "counseling" the academy cadets and pre-cadets as a way to disguise his dating Inzari.

Hiani had believed him. Gert bit his lip nervously, expecting her to appear and reveal at any moment that she knew he was sleeping with a ringel behind her back. Well... a ringel *and* a geordian, now. That didn't exactly compound the issue; when one dated a ringel one had to expect more to join in.

But he'd barely seen Hiani for the last three days, anyhow. Maybe he'd gotten away with it. This would all be over soon, and

Gert could break it off with Inzari and go back to normal life after experiencing something of a sexually liberating vacation.

At least, he kept telling himself that's what he'd do. He *had* to. As much as he liked Inzari, even *if* the Exit Plan succeeded, they'd eventually part ways and never see each other again.

The group's strands all laid face down in the middle of the table, though Moani violated the spirit of the custom by poking around on the much larger slate while everyone else talked and ate. They had situated themselves outside the deck's most popular breakfast bar, surrounded by a loud throng of geroo rushing about for all the things they needed before morning shift began.

When it turned out they still hovered over the yellow planet after three days, rumors spread that the ship was staying put. Ateri made nothing Pokokuro said official. He told only the senior-ranking subcommanders that a scanner ship was arriving at all, but mentioned nothing else about the threats Pokokuro made, that all of them would die. Nobody needed that kind of pressure on their heads. Gert didn't need that kind of pressure on his head, but he had no choice but to bear it.

Still, everyone knew they should have left orbit days ago.

A large marquee over the main entrance gate flashed several messages, the main one reading, WELCOME YOUR NEW ACADEMY ENTRANTS, along with eleven portraits and names few would remember. The academy accepted ten students on average every year, and so no one would notice an extra as out of the ordinary.

"I don't want to be eclectic either!" Yessi exclaimed. "I know there's a big waiting list, but I'd rather have the eye replaced…"

"Come on. Indari, what do you think?" Gert asked her.

Inzari paused, her mouth hanging open. She'd been practicing masking her accent over the last week since there was not much else for her to do. "Erm… What about piercings?" she asked. Bits of her accent still came through but, along with the noise, not enough to raise alarm bells—she was getting better.

"Piercings?" Yessi tilted her ears.

"Sure! It's a great way to work with asymmetry rather than against it. A row of piercings on the opposite eyebrow would look marvelous."

Yessi, with a disbelieving expression on her ears, dabbed a finger to the brow in question.

"I had an idea about that," Rotai said. He had a thick bandage tied over his ear while it was still healing from surgery—he shouldn't have been anywhere so loud, but he insisted they muffled it enough. "Right now we only mark officers by the small pin-on insignia on the strand holster—that's almost impossible to see from most angles. So, what if we marked officers with special piercings? Up high on the ear—three gold for captain, two for commander, one for subcommander, two silver for lieutenant and one silver for junior officer. Eh?"

"I like that idea," Inzari said. "Everyone needs more jewelry around here."

"Yeah, but," Jaki said, "everyone already knows who the captain is, for one, and I don't think he wants any piercings. Also if you make it required for officers, that means barring non-officers from wearing anything similar."

"Oh, right," Rotai said, biting his lip. "I wonder how other ships do it. Progressive tattoos on the ear lining?"

"That'd get difficult if someone's demoted," Jaki said.

"The turek do tattoos for their ranks," Inzari said. "For them, demotion and execution are synonyms."

"Really?" Jaki perked his ears. "I've never heard that before. There's no material in the system on the turek as it is. Where did you hear that?"

"Oh…" Inzari's ears fell flat. Her accent slipped back into her words, and she mumbled to cover it up. "Uh, around. I don't remember where. Maybe it was something someone made up, now that I think about it." She took a bite of her breakfast noodles to excuse her mouth from talking.

Yessi's strand saved her when, face down on the table with the others, it buzzed. When she checked, she sighed and pouted. "I'm sorry, my nephew needs me."

"Denali?" Gert asked. "What's wrong?"

"Computer system issues… En-den-to's too busy to help him out, so I gotta. It's fine—it's practice, isn't it?" She sighed again, picking up her disposable tray. "I'll see you later—" She looked down at Moani, who hadn't even made eye contact. "Moani? You've been quiet."

Moani continued to stare at her slate, which she'd been poking at rather than eating the still-full container of noodles drizzled with brown sauce. "I'm not hungry," she said.

Although Moani had come onboard with an inviting personality—partially inviting, in Gert's estimation; he wanted to believe she was trying—ever since that first day, she'd become frazzled. The change in plans necessitated she put in more work, and she'd barely been out of his apartment at all the last week. Gert was certain he was the only one who saw what was on her slate, and more certain he was the only one who understood its importance—a long picture list of starships, most of which were unknown to the crew, with color labels next to them. He couldn't glean their significance, but he hoped all the red wasn't that bad a sign.

"You haven't even been listening!" Rotai said. "Are you worried about the academy? I'm sure you'll do fine, you got this far."

"Academy is the last thing on my mind," Moani said. "I've…well, it's not important."

Yessi perked her ears. "Oh, I see… It's not your fault, you know."

"Huh?" Moani asked, her eyes darting around like she wanted to run.

"She's right," Jaki said. "You couldn't have known the coil overload was dangerous. It'd be stupid to hold something like that against you."

This was in part why they'd been having the meals together—Gert had felt awful, if on Moani's behalf, for what happened to the three cadets. They were two to three years class seniors to Moani, and so she would join them for at least some academy functions over the next few weeks. Gert had thought it a good idea for them all to get together.

Moani perked her ears straight up.

"What? What's wrong?" Gert asked.

"Something's coming through the gate."

"Are you sure?"

"I know that sound," was the only explanation Moani gave. Geordians had better acuity of ear than geroo did; Gert couldn't recall the gate making any noise but a low hum.

"What sound?" Jaki asked from across the table.

"What?" Rotai asked, louder.

Gert grabbed his strand from the table and looked at the screen. A message from Ateri:

Get to airlock four ASAP. Timestamped ten minutes ago.

"Shit!" Gert exclaimed. He shoveled the rest of his noodles into his mouth before standing up from the bench. "Moani, Indari, we're out of time!"

"The survey ship?" Inzari exclaimed, right when the dull roar of the crowd faded for a moment.

"Survey ship?" All three of the engineering cadets perked their ears at the same time.

Moani huffed with aggravation. She sighed at the list still on her pad.

"Probably?" Gert told the cadets at the table. "But if it's here, you know, duty calls and all! Moani, Indari, come on."

"You going to the gravity upwell?" Yessi asked, replacing her strand into her shoulder pocket. "I'll come with you!"

"Uh, we're gonna have to hurry," Moani said, twisting.

"Yeah, the captain wants us at airlock four," Gert said.

"It's connecting with us?" Jaki asked.

Gert's ears screwed up this way and that. "No," he said, after too long a beat.

"Then why—"

"I don't have time to answer questions, I'm sorry! It was nice having breakfast together. We should do it again sometime!"

Inzari yanked Gert over the bench so he stumbled before righting himself.

"I need the rest of my breakfast!" Gert said. "Who knows how long it will be before we get to eat again…"

"What are you doing up there?" Jaki asked.

"Hey, no!" Inzari said, holding a finger up at the cadets. "This is now a private conversation, no more questions!"

Jaki, puzzled, turned to Yessi, then Rotai.

"I didn't hear," Rotai said. "Say again?"

Inzari's camouflage did a nice job of capturing her eyeroll.

As Gert, Moani, and Inzari hurried their way past the crowd and toward the exit, Gert's throat closed up when he saw Hiani appear from between the crowd.

"Uh, Hiani!" Gert started, though his thoughts were racing, saying, *Oh ancestors, what have I done to deserve this?*

"Gert, I have fantastic news!" she said, ignoring the fact Gert was trying to walk past her. Inzari and Moani didn't wait; they both kept going, passing Hiani on either side.

"Catch up!" Inzari called back.

"Uh, what?" Gert asked, looking out and seeing the two non-geroo he was following disappear down the hallway. "What good news?"

"I have a gap in my work schedule tonight," Hiani said, "We can do dinner together! I was thinking Top Side Bistro again, cause it's your favorite, and they have—"

Gert felt like a complete fool, but once again, he had to say it. He didn't want to say it. His ears sank. "Hiani, I—"

She tilted her head. "Work again?"

Gert nodded.

"What if I shuffled that gap around and we went even later?" Hiani asked.

"This will take all night," Gert said. "I swear I'm not trying to blow you off, I…"

Gert's inner voice rattled on, *I've just been sleeping with a ringel for the last week and I feel heartbroken about it, but I don't know how to help myself. I want some kind of normalcy in my life I can't manage. I want you there but you aren't there—we may not even be compatible if we can't manage something so simple as a work schedule. And if I can't even manage something so simple as faithfulness to one female…*

"Gert!" Hiani exclaimed. "I can't believe this! You've barely been able to talk all week with this duty that sounded rather light to me, couldn't steal away even an hour for lunch or dinner… I've been trying to be patient, but it feels like you're not taking me seriously!"

Gert's contrite expression collapsed in on itself. Well, Hiani had done it. Gert didn't get angry often, but he did have his pride, and she's wounded it.

"I'm *sorry,* Hiani!" Gert said, significantly more forcefully than he'd intended. "I thought you *liked* me. But literally every time my duties come up, you want to kick dust all over them. I already don't get enough respect on the bridge, and every time I try to connect my problems with you, I get no respect from you either. *You don't understand how important this is!* All I can do is promise that it's not going to last forever but you seem driven to impatience so often, that it feels like you'd be happier with someone who wasn't going to be Captain! Because you certainly don't like it when *I* am!"

Hiani's expression turned to shock, her jaw dropping open. Gert had tears in his eyes. He knew much of what he said was unfair, especially when he only told a half-truth. He regretted his anger immediately, but when Hiani didn't reply, he just turned and stormed off, to follow Inzari and Moani to the gravity wells.

"Gert!" Hiani called back, her voice cracking among the noise of the crowd.

Gert should have kept walking, but he paused, his ear back and listening.

"... You're right," Hiani said. "I don't understand how important this is. I just know that Captain-to-be is a very demanding job, and I've been selfish. I didn't mean to lash out. I'm willing to wait. Don't worry about me."

Gert stood there, unmoving, tears forming in his eyes. *Tell her about Inzari. Tell her about Inzari. It will only get worse if she finds out on her own.*

"Okay, stop that." Approaching, Hiani pulled off her scarf and dabbed at Gert's face with it. She lowered her ears. "Is this still about how I got upset with you a week ago?"

Gert, not knowing what else to say, nodded.

Hiani sank. "You've been having a hard time letting go of that."

"It hurt, Hiani."

"You've never acted like this, I don't understand."

"I will explain when I get back."

Gert didn't know why it came out like a promise. He didn't have clearance to tell Hiani anything! He wasn't even about to claim he'd been with a *geroo* for the past week, let alone a ringel. But, how else could he resolve this? He still loved her, and yet...

Gert embraced her hard right there. It was more emotional a gesture than he intended. Hiani seemed only surprised at how emphatic the gesture was, with her paws spread out.

"Please don't hate me," Gert said.

"Gert?" she asked.

Gert let go, and looked her in her beautiful eyes for a while longer, before pulling away and rushing through the crowds toward the gravity well.

Chapter 19: Contact With The Enemy

In the airlock bay, sealed off since the pirates' arrival, Ateri seemed in rough shape. He was still as strong as he was when he was Gert's age, but it took longer for him to recover. Even a week out from his ordeal with Pokokuro, Ateri still carried an oxygen tank nearby. At least all the bandages had come off and his fur was sleek and flat, almost like new.

Given the captain was sitting down on a crate as a makeshift bench, it made Gert worry all the more. But the captain didn't seem in the mood to talk.

Gert's thoughts had been torn on his future. He tried not to think about the argument with Hiani; he wanted to remain positive and hopeful that his future would look like he'd always wanted it to. If they managed to survive all of this, then Ateri would survive too, and Gert would have more time than just a few days to prepare for becoming Captain. Maybe by that time, he'd be able to gain a little more respect.

But he also felt like he'd violated *Ateri's* trust in that time, especially with the captain's reprimand still on his mind.

There's a big difference between loss and losing.

Did it mean the captain thought Gert was due to let him down? Had it hurt their relationship? Was this the last time he could apologize, or did he just need to prove his worth? The more he looked at Ateri's rough figure, the more he thought, *this could be the last time I ever see the captain alive!* And Gert doubly felt like a fool for becoming emotional at the prospect.

He had to do this, and he had to succeed. For Hiani. For Ateri. For himself.

"Is something the matter, Subcommander?" Ateri asked, looking up with his one eye, his voice softer than usual.

"No, sir," Gert said, feeling as though he'd violated some sacred silence. "Just…I don't want to let you down."

"You'll do fine, Gert," Ateri said. "You always do."

Gert wasn't so sure now.

"So…what kind of ship *is* it?" Moani asked Ateri.

"Pictures we captured from the gateside camera," Ateri said, pulling them up on his strand. Quietly shielding his eyes, Gert glanced over Ateri's shoulder at the microscopic speck on his screen. Ateri pulled at the picture to zoom in closer. It was a full-resolution image from one of the surface cameras, and still didn't seem to get any larger the more he pulled in on it. Even when it took up a wedge of the screen, the shadows of deep space obscured most of the detail beyond the shape, leaving just a few mysterious, jagged edges facing the light.

"Hrm," Moani said. "Damn. Uh. Hrm."

"What's wrong?" Gert asked. "Is it not something you prepared for?"

"The computer systems I'm prepared for," Moani said. "The ship model is a Chinnok Arenia Class Five. Though it's hard to tell with the shadows."

"Aren't those personal cruisers?" Inzari asked.

"Yes, but they're modular. Meaning whatever computer they stuck in there is either factory Chinnok—which is dead simple to crack—or one of the modular upgrades, which can be more difficult, but doable. I doubt they put in military-level security on a ship not intended to face an enemy."

"So what's the problem?" Ateri asked.

"Modular also includes the cabin and habitation space," Moani said. "We don't know what kind of atmosphere we're facing until we're aboard."

"The environment suits can handle it though?" Ateri asked.

"Our suits, definitely. Yours, most likely. With how the Chinnok handles variable atmospheres, there won't be any rooms swimming in, say, hydrochloric acid or anything. Interior security might be a different story."

She tapped something onto her own slate and brought up a default layout for the ship class. The map showed the shape of the ship—something like a reverse teardrop with the rounded end shaved flat. Two corridors ran along both the port and starboard side of the ship, and met in the fore and aft sides. There was also a large, circular chamber in the middle that took up a third of the floorspace, with smaller paths outlining its circumference. Everything else was divided into chambers of fixed sizes that had a bunch of tiny, hard-to-read krakun labels on them.

"So how do we get aboard?" Gert asked.

"Same way as here." Moani gestured to the airlock doors. "Attach to their airlock, get in and out, erase airlock access logs to make it look as though we were never there."

"No way," Inzari said. "That thing is puny, at least compared to the *White Flower II*. I don't care how gently I touch down, there is *no* way they don't hear us attach to the airlock!"

"And even then," Gert said, pointing to Moani's map, "the outer airlock is facing the broadest side of the hallway. We open that, they'll see us."

Moani's ears flattened. "There is another way in," she said. "The belly access port, for maintenance. That would give us cover since we could come up through this room here, and most of the machinery in the underbelly will absorb the sound of touchdown."

"That's perfect," Inzari said. "Why didn't you say that first?"

"Because it has a catch," Moani said.

"Of course…" Inzari grumbled, stepping away to pace.

"It's intended for maintenance to open it in-atmosphere or drydock only," Moani explained. "There's no airlock pump attached to it. Once we open it, if there's any atmosphere onboard other than oxygen-nitrogen, we have no safe area to retreat to if we have suit issues."

Ateri glanced at them all. "Are you prepared for that? It could mean up to twenty-four hours in a pressure suit with no breaks."

"I thought you said I'd do fine," Gert said, feeling strangely hurt by Ateri's change of opinion.

"I mean, do you need to use the facilities?" Ateri asked. "Unless you want to hobble around a ship in secret in a spacewalk suit, the mobile environment suit we have in-paw has no waste reclamation."

Gert blinked. "I will be right back."

* * *

"This thing's a bitch to wear," Inzari mumbled as she tugged at the sleeves of the environment suit. Her dark blue suit had two layers to keep the body surrounded in a pressure cushion, but they were both thin and showed off Inzari's curves like she was five centimeters thicker all around. "I hate clothing, and this is the worst kind."

"Uh-huh," Gert said, failing to not stare at Inzari.

"Just watch where you're flying!" Moani said from the back seat. "I will not die from a stupid mistake just because you're a little uncomfortable…"

Gert's suit was different, in that it was one from onboard the *White Flower II* that had a purpose similar to the one that Inzari and Moani brought for themselves. Their suits had clear, even stitching, cool blue fabric designs surrounding stress points, and articulate gloves with precise grip. Gert's may as well have been an orange plastic sock.

At least they wouldn't have to be looking at it all the time.

"Got it," Inzari said, pointing up to the ship coming into view. "Now to just pray they make no more orbital adjustments while we're landing…"

She tapped several buttons to swing the tail of the ship around, and changed the view camera to that of the ones on the rear of the shuttle. Moani stepped up and peered at the underside of the ship—it was impossible to see anything with all the shadows.

"Well?" Inzari asked.

"Bit of light might help," Moani said.

"They might see us."

"They won't be paying attention to us," Moani said. "Trust me on that."

Inzari scoffed and turned on the rear lamps, which lit up the underside of the survey ship. Moani pointed. "The circle on the hull panel's right there. Should be small enough to pull the plate inside." She popped back into the rear cabin to make preparations.

Gert watched the screen draw closer to the faint outline of a circle on the black hull until Inzari shut off the light well before making touchdown.

"Inzari!" Gert squeaked.

"Keep your suit on, I saw where it is," Inzari said, pushing on the dual joysticks that were the shuttle's manual steering. "I just feel more comfortable if they can't see the light is all."

"Moani said—"

"She's right," Inzari said, "but just in case, you know? Cloaking technology is limited as-is. I mean, you don't need it for long distances in space, 'cause space distances are fucking enormous. They can't see you unless they already know where you are, and if they know where you are, they can fire on you anyway. So actual

disappear-from-view cloaking is for super close-range infiltration, like we're doing now. And shining a goddamn light through the cloaking field on the ship you're trying to approach would defeat the whole purpose of that!"

The entire shuttle stopped with a heavy *thump*, rocking Gert all about in his chair. His chest clenched tight.

"Perfect!" Inzari said. "Locking in the hatch now."

"Please don't say locked in," Gert said.

"Claustrophobic?" Inzari asked.

"No," Gert said, "but we *are* about seven thousand kilometers from the *White Flower II*, and that's the farthest I've been from it so far."

"Call your captain if you're homesick," Inzari said, unbuckling herself from her seat. "It'll take us a moment to get that hatch off."

Gert scoffed at such a suggestion, though the moment Inzari stepped behind the seats that separated the cockpit from the cabin, Gert reached for his helmet to tap Ateri's contact button. One feature his suit had that Moani and Inzari's did not was, like the spacewalk suit, the connectivity to his strand network. He wore the device underneath the suit and it synced up with the HUD inside the helmet. But it still counted as normal network traffic—Krakuntec could be listening. Still, he figured even a vague update would settle everyone's nerves.

Maybe he could think of what he needed to say to Ateri.

However, when he put on his helmet and tried to connect the call, the HUD gave him a big red, *Cannot Establish Connection*. He tried this several more times.

In the back, Moani opened the shuttle's rear door and Inzari prepped a large suction connector to unseal the panel behind. The whole disc of the hatch was two meters across; Gert could only guess at how heavy it must have been.

"Everyone's helmets on?" Inzari reminded the cabin. Moani grabbed her helmet from a box on the wall.

"Moani?" Gert said, "I can't seem to reach the *White Flower II*."

She perked her ears. "Really? Let me see…" She also removed her strand from the wall panel where she'd put it for safekeeping. She tried calling someone, but got a blaring "connection dropped" tone.

"Are we too far away?" Gert asked.

"Doubtful. There's nothing between us and the ship, and I don't think the gravity is affecting the carrier wave at this range. Which means… Ah shit, I didn't think of that."

"What now!" Gert said.

"The standard Chinnok antigravity generator is a lot bigger than the base ship needs. If they tore out its shielding to fit on more sensor equipment—not unheard of—it could be leaking."

Gert stared at her. "Leaking what?"

"It's called aetheric radiation, even though it's not radiation, but a selective form of residual gravity?" Moani looked to Inzari. "It's a byproduct of forcing artificial gravity into a localized area."

Inzari stared at her.

"It can bend radio waves!" Moani exclaimed.

"Yes, of course," Gert said, scratching his head. "But wouldn't that interfere with instrument readings? Scanners can be picky."

"They can compensate for it," Moani said, "but you must expect it first. We will be close enough that our radios should still work, but your strands have nothing built-in to overcome the signal drift."

"Oh… So we can't get a message back to Ateri to let him know how we're doing?"

"I doubt it," Moani said. "We'll need to play this by ear…and we can't stay here forever. We only have until they're finished with their scans."

Gert's ears fell. He'd messed up, he was sure of it—the last opportunity to say something to Ateri, and he couldn't even figure out how to sort the emotion in his chest enough to say…

No, you'll see him again, Gert thought. *You just need to finish this mission. He'll survive. You just need to end this in success.*

"Enough yakking," Inzari said. "Helmets on, both of you!"

Gert twisted his helmet on, which connected through a simple screw latch. Moani's snapped to latches around the neck. Once Inzari was satisfied they were both secure, she shoved the suction hose into the exposed hull plate. Moani jabbed a long, thin rod into several small holes around the inside the plate—safety pins, Gert figured—and when twelve of them had popped, Inzari turned on the suction device, and the plate rotated. The edges hissed as gas rushed into the cabin.

"Gert, get ready to catch this," Inzari said through the helmet radio. Gert scrambled forward to put his paws under the plate.

The moment the entire disc popped out of the hull and it fell into Gert's paws, he regretted it. While the surface was a black carbon-ceramic, the inside was twenty centimeters worth of various metallic alloy layers, ranging in colors from brass to silver. The thing had to weigh at least a hundred kilos, and Inzari was still taking part of the weight herself, and struggling to keep it upright. Still, Gert did his best to lower it to the floor so it broke nothing on the way down.

The second thing that happened was the blast of warm air radiated through the suits. Gert's suit had only a bare amount of insulation; it wasn't meant for firefighting.

"Savior of Vala!" Moani swore, backing away from the opening. "That's a lot more pressure than I wanted…"

"What's the air composition?" Gert asked, grunting as he shoved the plate aside to lean on the seats.

"Uh," Moani stammered, pulling a small device from her canvas bag. "Um…twelve percent oxygen, seventy percent nitrogen, seventeen percent…bromide compounds."

"Aw hell," Inzari said. "You mean this ship's staffed by anup?"

"Anup?" Gert exclaimed.

"Preferred room temperature, forty-three degrees, pressure one-hundred-thirty kilopascals," Moani said, reading from her slate. She rubbed at her neck as though the uncomfortable heat had already gotten to her, and the interior of the shuttle hadn't even absorbed the ship's atmosphere. "They seem to be running the ship cooler than normal; it's only forty-one degrees.

"Only forty-one degrees?" Inzari exclaimed.

Moani whimpered. "Oh, this is trouble…"

"Can you speak Anupian, Gert?" Inzari asked. "It might help."

"Uh…not as such," Gert said. "I started a course on it a year ago, but only got as far as learning a handful of words and some cultural aspects…"

"Why'd you stop?" Inzari asked.

"Erm… Hiani took up most of my free time."

Inzari barked a laugh. "That's cute, but not helpful."

"Gert, you're with me, remember?" Moani pulled on her personal cloak. "I've adapted the cloak to render us both invisible from normal view, so stay in contact with me."

"In contact, like," Gert took hold of Moani's tail wrapped up inside her tailored pressure suit.

"That should work. But for the love of the gods, don't tug. Keep it slack."

"Got it."

"So quick recap of the plan," Moani said as she also lifted her toolbag and pulled it over her shoulder. "First step is to locate where the survey data is being stored. That could be the bridge, or any of the computer rooms onboard."

She seemed to sink between the cloak and the toolbag, but she said nothing about it, so Gert didn't press.

"I'll shadow you," Inzari said, pulling on the other cloak. "Need to figure out how many anup are onboard and keep a lookout."

"Shouldn't someone stay behind?" Gert asked.

"In case…"

"Uh, in case we need to…get away fast?"

"Gert, if this thing goes tails-up we're all dead, getaway or no," Inzari said. "Keep it in mind, sugar."

Gert swallowed. He knew that all too well, the back of his mind still crawling with the consequences of failure. Inzari and Moani might be able to escape to the *Jet Black Sword,* but Pokokuro slated Gert to die if the planet proved inviable.

He tried not to think about the image he created in his mind. The mouth of the recycler opening to swallow him. Screams, cries, wailing. His thoughts re-purposed them from the video of his mother's death, and the audio recordings of the *Silver Mint III.*

He'd only ever watched them once apiece and regretted it both times, no matter how important it was. He could not bear it, as even now they felt like unhealed wounds inside his chest.

Good thoughts. Positive thoughts. We can get this done.

Inzari crawled through the access hole first, turning as she stepped into a different gravity field and crawling to find access to some room from underneath.

"You can let go of my tail until we're inside," Moani said.

"Sorry," Gert said, releasing. "Nerves."

"How'd you get this job again?" Moani asked, propping her paws onto the edges of the opening to climb in.

"Well, the captain and his mate would be missed, and I'm the only other geroo on board who knows about the plan."

"So, desperation then," Moani said, crawling inside with the shifting gravity. "It's so nice to know I'm working with the best of the best…"

Chapter 20: Under Pressure

I think it's safe to talk—" Inzari whispered over the radio. Her voice crackled over the line.

"Inzari, I'm having trouble hearing you," Gert said.

"I said talk, not shout."

Two hours after they boarded, Gert huddled in a low gap underneath what seemed to be a desk in one of the eleven rooms he was unable to tell apart. He secured Moani's legs in his arms, holding her up to reach the console, plugging in various small cards into the machine to gain just enough access to figure out how this ship mapped out its computer. Though she was invisible, he knew Inzari stood just at the doorway about three meters away.

Somehow Gert had gotten away on this mission without seeing even one of the anup onboard. He had a hard time picturing them, even though he'd drawn them in those lewd notebook doodles when he was a teenager, much the same as he had any other alien that looked appealing. He'd never gotten a sense of their scale until he had to hold Moani a meter off the floor to reach their control height.

As the map had showed, the ship had a simple layout—two corridors, one running down starboard and one running down portside, with connecting hallways at the fore and aft of the ship. The middle area bowed outward to fit the central habitat, which had small corridors circumscribing it, along with two doors—thick enough to be airlock doors—facing the starboard and portside halls, both locked. No other room on the ship seemed to even have a door, just a wide open doorway, even to the barracks or the bridge.

And the heat was getting unbearable.

"Ugh," Moani whispered, propping herself up on the console. "I'm getting light-headed."

"Nobody's approaching," Inzari said. "You can turn up your filter."

Moani twisted a knob on her helmet's muzzle, which created a small but audible hissing noise as the filter increased flow. The various humming instruments around the ship would muffle the noise, much like their landing, but Moani insisted they move cautiously.

Worse still, the filter on the mask only pulled oxygen from the atmosphere. She'd topped off her ammonia pump before they boarded, but she'd be pulling more than normal under the circumstances. They may have only had a limit of a few hours.

Her staticy, heavy breathing was audible over the link between the three.

"Moani?" Gert asked.

"Sorry, I was just… I was thinking," she lied. "This ship has multiple atmospheric combinations. If we can find a sealed-off room attached to an atmosphere pump, we could give ourselves a saferoom. And with temperature control…"

"Uh, I've looked," Inzari said. "The anup believe in open floorplans."

"Monumental architecture," Gert said.

"Huh?"

"Their planet has huge buildings. Ten-meter high roofs, even for residences, with similar doorways. They're not used to putting doorways on anything unless they're gates."

"That's nice to know, Encyclopedia Galactica," Inzari said, "but that means none of these rooms have doors, much less locks."

Rick Griffin

"But if nobody's gone in the central habitat," Moani said, "if we unlock that…"

"Someone's coming," Inzari whispered.

Moani twisted her breathing apparatus to silent filtering. Gert let her down, and they and ducked under the desk. The small gasp she made over their com link sounded as though she were holding her breath. Gert remained curled in the corner. He felt safe enough, if trapped, but should the anup bump into them and investigate, it was all over.

He didn't even feel nervous; it all exhausted him too much.

Two of the anup walked into the room, a male and a female, holding golden rods, one with a full-face breathing mask dangling off the end. They weren't as big as the krakun, but it was still alarming just how *huge* they were. Their thin body fur was all the same shade of shimmering black, each three meters tall with hardly a few centimeters difference between the tops of their heads. They had long, slender, canine muzzles to match their long, slender ears, but they were not slender in other regards—either one looked like they could break all three intruders in a single blow.

The female and the male argued. Gert knew next to nothing about anup languages, but hearing it fascinated him. Even as they spoke on top of one another, their tones seemed to match as though they sang a two-part harmony. However, as they spoke, the pleasing tones shifted, the female stepping back from the male's imposing monotone.

The female stopped talking altogether and folded her arms. She said one word to him—like, "Gih-dah,"—then turned and left the room the same way they'd entered.

The male huffed. It was often difficult to read expressions between species, but some expressions were close to universal—short staccato motions and impatience suggested frustration.

The male anup—Gert had no idea what his name was, but labeled him as "Gihdah" in his head—grabbed the face mask off the end of the rod. Then without even lining it up as one might when pushing a knife back into a sheath, he jammed the rod into a just-wide-enough hole in the wall, several centimeters deep.

This caused a monitor to flicker on, and the anup tapped several commands into the system.

"Oh, right…" Moani whispered, watching the proceedings. "No wonder I wasn't getting anywhere…"

Gihdah sighed and looked toward the doorway. He didn't leave. He instead walked right for Gert, and Gert inhaled. If the anup heard Moani, he made no motion to show it.

With anup paws five centimeters from his leg, Gert tried pushing himself farther into the corner, but he had already crammed himself in as tight as possible. Moani watched too, with her breath held so even her slight wheezing was inaudible over the radio. Peeking just under the edge of the desk, Gert glimpsed the anup typing something into the console that Moani was just at.

"We need one of those," Moani whispered even quieter, pointing toward the long, golden rod jutting out of the wall.

"One of what?" Inzari asked over the radio.

"Shh!" Gert shushed.

Gihdah stopped what he was doing, took one step back, and leaned down to look underneath the console where Gert and Moani squashed themselves. Moani stopped breathing. The anup sniffed, his lips almost on the edge of a snarl, like he'd been on edge and this was the final straw. Gihdah slid his paw backward into the small gap below, though he only moved it between Moani and Gert, stopping just before he touched their boots. He scoffed, and returned to typing at the console.

The uncomfortable heat and imminent threat made it a *little* easier for Gert not to feel turned on by an otherwise handsome alien again.

Moani was already panting hard over the radio channel, filling Gert's ears with static. But he said nothing else about it—all he could think about now was what the anup would do if he caught them.

Probably turn them over to Pokokuro, who would not cut their suffering short. Gert shivered, but he remained still, since that was the only thing that could save them. He and Moani huddled for what seemed like hours, but may have been less than thirty minutes in reality, before Gihdah removed his rod from the opposite wall and left the room.

Moani let out a loud sigh. "I mean I knew about the rods," Moani returned to a normal whisper, "but it didn't click until I saw it. We need one. That's the anup-preferred method of personal security; they do that instead of paw prints like other species use. Micro-etching on the end is their personal encryption key."

"How come they do that?" Inzari asked.

"I read about it once," Gert whispered. "They believe direct use of their paws is intimate. So they use the rod for everything else."

"That makes it convenient to steal," Inzari said.

"Kinda. They keep the rod on their person at all times," Moani said. "If someone steals it out from under them, they can change their access key. So we must steal it only long enough for them to not realize it's missing. If I'd guessed we would be on an anup ship, I'd have made a rod-reader ahead of time…" She groaned and slowly pulled herself out from under the desk. "Let's move toward the habitat chamber. We'll need more time."

"I'll scout ahead," Inzari said, followed by a brush of paw steps from the doorway.

"In the corridor around the habitat, there should be an access panel," Moani said. "I can find the lock override from there; they weren't built to be secure."

Gert clung onto Moani's long, covered tail as they both pressed against the wall of the doorway out, waiting for the signal. Moani was panting, leaning against the wall with clear exhaustion.

It struck Gert that he should have been carrying all that weight, given the circumstances.

"Moani, let me handle the bag," Gert said. He reached for the canvas bag at her side, but she brushed him away.

"Don't touch my tools," she creaked over the radio, voice distorted.

"You'll pass out," Gert whispered. "The less weight, the better. I'm just holding them for you."

"I need them—" Moani was mumbling.

"At least I should wear the cloak," Gert said. "Should have from the beginning."

"Don't have time to swap now, anyone might walk in at any moment... Would need time to recalibrate... Two or three minutes..."

"Moani, give him the damn bag," Inzari's voice came on over the radio after a good half hour of nothing from her. "We can't make a safe spot onboard if you get heatstroke! Who's gonna hack a solution for us? Gert?"

"Hey," Gert said as if to protest, even though he had nothing to counter Inzari's jab.

Moani paused, then pulled the strap from her shoulder and handed it by the shoulder back to Gert.

Gert peeked inside the bag and saw one of the tools she'd carried with her was the plasma pistol. It was stowed in a safety holster, but within grabbing range near the top of the pile.

He stopped and considered if he should say something about it. The pistol couldn't have been over three kilograms, but that was still excess weight they did not need on a stealth mission. Besides, if it came down to a firefight, they were all dead anyhow. There would be no way to keep their presence onboard a secret.

They shouldn't have even had it in the first place! But Gert said nothing while they were busy. He'd bring this up when they had time to discuss it.

"Inzari, did you find anything yet?" Gert whispered as he slung the bag around his own shoulder.

"I think this is the access panel we were looking for," Inzari said. "I'll try to jimmy it off. Do you see anyone coming down the hallway?"

"I saw movement up near the bridge." Gert peeked out the open doorway, up the starboard corridor toward the front of the ship. When Gert leaned into the hall, he had clear sight past the central habitat to the bridge. Way off in the distance, he could even see through a tiny window to C-18-3 as they orbited.

"Looks like they're taking their time. How many have you counted?"

"I counted five distinct faces," Inzari said, "but they're all similar-looking. Barracks has eleven beds, could be eleven. I suppose there could be twenty-two if they share them."

"Anup don't share beds," Gert said. "Not even mated couples; it's considered uncouth."

"Gert, that is fascinating," Inzari said, "but I was being hyperbolic. If there really were twenty-two onboard, we'd be tripping over them."

"I'm sorry, I'm trying to be helpful," Gert said. "Exobiology fascinated me, but I've never had chance to use it."

Moani slipped down the wall. Gert grit his teeth and caught her in both arms. The cloak strapped to her back, even insulated, felt hotter than Gert expected.

"Uh-oh," Gert mumbled. "Moani's suffering heatstroke."

"Shit. Get her out here, pronto. I'm in the aft-side corridor that's surrounding the central habitat."

Gert grunted and shook Moani. "Hey, wake up!"

"Nng," was the only thing she said.

Gert twisted the dial on her helmet to increase her oxygen flow, which let out a tiny hiss. She shouldn't have left it silent by default, but regardless, she needed the oxygen more than she needed to stay quiet. If things got too much worse, she'd be quiet forever.

Chapter 21: Gold And Water

Gert dragged Moani and the equipment bag toward the door and stopped. An anup had entered the hallway from the bridge and inserted a gold rod into the lock on the central habitat. The anup entered, and the door shut behind him, leaving the rod stuck in the doorway lock.

"Gert, are you coming?" Inzari whispered.

"One moment," Gert said. He approached the door, cradling Moani over one shoulder, and tried to pull the rod loose—but it stuck fast. His ears frowned. It was just as well; Moani wasn't in any condition to use it.

Since he was at the door, he put his ear to it. Or rather, put his ear to the inside of his helmet and put his helmet to the door, to see if he could catch anything. It was no way to listen. Two walls separating Gert from the inner chamber of the central habitat muffled everything besides the natural humming of the ship. He was about to give up when he heard the unmistakable whir of the hatch on the other side of the airlock open.

The voice he picked up was loud, even through the shielded door.

"I don't want you to bother me in person unless it's critical, do you understand? I know my job—you do your damn job, and if I need you I will call you, not a moment before!"

The voice spoke in krakun. Gert inhaled and dragged Moani away from the door—ducking under the rod sticking out from the wall before he banged his helmet on it.

His hurried pawsteps after he turned down the narrow branching corridor must have been loud, because when he approached to the open access panel, Inzari asked, "What kept you?"

It felt strange talking to someone who was invisible, but Gert said, "We need to change plans. There's a krakun in the habitat."

Inzari was silent for a moment. She swore in ringel—a feat, given how few taboo words they had. "I knew this was too empty with only five anup. A krakun...doing the bulk of the work, I assume?"

"Sounded like," Gert said. "But it also sounded like he wasn't too keen on having them walk into the habitat."

"Okay. Set Moani down and hand me her bag. We don't have much longer but I think I can make this work."

"You can hack it?"

"Maybe." Inzari sounded uncertain. "I know a couple mechanical basics for airlocks, but if you can revive Moani, that would be a lot more help."

Gert could not see Inzari, or the toolbox, only the way the panel floated off to the side and lay down on the floor, and then the occasional sparks as she cut some component with the minitorch.

Gert propped Moani up against the opposite wall. First aid was straightforward: a damp towel, cold water, and room for air. But the only water they had was in Moani's toolbag. It wouldn't be cold, and he had no way to get it to her mouth without breaching her pressure suit, which made the "make room for air" step moot.

"Moani, come on," Gert said, shaking her by the arms. Her head flopped to her shoulder.

He put his paws around her chest to be sure. Yes, her lungs still inflated and deflated. She would have said something if she'd sprung a leak; bromine was not a pleasant gas to experience breathing.

Actually…

Now that he thought about it, when he pressed his gloved paws against her chest, he realized he heard the texture of her fur through the membrane. The material was very strong, but it was thin. He might wake her up if…

"Inzari, let's swap camouflage," Gert said. "I need to find the ship's washroom."

"I thought you went before we boarded!" Inzari said, her voice coming in staticky.

"Not for that! Not yet, anyway. I mean to get cold water."

"Any water you find will be contaminated with bromine," Inzari said.

"It'll still cool her down. Shouldn't hurt the suit any."

Inzari paused a moment to consider. "Good idea. Let's swap and hurry." Inzari's pack fell to the floor and rattled, though she did not reappear until she removed the connected bracer.

Gert did the same with the bracer on Moani's arm, glancing back toward the curve in the small corridor they occupied. Only the slimmest sliver of the portside hallway was visible, and so long as they were quiet, it seemed a decent enough place to reset the disguises between the two.

Gert could not make out the interface on the camouflage bracer, and it was even less responsive to tapping it with his large gloves. Inzari took the bracer from him and tapped in a few commands. "There. One geroo body, your environment suit, and any object in your paws. Remember, if you grab something, it turns invisible with you in moments, until you break contact."

It relieved Gert to see her face through her helmet, even if it puffed up her cheek fur. He sighed and smiled at her. "Got it," he said, and strapped the bracer onto his arm. He hefted the very warm pack onto his back. "I'll be as quick as I can."

"Remember, our priority is not getting caught," Inzari said. "Try looking for a washroom connected to the barracks."

Gert tapped the activate button on the cuff, and the small display monitor gave him a blue light, showing he was good to go. Still, he turned around in front of Inzari and whispered, "Is it getting all of me?"

"You're good."

"Right!" He had an overwhelming urge to give Inzari a goodbye kiss, but the helmets would have gotten in the way. So he said, "Kiss kiss."

Inzari chuckled, attaching Moani's bracer. "Go before we all get caught, you dummy."

Gert hurried back to the main corridor before slowing his steps down to a tiptoe. He peeked around the corner, first toward the bridge where most of the anup seemed to gather. He saw movement, but no state of alert. They milled about in an all-too-familiar routine work malaise. He peeked the other direction—a long, curved corridor going all the way to the back, empty. He walked down the corridor toward the rear, heel-toe to ensure his soft soles would make minimal sound.

In the aft of the ship, the starboard and portside hallways met, with two of those doorways facing the furthest-back room. Both doorways appeared, from a meter away, pitch-black, save for the barest amount of light cast in from the hallways on the floor inside. The floor of the room was itself black, as if to capture and absorb all outside light. Gert wondered if actual doors that closed wouldn't be more effective at keeping the barracks dark.

He groped around the dark walls for a while, but found no doorway to a washroom. Then he ran into one of the bunk beds, tapping his helmet against the overhang. Gert froze when he heard a loud rustling. The room was too dark and his helmet muffled too much sound to allow him to pinpoint where it came from.

"*Eendie ora so a?*" A feminine voice asked—though with as deep as the anup voices were, he could only tell it was feminine because it was the same tone as the one he'd seen arguing with "Gihdah" earlier.

Gert said nothing. He held his breath.

The voice grumbled and a bed creaked, like she was standing up. Gert heard scuffling paws cross the room. He pressed himself into the corner between the wall and the bunk beds, trying to make his profile as narrow as possible. The steps grew louder, and he caught a glimpse of her from the light in the doorway—walking right at him. Gert bit his lip and waited for everything to go to hell.

The wall behind opened, and a light came on. The anup walked past Gert into the washroom.

Gert released a whimper that was more breath than voice.

The anup—Gert named her Eendie after the first word she had said—faced a wall mirror and groaned to herself. It struck Gert how nice she looked from the back, because her taut body shape, especially her rear, reminded him of Inzari, though much taller and with a much smaller, thinner tail. Not that it did distract him at the moment. One, it was much, much too warm in the suit to even consider being turned on, and two, she lived in a bromine environment, and Gert was already thinking about how much that would burn.

"*Eeesah,*" Eendie muttered, looking at her eyes in the mirror, pulling down the bottom lid to see—if it was bloodshot, perhaps? Her eyes didn't seem red or puffy, though Gert recalled from what he learned of anup that their blood wasn't red; from what he saw of her mouth, the flesh had a yellow-orange sheen to it. Very difficult to notice if her eyes were, he supposed, jaundiced from over a meter down.

Gert slipped into the washroom behind her, shoving himself into the empty corner nearest the door so he didn't need to walk behind her or brush her tail in the tight space. She tapped a panel in

the wall which clicked, and a large rack of various bathroom tools slid out of the wall, just low enough for Gert to catch the top of its contents at eye level. It included a stack of towels in the front and a small bucket near the back, both of which he eyed with need, and waited for Eendie to finish whatever it was she did.

Eendie picked out a small device about the size of a chip-reader. She regarded it for a long while. Pressing a button on the side to release a needle from its tip, she jabbed it into her lower gut. Gert winced, but she seemed to pay the pain no regard, instead holding the device there for a good twelve seconds before pulling it back out. She grabbed a wad of gauze from the open tray and dabbed at the splotch of bronze blood, regarding the small device in her paw all the while. It chimed a little beeping tune.

She tightened her grip, and her body tensed.

"Cheia! En soder…" She growled, baring both rows of sharp teeth. She hurled the device against the floor, and it smashed into several pieces—one tapped Gert's boot, and he pressed himself against the corner even tighter. Her balled up fist slammed against the wall, only a meter from Gert's head. He shook, and his whole body tensed and locked up. She had gotten way too close to his corner, though in that moment, he was much more concerned with her turning his face into a smooth puree. He could almost taste her breath, and felt the slightest bit fortunate he was unable to smell it.

She smoothed a paw over the top of her head, her ears falling back and popping up straight again the moment her fingers passed over. She sniffed and wiped her face. *"Nega…"* Then she placed a paw on her gut just below the navel.

Gert tilted his head at the scene he was missing context for. Eendie huffed a sigh, reached into the open rack for a small bottle, then dry-swallowed a pill from its contents. She leaned over the wash basin and slurped bromine-laced water from the faucet, before splashing it over her face.

After pushing the long shelf back into the wall, she turned to leave, then stopped and regarded the broken pieces of the device on the floor. She took a long, shallow breath, bent over, and picked up each one. Gert stared at the small piece touching his boot. That one was too close for comfort. The moment she turned her attention to a chunk in the opposite corner, Gert pushed the small plastic bit several centimeters closer to the center of the room.

Eendie turned back and tilted her head at the small piece. Gert could only think, *Shit, too far.* But she picked it up without further comment, then shoved them into another swinging panel, a garbage chute, before leaving the washroom. The light switched off behind her, and the door shut.

Gert released the breath he was holding and tapped a button on his helmet to turn on the built-in flashlights. He went to work, having wasted enough time already hoping not to die, and opened the same sliding wall panel the anup had used. He removed two of the towels, hoping the crew would not miss them, and soaked them under the basin faucet. The sink was about at his chin level, he could reach the faucet handle from the side, and standing tip-toe he saw just over the top.

Testing the temperature through his glove, he expected warm water, but he was pleased to feel it was ice cold—so much so that holding his gloved paw in the water for even a moment was a major relief from the oppressive heat.

The bucket was more difficult to fill; he couldn't see inside when he tipped the bucket over, and it would not fit all the way under the faucet. Still, he filled it until water spilled out its front, and he pulled the bucket back. The result was half-full, perhaps five liters, which he hoped was enough—he didn't want to risk spilling any on the way back anyhow.

He tucked the wet towels under his arm. Then, noticing they dripped as he squeezed them, considered a moment, then stuffed the towels into the bucket, bringing the water level near the top.

With his free paw he poked around on the wall until he found a shallow latch above his head he could barely reach and pull open. The door slid open, and Gert switched his flashlights back off before someone spotted the beam.

He stepped back into the barracks room, all ready to leave with the prize, when he noticed a small light still on in the barracks. Eendie sat on one of the low bunks, leaning over and tapping away at a strand-like device. Her ears were lowered in distress, and she kept sniffling and wiping at her eyes.

But in the low glow of the tiny screen, Gert caught a golden glint: Eendie's gold staff, tucked under her bed on top of a foot locker.

So he waited for Eendie to send her message. After only a minute she set the device face-down on the end table. She vanished into darkness, flopping onto the mattress.

Gert snuck low, very careful of his feet lest he catch the legs of a bunk, until he was once again close to Eendie. Slowly, he reached out his free paw and felt for the end of the golden rod under her bunk, until his fingers touched a cylinder. Even more slowly, he pulled it back out, trying to avoid the inevitable sliding sound. Having the rod in paw, he turned to hurry out the barracks door.

And immediately banged his boot against the bunk closest to him. Gert winced.

The mattress rustled. Gert spotted the glint of her eyes in the dark, on him.

"*Ora so a?*" she said again.

Gert waited, frozen in place. It was so long a wait, it amazed him he didn't keel over from holding his breath.

"…*En soder,*" Eendie mumbled, and flopped her head back onto her pillow.

Gert made his way out much more carefully.

Chapter 22: Plan B

Inzari," Gert whispered. "Inzari!"

"Right where you left me," Inzari said over the crackling radio. "Lemme tap the button so you can see." In the narrow bend around the perimeter of the central habitat, Inzari and Moani, slumped against her leg, appeared and disappeared. Gert would have worried the act revealed too much, but from her position they could only see the slimmest wedge of the portside hall. Just a bit farther and they'd be out of sight entirely.

"I'm here," Gert said, "I've got it." He hurried down the narrow corridor and knelt down beside the two where best he could figure. It was very difficult to judge proximity when he could not see either of the people he was next to.

His heart was still pounding so fast, and he wanted to embrace Inzari and have her comfort him—but he knew it was stupid. He knew there were more important things to do, and he knew he couldn't take the time to distract her. He laid the bucket and the two soaked towels on the deck in front of himself, releasing his touch so they would appear visible to her.

"Good, two towels," Inzari said. "Take one and wrap it around your neck under the helmet."

One towel vanished as Inzari grabbed it. Gert took the other and did as Inzari instructed. He sighed, at once experiencing an immense amount of relief as the overheating subsided the slightest amount. The HUD inside his helmet still flashed that small warning sign for overheating, but he might as well have stepped into a cold bath.

"Wait," Gert said, "what about Moani?"

The bucket disappeared. One beat later, *splash*. Gert jumped back as water pooled on the floor, and Moani sputtered to life over the strand. The water flowed in rivulets along the borders of the floor tiles, draining into ventilation grates that ran along either wall.

"Inzari!" Gert exclaimed. "We're hidden but not *that* hidden!"

"Gods of unknown space!" Moani bust out, loud enough to hear through the helmet. "Warn me next time!"

"Moani, you passed out," Inzari said.

"Oh. Shit. Moani's breathing was still labored, but she didn't sound on the verge of passing out again, at least not yet. Then she said, as if noticing for the first time, "You're not Gert."

"No, we swapped packs so he could get water," Inzari said. "Also, I think it's best you not wear this thing; it's nearing pan-sear."

"How are you not unconscious then?" Moani asked, indignant.

"I drank a lot of water before boarding," Inzari said.

"You? Water?" Moani cracked a laugh.

"Hey! It helps. However, if we want to get that water back out of me before I explode, we have a problem gaining access to the central room."

"Namely," Gert said, "we're sharing this ship with a krakun."

"Wonderful," Moani groaned. "How about some good news?"

"I got this!" Gert tossed the rod toward the moist puddle on the floor, presuming it would land where he remembered their laps to be. Instead, it clanged against Inzari's helmet. Gert winced.

"*Gert—*" Moani growled. She stopped, and the rod disappeared as she picked it up. "Where the hell did you get this?"

"Oh I…picked it up," Gert said, trying not to sound like he was bragging, because he still wasn't positive if he'd made the right move. He'd just known in that moment it may have been the only opportunity to grab one.

"And who will miss it?" Inzari asked.

"The anup taking a nap in the barracks. I saw her on my way in and out, and I thought—"

"That's good," Inzari said. "I need this for my backup plan."

"You have a backup plan?" Moani asked, deadpan. "Nice, tell the class what you brought."

"Alright, here's what I've been doing: I'm trying to gain access to an airlock that leads into the central chamber. We can't go inside the central chamber cause there's a krakun in there, but if the airlock is big enough for an anup or two, perhaps all three of us could fit inside."

"Those things are minuscule," Moani said. "You're saying we should take over one of those airlocks?"

"Right, and make it look in the system like it jammed. Since they have two airlocks they may toy with unjamming it, but they won't try too hard until they reach port for maintenance."

"Ugh, we'll be crammed in there," Moani said. "And we're still no closer to tracing the computer's layout or where they're putting all the data…"

"Hey," Gert said, breaking into their conversation. "Whatever you need that rod for, you need to do it first, because I don't know how long Eendie will stay asleep."

"Okay, okay, give me a minute," Moani said. "I think we can get away with only having to use the rod once…"

They were quiet for a moment as Moani rustled around in the open access panel. After that moment, Inzari asked, "Eendie?"

"Oh, that's what I named the anup in my head," Gert said. "She said that out loud."

"How close did you get to her?"

"Uh, close enough to watch her do something in the washroom. It was weird. Maybe it was a religious ceremony."

"What was it?"

"Some kinda device with a long needle she jabbed into her stomach… Then she became furious."

"And you're sure she was female?"

"Obviously," Gert said. "Their males have external genitalia."

"Well, Subcommander Obviously, that was a pregnancy test. Duh."

"A…" Gert started, then stopped. "What?"

"Don't tell me you don't have pregnancy tests on the *White Flower II*."

"Well I mean… Uh…"

Gert was even more confused than he had been standing just a meter away from the anup. Pregnancy test inside the washroom? Wouldn't it make more sense to check in a clinic? And why would she get so angry about it?

Or no, wait, maybe they didn't use regular birth control methods; not all slave colonies were so controlled. Still, Gert had a hard time wrapping his head around someone getting upset at having a *cub*. To the geroo, that was worth more than credits could buy.

"Hey genius," Moani said, "you're untethered now, so if all you're gonna do is sit around and yak about the developments in the latest anup soap opera, at least go be our lookout."

Gert scoffed. Whenever he listened to Inzari and Moani speak about hacking, infiltration, or subterfuge, he felt outclassed. He could tell himself that it was a matter of experience—he didn't have access to the vast libraries of information these two did. Gert was, compared to them, sheltered.

He sighed and leaned against the wall. What was he? Brave? Gert recalled what the captain told him in the medical ward—even Ateri was expecting Gert's luck to run out sometime. When that eventually happened, did he have anything to fall back on, if he didn't have practical skills like these two?

While the two bickered over the radio about the best way to set up the airlock, Gert wandered back down the portside corridor to peek into the main hallway. It was empty once again. There were so few anup running this ship, it seemed unlikely once the survey began that they'd even see any of the anup, so long as they stayed put in the out-of-the-way areas.

So far they seemed to have a terrible habit of turning up right when Gert was not expecting them. He headed toward the bridge.

The cockpit had a different look to it, compared to most of the rest of the ship's stark white. Like the barracks in the back, the bridge was painted dark so as not to create a glare over the bright curvature of C-18-3 and its rusty surface and thin atmosphere. It was otherwise well-lit, just not as bright as the hallways.

The bridge seemed to have no captain's chair, just several seats facing consoles both toward and away from the window, with hundreds of buttons on every desktop surface. Four anup sat upright at the monitors, their black pelts looking like shadows in the control room. On each console, the anups' gold rod jutted out and caught the scattered glimmer of lights from all around. And they all seemed focused on their work, not saying a word to one another the whole while.

So if there are only five, Gert thought, *that's these four and Eendie.*

He rather liked watching them all, though the benefit of this vantage point was he now knew where all five of the anup onboard were, and would not have to peek down both corridors.

Gert flipped the towel around his neck so the cool side was facing in again. He hoped Inzari and Moani, still discussing things with one another over the radio, would hurry and finish their hiding spot. He turned to look back down the corridor —

—and saw Eendie walking up, without her rod.

Shit. He'd just left her not fifteen minutes prior. He shoved his helmeted muzzle into the corner and whispered, "One coming port."

Moani and Inzari's voices quieted. Soon the only intermittent sound was that of Eendie's paws, stomping as she headed straight toward that bridge.

"*Eendar!*" she called out.

A pair of shining eyes turned in the dark as one of the anup heard the call, standing up out of his seat and peeking into the light of the hallway. Once illuminated, and this close, Gert realized at once it was Gihdah.

"*Nehsi e kah?*" Eendie demanded.

"*Mo so, orenjum,*" Gihdah said with a monotonous tone that didn't match Eendie's emotion at all.

"*Intekki a tora so e a mundu,*" Eendie barked. "*Etha!*" Gert noticed as she talked to him, she kept her paws balled up and arms stiff at her side. Lacking her rod to make her important gestures, she seemed trying to make a forceful show with just her shoulders and chest. It may as well have been she had both arms lopped off. Gert found the display fascinating, and not just because Eendie was rather well-curved. Her posture reminded him of Inzari.

Gihdah grunted and shoved his head back into the blackness. Gert heard a faint scraping of metal-on-metal.

He returned, holding his rod, and prodded her in the shoulder with it. "*Deis,*" he said.

Eendie slapped the rod away with a paw before returning it to her side. Gert had to duck to avoid the rod crashing into his helmet.

Gihdah looked surprised at this. Gert was too—the action was serious if Eendie would use her paw to reprimand him. Gert wondered, didn't it mean that Eendie was at least intimate with Gihdah? Family? Or—

Oh… Lovers, Gert realized. *Is Gihdah the father of—*

Stop thinking about that, Gert chided himself. *You're not here to catch up on the intricacies of their relationships. It doesn't matter! Focus on the job!*

Gihdah's lips narrowed to a pinch. "*Deis,*" he said.

"*Ondeta,*" Eendie said, and Gert felt the coldness in her voice. "*Noh. Indeh ra jo.*"

"*Deis—*"

"*Aigona wen* geroo *do jo.*"

Gert's heart skipped a beat. Did he hear her say —

"Geroo *onja?*" Gihdah said, looking past Eendie and glowering as he spoke. Gert turned to follow his gaze, though the only thing in view was the airlock door to the central habitat.

What do they know?

Gert only saw a little of the bridge since Gihdah towered over him and leaned forward. But he could swear he saw the eyeshine of two other anup turning toward the conversation when they overheard Gihdah's words.

Shit, shit, do you remember anything about their language? Anupian was one of those languages his teachers always told him was useless to learn; because geroo and anup were so different, the chances of it coming in useful were so marginal as to be zero. *Thanks a lot, Professor Mouda*, he angrily thought at his class four teacher.

But he remembered how krakun affected the languages of all species they came in contact with. In Old Geroo—that is, the primary language that survived to become Galactic Standard Geroo—the word "geroo" just meant "person". The krakun adopted it to refer to their species in particular, and so that word passed on to every other species they had under their empire as the official term.

Now, it might have been that the anup had a word like *geru* already in their language. It happened. But they were putting an awful lot of emphasis on that word.

"*Ingmagar ja sai gona e a* geroo *jeist, ba* krakun *on dan,*" Eendie said.

That word was definitely *krakun*, and it had the same emphasis placed on it as *geroo*. But why bring it up unless the anup somehow thought geroo applied to Eendie's missing rod? Did they think one of them snuck aboard, somehow? That seemed improbable, but that *had* to be what they were saying!

"*E so*," Gihdah grunted. "*Dah*." He pointed behind her with the rod, and she turned and walked down the hallway. Gihdah followed behind her.

Gert shoved his helmet back into the corner and whispered, low as he could go in case the other anup still attuned their ears to the hallway. "Bad news," he whispered. "Bad, bad news."

Chapter 23: Back Where You Found It

E^{*en dek*}," said Gihdah, shining a flashlight underneath Eendie's bed. They seemed to have no issue navigating a dark bedroom, but even so preferred having a light to see by.

"*Nee, sorbek a. Jai wen on do jo,*" said Eendie, her arms folded—so far as Gert saw in the minimal light.

He stood far outside the barracks and kept his profile close to the wall, trying his best to parse the discussion. Eendie knew her staff was missing, and Gert was sure she suspected a stowaway. Gihdah seemed more skeptical, but humored her.

Gert wasn't sure how much longer he could keep this up. Though panting through the heat, he still tried to keep his breathing quiet. If the anup passed close to him, they might even feel the heat radiating off of his back, with how much it burned. Several minutes had passed from the threshold of pain to just numbness, and he wondered if he'd lost all feeling where the camouflage backpack pressed into him.

"Gert, we have the airlock primed," Moani said over the radio. "We're going into the airlock to the habitat in the starboard hallway, since it wasn't the one the anup used to talk to the krakun. To get the airlock to open, we need to use this staff one time. Once we're inside and plugged into the override panel, we can control the airlock at-will, but the staff will stick out of the locking mechanism outside the door—"

"So you need me to grab it once the two of you are inside," Gert whispered.

"Wait a minute for us to plug in; pulling it out too soon will interrupt everything. Then once you have it, drop it somewhere inconspicuous."

"You're trusting me with that?"

"We don't have a choice," Inzari said, "but don't be so hard on yourself. You're doing fine."

Right until I get us all killed.

Gert tried not to think about the other consequences of failure: the certain death of everyone he'd ever met. Well, everyone except Hiani.

No, even Hiani. Pokokuro was prepared to execute the officers just because. But if she discovered they were actively sabotaging this mission…

Gert blinked. He was getting distracted, woozy from the heat. His neck, where he'd wrapped the towel, was the only cool part of his body—there was just too much heat to draw out, and the damp towel was itself growing warmer.

"We'll move in ten seconds," Moani said. "I'll give you to the go-ahead when it's safe to pull the rod out. Make your way back down."

"*Nichi ba so dek!*" Eendie continued arguing with Gihdah in the barracks. Gert didn't want to leave in case they ended up saying something critical, but then again, he couldn't glean any of what they were saying. He pulled himself away from the wall and sidled across the rear hallway to the starboard corridor.

The hallway toward the habitat seemed to expand in size until Gert felt a few centimeters tall. Though nobody was on this side of the ship, he still tried his best not to make too much noise as he padded his way down the corridor.

"We're going in," Moani said, once he passed the second set of doors. The rod popped into existence inside the locking mechanism aside the airlock door, jutting out suspiciously as the airlock door opened. Gert huffed and inched closer, though his movements dragged—he told himself he'd just been taking his time, but now he couldn't seem to make his muscles work any faster. After the faintest sound of feet shuffling, invisible pawsteps, he glimpsed the airlock door rushing closed, with the rod still stuck out into the open hallway.

Gert passed the gap that encircled the central room, as though stepping over an open hole in the floor. He clung to the wall, thinking he might fall over. He blinked and realized his vision had blurred.

"Moani, you need to hurry," Gert mumbled.

"You think I don't know that? I want this room as much as you do."

You're not the one out here…

Gert tried taking the towel still around his neck and flipping it, but it was no use; even though the towel was still moist, it'd warmed to room temperature. He leaned against the wall and tried to focus his vision on the gold bar jutting from the wall, or at the minimum, collapse it into just one bar rather than two orbiting one another.

Gert blinked. He forced himself to stand up straight. He forced himself not to throw up, since that liquid needed to stay inside him, and not clog his breathing mechanism.

Ancestors, what a way that would be to die. Visions of his own imminent death were the first things that seemed to work against his illness, forcing his stomach to quell.

"*O dah?*" said a voice from down the hall.

Gert turned his head only. The dark shadows against the white backdrop of the ship clarified that Eendie and Gihdah had wandered back into the hallway. The rod stuck out, visible to all.

She must have been pointing with her paw, because Gihdah slapped at her with his own staff and chastised her, setting off another exchange of harmonic arguments. Gert thought, the cloak would cover any object he was holding, right? But it wouldn't make parts of walls or floors disappear… What did the rod count as? Did he see it appear after Moani put it in the wall, or only after Moani had let go?

Gert didn't have time to figure out if it would work or not, so he reached out and grabbed hold of the rod.

He couldn't remember the last time he'd prayed, but he needed something—anything—more to hold on to in that one moment. He squeezed his eyes shut because he was certain he would fall over otherwise—and the first face to appear in his head was his mother.

It was startling how clear the image was; it had been so long since he'd bothered to even look at images of her, to avoid dredging up those horrid memories. But it was her, Sur'an, wearing that bright red neck scarf, smiling much like she used to, when she came in from her shift to bed. He remembered something she used to say, long before they took her from him.

Don't worry, little one. You are braver than you know.

Tears ran down his cheeks.

"Honored parents, and parents of my parents," Gert muttered to himself, more as a mantra than as a specific prayer, "in a chain unbroken like the necklaces we wear, leading us all the way back home…"

"…Gert?" Inzari asked. "Are you okay? Should I be concerned?"

"I'm…" Gert said, forgetting to end his thoughts as he trundled.

He heard the nails of the anup paws clacking against the floor behind him. Eendie still snipped at her counterpart. Even if he was hiding the rod, they might well collide with him at the pace they were making.

"O…*dah*," Eendie said not but two meters away. Gert didn't want to look, he didn't want to know how close they were to him—

he reached back with a leg and tucked in his tail so they might not trip over him.

Honored parents, and parents of my parents…

"*Eechi ben des,*" Gihdah said, matter-of-factly. Gert still couldn't tell just from that exchange if they saw the rod.

In a chain unbroken, like the necklaces we wear…

Footfalls clacked and padded closer.

Leading us all the way back…

"Pull it," Moani said over the radio.

Home!

Gert yanked the rod from the lock and stumbled into the side corridor. He couldn't tell what he was doing. But despite how he tried to remain silent, had metal scraped against metal? In pulling back, he might even have tapped Eendie in the ribs. But as he righted himself and opened his eyes back to the main corridor, he spotted Eendie scrambling around, looking back and forth.

"*Ai cha! On des unuch so—*"

"*Bei! Andah, e eechi ben des!*" Gihdah snapped back at her.

Eendie fumed. "*Noh, sesa!*"

Gihdah ignored her further protest, tapping at her with his rod as they devolved into yet another argument. Gert made his way back to the portside hallway though the thin corridor that surrounded the central habitat. He felt just clear-headed enough to keep going, the adrenaline rush giving him a couple more moments of lucidity, though he still had to grope his way around the central chamber by planting his paws against either wall.

He did not conceal his movement once he made it to the opposing hallway. One quick look to see nobody was emerging from the bridge, and once he pulled himself out, he *ran* down the corridor to the barracks.

That was a mistake—his lungs at once protested for better air, and though he had set his mask to maximum, it couldn't pull oxygen through any faster. His helmet HUD flashed vital warnings—heart rate too high, blood-oxygen thinning.

"Thanks, I know," Gert told the HUD.

"What's what?" Inzari asked over the radio. "Gert, are you alright?"

He tapped on the helmet lights and fell into the barracks, still gripping the rod. "No," he said, crawling on his paws and knees through the beds until he reached Eendie's bed and the foot locker tucked underneath.

"Get to a corner and I'll try to locate you once the hallway is clear," Inzari said.

"I got it." Gert looked across from Eendie's bed to another bunk leaning against the wall, with nothing underneath. He pulled himself up onto that bed—finding it firmer than the floor, he was certain.

There was a small gap between the bed and the wall. Gert pulled the rod over and tried to push it into that gap, finding it a millimeter too narrow to fall to the floor. He pushed down hard on the rod, planting himself against the wall to pry the gap a little wider. One end fell to the floor with a *tink*, leaving the other end wedged.

Shit, should have rolled it under from the other side…

He heard Eendie and Gihdah return. He tapped his helmet to turn the lights off before they noticed, and resumed shoving his shoulder against the wall.

"*Mes eques a so,*" Gihdah said, Gert glimpsing the flashlight as it ran over the floor.

Eendie argued with him again, and just as their voices picked up together, Gert gave one last heave against the wall, and the rod fell to the floor.

Although it landed with a tap, both the anup stopped at once and glanced at the bed.

Shit shit shit. Unlike Moani, Gert didn't have a knob on his helmet to turn breathing down to silent. He could only hope they heard nothing emanating from his suit or the camouflage pack.

Gihdah knelt down on the floor, and Gert caught sight of the light on the wall and floor as it shone underneath the bunk.

"*Ah!*" Gihdah said. "*A so, nehsi aranda.*"

Gert tilted his head up just enough to see Eendie and Gihdah standing right next to the bed Gert lay on, with Gihdah presenting the rod back to her. She was at first hesitant, then realizing it was hers, grabbed hold with both paws.

"*Deh…*" she said, uncertain.

Gihdah made a fitful noise that seemed analogous to laughter. "*Noh shu!* Geroo *onja…*"

He passed by her, slapping her on the rear with his rod as he left. Eendie jumped as he did and put on a dire face, though did not retaliate.

She stood there even after Gihdah left. She looked back, muttering to herself, "*Deh… So e a mundu…*"

Then she dropped to her knees and, taking a flashlight from her bedside table, shone the light underneath the bed Gert lay atop once more.

Please just go so I can get out, Gert muttered to himself. The adrenaline spike was already wearing off, and his head was not doing well at all.

"*Deh se sa!*" she grumbled. She slammed the flashlight back on the end table and lay back down in her bunk; from the light shining in through the open doorways, he caught a glimmer of her wrapping her paws around the rod tight.

Gert could not afford to wait any longer to see if she would fall back asleep. The bed did not creak at all when he climbed on, so he did the same in reverse—sliding off the mattress, planting both paws on the floor, and making his was back out into the well-lit hallway.

"Inzari," Gert wheezed into his radio, leaning against the wall to hold himself up. The hallway, not even fifty meters end-to-end, seemed to stretch on for an eternity. "I need in."

"Are you outside the door?" Inzari asked.

"No, I'm in..." He slid down the wall, but tried to paddle himself forward with his paws. "Starboard hallway...heading toward your—"

He lost consciousness before he finished.

Chapter 24: River's End

Jakari entered the apartment at a tiptoe, presuming the captain was napping. He was, for the moment, hooked up to an oxygen generator, to help his lungs after the sulphuric ordeal. She waded through the perpetual mess on the floor, across an open path around the bed, and removing her accoutrements, stepped into the shower for the first time that day.

She felt exhausted worrying after what Gert was doing. It was strange to think this could be her last day alive, and yet, what could she do?

After several minutes of relaxing hot water, she left, drying her fur with a towel, re-entering the bedroom, and jumped when she saw Ateri sitting up in bed, removing the breathing mask from his muzzle. He panted with a paw clutched to his chest.

"Hon, what's wrong?" Jakari asked, hurrying to his side.

"I... How long has it been?" Ateri asked, patting down his head in a frightened rush.

"About four hours now."

Ateri squeezed his eye shut and slowed his heaving breaths. The missing eye, even uncovered, didn't have the muscles to close.

"Are you feeling alright?" Jakari asked as she wiped herself down with the towel, stepping around the mess on the floor to get to Ateri's side of the bed. "Another panic attack?"

Despite the fact that he'd been given a stay of retirement, Ateri still needed to acclimate to the fact that he wasn't going to die on his sixtieth. Panic attacks and nightmares were common for geroo who were approaching the end date. Some thought it was a symptom of old age, but Ateri was certain it was the body anticipating the fixed date of recycling, and reacting with a fight-or-flight response. Acceptance of the sixtieth had never been entirely bred into their systems, and even someone as stoic as the captain had suffered more than a dozen bouts of panic since his fifty-ninth birthday.

But that wasn't the case *this* dream. Ateri shook his head shallowly.

"Gert?" Jakari asked.

Ateri nodded. "It's hard for me to say… But I am terrified. Why am I doing this to him? Why send him alone out there into a place he's never been? He's barely had to training to be…"

Jakari sat down on the bed next to Ateri. "What happened in the dream?"

"I saw his suit breaching and him suffocating in the air…" Ateri pressed a paw to his forehead. "What if something's happened to him? Why did I agree to any of this?"

Jakari pulled Ateri close and wrapped her arms around him. He leaned into her shoulders.

"My captain," she said, "I admit I had misgivings when you first told me about the pirates, but this is how I see it—if we *didn't* take up the pirates on their offer, Pokokuro may have just restructured the command of this ship anyway. The coil blowing was just a convenient excuse."

"But I want it to succeed. I want… I want everything to go the way it should. I want to win something we've earned. And I don't want Gert to die. I don't want to lose anybody, but…"

"As captain, you know that is not always something you have a choice in."

Ateri nodded. He rose from the bed and waded through the junk on the floor, paws stepping in the spots Jakari had taken. He opened the shrine box that sat on a long base cabinet at the end of their bedroom. The place was one of the few spots they could keep clean, given they almost never had the spare energy between them for household chores.

The family shrine was rather robust—not elaborate like some of the wealthier crew, but the beaded necklaces and family portraits between them were filled-out. Jakari's side was far fuller, containing the original necklace of Captain Idal, and Jakari's mother, Jakari's older sister who recycled over a decade ago, grandparents on both her father and mother's side, and great grandparents. Ateri's side had his father's necklace, a placeholder for his mother's lost necklace, and one for his grandfather on his father's side.

So Ateri had filled the space on his side of the shrine with another he considered family. Gert had the first copy, but Ateri had another reproduction of Sur'an's necklace there, with a flattering portrait taken over thirty years ago.

Jakari put an arm around Ateri's shoulders. "Do you want to pray together?"

"Please."

They knelt down together in the clear space before the shrine, facing one another, and pressing their heads against in another so the bridges of their muzzles touched and faced the floor. She closed her eyes, to focus her thoughts on the warmth of Ateri against her. Jakari waited for Ateri to start, but when he hesitated, she spoke.

"Honored parents—"

Ateri picked it up with her, and they finished the line together, "—and parents of my parents, in a chain unbroken like the necklaces we wear, leading us all the way back home."

"Grandfather watch over us," Ateri began.

"Grandmother, care for us," Jakari said.

"Though I never knew you, I revere you. I know you likewise cared for me though you never knew me. And as kin I pray, all geroo need your help, oversight, guidance, and love."

"As all geroo are of the same family, we petition you before the common ancestor, all your cubs need you in the hour of fear."

Ateri paused a long moment before continuing.

"Captain Idal," Ateri said.

"Dad," Jakari said, smiling.

"I don't know if you were ever in a position like this before. I…I've been reckless with the responsibility you've put on me. You believed in me when you appointed me your successor."

"I know you still believe in my mate," Jakari added.

"I'm not asking for you to take it back, but you warned me to be careful, and I've failed on that front so many times, and I fear another failure will bring an end to everyone."

"But we also know success could reap a greater reward than we ever imagined," Jakari said. "So please watch over us and our mutual foolhardiness. If you can see to it, as you blessed our pairbonding, please give your blessing to this mission and its crew."

"And to Gert," Ateri said, "because I fear I will lose track of him if I have to keep an eye on him myself. I only have the one left."

Ateri quivered in Jakari's arms, and so she held him tighter. Ateri took a deep breath and continued.

"Sur'an, in life I loved you as much as I love my mate," Ateri said. "And even now…"

"As did I," Jakari said. "And you still bless us with your memory of the good times and your intimacy, and honor the sacrifice you made to save us."

Ateri was silent again. Jakari gave him longer to collect himself and continued for him.

"Sur'an, please watch over your son," Jakari said.

"Sur'an, I'm so sorry," Ateri cried. Jakari heard tears falling to his lap. "I have wanted nothing more than to protect him, but I can't shield him from this awful place or the necessities and burdens of action in a dark time. He can do it; he's smarter and braver than he knows. But I am so scared what will happen to him even if we succeed."

"Sur'an, give Gert strength to face all trials," Jakari said.

"And please don't be angry if we should join you too soon," Ateri said. "Because no matter the cost now, we have to try."

This time, when Ateri fell silent, Jakari shifted her stance, pulling her head away from Ateri and instead just wrapped him in a tight embrace. Ateri hugged her so fiercely he might have pushed the wind from her, were she not long since used to his strong grip.

"My love, I will not abandon you," Jakari whispered in the dark. "We're in this together, and we always have been."

Chapter 25: The Geroo

*M*om, mom!

What's wrong, Gert? Why are you crying?

Some other cubs from school pushed me off the platform in the gravity well...

Are you hurt?

No... They laughed at me cause I spun in the air and landed on my tail.

I'm sorry, love. You know they're jealous.

That's what you always say. They're not jealous of anything. They just wanna pick on me.

Then I'll speak with their parents.

No! Then they'll just pick on me more.

What do you suggest we do, then?

I don't know. I want a hug.

Then I'll hold you as long as you like, how is that?

Okay...

* * *

Gert sputtered as he came to. His vision was unobscured by his helmet, and for a moment he panicked, but the air he hyperventilated tasted fine. In fact, it was more than fine, with correct pressure and temperature and everything. He was staring up at a light over the ceiling only a few meters above his head.

He sat up and thought he was still dreaming. The room—just a little wider than his arms at full spread, and under ten meters long reckoning by the length of the ceiling—had all of its walls covered in murals of a blue sky and green trees.

The lighting in the room was not flattering, with a single overhead lamp covering the whole space. Someone had set two side lamps up on the fore and aft of the room, lighting the corners and giving a bright look at the green hills and a crudely drawn citadel, like out of a cub's storybook.

It smelled a little wrong. The paint, whatever they had painted it with, had been there a long while, and some of it had dulled underneath a fresh coat.

The only part of the room untouched was the large, circular airlock with the heavy trim jutting out of the wall. Gert dismissed his first thought that Inzari had pulled him into the airlock she'd intended. But if that wasn't the case, what was this place? He glanced sideways, wondering if he was hallucinating from having deep-fried his brain.

He didn't see his helmet anywhere, and so he had no radio to contact Inzari—and his strand, still on his shoulder band since he'd never taken it off, was useless. Tension rose in his chest. What the hells was he going to do now?

At the back of the room, a curtain the same color as the painted sky opened. Gert turned his head, and his ears perked in astonishment.

"Fancy seeing another geroo here," she said. The female geroo was gray all over, though it was the kind of gray that made it impossible to tell her age. She could have been twenty or fifty, though the way she carried herself, Gert was certain she was on the young side. And her words—closer to the refugee dialect than standard—were strange, with clear vowel drift, but still intelligible as the geroo language.

But for the split-second when Gert first caught sight of her, she looked just like Hiani, with the way the white under her cheeks highlighted her eyes. She could almost have been Hiani in twenty years.

"Wha— What the... Where..." Gert stuttered.

"No, do not move," she said, her ears turning dire. "I need to know what in the hells you're doing on this ship." Gert only then noticed that she wore a belt around her waist, with a holster for...some kind of gun? She leaned against the wall, keeping it ready to draw at any moment.

Gert paused and swallowed. "I'm...I'm sorry."

"Is that it?"

"I am very confused," Gert said.

"Let's start with names," she said.

"Uh...my name's Gert. Hi." He wasn't certain whether to offer his rank aboard the *White Flower II*; for all she knew, he could have been a rogue agent.

"My name is Aride," she said.

"That's...a lovely name." A smile spread across Gert's ears.

She narrowed her eyes, but even so there was a warmth to her expression.

"Where am I?" Gert asked.

"Aboard the spacecraft *Ervichzidak* of the Starship Technology Corporation."

"I figured I still was. I mean, if it is the one... I mean, *where* aboard am I?"

"My quarters," she said, looking around as though filling the room with her gaze. "I figured the breathable air would give you a clue there."

"It did, but I thought anup staffed this ship."

"They're the ones piloting it. My job would be to clean the habitat—and the rest of the ship if they don't want to do it themselves."

At least that was what Gert gathered from context—the word she used for "the habitat" took him three seconds to parse, since it was based on an Old Geroo word that meant *mansion*.

"So we're in the habitat?" Gert asked.

"Okay, enough questions from you," she said. "Answer mine. What are you doing aboard?"

"Why did you rescue me?"

She put her paw to the pistol's grip.

"Hey! Hey!" Gert said, putting his paws up. "I meant nothing—"

"Answer my question. What are you doing aboard?" She glared at him, but despite that, there was a sadness to her eyes. Gert had to conclude—no, he hoped—she meant him no harm. Why go to all the trouble of pulling him out of the hallway and into this place rather than turn him over to the krakun?

"I… How did…" he began, but looking again at where her paw was, he thought better. He had no lie prepared because the presumption was capture equaled death. Even then, what lie could he tell?

It may have been because of how much her face reminded him of Hiani, but something inside him screamed, *tell her the truth.*

He took a deep breath.

"I am Subcommander Gert of the *White Flower II*," he said. "My mission is to infiltrate the Erv…the Everi…this ship, hack into its systems, and make the…scanner results say what we want." He was certain his words could have come out cooler than that.

"*White Flower II*… Is that a pirate ship?" she asked, twisting her grip a little.

"No, that's the ship that's floating over the planet. You came here through its gate."

"Hmm." She relaxed her grip. "A geroo-crewed gate ship?"

"Yeah! Uh, I take it they didn't tell you very much about this mission."

"They rarely bother to tell the custodian where this ship is going, no," she said, shaking her head. "I overheard it was scanning some remote system for Planetary Acquisitions, and I can at least line up my divisors from there."

Gert had never met a geroo from elsewhere than the fleet, and had worried she was too uneducated to understand what he was even talking about. But if she could follow that much, Gert could feel confident—and relieved—that she was aware of at least her own situation.

"If you're hacking to change the results," Aride said, "what results do you want?"

Gert figured if he'd already told her the basics, then her knowing the details of the plan couldn't hurt any more.

"To make the planet we're over appear viable for terraforming," Gert said.

Aride seemed to pause, and her posture changed again, ears up and forward like Gert had captured her attention. "Ancestors slay me," she said, and yarped. "you have got gall to try that!"

"It's a huge gamble," Gert said, falling back against the bed. "If we fail, there won't be words to describe how angry the commissioner will get. In all likelihood, she'll purge our ship... All ten thousand geroo."

Her ears wilted rapidly until her mouth fell open too. "I...musta not heard you right. Ten..."

"Thousand," Gert said.

She looked down and about, as though trying to distract herself from a magnitude she'd not expected to hear. If she could even picture ten thousand geroo.

"Oh my..." Her words were distant.

"Sorry to drop that on you," Gert said, though he felt better seeing she cared enough to try and comprehend the scope. He'd needed to confide in another geroo.

"It's fine." She shuffled her paws. "I'm glad you told me. I wasn't even sure there were another ten thousand out there."

She stood in contemplation a moment longer.

"Do you mind if I get out of this suit?" Gert asked. "It was hot enough in the rest of the ship…"

"Let me help," she said, approaching.

"Do you have any clean water?" Gert asked. "I'm parched."

Together they undid the snaps and zippers that comprised the top of the pressure suit, until Gert could fully step out. He took the canned water she offered him. As he drank, her eyes swept up and down his entire body.

"Something the matter?" Gert asked.

"Damn me, you're handsome," Aride said. "An officer, you said? Over a crew of ten thousand?"

"Er…really?" Although he'd always had something of a steady girlfriend—for whatever that seemed to be worth—he'd taken his homeliness for granted. His spotted coat was weird and uneven, and that seemed to be all anyone looked at when they saw him. Even Hiani never seemed to bring up his appearance; she always seemed more interested in what he had to say than what he looked like.

In fact, Aride's words brought him back to just that morning, when he insisted that Yessi should be okay with one dilated pupil because it made her eccentric. He never even used himself as a comparison because he didn't have the confidence to pull off "eccentric" either.

He was just Gert. Weird, awkward, juvenile Gert.

"I've never even seen a geroo with that kind of mottled coat before," she said. "It's striking."

"It's chimeric," Gert said. "I have two sets of DNA. Ends up creating a strange pattern."

"DNA, now where did I hear that before…"

"You know, genes. Genetic material."

She tilted her head at him. Gert thought about this for a moment, then repeated the word, but in Krakunese, to see if it would take.

"Oh, DNA!" she said—though she pronounced the abbreviation *die-nuh*. "Course I know what that is! So, you have two sets... Like, two fathers?"

Gert chuckled. "No, I don't think it'd work like that. I think the doc said my father fertilized my mother's egg twice. Just one of those weird things that happens."

"Like, two geroo of different histories meeting aboard a krakun ship in the middle of nowhere."

"Yeah," Gert said. "Weird."

They sat down on the bed together. It was quiet for a moment, but as Gert looked over Aride, she didn't seem to mind. Even without words she seemed to convey a certain bubbly happiness—relief, even, as she sat next to Gert and leaned in toward him with a very attuned expression across her ears.

"They let you keep guns here?" Gert asked, the thought crossing his mind.

"Only specific kinds of guns," Aride said, pulling hers out and holding it with her fingers far from the trigger. "This here's a sonic pistol. It can't kill a krakun. It can bruise one, although that would make it furious. You ever see what sound waves can do to a slab of meat?"

Gert winced. "You weren't really going to shoot me, were you?" Gert asked.

"Only if you were dangerous. But you're not even armed. Plus I'd hate to turn a cute face like yours into chunky stew."

Gert bit his lip. "Can I...get my radio?" he asked. "It's in my helmet."

"I don't know yet," she said. "You being onboard is dangerous as it is. I had half a mind to turn you in, but right now I'm glad I didn't. It's been awhile since I've seen a friendly face that wasn't from the colony."

"How did you find me anyway?" Gert asked. "I thought I was invisible."

"That's a curious device," Aride said. "Ain't never seen that kind of technology before."

"Neither have I," Gert said. "I was just using it."

"Well, since you seem like a nice enough geroo, I'll tell you. I was in the habitat's sitting room, polishing metal surfaces, when I noticed the starboard airlock was acting up—giving a flashing 'prepare to enter' message over and over. Well, I went over to check, but the door would not unlock."

"Oh," Gert said. He wondered if it would have been good to tell Moani what the effect of her airlock hacking had been on the inside the chamber, or if she would beat herself up again for a crude mistake.

"My master, Totaikona, is sleeping, and the only way to the other airlock out of here is through his bedroom. Fortunately, I am soft-pawed and these habitat airlocks are quiet."

"I noticed," Gert said. "At least, I think I did."

"So I snuck out the port door and made my way around to the starboard hallway to see if something had jammed the airlock. That was when I heard you collapse to the floor. I looked around, but saw nothing. I searched the hallway where I was certain I heard something, when lo and behold, my knees bumped into nothing at all."

"Sorry," Gert said. He wasn't certain he needed to apologize for taking up space, but it was a habit at this point.

"Now I wasn't certain what I was looking at, but the heat it gave off made me think it was some kind of creature made invisible. I've heard about some animals from Turektec with a natural invisibility, and at first I thought something like that had somehow gotten aboard and suffocated in the bromine air. I was gonna leave it alone, but my curiosity got the better of me. I touched it to feel its shape, and found it wore a helmet and an environment suit, to the best of what I could feel through my gloves."

"And you dragged me back here?" Gert asked.

"I would inform the crew," she said, "but me and the anup have never gotten along anyhow. I might have told Totaikona, but he's sick, and that's made him grumpy. So yeah, I brought you back here. I ended up switching off your disguise by accident, and to my surprise—"

"I was a geroo," Gert finished for her.

"Well, you were a male. I already figured by that point you might have been a geroo, by the shape of your tail."

"You felt my tail?" Gert's ears reddened.

"It's a nice tail," she said, putting a paw on it and stroking down its length.

Oh ancestors, stop! Please, she only looks like Hiani, I shouldn't be so attracted…

His neck-fur stood on end. This time, Gert didn't have the heat and pressure to take his mind off his overpowering hormones. This spot on the bed, with cool air all around and with his thirst quenched—despite the place's crudeness—was a thousand times more relaxing than being anywhere else on the ship.

"I need to get my radio," Gert said, "If my partners can't find me, they'll panic…"

"One last thing before I do," Aride said.

Gert was sure he could overpower her since she was now close enough he could grab her gun from her holster before she did. But he wasn't going to. She smelled far too nice.

"Do you understand how our colonies work on Krakuntec?" she asked. "See, they use many species for running minor matters in place of AI. I'm sure you know, being from a gate ship."

"I do," Gert said.

"Our colonies are a lot smaller, though. Sometimes just forty to sixty, only enough to keep things stable. If we die out, they don't care; they get replacements from somewhere. My colony's population has been declining… Over the last two hundred years, we've developed an infertility disorder."

"That's awful," Gert said.

"Like I said, they won't care much when we die out. We're one of a dozen species they use, and they consider us some of the least useful, as though geroo are only suitable to be janitors. Maybe they'll inject us with new blood sometime soon, but I'm not hopeful it'll be in our time."

"Inject with…DNA," Gert repeated, getting the drift of her meaning.

She put a paw on his leg.

"It would mean the world to us if I could get pregnant," Aride said.

"Oh," Gert said. "O-oh."

Is she asking that? Gert had no clue how colony geroo lived—he only had the barest understanding of refugee life, but even less about the geroo who lived on Krakuntec. Was this normal for her? Or had things gotten so bad it didn't matter who she asked?

"More of our males are sterile each generation. I've been taking fertility drugs just to increase our odds…"

"Like multiple cubs?" Gert asked.

"Four or five," she said. "Even if only two of them grew up to be fertile males, that would help a lot. You'd help a lot."

Four or five? Can a geroo womb even hold that many? The number of times that a couple on the *White Flower II* even ended up with twins, Gert could count on one paw—and in those few cases, the krakun insisted that the doctors euthanize the "extra". He figured geroo didn't have the capacity for whole litters like some species, but he must have been wrong.

At that point, Gert should have said no, that he was in a committed relationship with someone that looked a fair amount like Aride. Then he thought about Inzari coming in here to meet Aride and saying, "Naw, we screw all the time," and Aride getting upset that Gert lied.

Ancestors damn me she smells so nice, and I am so tired, and I want to take hold of her and feel her against me for a while...

"Do this for me and I'll give you your helmet back," Aride said. "What do you say?"

"But, what about your mate?" Gert asked, gesturing at the one mismatched bead on her necklace.

"What about him?" she asked. "He wants cubs almost as much as I do."

"But did you speak with him about you having sex with other males?"

She gave him a look. "Gert, when we realized we had a genetic issue, what do you think is the first thing we tried to resolve it?"

Surrogacy, Gert thought. That'd help keep the population up via the geroo who did not have such an issue, but would rapidly diminish the gene pool. He tried to think of some other excuse.

The only other one that came to mind was Hiani. But it shouldn't have mattered! Hiani would just have to understand. As future Captain of the *White Flower II*, sometimes it was Gert's *duty* to sacrifice their relationship and sleep with the enemy and/or neutral parties.

Gert had to internally kick himself for inventing such a brazenly ridiculous justification. Why would he even think that? The problem, though, was that this was *literally* his job at this moment. Aride was armed and not handing over his helmet unless he did her this favor. What could he say to Hiani then? *Sorry, hon, but the krakun are going to kill us all because I decided my faithfulness in our relationship was more important than our lives!*

He imagined Hiani's counterargument. *You could have overpowered her!*

No, that wouldn't work, either. He might have needed Aride's help! It was impossible to know. The only thing Gert could reasonably do is look at this situation at this moment and choose the most practical course of action.

… I'm so sorry, Hiani. I know you hate it when I say duty comes first, but…

Gert said, "Then, I'd be…happy to help."

"I can see that," she said, looking down, then leaning in and pressing her head into the scruff of his neck fluff. His skin tingled and his fur stood on end.

I hope Inzari can wait a few more minutes…

Chapter 26: Give and Take

Gert squirmed in place as Aride snuggled her face into the crook of his neck. He felt good, but strange. So far he was two-for-two with sudden sexual flings: sit down on the bed of a new female and poof, she couldn't keep her paws off him, and he was in no position to complain.

Maybe he could bottle this effect and sell it on the black market.

"Can I have my helmet now?" Gert asked, still panting and fuzzy in the head. Ancestors, did he want to stay right where he was for a good hour, but he couldn't wait that long. "They're worried about me."

"Oh, you don't want to cuddle?" Aride asked.

"Yes, but it's kinda a life or death thing," Gert said. "When I left them behind we were all overheating out there. I don't want to seem like I'm brushing you off or anything… I mean, that was great, it's just that I'd prefer them to…not die."

"No, I understand…" Aride said. "Just promise me we'll go at it once more before you leave, to make sure it takes."

"Are you in heat?" Gert asked as Aride crawled over him to get off the bed. He could smell her desire, but that was not always distinguishable from being on one's estrus cycle. Besides, young adult geroo smelled like that all the time.

"Hmm, pretty sure." She sauntered to a door that hid a shallow closet, no bigger than the pantry from what Gert could see—though he was watching her hips sway more than anything else.

"So they sent a female in heat on this mission from your colony?"

"We have more things to do than this one mission," Aride said from the closet. "Some weeks, half of the geroo are out doing work, sometimes for weeks at a time… We only supposed this mission to be a day at most."

"Oh. I guess I don't have a great idea what things are like on Krakuntec."

"No, you don't."

Gert bit his lip.

Aride returned with the helmet in her paw and tossed it to Gert. He caught it and fumbled with it before pulling out the tiny pocket radio velcroed to the gap inside. He swallowed, too, because he was certain that Inzari would be so furious when she learned he was doing just fine himself.

"Inzari, Moani, are you in?" Gert asked.

"*There* you are!" Inzari said. "We've been sitting around the last three hours trying to figure out what the noises were. Cause it didn't sound like someone had caught you. Or that you died."

"You could hear that?" Gert exclaimed.

"Who is that with you?" Moani asked. "Last twenty minutes we heard another voice talking in geroo. Don't tell me you went back to the *White Flower II* somehow."

"Uh," Gert said, looking up at Aride. Her ears spread out with enthusiasm. "I think we have an ally onboard."

"An ally?" Moani asked. "Gert, are you sure this is—"

"She's a geroo!" Gert said. "Cleaner for the central habitat. I think she can help us." He looked up at Aride. She tilted her head as though she still weren't sure.

"Come on, please?" Gert said. "I *am* helping you out."

"Is that what all those hushed moaning noises were?" Inzari asked.

Gert flushed. Aride burst out in loud yarping laughter.

"Inzari," Gert started, "I—"

"It sounds like you lucked out again, pipsqueak," Inzari laughed over the radio. "You in a safe room together?"

"Y-yeah, we are."

Aride waved her paw in a beckoning gesture, then snatched the radio out from Gert's fingers.

"H-hey!" Gert said.

"Howdy, I'm Aride," she said over the radio, "If you need to escape the confines of the ship, you can come to the confines of my little room here… How long you gonna be aboard?"

That was how Gert understood her, at least. Her actual words were more like: *Long life to yah, Aride ah am! If'n be yah needin' respite ov'r this dory's en-virons, yah can alway park yer tails in this here wee flop o' mine… what so long be yah em-barked?*

"The hell is she saying?" Inzari asked.

"Something about sitting on our tails," Moani suggested.

"She said you can come over," Gert translated, "and wanted to know how long we plan on staying."

"I still don't have the computer data I need," Moani said. "I mean… By the process of elimination, I can guess that, as the only remaining computers, the data is either in there or on the bridge, and I'd prefer not to go on the bridge. I've been trying to gain access from this conduit panel, but there're no options for data interruption."

"I don't know about that thing," Aride said, "but I wouldn't mind the company."

"You have a toilet in there?" Inzari asked.

Aride puckered her lips in a concerned expression. "You didn't think this whole infiltration thing through very far, did you?"

"We had to improvise," Moani said.

"Well," Aride said, "they split the central habitat into two rooms. Totaikona's been sleeping off an illness in the bedroom, but that's only from port side. If you can come in from starboard, the airlock to this chamber is on the left side, behind the sofa. The outer door should be unlocked."

"Thank all gods of unknown space," Inzari said. "We're coming in ASAP. Keep the path to the restroom clear."

"Wait—are you sure?" Gert asked Aride.

"Gert, any friend of yours is a friend of mine," she said. "That's called hospitality."

"But…" Gert hesitated, and bit his lip as he considered. He'd been given this opportunity here, and if he did something Aride didn't like, he had no idea how she'd react. She was a loyal geroo through and through, but it was just that—loyalty to *geroo*.

There wasn't any way around that fact. He had to chance the possibility of the truth upsetting her, and before either of his partners surprised her.

"They're not geroo," Gert said, covering the mouthpiece of the radio.

Aride perked her ears. "But I thought—"

"It was part of this whole infiltration package," Gert said. "They *are* pirates. I'm technically a pirate now that I'm working with them. They provide things we don't have, including the whole plan I mentioned."

"That's fine!" Aride said. "Hells, I've been around at least a dozen species, and not all of them are like anup. If they can breathe the air in here, all the better!"

Gert sighed. "Okay. Thank you for trusting us."

"It's for the geroo, sweetie," she said with a cute pinch to his ears and a kiss. "You'd do the same, right?"

"I *am* doing the same."

"There you go!"

After that, Gert replaced the radio into the helmet and then placed it with the open side down so that his voice wouldn't carry inside anymore. Since they had time to kill, Gert decided he'd like to settle some of his curiosity with her.

"So what's with the mural?" Gert asked, looking around at the painted trees.

"Don't you recognize it?" she asked, looking up with sparkles in her eyes. "It's Gerootec."

"Oh," Gert said, tilting his ears. "I think I see it. Did you paint it yourself?"

"We all did," Aride said. "All our chambers have these… Don't you tell each other stories about the blue sky and green grass? The outdoors of Krakuntec are awful, unnatural…"

"I wouldn't know," Gert said. "I've lived all my life in an aluminum can out in space."

"Oh, that's right," Aride said. "Never even seen a tree, even if it is a crude Krakuntec mockery of a real one."

"I'll have you know I have seen a real tree!" Gert said. "Aboard there's at least…three? We have a garden! It's huge—it takes almost twenty minutes to walk end-to-end. If you take your time."

"Uh-huh," Aride said, turning her nose up as she stood from the bed. "I'm sure it's technological and fancy and all that."

"Oh," Gert said, feeling flush. "I didn't mean to rub it in your face or anything."

"I'm sure you don't even need to tell each other stories," Aride said, sighing. "You have everything you want in your little aluminum can."

"I…"

Gert thought about this.

Aride seemed hurt by the insinuation that he had what she could only dream of, but even then it was only crumbs compared to what they'd both lost, and never knew. Gert had never even been inside a real atmosphere, but looking at the wall he could see they'd gotten aspects of painting correct. The hills faded blue into the background, creating illusory distance most had forgotten was a real effect of living on a planet, and not just an artifact of old videos.

But, Gert realized, he *was* complacent. Was that what Ateri had chastised him for? Because Gert understood he was complacent, and he hated himself for it. Did he act brave because he was striving for a better future, or was it because the captain and crew expected it of him? If Ateri had not taken on this plan with the pirates, would Gert float along unchallenging of the life he lived, or would he act of his own volition? Did he understand the importance of what he strove for, like Aride seemed to?

He was the one at a disadvantage here. She'd stared at the same scene on that wall a hundred times, yet he could see in her eyes she was trying to picture herself there, and muttered to herself like a quiet prayer.

"See within your mind's eye, the verdant fields and azure sky, cool and clear like water pure, stand on the gleaming crystal shore…"

"What's that from?" Gert asked.

"That's the story," Aride said. "First several lines. We all have it memorized."

"I'm sorry, I don't know it," Gert said. "But it's weird, it reminded me of this one hymn we have, but—"

"I'd like to hear it!" Aride said, sitting on the bed and sidling up to Gert again.

Gert stammered in shock. "I uh…I can't sing."

"Nonsense, anyone can sing," Aride said.

"Sing for us, Gert!" Inzari said over the radio.

"Would you stop eavesdropping!" Gert said, picking the helmet up. "You never even told me how to turn the radio off."

"Well now I'm not gonna," Inzari said. "Sing! Siiiing."

Aride yarped and giggled.

Gert sighed and flopped his head down on the thin pillow behind him. "Ugh, I don't even remember how it goes… Erm…"

Past the falling water on the river's end
Will we ever see that home again
Flocks of birds that pebble o'er the open sky
Maybe we can glimpse it if we close our eyes
Calling to the loved ones who have gone before
Standing, looking distant past the open shore
We'll join them in the comfort of forever-time
Blessings on the ones who keep this hope in mind
Hold on to that hope no matter how it pains
And someday once again we'll feel the sun and rain

He sighed. "I know, my voice is stupid—"

Aride cried openly. Gert sat up in surprise.

"Oh ancestors, that was beautiful," she said, sniffling and wiping an eye of tears. "Your words are strange, but I got your meaning just fine…and I…"

Fearful that she would break into an open sob, Gert held her close. It was weird. Although he'd gotten the meaning of the song when he was a cub, it never hit him so hard. Though seeing Aride weep about it, he felt stupid, like he'd missed something staring him in the face the whole time.

"I'm sorry," Gert offered.

"Don't be sorry," Aride said, sniffing back tears. "Crying is good for you; it means you have a soul, don't you know?"

Gert pondered that with a tilt of his ears. Had he ever seen a krakun cry? Even in a video?

He heard the outer airlock door whir as Moani and Inzari made their approach. Gert just continued to hold on to Aride as he waited for the airlock to complete cycling.

"Thank you for being so accommodating," Gert said.

"It's nothing," Aride said. "You're kin. All geroo are."

The airlock cycled. Aride wiped her eyes and stood to receive the guests. She seemed even more pleased than she had been, like she was so very starved for attention. The inner door opened.

"Howdy!" she said, her paws clasped. "I'm sorry I have little to offer you for food—there's only canned karbaroot in the pantry and little else. You can put your suits down anywhere, there's not a lot of space for—"

She stopped, noticing their body suits for the first time. Gert glanced at her alert ears. He told her to expect non-geroo, right?

Inzari had already pulled off her helmet at that point. "I'm sorry, I didn't catch that," she said, her ringel face there for all to see. "Between you talking, and the radio talking, and your weird accent—"

"Oh, a ringel!" she started. "Of course! For a second I thought you were…"

"What?" Inzari asked.

Uh-oh, Gert realized too late.

Then Moani took off *her* helmet, revealing a geordian face. Aride's ears went from a tilt of confusion to jutting back in rage.

Aride snatched the gun from the deck and backed into the rear corner of the room. Inzari reacted, reaching into the pack that hung at Moani's side and pulled out the plasma pistol, aiming it at Aride. Moani, shocked and clearly recognizing what kind of gun Aride held, dove into the corner near the airlock and pressed her paws over her ears.

"Whoa, hold up, stop!" Gert said, standing up at once and placing himself between the two. "What the hells are you doing?"

"What the hells are *you* doing palling around with a geordian!" Aride snipped.

"She's here to help us," Gert said. "Inzari, put that gun down."

"Gert, you're sweet, but I won't ever lower a gun while someone has theirs trained on me," Inzari said.

"I have nothing against you, ringel," Aride said. Her voice shook. "Step out of the way."

"I happen to like Moani for the record!" Inzari said. "And I don't appreciate it when someone threatens people I like!"

"Just stop trying to kill everyone for a moment!" Gert said, his voice getting louder. "I promise she will be no bother to you. Put the gun down."

Aride huffed and whimpered, the strain of emotion palpable on her ears. "But—ancestors, Gert, *a geordian?*"

"What is the problem?" Gert asked. "She's our hacker. We *need* her."

"You trust a geordian to help the geroo?"

"She's done a great… She's done an okay job so far," Gert said. "She's smarter than any of us by at least an order of magnitude."

"That's not it," Aride said. "Her kind's responsible for everything! Or did they forget to teach you that on your ship?"

"Moani's not responsible for anything!" Gert said. "She's only *twenty-five*. You gonna shoot a twenty-five-year-old for four-hundred-year-old crimes?"

Aride scoffed. "Gert, you know what I mean."

Gert flattened his ears out. "I do, but that doesn't make it right. Her people took orders from the krakun, and to do otherwise would have been suicide. I've been doing much the same all *my* life, but you don't hate me or the other geroo for that, do you?"

"You—" Aride said, tripping over her words. "That's different! You're trying to do something about it."

"Yeah," Gert said. "And now, so is she. She's *helping us.* "

"But I—"

"Aride, I trust her. Please believe me, if you trust me you can trust Moani."

Aride broke into tears—more bitter than the ones she expressed moments before. She lowered her gun. Inzari didn't lower hers until Aride placed the gun on the deck, and then Inzari relaxed her aim.

"I guess I have no choice but to take your word for it," she said. "Ancestors, what have I gotten myself into…"

Gert stepped closer to her and opened his arms.

"I'm sorry," he said.

She seemed hesitant at first—why wouldn't she be—but then she jumped at him and held him tight. Gert wrapped his arms around her as warmly as he could manage.

Inzari replaced the gun back in Moani's bag. "Are we good?" Inzari asked. "No shooty pew pew going on?"

"No shooty pew pew," Gert said.

"I wish you'd warned me!" Moani said, uncovering her ears as she came down from hyperventilating. "Gods of known space! I don't want to be in the room if you're gonna shoot each other—"

"We're done with that!" Gert clutched Aride tighter. "Nobody's gonna get shot today!"

"In that case," Inzari said, gesturing for Gert to move them out of the way, "I need at your toilet back there, pronto."

"Hey!" Moani said, struggling to get her suit off. "I've been holding it in for ages!"

As they scrambled to the partition at the back of the room, Gert picked the gun up off the floor so they wouldn't step on it, and he sat down on the corner of the bed. He turned the gun over in his paws, uncomfortable with it there. Aride wrapped her arms around his midsection, her body somewhat limp.

"I should have been forthcoming about that," Gert said.

"That's not your fault," Aride said. She still huffed, holding that tension in.

"It is. When you said you were fine if they could breathe the atmosphere in here, I assumed that Moani counted, because she has a breathing device installed." He paused a beat. "Are *all* geroo that distrustful of geordians?"

"I've seen their kind around the colony space," Aride said. "We're not on good terms…"

"Space is big. I'm sure there's enough room out there for people who defy the stereotype."

Aride stayed quiet for a long moment, but at the least she seemed to contemplate his words rather than dismissing him outright.

"Gods of known space, I could use a nap after that," Inzari declared as she barged out of the partition, out of her suit. She looked stunning, even though undressing had roughed up her fur, sticking out in random places. "Gert, what time is it back on the ship?"

"Fifteen hundred hours."

"Gotcha. I'll catch some shuteye. Could you make sure miss itchy trigger finger doesn't kill our only hacker?" She frizzed Aride's head with a wiggle of her paw.

"Not helping, Inzari," Gert growled through his teeth.

Aride fumed and shot a look at the ringel, but Inzari had already passed behind them, and flopped down onto the cot face-down.

"Hey!" Aride said, standing up as Inzari's knees fell on her tail. Gert shifted his own tail out of the way, to lie on the spot Aride had been sitting.

"Ow. This thing's hard as a slab of sheet metal," Inzari said, "How the hell do you sleep—" And she was out, snoring.

Aride shot Gert a nasty look. "How do you stand them?"

"She's blunt, and that's refreshing," Gert said. "I think you know where you stand with Inzari."

"The ringel is one thing…" Aride said. "I can hold my tongue for her kind's rudeness. But while I'm going to try and be civil, you'd better make sure that geordian doesn't come near me."

Gert put a paw on her thigh. "Aride, please—"

"I know," Aride said. "Trust you. I do. But I'm not sure I trust myself around her."

Chapter 27: What Was Broken

Moani was exhausted and more than a little frustrated that Gert seemed to have all the luck. She felt horrid, queasy, and if breakfast hadn't already left her stomach, she would have thrown it up an hour ago. She wasn't even hungry despite not eating for hours—though she must have drunk several liters of awful-tasting but cold-enough water. The strange and crude murals on the wall had been painted with unstable organic paints. Something in them rotted away long ago, polluting the room with a dirty, musty odor. And this "Aride" pulled a gun on her, terrifying Moani out of her mind and dredging up memories she didn't want to revisit—ever.

She wanted to curl up into a little ball and cry, but she'd broken herself of that habit years ago. She much preferred to think of herself as a cold, hard machine; these feelings were to flow by and not bother her when she still had a job to do.

It is necessary for your survival.

To give the camouflage packs time to recharge, Gert convinced Aride to let Moani wear her environment suit into the central chamber. That way, she could check the computer in the office-slash-sitting-room without raising too much suspicion.

The thing was bulky and ill-fitting, but it allowed her some time out of her own environment suit and did a decent job of hiding the differences in her physique. It was also just as stuffy as Moani's own environment suit, save that it was loose enough to allow air flow around her fur.

Gods, please don't throw up. Passing out once already was hard enough on her constitution, and she'd been queasy since she'd revived.

"You're certain that it's okay for her to wear your suit?" she heard Gert talking to Aride behind her. "We can figure out a different plan."

"I can clean it out later," Aride said. "She already smells like ammonia, shouldn't be too hard."

"That's not nice," Gert said.

"I ain't trying to be."

Gert rarely seemed to know what he was talking about. He was, in Moani's estimation, a naive idiot. But there were worse things to be, especially when it had made Gert particularly fearless. Especially the way he'd dived in front of her to save her from Ateri. It just made him seem all the more naive, if a useful kind of naive.

Still, she wondered why someone like Captain Ateri would choose someone like Gert for this job, regardless of their relationship. She'd learned a long time ago that the only way to make it in this universe was to be the best at something invaluable, and then they'd have to let you live.

Gert was decent at a lot of things, but few were all that valuable. His primary positive quality was bravery, and she supposed that was a requisite trait for dangerous missions. But the universe was filled to the brim with meatheads who were stronger and smarter. Why did *Gert* get to survive?

Moani leaned over to speak with Inzari, but the ringel was out cold, her muzzle half-open and drooling. Inzari was tough; she'd power through anything, though even these last few hours took their toll on her. She shook Inzari by the shoulder, but Inzari refused to wake up. Moani doubted that anything would rouse her short of the promise of some strong alcohol. It was just as well; Moani had expected to do without the company. Inzari already went to the trouble of sitting up with her for the last several hours inside the jammed airlock, trying her best to cure Moani's heat stroke with the wet towel and a cold air vent.

We need you alive...

It seemed those were the kindest words she could expect to hear.

She didn't say much else. She put the helmet on and threw the tool bag over her shoulder before she left through the airlock. The suit scrunched inward from the pressure at all angles, and the boots, much like those on the pressure suit, were too large for her small, geordian paws. When she walked, the whole bottom shuffled about, but she coped.

Her radio was on, so if she wanted, she had Gert or the strange geroo female to talk to, but she was already poring through options in her mind of how to get into the krakun computer system. First, however, as the outer airlock door opened, she faced the high-pile carpet.

Oh yeah, this stuff.

She had waded through it on the way to Aride's chamber, but it was difficult enough with the pressure suit on. With the awkward environment suit it seemed even harder, with her paws threatening to slip out of the leg holes if the rubber treads got even a little caught in the friction.

Her first intent was to lock the starboard airlock of the habitat again, but it took so long to get even halfway across the carpet, she abandoned that idea. Who knew how long that would take if she even found the access panel on this side of the door? She considered going back and dealing with the pressure suit, which at least gave her the profile to shuffle through the carpet easier, but she was already halfway to the computer console.

She kept going.

The desk was also three times her height off the floor, being sized for a krakun, but the ventilation panel along its side was plenty suitable for her to climb, even with the awkward suit. She took far too long, though, to pry open the connector panel—a large, flat piece of plastic about as large as she was—to reveal all the sockets for direct wired connections. They were the best way to get computer access without a krakun keyboard.

There was no way to lug around krakun-sized cables in her bag, so she always did the next best thing—sticking conductive paste to a bunch of smaller wires and shoving those in a socket big enough to fit her entire arm. She had to reach deep inside, as the plug she needed to mimic was a meter and a half long and had fifty-five points of connection, not counting power draw.

Don't touch the power connector… she thought, reaching in deep to glue on the third wire. It wouldn't kill her, but the subsequent fall might.

"Moani, you doing okay?" Gert asked over the radio. "You've said nothing."

Moani huffed, more bothered she was being interrupted than anything. "Kinda busy not getting electrocuted," she said, pushing the flat copper ring to the open pin until it stuck.

"Okay, don't hesitate to call if—"

"I know, Gert," Moani sighed, pulling her arm back out before her glove also stuck to the pin. "Just let me do this, okay? I know what I'm doing."

The mistake she'd made with the spectrometer array never stopped haunting her. She'd come up with a brilliant and creative solution, like Jain expected, but she had rushed the next step. She didn't consider whether the line was big enough that the capacitor would explode when faced with its maximum energy draw.

Just like Jain warned her.

This was her punishment, or at least the next step of the forever-punishment she would endure for the rest of her life. Instead of getting cozy on the *White Flower II* for the next several months, they stuck her on this gods-forsaken ship, trying to salvage the operation and continue living another couple of days.

She worked her way up to the shallowest level of connector pins, though at that point she had to double-check her labels for each of the wires she was using. Moani didn't need to look up which ones to put where—she'd long since memorized the correct order and sequence to attach individual wires for all seven hundred fifty-three krakun cable standards. Her adapter would figure out which wires meant what from there. But the wires themselves still always looked the same.

Getting into the tedious work always made her feel better, safer. In it she could forget the pain she'd been putting herself through; it focused her mind, made her quick and efficient, not bogged down by crass feelings that threatened to cloud her mind with doubt and fear.

Which was why she missed seeing the anup come in through the airlock door.

She stopped when she noticed movement from the corner of her eye. The anup wore breathing masks inside the krakun chamber—black, polyvinyl ones with dark, flat eyepieces that obscured their faces. She should have been too far away for them to notice, so long as she didn't move or make a sound.

Why did they come in here? They stood next to each other, waiting for something—

Shit, what if they expect the krakun to come out of his room?

"Gert?" she whispered over the radio. The receiver fuzzed; she got no response. "Gert, come in, the anup just walked inside…" Still no response.

Only three left to go. She slicked the next wire with the conductive paste, then reached into the socket and pressed it against the node. She craned her head back. The anup standing to the left had an itch under his mask and tried in vain to scratch it without breaking the seal. The other was chastising him for…Moani couldn't tell. Using his paws, perhaps?

She slicked another wire and pressed it to the open node. She turned again. Still saying nothing, making idle, muffled chatter in their gibberish. She attached the final node and looked into the open socket with a flashlight to ensure everything was in place. She hoped everything was correct; the wires still all looked the same, and all converged into her rather hefty adapter.

There was no way she could stay up here if the krakun was coming. She pulled her slate out of her bag and connected that to the adapter, turning it on but leaving the wireless signal active. Even with degraded signals it would connect over a couple meters, though the connection would lag. So with all that in place, she closed the lid on the console, hiding the rest of her equipment inside with it.

The whole door-sized panel settled with a loud *clack*. Moani winced.

"*Ayo!*" one of the anup said. "Geroo *do ee aindata!*"

Moani swallowed hard. She did not know if Aride even knew how to speak their language. "Gert, I need help," she whispered. "I might be in trouble…"

The anup, a young and somewhat small male who held onto his golden staff, walked to the base of the computer desk. His height was still greater than Moani's, though even then he came nowhere near the top of the desk. "*Bogodai or dea Totaikona ama de su! Se!*"

"I don't understand you!" Moani insisted, standing up and backing away.

The anup snorted. "Stupid geroo, have insisted, learn language! All time, learn Geroonic, will not speak Anupian."

Well he knew *something* at least.

"I am busy…cleaning! You wouldn't want Totaikona to come in here and everything be dusty, would you?"

"No dust!" the anup snapped. "I am demand know, did you be seen in *soida*? Messing with *nehsi*?" He waved the golden rod around.

"I don't know what the hell you're talking about!"

"She said geroo messing with *nehsi*, you are only geroo!" the anup demanded. He climbed up on the desk—and he took far less time than Moani to do the same thing. She retreated until her back collided with the wall; it was so hard to move in the suit! The edge of the desk was just two meters to her left, but that drop could kill her if she fell wrong, high-pile carpeting or not. Geordians had a preternatural reflex that let them land safely, but not in *these* suits.

The light of the room shone behind the anup and cast him in darker shadows as he stood up to his full height, right on the edge of the desk. If she had the weight of a geroo, a well-placed tackle could knock him down, but she was lightweight, powerless.

"I want know!" the anup demanded, the mask only moving a little with his jaw, just enough to allow speech without expression. "Saw you in hallway—were you in *soida*?"

"I was not!" Moani shrieked, almost in geordian too, rather than Geroonic. "I'd have no reason to go in there!"

The anup stepped forward—two strides, and he was already on top of her.

"Liar," he huffed. The anup lifted the rod and struck her across the face.

CRACK. The tinted face shield of the environment suit took the large part of the blow, but it resulted in a thick spiderweb pattern across its right side. Moani yelped in shock, more rattled than hurt—but already panic gripped her.

Chills through her body forced her fur to stand on end inside the suit. *Oh gods, don't let the helmet break,* she swore, not wanting to face the slow and painful death *that* would bring—suffocation in krakun air would be preferable to a late rescue.

Without thinking she scrambled back, away from the anup, until her paw on the desk hit nothing, and she caught herself from toppling over the side.

Moani felt so very, very small, whimpering and looking up at the shine of the eye-guards on the anup's breathing mask. She heard him breathing—or was that her own breath? Moani shook so hard it numbed her; she couldn't tell what she was feeling.

Gods, please…

The anup planted a paw on Moani's chest and pressed down, just short of breaking her ribs.

"What were you doing there?" the anup said.

Oh gods, she couldn't even think of a good lie! She couldn't even speak, it paralyzed her throat. All that came to mind of was…

Her sister.

Gods, let me die.

And with that, the anup shoved her off the edge.

The carpeting pile saved Moani from breaking her neck, but she ended up bashing her knee regardless. She scrambled to get to her paws, but now she could not stand. The anup leapt down beside her, landing deftly as she might have were she unimpeded.

He didn't even say anything at that point, waiting for Moani to partially stand, before swinging his rod at her again. This time he hit her in the side—right on her hip. She cried out in pain.

"Gods be damned!" Moani yelped. "Just kill me already!"

"I am not kill you!" the anup said. "I want answer. You distress she, already she upset, she *debah*, will not leave *soida*, and you go into *soida*—"

"I told you I didn't go in there!" Moani cried. "I never went near the place, damn you!"

WHACK on the back of the helmet. The helmet took the blow and held the seal, but Moani was in so much pain it did not matter.

"*Gya!*" the other anup from across the room shouted.

The one assailing Moani turned. "*Dai e?*"

The one across the room turned and searched the ground below, even kneeling down and peering under the table and the couch. Moani was just holding herself up in the thick jungle of carpet fibers, breathing now labored with the pain. She could only see through the left side of the helmet, but saw what the two anup missed: the pile in the thick carpeting parting, someone walking through the room unseen.

"*Sagha—*" the anup across the room muttered.

"*Mai so ko rai du?*" the other rasped in an exasperated tone.

From the other room there came a rumble. Both the anup, hearing it, turned toward the bedroom as the door opened, and out came the head of the enormous krakun. His neck was long, and the scales all over his back speckled from red to orange to yellow.

"Why are you out here making all this noise?" Totaikona bellowed at the two anup.

"*E se dei e ai da!*" the one nearest him stammered, more than usual, so taken by surprise he gestured with an empty paw. "*Nensuk aredia a cho men!*"

"And you were to wait until I woke on my—" Totaikona stopped. His massive, broad nose wrinkled, and twitched. Suddenly he sneezed, and the force hit Moani like a shockwave. Thick spittle flew everywhere, largely onto the two anup, even all the way across the room. Moani realized the corner of the desk hid her, but that wouldn't be enough if Totaikona came over to investigate…

Then she felt two paws under her arms pull at her. It was painful, but she suffered in silence. Gert dragged her into the narrow space underneath the computer desk. "Shh," he whispered, "I don't think they spotted me."

She could barely hear him. It was only then she realized that the rod to her helmet had shaken the radio off its clip, and it had fallen into her environment suit under her right arm.

"What did you do?" Moani whimpered, trying to speak loudly enough for the radio to pick her up without her voice carrying into the room.

"Slapped Gihdah over there on the back of the thigh," Gert said. "Thought it'd distract him long enough."

Moani sniffled. She hurt so much still, and it was hard to take comfort from Gert.

The other anup noticed her disappearance, and peeking under the desk, realized he was too large to reach her. If he could even see her anymore.

"No. No more moving about! Get over here!" the krakun shouted. "You woke me up, give me the report, and then get out of my chambers! No more loitering!"

The anup glared at Moani's form in the dark a second longer, and left. Gert held Moani tight.

"Gods, it hurts," Moani whimpered. "I think they broke my leg."

"We'll get you back to Aride's room soon enough," Gert said. "You don't have to do anything else, we'll handle it."

"Oh gods, no, you can't," Moani sighed, shuddering. "I'm the only one who can—I need to…"

She tried to stand again, but couldn't. Her left leg didn't move at all anymore; it had already swollen at the hip. Would she even fit back in her regular suit? And who knew how long it would take that to heal?

Not that she could let it stop her.

Chapter 28: Responsibility

They roused Inzari, who made way for Moani, who they had to peel from the suit. It was fortunate Aride's suit was so loose-fitting, because Moani's hip and thigh had swollen.

"Dammit," Inzari sighed. "I'm sorry. I should have been awake to escort you…"

"I don't know what you could have done," Moani grunted. "Besides lock the airlock door from the outside, if that were even possible…"

"What in the five hells did they do to my helmet!" Aride stared in shock at the cracks.

"I think they're upset with you," Moani groaned. "Consider investing in armor."

"What did I do!"

"I'm not sure," Moani said. "They think you invaded their space or something…"

Gert pulled Aride aside to keep her from killing Moani. Aride growled, "She's lucky I have a spare! But that's one less the colony has. The company hates it when we requisition equipment!"

"Blame me for this," Gert pleaded. "A helmet's replaceable, at least."

"And it's not like we and the anup are on good terms as is," she grumbled. "I can just imagine the trouble this is gonna cause at home…"

"I'm sorry, Aride."

Her ears wilted. "Ancestors, Gert. You don't have to look so pitiful. I… I said I was willing to help and I mean it, especially if this helps our people. Hells, I'd break a hundred helmets to help our people."

"It shouldn't have gotten this messy," Gert said. "But I promise this is worth it."

"All right, all right," she said, putting her paws up. "I'm still mad, though. Especially at the geordian."

"I can live with that," Moani said. "If I live, anyway."

Meanwhile, since Inzari had trained in field medicine, she looked over Moani. But there was nothing she could do besides give Moani painkillers—which she left in the bag over the desk.

"I'll go get it," Aride said with a furious huff as she removed the spare helmet from the pantry. "I need to walk this off anyhow."

It took her ten minutes to fetch the bag, this time without incident. By the time she returned, Inzari was cooling Moani's hip with tap water, trying to reduce the swelling.

"Best-case scenario," Inzari said, "thigh bone shifted out of place and the swelling is from bruising. Worst case, thigh bone or hip bone—or both—are cracked."

"Gimme pills," Moani said, holding her paw out. Gert dispensed a few from the bottle, which she dry-swallowed. "Now, caffeine," she held out her paw again.

"Is this a good idea?" Gert asked Inzari as he held the food bar with the ringel *caffeinated* symbol on the wrapper.

"Regardless of if it's a good idea," Inzari said, "she does need to finish what she started."

Gert sat in the corner for the next hour as Moani hacked her way into the ship's bridge. After a few more minutes of checking whether Moani was comfortable, Inzari also sat down next to Gert. She dozed off again, her head nestled in the crook of Gert's neck. Gert, without thinking too much of it, put his arm around Inzari and held her tight.

Aride sat on a chair—rather, a small box acting as a chair—opposite them, giving Gert the most curious look. But he owed her nothing else, right? Once they left, it was unlikely he'd ever see her again…

Gert awoke, not even realizing he'd fallen asleep. Moani was poking him in the face with the end of a floor sweeper she'd lifted from behind the bed.

"Everything's in place," Moani said, her voice low as both Inzari and Aride had fallen asleep in the meantime. Gert still found it amazing Moani had stayed awake with that fine line between the pain and the opiates.

"You found the data storage location?"

"The habitat computer had everything. Totaikona's job is to compile and analyze the data, but he hasn't begun yet. He may be waiting until they return planetside."

"I noticed he was sick," Gert said. "I didn't even know krakun got sick."

"Everyone gets sick. And then your boss makes you work through it anyway because it's too inconvenient to acknowledge."

Gert winced, believing Moani referred to her own situation.

"That's just the way of the universe," Moani said. "No sense getting upset over the truth of things."

"We're done then?" Gert asked.

"Almost. I need you to smooth out one final snag. There's a security lockout from the bridge. I can't initiate a data overwrite without confirmation from there."

"Really? You can't do it from the krakun's console?"

"That requires a code I don't have. But I still have the anup code from the rod you stole, so you can access it from the bridge. You need to find whichever monitor has the confirmation written on it and make sure it's accepted before any of the anup find out it's there."

"But there were four on the bridge last I saw," Gert said.

"Yeah, that was six hours ago now. Security footage shows they've gone to bed, so the bridge is empty."

"And how am I gonna get back?" Gert's ears flattened back in a light, mild panic. "If you aren't set up to override the airlock from this side."

"Manually, I suppose. They don't require the rod key from this side, so Inzari can wait inside the airlock."

How did Aride use the airlocks without a rod? Maybe there was something in her suit. But he didn't want to ask her to borrow it again.

Gert glanced over at Inzari, who had fallen over and was snoring on his lap. His attitude about the mission had gone up and then down again, and now he felt guilty about complicating matters for Aride. It relieved him, at least, that this step of the plan was almost over. If it would only take a few more minutes and they could be out of this hellscape, he had to find the energy to finish.

"I'll go," Gert said. "Let Inzari sleep as long as you can let her. She needs to fly us back after all this."

He rolled Inzari off of him and climbed to his paws, then pulled on the pressure suit. He looked over at Aride's sonic pistol hanging by the doorway. Gert stowed that too. He hated admitting it to himself, but he didn't trust Aride to be alone with Moani. And if something happened to him while he was out there... At least Inzari would have a chance at overpowering Aride.

It seemed a cruel calculation. He hooked up his radio to the inside the helmet, donned the recharged personal cloak, and stepped over Inzari's sleeping body on the floor as he exited through the airlock.

"Gert," Moani said, just as the airlock door closed, her voice crackling over the radio.

"What is it?" Gert asked. "Did I forget something?"

"Thanks for rescuing me," Moani said.

Gert wasn't sure how to respond. He was still feeling self-conscious, even as he left the airlock for the central chamber and entered the warmer, higher-pressure air of the rest of the ship. The lights had dimmed from their wake cycle, though the hallways were still well-lit from lighting strips lining the hallway floors. Gert followed those strips to the still-darkened bridge. Bright images of C-18-3 glowed from various monitors.

"I see no one," Gert said, glancing around. "Let me get a good vantage point and you can activate the overwrite."

"Got it."

Gert climbed on top of an anup-height seat, which was higher than comfort allowed, then climbed onto the console in front. He balanced on the edge so he didn't plunge his boot into a screen. He doubted they were flimsy, but he worried about hitting any buttons should the bottom of his boot be touch-sensitive.

At least two dozen monitors were lit up all around the bridge. From the sufficient height he at least saw them all, even if he couldn't read any.

"Ready?" Moani asked.

"I think so. What am I looking for?"

"Anything that changes on any screen. A pop-up notification, a red blinking light, fanfare with confetti and balloons."

"Got it," Gert said. "Ready."

"I already activated it," Moani said.

"Shit. Um..." Gert looked around at every screen again, realizing the ones on the console on the other side of the walkway were too skewed to see anything. After checking all the monitors on the console side he could see, he jumped to the floor and tried to climb a seat on the other side.

"I'm still not seeing anything," Gert said. "I didn't even hear anything, not an alert sound, or..."

"Gotcha," said a voice from behind, saying the word in krakun.

Gert jerked his head to the sound of the voice. With Gert up on the console, Eendie—her deep blue fur lost in the darkness save for her golden eyes—leaned over face-to-face with him. She spread her arms out wide and snapped them in. Gert jumped back at once, wobbling as he landed on a chair, and it swiveled under his feet.

Shit, shit, shit!

Gert scrambled to right himself, the chairback swinging as it swiveled. Eendie turned her attention in his direction again. Gert spotted the indicator on his armband—he was still invisible. But she'd sussed him out anyhow.

"*Se ga!*" she shouted and lunged at him again. Gert fell to the floor this time trying to dodge her.

"Gert?" Moani asked over the radio. "What's happening?"

"Small problem," Gert muttered. "Smallest of problems." *Why isn't she asleep now? Oh… Oh Gert, you idiot. She was sleeping all day!*

Eendie's ears swiveled, trying to pinpoint where he was on the surface below. Her nose twitched. After a moment of trying to detect him with her eyes, she pounced at the floor. Gert rolled out of the way just in time to avoid being crushed, but her arm, reaching out wide, caught him around the shoulder.

"*Isedo e!*" she hissed, her other arm snatching Gert's neck in the crook of the elbow, pinning his back to her chest. She gave no consideration to the camouflage unit on his back, but it was the only thing between them that gave Gert room to squirm. He tried swinging a kick behind himself, but only ended up tapping his own tail.

Well, it was a good try, but we're all dead now, because I couldn't be bothered to pay attention. Nice going, Gert.

"Gert, get to a hiding place," Moani said over the radio. "Inzari will be there to extract you in a moment."

"A little late," Gert wheezed.

He had one last option. As Eendie stood, clutching his bulky body in her arms, Gert still had his lower arms free to reach into Moani's canvas bag. The space was tight, and he couldn't tell right away which gun he'd grabbed. But as Eendie pressed her jaw against the dome of his helmet and sniffed him, her sharp fangs coming into plain view as she snarled, Gert was out of time.

He pressed the end of the gun into the soft flesh under her chin.

"*O…deya?*" Eendie's tone curled into realization.

Gert pulled the trigger.

For a moment, he heard nothing but pain. It turned out that firing a sonic blaster right next to his own head was not the best of ideas.

He'd never even fired a gun before, though he knew the general mechanism—hold the handle, squeeze the trigger. He expected something like bang or zap or zorch to follow, like in the videos, but the sound the sonic blaster made was more like someone banged a massive brass gong, and he was the gong. The low bass noise sucked all the ambient sound out of the room.

Gert felt fortunate he was wearing his helmet. When his head stopped buzzing, he sat up and shook himself alert.

"…Shit," he said, when he saw Eendie's body on the floor in front of him. Her bronze blood had spilled all over the bridge. *Everywhere.* Even under low ambient light, spatters plainly coated the viewscreen and the computer monitors.

Eendie had fallen away from him, her upper half thankfully obscured in the dark. He didn't want to see what happened to her head.

"…Gert? Gert!" Moani's voice came from his radio. Only then he realized his ears were ringing.

"W-what?" Gert replied, cringing and clutching his paw to his helmet. Hearing things hurt suddenly.

"Are you okay?"

"I don't know," Gert said. "But the anup definitely isn't. She's… She's dead now." Ancestors, that felt so wrong to say.

"I can see that!"

Oh right, she's looking at the security feed.

"I didn't have a choice!" Gert said, regretting speaking—his own voice inside the helmet was far too loud. "She'd known I was here somehow! It was the anup I stole the rod from earlier."

"What'd you hit her with? The picture on this is too grainy to tell."

"The sonic gun… Shit, does the sound carry?"

Silence. Moani came back, "I don't know. I couldn't hear it over the radio."

Gert had to think in case the others were coming up the hall right now. "What paw do anup use guns in?"

"What?" Moani asked.

"Like with the rod. Do they use the same paw they hold their rod in?"

"I think you'd know better than me," Moani said. "Why?"

"Because this was a suicide," Gert said.

"Oh. Oh," Moani said. "Be sure to wipe the gun before you give it to her."

"Why?" Gert asked.

"Uh, fingerprints! Forensics stuff, you know…"

"What the hells are fingerprints?" Gert asked. "Like a pawprint? Why would they run forensics, this isn't a detective story. Also, I am wearing gloves."

"You can't!" Aride's voice came in over the strand. "Gert, what in the five hells are you doing? That's my gun! They would figure that out in an instant!"

Well, she was awake now.

"I'm sorry, Aride," Gert said, crawling toward the paw that still had a death-grip on the gold rod. He had to work to pry open her fingers, his thick-gloved paws slipping on the gore that had coated everything. "I'll figure something out! I don't know. She took it from you."

He pulled the gold rod out from Eendie's paw. He had to reach over and place it in her other paw as though she'd swapped them. His paws shook, and he willed them to stop. *Not now.*

Just as Gert curled Eendie's fingers around the gun, he looked up. One of the other anup peeked their head into the bridge, a young female Gert had not seen in full before.

The anup spoke, "*Gih—*" and stopped mid-utterance, her mouth falling open in shock. She sprinted back the way she came.

Gert exhaled a sigh and prepared to sneak his way back out.

"Gert, not to throw a bug in your wine," Moani said, "but did you confirm the overwrite?"

"Erm…"

Gert scrambled back to the top of the monitors, dodging every puddle of blood he could lest he leave a distinct boot-print in it. On the third try, he found the blinking pop-up box with the unintelligible anup text inside, Eendie's blood and bits of brain matter smeared over the whole monitor.

Gert had no time to feel sick—*have a physical and/or mental breakdown on your own time!*—and he tried his best to press the "accept" button below the dialog box, marked with an elaborate Anupian symbol. The screen refused to accept his input.

"Shit, shit, shit," Gert muttered. On the adjacent screen, not covered in blood, he tried tapping an icon with a clean finger, and it also did not respond. "Moani, I can't activate the touchscreen with these gloves."

"That's weird," Moani said, "Any environment suit should allow your bioelectric field through for that exact purpose."

"Anup have a different bioelectric field," Aride said. "I've never been able to use a monitor made for them."

"That would have been nice to know," Moani groaned.

Gert glanced up and saw a fleshy shred of Eendie's ear pasted against the viewscreen monitor that displayed C-18-3.

Oh… Oh ancestors no, this is wrong. This is all wrong.

"Does a bioelectric field work after someone is dead?" Gert asked, regardless of how his instincts were screaming at him.

"Maybe," Moani said. "Just try it and hurry!"

Gert had little time to try anything else. He reached up and grabbed the ear off the monitor—sticky and slick at the same time—and jammed it down on the screen above his knee as though forcing the monitor to accept the input.

The dialog box flashed and discolored like he'd dragged a finger across the screen to highlight everything. He winced, but moments later the box disappeared. Gert, hesitant, let the ear fall to the floor, and waited for something else to go wrong.

"...Gert?"

Just then, three anup entered the bridge from the port side door. Gihdah was among them, staring down at Eendie's corpse. "*Seh... Seh! Se-eh! Go deh seh!*" He shouted as he fell to his knees. His irises contracted in shock.

Gert could only remember Gihdah's past behavior toward her— his flippant dismissals, his surly attitude—and had come to the conclusion that Gihdah *didn't like* Eendie. Gihdah, instead, burst into tears and sobs, emitting a broken, high-pitched whine of sorrow.

Ancestors... Maybe Inzari was wrong. Maybe she wasn't pregnant... Gert tried to tell himself comforting lies.

It took all of Gert's strength to climb down off of the console without touching the chair, lest it move. He stumbled away from the sight, out the starboard side door.

As the habitat airlock door opened, he collided with Inzari as she was on her way out. He knew it was her because nobody was there.

"There you are!" Inzari said. "You're trailing blood!"

Gert looked back behind himself. The edge of his boot had caught a puddle somewhere, leaving a clear imprint behind him.

"I...I'm sorry," Gert said.

"Don't apologize!" Inzari said. "You get back inside, I'll do the clean-up. Gods of known space, Gert, don't scare me like that." Inzari's paws grabbed at his legs, wiping the heel of each boot with the damp towels they'd stolen from the washroom, before she shoved him back on his way.

It took inordinate effort to move. Gert stumbled through the open airlock door to the central habitat, nearly giving up and just falling face-down on the thick carpet. When he was inside, he trudged his way through the carpeting, making his way to Aride's chamber. And once inside there, he stood blankly until he made himself release the latch on his helmet.

"Gods, Gert," Moani swore, still unmoving from her spot on the bed. "You look like hell."

Gert panted with long ragged breaths—it was only now he realized how watery everything sounded. He tried to unclasp the rest of the pressure suit, but found he couldn't put any strength into his paws.

"Ancestors no…" Gert whimpered. "It wasn't supposed to go like this…"

"Gert, she was just an anup," Moani said.

"I don't care if she was an anup!" Gert shouted. "Damn it all! She was just defending her ship! We came in here to disrupt things—she was innocent!" Gert nearly tore the zipper trying to undo it.

"You did what you had to do," Moani said.

"That doesn't mean I have to like what I had to do," Gert said.

"Gert," Aride said, moving in to undo the clasp on his suit. He didn't notice at first when she reached her paw into Moani's handbag and pulled out Inzari's plasma pistol.

Aride stepped back, aiming the gun at Gert's head.

Gert froze. He looked to the side—the inner airlock hatch was still open. Inzari wouldn't be able to open the outer hatch until the inner was closed once more.

"I want to hear one good reason I shouldn't kill you all," Aride said. Her face had shadowed over with rage, ears down and lips pulled back in a snarl. Tears formed in her eyes. "You come in here saying you'll stay secret, you get *me* in trouble, you frame *me* for murder… What the five hells am I supposed to do now!"

Gert didn't have a good answer for her.

Chapter 29: Traitors, Thieves and Liars

Gert didn't know how to feel with a gun aimed at his face. He supposed he should have felt frightened, but given everything he'd just been through, fright was such a minor concern.

And he agreed with Aride. After everything they'd done, it all fell on her head. He'd violated her trust. And now, to pay for it, he would die. And he didn't care—not about that, at least. He cared that every crew member aboard the *White Flower II* would die now because of his mistakes.

He'd just kicked off another *Silver Mint III* incident, fifty times over. The full purge that would surely follow once they realized the full extent of the deception would be all his fault.

And he realized, facing down the barrel of a gun, he had no recourse. Aride would be in the right to kill them to save herself, because what motivation could she have for caring about a few thousand geroo she never met?

Gert then looked past her shaking pistol, at the bright blue and green murals covering the walls. And he had a thought. It was awful, and it was honest. Gert didn't care if he succeeded as long as someone's life was saved.

"You're right," Gert said. "I deserve to die."

"What!" Moani started, still unable to move her lower half even though she scrambled for purchase with her paws. "You can't be fucking serious! I don't want to die!"

Aride, though, hesitated. She brought up her other paw to steady the weapon. She was so, so angry, Gert wouldn't have blamed her if she shot him right then in her fit of rage.

"I fucked up," Gert said. "I didn't tell you what you were getting into. We were gambling with our lives."

"What the hells for?" Aride demanded. "What could be so important!"

Gert cast his eyes to the deck. "It doesn't matter now, but I'll tell you the whole story. I don't need to explain what life is like under the krakun. Even for us on gate ships, we're still subject to the whims of the masters. Our lives are still under their control. And then a week ago, the pirates of the *Jet Black Sword* appeared and made us an offer, a plan to steal one of the terraformers, in exchange for a way to take the gate ship for ourselves, so we could be free. There's never been an opportunity like this before in the history of the fleet. My captain had to take it. And I love and trust my captain, so I followed him, and would still do so, because every geroo I know deserves to be free."

"You put everyone's lives on the line for—" Aride started, then stopped when she saw Gert looking up at the murals on the walls. Gert didn't have to say it outright—and it might have been too garish to—but Aride at once understood what that kind of freedom meant to them both, and every geroo in the galaxy.

"The first attempt to fix the data failed," Gert said, staring at the green hills and sky like they were a real, long-distant land he could step into. "And our commissioner was angry. She wanted to recycle *every officer*. She couldn't, because company policy says she's not allowed to execute any of us so long as the planet could be viable, no matter how remote that possibility. But the moment that the planet data comes back as a dead world…"

Gert turned back to Aride and fell to his knees in front of the barrel of Aride's weapon, which had lowered several centimeters. Aride gasped, but she did not move, still watching him without blinking, her own features trembling. He was crying at this point. No, he didn't want to die, but that was not something anyone should ever have to live through.

"Gert, are you out of your goddamned mind!" Moani screamed as she scrambled on the bed, though her voice seemed muffled like it was underwater. Neither Gert nor Aride responded to her—she may as well have been on the other side of the galaxy.

"I fucked it all up," Gert said. "I used you. And I know you don't owe me it, but I have to beg you for one last thing. Don't tell the krakun I was here. Toss my body out the airlock. Or if you find it better to let Inzari and Moani go, let them drag my body back to their ship. Because if they discover we tampered with the data, she won't just recycle the officers. The company will demand the whole ship be purged."

Inzari demanded something over the radio, but Gert didn't catch any of her words; he studied Aride's eyes and ears.

"Ten thousand?" Aride asked. "You weren't lying?"

Gert shook his head. "No lie. I deserve this, Aride. I failed. But don't let them be punished for my mistake too. I can't bear ten thousand deaths on my soul. I can't even accept one."

"But if I don't give you up, they'll blame me!" Aride said. "They'll want to kill me!"

Gert sighed, his ears limp. "Then do what you must. There's no denying that I deserve it. At least you'll spare me from being there for the full purge. I've heard they make the officers go last. So at least I won't have to watch the rest of the crew file in for the recycler." Gert turned and stared at the mural. Moani shouted something else. What it was didn't matter. "Just give me another moment longer, okay? This is the closest I'll ever come to home. Let me go out imagining what might have been."

Gert reached touched his fingertips to the paint, and thought about the feel of the grass Top Side.

Aride tensed her fingers as her eyes brimmed over with tears, and then she slumped—first her shoulders, then her entire body. "You asshole…" she said, crying, those tears pouring down her face in a torrent. "You damned asshole…" She pulled the gun back and tossed it aside, where it chipped some paint off the wall before clattering to the floor, leaving a plain, gray scar in the middle of the green. "How am I supposed to kill someone like you!" Her voice creaked. "I don't even care if you're telling the truth or not, just leave! Get out, and may the ancestors throw you in the hell of all traitors, thieves, and liars!" She turned her back on them and stormed behind the washroom partition where she burst into loud sobbing.

Moani exhaled a sigh of relief. Gert collected up everything and put it into Moani's bag.

"Aren't you going to kill her?" Moani whispered, as Gert picked up the plasma pistol from the floor.

Gert stared at her, ears down with grief. "I think I have."

"No, I'm serious," hissed Moani. "If she talks, it'll ruin everything. You can't believe she'd throw in with us after such a short speech!" Moani sat up, though that only amounted to her propping herself up on her elbows. "All you did was make her feel self-conscious about killing us herself. The moment we're gone—boom! She's contacted Totaikona and we're still dead! And even if not, you're asking her to keep a secret like this for the rest of her life?"

"I couldn't cover up her death even if I wanted," Gert said as he pulled Moani's pressure suit up her legs. Her thigh had become so swollen that, after a few moments of struggle and Moani wincing as the suit crushed her, he gave up trying. So instead he took the cracked helmet off of Aride's paws and put Moani into the spare geroo environment suit. Moani didn't struggle. He had to be extra careful lifting her backside up to slip her tail into the sheath.

"But she won't tell," he said.

"How can you be so sure?" she asked.

"Because of that." He pointed behind himself to the murals on the wall, the sky and trees and grass and the white citadel.

Moani blinked. "What the hell's that got to do with anything?"

"I'm sorry if you don't understand," Gert said, zipping up the suit's front. "But you're not a geroo."

He popped his helmet back on. Inzari came through the radio.

"What the *hell* is going on!" she demanded, "What were all those noises about?"

"It's fine," Gert said. "Get to the shuttle. We need to be ready to lift-off as soon as we're able."

"I am going. I'm waiting for you, assuming you're not—"

He slung the cloaking pack on his shoulder, Moani's bag of equipment, her useless pressure suit, and, after popping on her helmet, picked up Moani herself, holding her close. She wrapped her arms around his neck and pulled herself up to avoid putting pressure on her leg, though putting even more pressure on Gert's shoulders. The weight between everything was ridiculous even for him, but he put on a stern face behind his helmet and left Aride to cry.

* * *

"Gert?"

Underneath the ship, Gert had handed Moani off to Inzari when he heard Aride's voice come on over the radio. Moani was in no mood to talk, so neither of them realized they left Moani's radio behind when they switched suits.

"Aride?"

"Listen," she said. "If you have a moment."

"What's she doing on the line?" Inzari asked.

"Give us a moment, please," Gert said, sitting outside the access hatch and letting the shuttle's different gravity pull at his boots.

Inzari sniffed. "I suppose… Radio off."

Gert sat in the dark as Inzari strapped Moani down to a seat inside. They were about to make a pit stop back at the *Jet Black Sword* so that their doctor could treat Moani, since he had a working knowledge of geordian physiology, and no doctors back on the *White Flower II* were in on the scheme. Gert doubted she would stay on the mission.

"What...what happened on the bridge?" Aride asked between sniffles. "So I know what to say."

"The anup who Inzari assumed was pregnant found me out there. I think she'd become paranoid after her rod disappeared from the bedroom. Then I shot her with the sonic gun because I had no other recourse."

Saying it clinically like that made Gert feel hollow. His panic had spiked so high he still couldn't give any thought to the events beyond their mere details.

"She was..." Aride started.

"I saw her in the washroom with a device, I suppose to test for that kind of thing. She was furious and upset, but I couldn't tell what the actual results on the device were. In fact, they have depressed her, if that's how anup express depression."

"And then you put the sonic pistol in her paw..."

"Yeah so it'd look like..." Gert's ears perked, then sank again when he realized what he'd been saying. "...suicide."

Aride was silent for a long while. So long, Gert became concerned.

"Aride?" he asked.

"It's a long shot..." Aride said, "but I might survive this."

"You might."

"Whatever happens, the anup will still blame me for what happened," Aride said. "But I could mitigate some of that. They might not try to kill me."

"I see," Gert said. It didn't seem like enough to counteract all the evil he perpetrated.

"Listen. I don't think I can ever forgive you...at least not like this. But if, somehow, someday, this all pays off and you find New Gerootec... Promise you'll come back for me."

"I swear on my mother's memory," Gert said without hesitation. "It is the least I could do."

"Gert, we need to get going," Inzari said over the radio. "Unless you want Moani to stay in pain much longer."

"Alright. Aride...goodbye." Gert swallowed, like he was trying to catch the word he said and put it back inside.

"Long life to you, Gert," Aride said. The background static fell silent.

Gert pushed himself into the hole below, righting himself to the different gravity inside the shuttle, and helped Inzari lift the hatch cover and screw it back onto the bottom of the survey ship.

"You okay?" Inzari asked, noting the blank expression on the subcommander's ears.

"Just thinking," Gert replied flatly. He realized then, the captain was right. Despite all the loss, until this moment, he hadn't known what it was like to lose.

There were words written on the hatch in krakun, which Gert could read now that they were the correct orientation. *Property of the Starship Technology Corporation of Krakuntec Prime.*

"Starship Technology Corporation on Krakuntec," he whispered to himself, to cement it into his memories. "Aride."

Don't forget. Ancestors, don't forget.

Chapter 30: Thicker Than Blood

It was well after evening shift by the time Gert and Inzari returned aboard the *White Flower II*. They'd spent thirteen hours aboard, including the additional hours docking with the *Jet Black Sword*.

Ateri met them at the airlock alone. When he saw Gert remove his helmet, Ateri hesitated. Gert's frazzled features looked not unlike Ateri's own that day he looked in the mirror after Sur'an had died—though Gert appeared uninjured. His suit looked a mess too, like it had been scrubbed clean, though there was still an unusual polished-copper caking between the glove fingers.

"I hope the lack of progress updates didn't worry you," Inzari said.

"One message about strand outages got through," Ateri said. "All I could do was pray for your success all day."

Gert nodded shallowly.

"Erm… Mission report?"

"Success," Gert said, just above a whisper. Turned away and facing the wall, he unlatched the top latch which kept the helmet seal in place, and dragged off the suit.

"Moani was injured during a scuffle," Inzari said. "We returned her to the *Jet Black Sword* for treatment."

Ateri's ears perked up in alarm. "What do you mean a scuffle?" he asked, voice lowered. "Did someone see you?"

"Nobody who's left to talk about it," Gert said.

This also concerned Ateri greatly, but relieved him nevertheless. Still, if they reported the mission a success, then they must have mitigated the potential fallout…right?

Gert pulled his strand out of his armband. "I'm sorry, Captain," Gert said, trying to regain his composure as he turned his strand over in his paws.

"You'll be fine," Ateri said. "I'm betting you're exhausted."

"Very, sir."

"I can make my way back to the saferoom," Inzari said, switching back on her geroo camouflage once she was out of suit.

"You're not—" Gert started, somehow assuming she would force her way back to his apartment.

She shook her head. "I can tell when someone needs time to themselves for serious. Listen. Call me whenever you're ready; I'll get you anything you need." She hugged Gert around his shoulders and then left though the door to the hallway.

Ateri turned back to Gert. "What happened?"

"Can I give the rest of the report in the morning?" Gert asked. "I have something I need to do before I can sleep."

Ateri nodded.

* * *

Hiani found Gert slumped over next to her apartment door. She gasped and hurried to his side.

"I'm up!" Gert exclaimed. "I'm… Oh, Hiani. I thought you were off shift… I came by, and…"

"Gert, you look like every hell!" she said, helping him to his paws. "Inside, please."

Inside, Gert sat on the soft couch and tried to keep his head up. Hiani poured him some tea, and he drank it. He wasn't fond of tea, but he appreciated the gesture more than his life.

Hiani sat down next to him. She'd removed her strand holster, likely tossed it in the other room, as to mark her complete and undivided attention.

Gert couldn't even bring his shoulders up.

"It's a long story," he said. "But here it is."

And he told her everything. Gert remained in his spot for the next half hour as he explained the emergency, the pirates, the Exit Plan, the deal, and every situation he'd had to handle with Moani. He showed her proof—a series of photographs taken on his strand of the inside the pirate ship, which he took while on the Jet Black Sword two hours before. He would delete them right away, but first he needed these to show to Hiani.

She said nothing the entire time, but her ears expressed everything—disbelief, shock, confusion, fear, distress. Gert couldn't be certain, though, that the way they turned upward near the end—perhaps a little hope.

He wanted to drag Hiani back to her bed and kiss her and make love to her, but now he realized there would only be false pretense to it. He couldn't make things better.

"I, um…" Gert said, his voice trembling. "You'll probably hear about this from someone soon enough, and I've run out of time thinking about how to approach you about this. I…I need to come out and say it."

"Gert…" Hiani put an arm around his large shoulders. "Don't cry, okay? This isn't any of your fault; I understand what the captain's done is crazy, but you trust his judgment, right? That's good enough for me."

"That isn't…"

Gert broke into tears and hated himself for it.

"Sorry, I'm sorry," Hiani said. "Please, go on."

"I can't," Gert said, crying. "I can't. I'm horrible for what I've done to you. I—"

"What happened?" Hiani took Gert's paw in both of hers and she squeezed it tight. "Please, Gert, I can tell this is eating at you. You kinda make it obvious."

Gert's ears twitched into a smirk for a moment.

"It's that…" he said, without looking up. "Right before I left to come here the first time, we had that strand call, and you were angry at me, and you had every right to be so, so I thought the way you worded everything that we'd broken up…"

"I thought so too, but I'd cooled off in about an hour," Hiani said. "Then there was the explosion at the scanner array and you were a hero, and I felt stupid about everything I said."

"Well," Gert said, trying to clear his voice. "That's when I did something on the assumption we were no longer a couple."

Hiani perked her ears. "I…I understand."

Gert shook his head. "This is more complicated than that."

"Well let's start with… Who was it?"

Gert pulled out his strand again and showed her the picture with Inzari.

"You're joking," Hiani said.

"I don't know! She's attractive!" Gert said, his paws stiffening into claws as he gesticulated without aim. "I don't know how to explain it. I've always been kinda attracted to aliens. And then she shows up, and you'd broken up with me, so I…"

"So you had sex with her. Just like that?" She tried to make her vague statement sound more charitable than accusatory by bending it into a question, which Gert appreciated to no end.

"It wasn't just like that, there was a lot of… Well there was drinking involved, but neither of us were drunk."

Hiani blinked. "This was over a space of what, nine hours? How was drinking involved without either of you getting drunk?"

"That's beside the point and also a long story," Gert said. "The fact is, after an hour or two on this ship, I had sex with Inzari. I've had this monumental crush on her that is not going away."

"Well I mean… It's kinda weird, but—"

"And then I did it again," Gert said. "And again. And again. Hells, I had sex with her yesterday."

"I…" Hiani's words trailed off.

Gert nodded. "I've been doing it behind your back. I couldn't even tell you because you needed to know all about this first—" he shook his strand. "And this was supposed to be a secret by order of the captain."

"Then why are you even telling me this?"

"Because after what I did, you deserve to know. You even said at first this wasn't my fault, but it *is!* I lied to you and to myself to avoid admitting it." Gert exhaled. "I am honest when I say I love you, and I want to be with you, but when I look back on my motivations for loving you, I keep seeing myself as Ateri and you as my Commander Jakari. And I realized… that's unfair to you. I wanted you to be someone you are not; I was keeping you in the dark as though it could somehow mold you into becoming the geroo I wanted. I should have wanted the Hiani you are from the start, but I couldn't do that unless I was first honest with myself."

Hiani sat quiet for a moment, though the expression on her ears seemed calm more than sullen or angry. "And you weren't?"

"I don't think I was." Gert's shoulders sank. "I originally assumed I was, and then today happened and… I have a lot to think about. I think, maybe, if I'd been honest with myself sooner, we could have made a good couple. But… I think I ruined it. It *is* all my fault." Gert's ears wilted. "I'm so sorry, Hiani. I think we need to break up, but… it'd probably sound better if you got angry at me, and you said it."

"Gert…" Hiani started. "You know… I always knew you were brave, but this is another level. I *am* upset that you lied to me. You figuring out at the last moment that you've grown as a person doesn't undo that. But…" She pulled herself closer to him. "I did love you, too."

Did. Gert was now three-for-three in breaking hearts. At least this time it wasn't a shallow reason.

"Do you want to separate?" she asked.

Gert sighed. "I want you to be happy. I'm not going to help you achieve that by remaining your boyfriend, not after what I've done."

"You might be right," Hiani said. She choked back tears.

"It would be for the best," Gert said. "I promise though, someday I will make up for this."

"I know you will. Because no matter what else you've done, that's the kind of geroo you *are*. I can't love you anymore, Gert, but I've always believed in you. I'm sorry I failed to let you know that sooner."

Hiani and Gert sat for a long time, saying nothing, but clasping paws. Hiani then pulled Gert over by his shoulders to face her, and he embraced her.

"I love you, Hiani," Gert said. "I'm so sorry for breaking your heart."

"I know, Gert. For that at least, I forgive you."

* * *

It was nearly 0130 by the time Gert entered his apartment with every intent to fall down on his bed and sleep for the next thirty days.

"Gert," he heard. It surprised him at first, but it was the commander's voice. He hadn't given them permission to enter, but he didn't care if they did. "Can you come in here?" she asked.

He turned toward the kitchen, and Ateri turned on the light. Gert blinked, too tired to react. Jakari sat at the table before a green-frosted cake. The writing on it said, *To Gert's Success.*

"Surprise!" Jakari said. "Ateri told me how you were feeling after the mission, but since it was a success, I thought you might need something to cheer you up!"

"It's been a long day," Gert said. He accepted the scene at face value and shuffled toward a seat where he plopped his tail down.

"It's chocolate," Ateri said. "Just got it from Theseri's Kitchen. Your favorite, right?"

"It is," Gert said. "The cake smells delicious."

Jakari paused and turned silent as she contemplated Gert's expression. She looked so concerned. Gert wanted more than anything to assuage her worry, but he couldn't muster up the strength to change his expression.

"Gert," Ateri said from behind. "Erm… Sorry. This was my idea. I thought… It would be in part an apology for how I treated you last week. We were all under a lot of pressure."

"Okay," said Gert, his voice on the verge of breaking.

"Dear…" Jakari put the cake slicer down and leaned over to Gert to put a consoling paw on his shoulder. "Do you want us to put this away for now?"

"No, it's just…"

The full weight of everything hit him. He'd just saved them all from an untimely death, but it didn't even seem to matter, given the price he paid.

Mathematically, the equation fell in his favor. The life of one anup and her unborn cub, and the potential life of one geroo and her—*his own* unborn cub, plus any chance at happiness he might have had with Hiani, to save the lives of two hundred, maybe even ten thousand geroo, to secure their freedom.

And he couldn't convince himself it was worth it.

Gert burst into open, loud, terrified sobs, burying his face under his arms so they wouldn't have to look at him in shame.

"Gert!" Jakari cried, "Ancestors, what's wrong? Gert!"

Jakari was first to take Gert in her arms and hold on to him tight. Ateri stepped around and held up Gert to embrace him from the other side.

"Gert, I'm so sorry," Ateri said, his voice quiet.

"I should have… I should have been able to save everyone," Gert creaked between fits of tears. "I—I had to do something…terrible…"

"I understand," Ateri said. "So have I. I'm still paying for it even to this day. Don't hold it in, Gert. I'm right here. I can't promise I can make it better, but I'll listen. For as long as you need."

Given the circumstances, it was the best Gert could have hoped to hear. It fixed nothing, but maybe for a little while he could fool himself and pretend Aride and Hiani both forgave him, though he knew that, too, was fleeting.

So he cried, and cried, as the cake on the table cooled, and his crying seemed to go on endlessly.

"Sir…" Gert said through a break in his tears.

"Yes, Gert?" Ateri asked.

"I didn't say so earlier, because I didn't want to sound selfish…but when I learned you wouldn't be retiring on your sixtieth, I…I was so relieved. I didn't want you to go. I'm not ready to be left without you. And after today, I know for sure. I don't want to be captain anymore."

Ateri was silent for a long time, but to Gert's surprise, he didn't object. "I understand," he said. "It's a horrible job. The worst. But for what it's worth, I think you've done great. But if you still feel that way in the morning, I will inform the academy."

"Thank you, sir."

Gert hated himself for giving up. But a great pressure lifted off his chest. For the first time in hours, he lifted his ears up in the briefest smile as he held on. At the very least, he got something he needed—his captain, his family, for a little while longer.

Maybe he would be okay.

Epilogue

Pokokuro had a proper office, unlike her predecessor who only worked in a cubicle. While it was not a nice corner space with a big picture window, it still had marble amenities, with a gold-edged fountain that burbled water into a kaoki pond just aside her desk.

She was not looking at her nice pond. She was glaring at her cousin, Totaikona, as if to cut a hole in him.

"What." She said the word with all the intent of a question, but all the force of a reprimand.

"It's viable!" Totaikona said. The krakun wore one of those ridiculous breathing masks, as he was still getting over his flu. "I've already put up the estimations for the projected landmass size... What's wrong? Uncle will be thrilled!"

"I will tell Daddy before the day is over," Pokokuro said. "Once I have looked over the data myself."

"I know what I'm doing. The numbers are all there."

That's what bothered Pokokuro so much. She was intent on, at the least, giving Captain Ateri his due punishment that her predecessor neglected. And now company policy was standing in her way! It was almost insulting how the moment money got involved, the krakun had to pretend to be sweet and supportive to such creatures. *Geroo,* at that.

"Wasn't there an incident aboard your vessel?" Pokokuro asked, as though changing the subject would salvage her pride. She picked at any corner she could to try and peel the whole sticker off.

"Uh, yes," Totaikona said. "But there wasn't anything interesting about it. One of the anup committed suicide. It happens."

"And something convinced the others it was murder."

Totaikona scoffed and laughed, before rearing back and sneezing into his mask. Pokokuro pulled an antiseptic wipe from a box near her talon and swabbed it across her face, just in case.

"Who cares if it was?" Totaikona said. "Looked like suicide. Was even in the security feed. She entered the bridge, thrashed about in a fit of grief, shot herself under the chin with a sonic blaster stolen from the janitor sometime earlier that cycle. I don't care if the anup don't believe that, it's just their job to clean it up when it happens. Damaged no equipment; that's the important part."

They had not set up the video feed to capture a low-light environment. Totaikona had a bad habit of cutting corners in his fleet, "specialty ships" made from out-of-date overstock garbage.

And she wanted that fact to somehow overturn the bare truth of the matter. All his scanning systems worked as intended. There wasn't anything in the security feed that contradicted the incident aboard. And even with her suspicion that the incident indicated *something*, unless she had some idea what that something could be, she was thrashing about at open sky trying to find purchase.

She could always request another scanner ship, but Thrull would turn it down. The company *needed* a success after four centuries of turning up so little from their exploration division. Even if she had time to come up with some excuse to throw the data out *again*, the cogs of capitalism would not wait for her.

Pokokuro inhaled and sighed. "All right. As promised, you'll receive one percent of the finder's bonus."

Totaikona twisted his talons, looking far too thrilled at the sum. Pokokuro didn't even need the golds, but she wasn't about to give her cousin too much of an unearned cash injection. Nine hundred fifty-five thousand golds could buy a couple more ships at the rock-bottom prices he purchased them at. At the very least, he wouldn't need to scrape for change under the couch to replace that anup he lost.

"*I* will deliver the news to Daddy, however," Pokokuro said, "so get out of my office. I have work to do."

"Yes, Cousin," Totaikona said, turning to leave. "I'll see you next Emperor's Day."

"Mmm," Pokokuro grunted, pretending to be interested in her computer console. Once she was alone again, her thoughts turned back to Ateri. She would not let him squirm his way out of a well-deserved execution, company policy or not. There had to be some way around it all.

A long grin spread across her lips, and she wrote up her next proposal, to deliver to the board once the excitement over the new planet quelled.

To be continued.

ANOTHER STORY:
Whatever Happened To Commissioner Sarsuk?

By Rick Griffin

One.

Sarsuk, you will step back this instant!" roared Overseer Saqqadr. The thick green female krakun marched down the space station platform to where Sarsuk's company shuttle waited.

Sarsuk stopped at the open bay door. He'd almost gotten through the station without notice…almost. Turning to his immediate boss, he put on a plastic smile.

"I sent a message about—" he started, knowing he'd get nowhere.

"Do I sound like I care?" Saqqadr said, pushing past the other krakun on the platform and stopping a meter away from Sarsuk's face.

Sarsuk backed off. "I—I didn't—"

"You know I cannot respond to those messages," she snapped, lowering her voice to a hushed whisper. "We're trying to recover from *espionage*. I'm not even supposed to breathe a word about it in such a public area!"

Sarsuk shrank. "Then we can't talk about it here, can we?" he asked, grinning.

She snorted hot breath on his head and sat back on her haunches. "I have to only because none of this can be on the network. So you had better be in the Sensitive Room tomorrow morning with your fleet proposal."

"Wha-but…it's festival night!" Sarsuk stammered. "And for once, I have a date!"

Saqqadr considered Sarsuk's face. She burst into uproarious laughter. Sarsuk, embarrassed, curled in on himself.

"It's true," he said, muttering under his breath.

"I'm sure! Where's she live? Krakuntec II?"

"No!" Sarsuk said. Though the truth was he didn't know where she lived, he figured she must have lived somewhere in the city. "I met her online. She's local. We're going to go to the park tonight."

"Well then, loverboy, you'd better see her home at a reasonable hour. I expect your proposal tomorrow, oh-seven hundred sharp. And that's the fleet proposal, not mating."

Sarsuk snorted.

"Do I hear a *yes, Overseer*?"

"Yes, Overseer," Sarsuk said.

"Be sure to set your alarm so you don't oversleep again." Saqqadr turned, smacking Sarsuk in the face with her tail before she tromped down the station platform again. Sarsuk, keeping his head low, hurried into the shuttle lest she thought of something else and turned about again. He tapped in his clearance to Orbital Defense and the shuttle began its several-thousand-kilometer flight toward the enormous, honeycomb-like array of Planetary Acquisitions gates.

The day's review was on the gate ship *Lost Palisade I*, which Sarsuk wanted more than anything to hurry through. He couldn't display any form of weakness to the geroo, however. They talked. The indignity he suffered on the *White Flower II* was already too well-known among them to let them latch onto anything else.

Captain Pippa, a safe, wearying, boring geroo, would meet him at the bay. Overly fat even for one of his kind, Sarsuk could already hear the pudgy captain droning on and on about ship operations in a memorized manner. Sarsuk saw himself falling over asleep as he breathed in the stale, oxygen-rich compromise air. Ugh, it gave him a headache these days. He could see himself as an old wyrm now, a hundred fifty major-years hence, brain rotted from sulfur deprivation. He was certain it was one part of what degraded his job performance.

The other part was that Saqqadr just despised him. He couldn't fathom why. He used to find her attractive, but that was a long time ago.

When Sarsuk arrived, his ship docked in an empty landing bay. Pippa was not outside the bay door, either.

Sarsuk, snorting out the awful compromise air, snapped a talon onto the bay operator's intercom. "What the hell is taking the captain so long! You know he's supposed to meet me here as soon as possible!"

"I-I don't know, sir," the officer responded. "I believe he's on his way—"

"I don't want him *on his way*, I want him here! Now!"

Dead gods, these geroo have no respect! I have a schedule to keep! Do I have to spend every day waiting on them to get their worthless personal lives in order?

It took three minutes for Captain Pippa to arrive, huffing and frazzled with his filthy mammalian fur sticking up about his head. The compromise air depleted the stamina of geroo even quicker than that of krakun.

"M-my apologies, Commissioner," Pippa said, the minuscule geroo bowing his head low. "We had a terrible accident this morning. S-six of the crew are dead, fifteen injured."

Sarsuk strummed a claw. Was this one of those rhetorical statements the geroo were fond of? "So issue six birth tokens and make more."

"Oh, ancestors, I can't—"

Sarsuk knocked the fat geroo onto his back and pressed the blunt end of his talon across the captain's throat. Pippa cried out, though Sarsuk was already crushing him just hard enough to give him trouble breathing.

"Listen," Sarsuk growled. "I don't care. If six geroo died, then you put it on the report. If the outcome is still uncertain when you file, then you amend the report the moment you receive the final numbers. But when I land, I want that report in my claws. I don't want to sit around here, wasting my precious time just so you can dawdle over *six geroo*."

"S-sir—" Pippa croaked.

"Do you know how much your kind costs?"

"N-no, sir."

"One gold per head, maybe two. Do you know why so little?"

Pippa shook his head.

"Because unlike pets, you're supposed to take care of yourselves. Given a sufficient environment, you grow, reproduce, handle your own matters. You're more like mold than animals in that regard. A mere six of you dead is not a concern of mine. Do you know what would concern me? Forty. Perhaps fifty. But only if they were critical crew. Is that what you want? Would you like me to retroactively amend the report to fifty dead crew members?"

Pippa shook his head faster. He might have nearly cried. It would have been pitiable if the geroo weren't so ugly and incompetent.

"Marvellous." He let go of Pippa's throat, and the captain wheezed as he stood. In truth, Sarsuk didn't have the time to carry out that many executions, but the threat was often more effective than the punishment.

Once he received the report on his mobile com, he looked it over and memorized it as the captain escorted him down to the commissioner's chamber. Then, once he was alone inside the small single room, Sarsuk tossed the report aside. He pulled up the station computer and started work on the next morning's fleet proposal, which he'd promised Saqqadr he had finished a week ago.

Two.

"So you work in outer space?" asked his date as they lounged on the veranda of The Nova And Comet, the trendiest restaurant Sarsuk could afford without going into debt. "That sounds amazing, tell me more!"

Nyakkat was long and slender and glossy, with a color that shifted from her belly white to yellow to bright orange to red to coal black on her back. Her scale polish had a sheen to it with bits of well-placed ultraviolet reflection, creating an illusion that her excellent, well-bred color pattern was flickering like flame. Her perfect teeth seemed unnaturally burnished to pearl yellow, and when she talked, she clicked her tongue like she was tasting the air.

She is out of your league, Sarsuk thought to himself. *Do not mess this up.*

Sarsuk was frumpy for a krakun: a bright but flat muddy yellow with blue-green undersides. Being male, his patchiness was easier to overlook, but it didn't make him appealing. He'd tried things like scale polish and perfumes and bits of plastic surgery here and there, but it was so time-consuming and expensive to maintain. If he had a better-paying job, perhaps it wouldn't have been a problem.

He couldn't tell her his actual job, of course. Slave wrangling...one of the least appealing jobs that didn't involve actual manual labor.

"It's classified," Sarsuk said, strumming his talons on the slab between them. "Government contract work...secret clearance, gag orders, that sort of thing." That was all true, but misleading. There was little daring about having privileged access to dull and tepid government secrets, especially of non-military fleet movements. It didn't make him a spy or a secret agent.

"Oh…" Nyakkat stirred her drink bowl with the little glass stirrer they provided. "It sounds interesting though…"

"Ah, my title is commissioner," he blurted out.

"Oh?" She perked up. "Like, commissioner of a fleet?"

"Yes! I can't tell you which fleet of course, that's the classified part." He bit on his tongue and hoped she didn't jump to the conclusion he was the commissioner of an orbital cleaning scow or something.

"Hmm…" She peered at him as if to size him up.

"Sometimes it's dangerous," Sarsuk offered. "On one mission not too long ago, I ended up losing my talon to the elbow."

"Oh my!" she exclaimed, casting her eyes down. "Which one?"

Sarsuk boldly showed off the replacement arm. Truth was, the entire incident was embarrassing, and he was still bitter about the whole affair. But she didn't need to know that part.

Nyakkat held up a talon of her own, reluctant. "Do…do you mind if I…?"

"By all means," he said, holding his arm out. "It's long since healed up and I hired the best surgeons. The new scales line up so well with the original I doubt you could find the scar."

She took his arm in her talons, stroking her fingers and thumb down the wrist like a professional masseuse. "Hmm, all feeling back?"

"I had phantom pains for a few months," Sarsuk said as suavely as he could muster. He tried not to tremble around the lips as she touched him. *Play it cool. Act like this is normal for you.* "But it's gone now," he lied. "Doctors said I healed remarkably well."

"It must have been a terrible ordeal."

"Oh it was," Sarsuk said, trying not to bite down at the thought. "But one soldiers through it. Line of duty and all."

"Don't be so modest." Nyakkat ran a claw up his arm to the inside of his elbow, and he twitched as she touched there. An unexpected shot of pleasure ran through his hearts, despite the ache. He still had fiery nerves up to his shoulder; it had been a decade and nothing had removed them entirely. The pains weren't crippling by any means, but they made it troublesome to walk whenever they flared up.

Sarsuk smiled anyway.

"I think I see the seam…" she said, flashing a devious grin.

"What!" Sarsuk said.

"Right here, isn't it?" She brushed a claw across his elbow, turning it to the light. "Amputated to the elbow so they could replace the entire forearm. You have a line right here, greener than the upper arm. Near perfect delineation for a whole meter."

Sarsuk pinched his lips together and pulled his arm back to his cushion. He felt like an idiot. That point just under his elbow was almost impossible to notice, especially since it was inconvenient to look at without a mirror. But he'd hoped she wouldn't spot it.

"What?" She said. "Sarsuk, there's nothing wrong with having a scar."

In some sense, she was right. But despite what he said, Sarsuk didn't see himself as some battle-damaged soldier, it was just too crude and unrefined. He was one of the pretty ones! Beautiful and flawless! Or at least he should have been.

"It's not…it's not the scar," Sarsuk lied. "Can we talk about something else, please? How about you? You haven't said much about yourself."

She gave him a concerned look. "I like it."

Sarsuk blinked. "You do?"

"I mean, soldiers have always attracted me," Nyakkat said. "Sometimes I think Krakuntec is too much of a paradise. All we ever do is lounge and gossip far away from the war."

If you have the money to do so, Sarsuk thought.

"Working in space, that's different. It's fascinating! It's almost…" She rolled her shoulders. "…dangerous."

Sarsuk squeezed his talon tight and he cast his eyes at his elbow. His lips parted into a broad grin.

* * *

The Festival of the Last Chorus ran all week, though Sarsuk could only manage enough time off work to attend one evening, with Nyakkat at his side. Fairy lights decorated the park between the overpriced booths, most sponsored by Trellis Corporation or Stella Vista Incorporated, which gave away just how expensive the stalls fees were. Nyakkat was most interested in the musical performance at the amphitheater. Kharmanuk was in the city and she insisted on a live rendition of *That Which The Last Chorus Played*. Sarsuk couldn't get them closer than the outer row. She seemed happy enough.

Somehow, she ate a slab of roasted hikkfowl without getting her claws or mouth dirty, then with barely a glance, tossed the roasting spit into a garbage can from fifty meters away. Sarsuk, meanwhile, had to wash himself in the brook feeding into Chyerno Lake just to get the char crumbs and oil off his face. Rental boats filled the lake end-to-end, all still too expensive to take Nyakkat out on for even an hour.

"Sarsuk, would you cheer up?" She said—not accusingly—as they crossed over the concrete bridge that connected the west side of the park. "It's festival time and you're acting like it's paining you."

That was the entire problem. This date was going far better than he'd hoped. She was *interested* in him. And he still had work in the morning! He could at least tell her that.

"Just work stuff," he said. "Sorry."

"You need to get it out of your head when you're home," she said, encouraging him forward with a wrap of a tail around the nape

of his neck. "I know it's hard for people to stop calculating all the time. Have you tried meditation?"

Sarsuk scoffed, then regretted scoffing at her suggestion. "Doesn't sound like my style."

"It might surprise you," she said. "I go to this parlor downtown where they combine that with deep tissue massage and aromatherapy—"

"Oh, I suppose you pay a lot for them to drop hot stones on your back."

She considered this and tilted her head. "I never thought about the cost."

Sarsuk bit his lip. *No, of course not.* That was the way it was for krakun of means. If you have to ask…

"But I could take you there sometime. Oh, our next date, perhaps!"

Next date…

"Perhaps," he said, perking up.

He lifted his foretalons up to lean on the railing on the bridge, just as another round of fireworks lit up the sky, their smoke obscuring the moon Hyulda.

Nyakkat leaned on his shoulder. Sarsuk did his best to not appear so aroused at her closeness.

"It's getting late," he said.

"Going to invite me over?" she asked.

His hearts seized in his chest and gut. "I…"

Damn, I want to. But I can't afford a reprimand or a paycut!

"I wouldn't want to take advantage," he lied.

"Oh pah," she said with a trill. "I'd like to see you try. Come on! You won't offend me."

"I mean, honestly…" Sarsuk sighed. "It's work. I would love to ask you home, but…"

"Oh," she said. "Can you talk about it, or is it one of those high security things?"

"They've packed my mornings full of meetings," Sarsuk said. "Have one compromised document, and now we must rearrange the fleet movements for the next five hundred years. They overreact to any little surprise like a bunch of baying whelps."

"You've had more than one meeting?" she asked. "Sounds like they should have dealt with such a minor thing in a single discussion."

"I wish, but it's so much more challenging in practice when the fleet covers so much space," he said. "And we have to memorize the fleet patterns so that nothing gets recorded. We can't spread the meetings out over a year or two. We have to hammer down the new plan within a month or they're afraid someone will take advantage of the situation. I'm barely even a part of the decision-making for that, but they expect me to make a report anyhow."

"It sounds like an opportunity to get noticed," she said, yawning as she rested on him. "Maybe you'll impress them."

Sarsuk snorted. "More like they want a paper trail so they know who to blame when things go wrong again."

Sarsuk wondered if he should talk so much about work, but he said nothing outside of what anyone with fleet responsibilities would face. Besides, he liked talking to Nyakkat, and he liked smelling the tikkwood fragrance she wore.

"I don't want to keep you from work; it sounds important."

"But—"

Nyakkat lifted her head and met Sarsuk's eyes. Hers seemed to glow with marvelous heat.

"How about this," she said. "I promise, next time, I'll come over to your place after. Then we can do…whatever."

Sarsuk stammered over his words, but didn't need to say anything as Nyakkat nuzzled him under his chin.

"And a little taste of what to expect, big guy," she said, dragging a claw up the inside of his thigh.

Sarsuk tried to suppress a stupid grin. "I-I should be done with these meetings in three weeks."

"Three weeks," she said. "Massage, then your place."

"O-okay. I'll hold you to it."

"I'm counting on it."

Three.

Nyakkat…" Sarsuk sang to himself in the vague approximation of a showtune he had once heard as a whelp. "Gonna become her loving mate, Nyakkat…gonna nip her up her neck and make her shiver, gonna have a clutch and we'll be happy, Nyakkat…" The front door of the apartment building unlocked and slipped open for him.

It had been a good two hundred years since his last successful date. In fact, he wasn't certain if a date of his had ever gone that well. Farryhsal's departure had been too painful, and to think of her still infuriated him. He would rather forget she ever existed now that he had Nyakkat.

As his front door swung open and he considered the look of his place, he felt a twinge of self-consciousness. Steel-fiber laminate flooring in the kitchen? How tacky! Plain solid-painted walls? Boring! And what was that weird smell in the guest bedroom? Unacceptable! The place was clean, but clean would not cut it anymore.

It was a boon that he'd missed inviting her over! He'd have recalled too late how terrible his place looked. Any of this stammering, "Oh, no, see, my apartment is being fumigated for sourang," she would see for the obvious lie it was.

He'd have loved to go see her place. But he didn't think to ask her. Maybe he should message her now.

No, you said your place, so she's coming here!

He sighed and, as he lay on the living room couch, took his mobile com to call a consultant. While he waited for someone to respond, he checked his bank account. *₲25,506.*

It wasn't a lot of golds, just enough of a cushion should he need to move out at a moment's notice and couldn't sell the place fast enough. Not that it would have been a good idea. This was the best apartment he could get near the FennWorks Elevator, the most cost-effective way of commuting to space.

But he'd long since grown to hate the job. He *hated* geroo. And he hated, looking at his email inbox, that work was still exploding every moment he wasn't there.

Presence required 0600, face-to-face commissioner meeting aboard Fheighr-Alpha in the sensitive discussion room. All commissioners required to attend and telepresence is not an option.

Sarsuk groaned. They moved the schedule up an hour! It was already 2200, how could he get any sleep tonight if he needed to be up at 0400 to make it to the elevator in time? Why did this have to happen after his first date night in six years? *They had better provide breakfast.*

Almost seven major-years without a promotion…

A tone sounded from the mobile com and a blue-green krakun appeared on the screen. Sarsuk flicked it to his broadcast monitor on the far wall to make better eye contact with the associate.

"Hello, thank you for calling Fashion Elite!" said the krakun. "Please state the consultation you desire for—"

"Is this a robot?" Sarsuk asked, peering at what had to be a computer-generated face. It was so hard to tell at first glance.

"If by robot you mean automated customer assistance manager, then yes," said the robot.

"I want a real consultant," Sarsuk said. "I don't want an AI giving me life advice." Whether it was a true AI or a glorified dialogue tree, Sarsuk didn't care.

The krakun smiled and turned his head. "Live consultants charge an additional fifty golds per minute." He said it in the same cheery tone, but the delivery had become almost sinister.

"Automated it is," Sarsuk said. "I'm looking for advice on improving my living space."

"I can see that," the robot said.

The robot's brazen comment would have appalled Sarsuk if it hadn't been so honest. He scoffed in annoyance instead.

"Please approve Fashion Elite to access any additional device cameras you require. Then, as directed, point the camera into all walls and corners of your living space, capturing the full height of each wall and item of furniture."

Sarsuk did as instructed, the whole process feeling slow and boring. He should have just been able to give them apartment layout plans from some database. His home computer should have kept track of every stray item in his apartment with no need to catalog them. What good was this technology of convenience when he had to do so much manually anyhow?

"Excellent!" The robot returned Sarsuk to his living room. "We have rated your living space as: dingy."

"You're doing this on purpose, aren't you?" Sarsuk sneered.

"Oh? Let's begin here," it said, pulling up a picture of Sarsuk's bed. "When was the last time you replaced these bedsheets?" It zoomed in as far as Sarsuk's camera resolution went, which was too far. Plenty to see the individual fibers had stretched, frayed and become uneven.

Sarsuk opened his mouth and closed it again.

"Go on," the robot said. "This consultation is confidential and for your benefit, remember."

"…About one major-year," Sarsuk said.

"And the mattress?" a wire overlay appeared on the bed, showing how large of a divot Sarsuk had made.

"…Not since I moved in. But I can't afford a new mattress all the time!"

"I am getting this impression this will be a budget consultation. To save golds, you can, for instance, swap out your guest bedroom mattress for your own, given the one in the guest bedroom appears to have never been touched."

Sarsuk's jaw hung open at this computer's audacity.

"So, let's talk specific improvements. What is your budget for this project?"

"Sixteen thousand," Sarsuk said.

The robot huffed, hemmed, hawed, and glanced to the side. "Hrm, well… I don't…"

Sarsuk sighed. "Twenty thousand."

"Better. Given your hue, your preferred decorating scheme's primary color will be black."

"I don't like black!" Sarsuk said. "It's too moody. And it reminds me of work. Can we go with ultraviolet? That's a nice natural color."

"We do not recommend ultraviolet for your complexion," the consultant said.

Sarsuk grumbled, but he didn't have much recourse. They were the cheapest service in the directory…

Four.

The military police all wore smooth black masks covering their faces from the tip of their snouts to the base of their horns. Their lack of expression made for an unsettling atmosphere. Despite Sarsuk having known many such police in his time, the moment those masks came on it was like they became different krakun, almost robotic.

In the classical sense, at least. Not like the robot he had to deal with last night. *Dead gods* was he overtired.

The huge dark red MP tapped the small chute next to him. "Your computer goes in the holding bin. Please wait for the scanner."

Sarsuk yanked on the computer around his neck until the magnetic clasp came off, and he tossed it in the bin. This was the most annoying part of the meetings. No matter what notes he had on that thing, he'd have to recreate them from scratch inside the secure room. That took more practice than he'd given himself time for.

"Come on, Sarsuk, we don't have all morning," Saqqadr said. How fortunate he was to be just ahead of his boss in line. He was already cranky from his lack of sleep and her prattling wasn't helping his headache.

Sarsuk sighed as the white lamp lit up over the scanner door and he stepped through. An agonizingly slow green beam swept down over his entire body. Sarsuk did his best not to nod off, and failed. The MP rapped on the window to the booth to usher him along. Sarsuk shook himself so he wouldn't pass out while standing up.

"This had better not have made me late," he muttered as he emerged on the other side into a similar wide hall with more rope barriers. "I had to get up early enough as—"

He couldn't finish his thoughts, though, as another MP, dark blue, mask fitted around the huge ugly horn on his nose, seized him and groped Sarsuk under his forearms. Sarsuk yelped and flailed, but knew better than to struggle, and ended up falling into the belly of the MP. The huge krakun wrapped his arm around Sarsuk's neck as his gloved claws swept under the crags of Sarsuk's armpits.

"Manual pat-downs?" Sarsuk grunted. "What is this, the atomic age?"

"Just an increase in precautions," said the red MP. "We are re-assessing our security procedures for weak points. In the meantime, we're reverting to older methods."

Yeah, you won't admit that the security breach was your fault, or that your scanners aren't perfect. Always a work in progress, but you sell it like you're infallible…

Sarsuk squeaked as the dark blue MP's claws dipped under his crotch. *Not there, not there, not there!* Oh, but the blue MP's gloved claws went there. Sarsuk dug his own claws into the shallow carpet pile of the station floor and grit his teeth, both trying to pull himself away and forcing himself not to move.

"I don't deserve this treatment! I've been loyal to Planetary Acquisitions for years!"

"That just makes you a contractor," said the blue MP. "You're subject to the same procedure as any civilian with security clearance." Those dirty claws of his raked over where Nyakkat had touched him.

Sarsuk grumbled. They'd always blame the contractors. The government employees weren't subject to these procedures! How else would these goons get their jollies? At least he took comfort knowing Saqqadr would be subject to the same invasion of privacy.

"What the—!" Sarsuk exclaimed. Saqqadr walked out of the scanner booth without so much as the pale white MP standing at the other side of the hall touching her once.

"She has pre-screening clearance," said the red MP.

"What does that even mean! She pays more to not get groped, and then can walk in with as many bugs as she wants?"

"Is that an accusation, Sarsuk?" Saqqadr said, turning in the empty part of the hall. She took pleasure in seeing them torture Sarsuk like this, if the creepy broad smile was any sign. "The War Authority has researched me enough to trust I would not walk in with a bug at all."

She was practically *laughing* at his misfortune! Sure, she wasn't literally laughing, but the tone implied how little concern she had for her employee of so many centuries. It was constant, it was grating, and it was getting on his damned nerves.

He blurted out, "I bet one of your slut boyfriends could plant a bug on that fat ass of yours and nobody could find it!"

Sarsuk immediately regretted saying it. Out loud, at least.

Saqqadr's expression dropped. "Hmm. I was about to tell them they violated you enough, but now I'm not so sure."

"Hey!" Sarsuk exclaimed as she continued down the hallway without him. "I didn't mean… Saqqadr, come back!"

* * *

Sarsuk shifted uneasily behind the table with the other low-ranking commissioners. The company bigwigs, including Saqqadr, sat at their own table with their own discussions just within earshot. At the head of the table sat Commandant Chekohinok, an ancient silver krakun who had so many major-years under his claws, he'd lost much of his natural color. He would act as the War Authority's liaison for these weeks of meetings.

With as little as he moved, Sarsuk could have sworn the commandant fell asleep with his eyes open. He turned to make a crude remark under his breath to one of his tablemates, but then realized that the doors to the secure room had shut and locked with one commissioner still absent.

"Where is Commissioner Orensan?" Sarsuk asked out loud, shifting again. Several of the other commissioners his rank expressed the same question. Until that moment, everyone presumed the young and frail krakun had just risked coming in late again.

Saqqadr, lying nearest the commissioners' table, turned her head to address them. "It would be better if we didn't speak about Orensan."

Sarsuk didn't like the sound of that.

"Naturally," Sarsuk said. "You always hated him."

Sarsuk knew he'd regret his remarks, and the ones previous, the moment that Saqqadr had him alone, but so long as there were other krakun present, there was a limit to how much aggression she could properly express. And he figured, she was going to bully him anyway, he might as well work in his snipes while he had freedom to speak.

Ellyandris, a high-crested bright blue krakun that Sarsuk would have considered handsome if he were even a little inclined, and the only commissioner at the table he could call a friend, shushed Sarsuk.

"We're talking about major security breaches," Ellyandris said. "For all we know, Orensan could have sold information to our enemies. Or Founder of Worlds Technologies."

Sarsuk snorted. "Yeah, and perhaps they'd be willing to buy next month's menu plan from the cafeteria. How much do you think he sold it for, and was it enough to get *two* stone rolls out of the vending machine?"

Commandant Chekohinok spoke. His voice startled Sarsuk enough he jumped from his cushion.

"I will say this once to this room so there will be no further rumors," the commandant said. His voice crashed about like waves on the ocean, terrifying and hypnotic. "After the recent investigation, we found Orensan to be a common element in the recent data leak, and so the War Authority has taken him for further questioning."

"It is unlikely he will return," Saqqadr said to finish the point. "So put him out of your mind."

Sarsuk blinked. Orensan, gone, just like that? The War Authority couldn't have been *that* concerned. Sure, the gate ships had an instant path right back to Krakuntec Prime, but those ships were in the middle of vaguely-to-un-controlled space, often hundreds of years away from any direct contact. The company could always shut off their side of the gates should they be compromised. Loss of material was on the company's head, not the War Authority's.

Right?

Under his breath, he groused to Ellyandris. "That's not how leaks work. Anything that Orensan would have known, so would Saqqadr, but they let her off the hook."

"I'm sure there was more to the investigation than just that," Ellyandris said. "Now hush, before—"

"Oh, are we not done with the discussion?" Saqqadr snapped her head back, her eyes on Sarsuk again. "Sarsuk, you seem talkative this morning, why don't you give your presentation first?"

Sarsuk swallowed.

* * *

Saqqadr didn't say a word as Sarsuk gave his slapdash presentation on the operational schedules of his specific portion of the geroo fleet. He'd done his research—he had no choice—on the risk assessment of changing course plans when several such gate ships hovered around the turek's infamous Hole Facility. Since they had no idea *which* fleet movements the breach had compromised, they had to continue on the assumption they all had been.

"So what you're saying," Saqqadr said, tapping her talon down on the low table, "Is that we'd have to cede most of Qwan Sector to the turek."

"N-not in so many words," Sarsuk said. "But the turek may already know we have four such gate ships approaching within fifteen light years of their outpost. We will have to change course or risk significant material loss. But regardless of how we react in the Qwan Sector, the best we can do is delay passing within that fifteen light year range for two hundred years, plus or minus a major-year. I ran the astrometrics through—"

"But you are talking about a hundred star systems!" Saqqadr snipped, fangs showing as she rapped on the table. "Besides our primary business, the War Authority needs data on those systems."

"I am pointing out the cost-benefit exchange!" Sarsuk snarled. "Or do you believe losses to turek hurt less than losses to the lio? Because if this was a lio outpost you would not object." Sarsuk stomped toward the conference table.

"Sarsuk, propriety!" said Ellyandris. He placed a claw on Sarsuk's chest, as if to stop him from marching across the table to strangle Saqqadr. "You're speaking to your boss."

Sarsuk was running on too little sleep. Besides being tired, they'd frustrated him to the point of illness. He stopped and let himself fall back on his haunches. Ellyandris nudged Sarsuk up again and away from the table, all the way to the corner of the room. The committee of importants returned to discussing options, other sectors, and so on.

The entire station had the same false windows as their gate ships had. Tall screens projected images captured by outward-facing cameras. This was a silent room attached to the space station, enclosed in such a way that no one outside could capture any sound, not even from the trick of shining a laser on the hull or windows to capture vibrations.

"Are you mad?" asked Ellyandris. "They'll never accept what you're telling them."

"I am making my case known," Sarsuk said, sulking. "I need to convince them I took this seriously. I don't expect her to accept the proposal. I don't want her to accept the proposal!"

Ellyandris blinked. "Why not?"

"Because if they choose my proposal, then its success or failure is my responsibility! There's *countless* ways to redeploy the fleet. They just want someone's tail to pin to the plan, so if it goes wrong, there's someone to blame for it. That's why they make us do this."

"But they are your ships, too," Ellyandris said. "Surely you don't want to suffer property loss either."

"I don't care," Sarsuk said. "It's lose-lose-lose. Either I'm blamed if something goes wrong, or the turek destroy my ships and I'm blamed for not being more cautious, or I have to keep working this gods-be-damned job."

"Sarsuk, over here," said Saqqadr. Sarsuk groaned, turned and sat down at the foot of the conference table.

"We have accepted your proposal, with modifications," she said. "We will hand it over to the War Authority, but we expect that the alternative will be to send automatic probes into the systems we must avoid. So, nice work."

Sarsuk grumbled under his breath. "Damn."

"What was that?"

"I said, thank you, Overseer."

Five.

"So, what do you think?" Sarsuk asked as he marched partway into his apartment, pivoting his back end around in a sweeping gesture.

Nyakkat tilted her head at the look of the place. Gold detailing inched up the dark teal walls, with matching ever-so-elegant touches on the new kitchen fridge and countertop. It ran between every room, with slight color changes from there to the sitting room to the bedroom. Matching his own color scheme but in reverse intensity was considered indelicate, but viable.

"It's smaller than I expected," she said.

Of course. Sarsuk tried not to cringe.

"My apologies," he said, as he sprung open the fridge with his tail. "But proximity to work was a most considerable factor. When one spends so much time in space, it's hard to justify a large apartment planetside." He pulled out a tall decanter, placing it on the table, a polished stone-slab table with a mirror finish.

"Now though, knowing such a charming female, I should go back in time and tell myself to find accommodations more befitting her. Redmead?" he asked, producing two drinking bowls.

"Oh please," Nyakkat said, stepping forward and taking the bowl under her claw, stopping Sarsuk when he reached halfway. She sipped as Sarsuk downed a full bowl. It was the savory kind, with a strong bitter start but a thick, rich finish, which he clearly couldn't afford.

"Oh!" Nyakkat said. "Pilzarian!"

"More?"

She held the bowl out. Sarsuk filled it up.

"I love this stuff when you scrape burnt meat tips into it," she giggled as though she were already tipsy. "Oh it's heavenly when it gets smoky and there's a thin layer of hot oil still cooling on the surface."

"I didn't prepare—" Sarsuk started, feeling dumb for not having thought of it.

"It's fine!" she said. "We've eaten…it's not appropriate for afters either, but I'll take it!"

Sarsuk suppressed a groan. He was making mistakes left and right. Then he noticed a slight trickle down her chin as she drank, and he smiled to himself. Producing a napkin from the nearby drawer, he daubed the cloth up her neck to the edge of her lip. Nyakkat grinned and swirled her claw in his bowl teasingly.

He shouldn't have drunk anything. He was exhausted. But it wouldn't have been proper to just pass a drink to a lady and not share. Especially if he wanted to bed her.

And he desperately wanted to bed her.

"So, your meetings went well?" she asked.

"Hmm? Oh, yeah, yeah," he said. "I can't talk about them, of course."

"Of course."

He realized he shouldn't even have mentioned how many days the meetings went on. Well, there were still more in the morning, despite what he'd told her. But he didn't care at this point. He wanted her here, and he would not wait another three weeks to have her.

"Would you care to recline for a while?" he asked, gesturing toward the sitting room, terrified his politeness came across as cloying. Though on second consideration, perhaps he wasn't forward enough.

"Actually," she said, brushing a claw along his cheek, "Would you mind ever so much if I stepped into your shower?"

Sarsuk blinked. "Really?"

"It's been a long day and I haven't had time to wash up."

"I couldn't tell," he said. That morning he had scrubbed himself raw and clogged the shower drain with scale residue. The cleaning crew had better have attended to that or he'd pop heads.

"How about you wait for me in the bedroom…"

"Take all the time you need," he blurted. As much as he wanted to show off the new stonework false fire pit, he was more than happy to skip to the end. He couldn't help himself; as she sauntered into the bathroom, he glanced at Nyakkat's rear end, trying his best to catch her scent from that side, though he only smelled her perfume. It would have been a shame to wash that all away, but he was minutes away from touching her, so who cared about the scent?

Swooning, he launched himself into the bedroom, adjusting his position on the firm mattress over and over, trying to find the best position to meet her in.

And he yawned, surprising himself with its ferocity. Ugh, work keeping him up so much, and he still had work in the morning too. Even with the nap he caught while doing his rounds on the *Boulder Meadow II*—the geroo had such awful names for their ships—barely made a dent in his fatigue. He'd nearly fallen asleep during the massage Nyakkat had taken him to for their date as well…*dead gods*, it felt good to get that tension out of his system.

But he was in bed now, listening to the rush of the shower in the adjacent room, reminding him of the massage. All he needed to do was place his head on his pillow, and—

* * *

Sarsuk awoke to light pouring in the window. He was alone in bed.

"*Dammit!*" he yelled at the room. "*Dammit, dammit, dammit!*"

He caught himself before he raged and marched around the apartment to see if Nyakkat was still there. When he couldn't find her, not even in the bathroom, he resumed his swearing spree.

"*Damnation to every god!*" he screamed. He huffed, turning his thoughts over in his head. He didn't even remember falling asleep. He couldn't have been that tired! It was only 2200 when he'd returned home with her.

What time was it now? He checked his mobile com.

"Oh-seven-thirty!" he exclaimed. Oh...this was trouble.

He forced himself to not break the furniture; half of everything in the apartment was new and he had a couple hundred payments yet to go. He took several long, deep breaths and opened the email client, all the while probing his brain for a suitable work excuse.

He found a message from Nyakkat.

Sarsuk, I'm so sorry! I would have remained, but I couldn't stay overnight anyhow, and you didn't respond when I tried to wake you...and well, I got to thinking. I need to tell you the truth before this goes any further. Tonight, Leeward Dock in the old city at 1500 or whenever you can make it.

Sarsuk's hearts beat out of sync for a moment as he read the rest of the letter. Truth? He did not understand. She'd kept her personal life close to her chest, yes, but krakun did that as a matter of course; nobody wanted to admit if their living situation was less than ideal. How was one supposed to move up in the world if they didn't engage in the necessary lies?

That she admitted to this...something was wrong.

He would make that rendezvous and did not care what the company thought.

Six.

Sarsuk spotted her, though she wore an opaque rain cape in the drizzly weather. That still-vibrant tail of hers poked out from underneath as she sat with her forearms draped over the concrete wall of the pier, looking out at the misty gray bay.

"So what is this about?" Sarsuk asked, approaching.

Nyakkat pulled back the hood so it rested on her horns, and the mist of the rain scattered over her face. She said, "Didn't you think it odd I was so insistent you don't come home with me?"

"We've only had two dates together," Sarsuk said.

"I know. I didn't want to…listen, it's hard to talk about this."

Sarsuk looked back and forth along the dock. Krakun congregated under an awning some hundred meters away, then others even farther out. "Nobody's here but me."

"I don't want word getting out."

"Nyakkat, I was so exhausted last night I overslept. That resulted in a reprimand this morning. They docked my pay! Again! So if you have something to tell me…"

After a long pause, she said, "My family's been out of golds for a long while. Scandal. My grandfather's held onto the estate for the last three major-years out of inertia, but it's been slipping out of his claws."

"Who's your grandfather?" Sarsuk asked.

"I don't want to say," she said. "My real name's not even Nyakkat. I've been using that so people don't recognize me."

Sarsuk was uncertain how someone of her striking color could avoid being recognized unless one or more parts of her gradient were false color. Damned good false color, though.

"What's your real name?" he asked.

She stared toward the water. "I'd like to tell you someday. But I've been considering keeping Nyakkat."

"How come?"

"Because I need out of my family's affairs," she said. "My entire life is being dragged down with that of my family, and it's been so prolonged. But I don't have the resources to get out of here. Just a plan."

"What is it?" Sarsuk asked.

"I acquired a small cottage on Krakuntec II," she said. "A village called Mesmar on Sweet Water Island, near Corsicova. It's tiny and doesn't have much in the way of modern conveniences—electricity, network—that's about it, not even sure it has running water. Single room. But aside of hurricane season, it's beautiful. Deep glass sand all around, ocean view facing the west so you can watch the starfall near every day. It's a kilometer away from this tacky swim shop that looks like an old shipwreck, but there's a restaurant attached with the best fish fry I've ever tasted. Such intense saltwater flavor." She sighed. "I've been trying to keep up with the property taxes but it's so hard when I'm not there; they charge you double for leaving a residence unattended. And I'm two years behind as it is. I want to just go there right now but I have nothing ready."

Sarsuk lowered his brow. "Why didn't you go the moment you bought the place?"

"It was two and a half major-years ago," she said. "At the time I supposed it to be a small summer thing. I wasn't ready to just upend my life and go work as an attendant in a tourist trap. I've gotten used to a particular style of living, and the thought of throwing it away scared me. Now I wish I did."

No. No, he'd heard this before. This was a grift. This *had* to be a grift.

And she's so cute, too.

"How much are the property taxes?" Sarsuk asked, playing along for the moment.

She turned to him. "About twenty thousand golds now. But—"

Sarsuk *knew* money was going to be a part of this. He didn't have a bank account worth mentioning anymore, just a few hundred golds after all those renovations that barely added to the value of his home. That money he might as well have set fire. But if she wanted the money, then she would expect his next words to be, "oh darling, I will sell all I have to see you safe." So he said it, calmly, but tried to refrain from sounding like a cheesy serial.

"That's at least as much as my apartment costs, especially with the improvements I've made as of late. I could sell it off. It might take a year or two, but it shouldn't be too long a delay to get the money. I mean…if you'd have me there with you."

She turned away again as if to consider. "We don't know each other," she said. "I shouldn't have obligations toward a male I've barely met."

"No obligations!" Sarsuk promised. Though, if she were sincere, he imagined a make-up night, or many, for the missed sex.

He *wanted* this to be sincere. He wanted to be wrong that this was just a set-up because she was just so beautiful and charming and *nice to him.*

I offered the money, now say you'll take it, he thought at her. *Prove you are what I think you are.*

"Really?" she said. "You'd upend your entire life and throw away a stable job just for me? No, that won't work. You'll run out of golds."

"I—" He sighed. If he really were to follow her, hypothetically, would he give up the job? Maybe his golds would stretch farther on Krakuntec II. "The commute will be longer, sure. But I don't have to give up the job. I could make a connection from Krakuntec II to Krakuntec Prime every morning; that should only add an hour onto the trip."

"Sweet Water Island isn't anywhere near a space elevator," she said.

"Two hours!" he said.

"Two hours there and back. Plus Krakuntec II's local time being an hour short of standard time every day would erode your sanity."

"I don't know!" Sarsuk threw his talons up. "Okay, maybe I will have to abandon the job, but I want this. I don't want to be commissioner to a bunch of ingrates anymore. I've been sick of the job for two centuries now. They promised opportunity for advancement and I've had nothing. I'm nearly eighty-three major-years old! I'm not getting any younger."

The worst part was, Sarsuk was telling the truth. It was only his sense of self-preservation that kept him going, as being left jobless and on public housing would be worse for his reputation than the meager amount he'd scrounged together as it was. There weren't enough jobs! He'd been lucky to get this one! As awful as it was, *it was a job.*

And for over a major-year, he'd been looking for an excuse to just drop it all and leave. But not for this. *Not this.*

Nyakkat cast her eyes to the pavement.

Come on, you made the pitch, Sarsuk thought. *Ask for the money.*

"Okay," she said. "When I'm able to move, I'll get a shuttle ticket to depart from Fheighr-Alpha Station. When I have it, I'll send you a copy so you can get a shuttle ticket too. Hopefully it's not too long. But it might be a while…"

He blinked. No "send it to my bank account"? No "I'll get the tickets for you"? No "Let's leave right now"?

Was he wrong? Was this real?

"O-okay," Sarsuk said.

Nyakkat pulled him closer and kissed him, clinging to him and nipping down his neck. He inhaled sharply, surprised at the public display, but for the moment he didn't care. He pulled her close, held her tight, and tried not to think *too* hard about how much he still wanted to have sex with her, even with her claws scratching him around his inner thigh.

When she pulled herself away and departed, Sarsuk waved after her.

He was certain it was his own latent sense of worthlessness and insecurity telling him he didn't deserve someone like Nyakkat. But he couldn't shake the feeling that this was a con.

"Dammit!" he muttered to the ocean. "If she gave me a straight clue to her motive, I could dismiss her…"

Or follow her.

He pondered Nyakkat's story as he trudged back up through the old town between tall towers of steel and rough-hewn stone, which housed endless tacky tourist shops and gallerias. Stopping at a small cafe just across the avenue from the parking deck, Sarsuk pulled his mobile com from his neck band and checked map data from Krakuntec II for the small village on Sweet Water Island. Just a kilometer away from a shipwreck-looking shop, down a small unmarked path just off the main road, he found a single room cottage standing on a thick frame above the tide water.

That just proved she didn't invent the place whole-cloth. But did that mean he could trust her? She didn't ask for his money; in fact he'd only pledged it, he had not produced it or sent it to some mysterious account of hers. She hadn't demanded he quit his job, give up his life. And why should he?

There was all those golds he spent on decorations. But that was just the cost of pursuing a lovely female, wasn't it? That part was a scam he didn't dispute. He still would have dove headfirst into it whether or not he saw it coming.

But at least it was all still his own. So far, she'd taken little but some of his time.

Seven.

For months, Sarsuk didn't hear much from Nyakkat. Every so often she sent a message with an update, but as Sarsuk returned to his work, he wondered if she expected him to take initiative. He would not fall for this unless she proved she was legitimate. He'd poured his savings into this apartment for her! He promised to sell it all off for her!

And he still pined for her all the time. He listed his apartment provisionally for-sale simply to lines someone up to take it the moment he decided if he would vacate. The waiting list grew long and impatient.

Then, one year and two months later, when he'd nearly decided he'd give up and return to his old rut, he was jolted awake by a particularly loud message tone. Not from Nyakkat, but from his boss.

THERE WILL BE AN ALL-COMMISSIONERS MEETING IN THE FHEIGHR-ALPHA SENSITIVE ROOM IN FOUR HOURS. BE PREPARED FOR THOROUGH EXAMINATION ON ARRIVAL. TARDINESS WILL BE PUNISHED.

For a while, Sarsuk had imagined he'd seen the end of early morning meetings. Glancing at the time on his mobile com—0340— he groaned, rolled over, and pondered whether it was worth it. It was his job. Nyakkat hadn't contacted him in four months. He needed to get up and get going on the assumption she wasn't coming back.

Even in the early mornings, the drive was painfully slow. Sarsuk napped in the autocab until it shook him awake and dumped him out at the elevator station. Sarsuk groaned, picked himself up off the pavement, and yawned. He flashed his daily pass to the sensor and waited for the next car, his head drooping among the sea of dozens and dozens of other krakun.

Nnng, should have just sprung for a direct flight, Sarsuk thought, trying to keep his eyes open. *Still don't have my savings back up though...still paying off creditors...stupid females...*

The gates opened and he crammed inside. The cab lurched and sped up to extraordinary speed in a matter of moments. The G-force only made Sarsuk feel more fatigued, like he could lie on the floor and nap right then. So he glanced here and there about the cab to find something to focus on.

There were an awful lot of military police on this trip. They all wore the eye-concealing face masks and black neck bands. At least a dozen congregated in the far corner, though Sarsuk only noted one or two during previous trips. Maybe he'd arrived early enough for their shift rotation.

On reaching the top, the doors opened and Sarsuk staggered out. He was an hour early for the meeting, which was fine with him. He made his way to the station cafe and bought a giant draught of blackmead to wake himself up. It only gave him palpitations while he nearly nodded off in the adjacent washroom.

This only killed twenty minutes. He didn't want to fall asleep in the terminal and miss the meeting, so he went in early. He took the fast sidewalk toward the sensitive discussion room, unclasped the necklace to hand his mobile com to security...

...When he saw fifty MPs swarming around the security checkpoint. He'd never seen over *four*.

Recalling the "manual search" treatment they had subjected him to *last* time, he made an about-face at the end of the sidewalk and retreated down the hallway.

This is…normal, right? If there was a breach, security must once again be embarrassed and is overcompensating for their weaknesses. They—

He collided with Ellyandris.

"Hey, what's the rush?" Ellyandris said, righting Sarsuk before he fell over. "Secure room's that way."

"I uh, well—" Sarsuk stammered. He glanced back behind him to the end of the hall. So many black facemasks.

"What, didn't you hear?" Ellyandris said.

"I got the message. Saqqadr's pissed and is taking it out on us."

"I mean the news. There was another data leak. It was public, all over the broadcasts."

Sarsuk sighed. "So…we go back to early morning meetings for another three months, invasive checks…"

"Here."

Sarsuk froze. "Here, as in…"

Ellyandris bobbed his head like the prospect excited him. "They traced the leaks right back to this room. So someone in our meetings within the past year and change had passed on classified information."

Sarsuk blinked. He looked back at the gaggle of military police. Right then, two walked back toward the main concourse directly at Sarsuk.

Ellyandris didn't look nervous in the slightest. A little chatty perhaps, but unconcerned about the implications of his words. "That still covers three months worth of commissioner meetings. Several dozen krakun to interrogate. But at least they've narrowed it down…maybe they can put an end to these leaks."

"Wh-what *leaked*, though?" Sarsuk asked, feeling his spines stand up as those MPs approached behind him. He forced himself not to turn and look.

Ellyandris shrugged with his talons open. "If I knew, I'd tell you. Would make the next week easier, what with yet another fleet redeployment proposal. At this rate, we'd just be better off choosing a random direction at each star system arrival, am I right?"

This isn't *just a firing offense, is it?* Sarsuk thought. *You don't bring up fifty MPs if the leaked information wasn't the War Authority's own intelligence.*

"Sarsuk?" Ellyandris asked. "You all right?"

"I'm underslept," Sarsuk said. "I need to make a call."

"Oh, okay," the bright blue krakun moved out of the way just as Sarsuk hurried past him. "Don't be late again! Saqqadr was serious this time!"

Right where the concourse opened into sitting areas and shops, Sarsuk stopped and peeked back down the hall to ensure none of the military police spotted his unusual behavior and followed him. He froze when two more MPs approached from the opposite direction of the ones at his tail. On meeting, the four gestured with their foretalons. Was it at him? No, they were gesturing at the blackmead shop at the other side of the hall.

Of course.

Of course.

Shoving himself in a private call booth, Sarsuk fumbled with his mobile com and dialed for Nyakkat. These booths were so small! His rear end and tail still stuck out the back. The lockable secure call booths ten meters away cost golds per minute. What if someone heard him? It was sound-blocking, wasn't it? Nobody would overhear him, right?

It didn't matter. Nyakkat didn't pick up. He got an automated response. "The code you entered has been disconnected."

"For how long?" He asked, worried he'd lost contact with her. She hadn't yet closed the deal! Why drop contact with someone so infatuated with her?

"This code is not in our official records," said the automated call bot. "Can you please say the name of the individual you are trying to contact? We will attempt to look up their current contact code."

"She didn't give me her real name!" Sarsuk exclaimed. "She was the color of an oxygen sunset with a white underbelly, yellow orange and red up her sides, and coal black on her back, and she went by the name Nyakkat!"

"I'm sorry, this system is not primed to investigate the identities of individuals by alias or description," the robot said. "Would you like to see listings for private investigators? Or, if you believe a crime concerning this individual has occurred such as kidnapping or trafficking, I can put you in contact with your local police authority."

"Dammit!" Sarsuk slammed his head into the padding on the booth's far side. "Nyakkat, please! Saqqadr has it out for me! If they dragged away Orensan over spurious charges, what are they going to do to me?"

He looked up to that far wall, which featured a poster that read *Visit Beautiful Krakuntec II!*

Sarsuk pondered his options.

He could march right back into that secure room with the fifty MPs. He'd be nervous. If there was no obvious evidence by now, Saqqadr and the War Authority would need to frame someone. With Orensan now gone, Sarsuk was certain he was at the top of Saqqadr's hit list. Leaked War Authority intelligence was likely to bring the death penalty.

On the other claw, Nyakkat had given him a hiding place. Nobody knew but himself; even if they traced him to Krakuntec II, that was a whole planet to search. But it could have still been a lie, a scam to rid him of his money and leave him stranded with a worthless piece of property.

Even if it was a scam, it'd have to be better than whatever fate awaited him behind the wall of MPs, right? Though he wasn't absolutely *certain* that Saqqadr would point the talon at him. This could blow over. Then he could return to his regular life, his regular job, all those regular geroo…

"God in hell!" he muttered. "Operator, are you still there? Give me the flight times out of Fheighr-Alpha Station."

Eight.

Sarsuk leaped out of the taxicab when it reached the barren corner of the city street. He waved the cash card over the payment bot that followed him out. He snarled, since the cash card was not as secure as his bank account had been. What could he do though? The bank was tied to his identity, and he couldn't let anyone know he'd come here to this kitschy island in the middle of Mohowain Gulf.

But he'd made it without being spotted. He'd transferred everything to a cash card before he made a single purchase. And he would stay here for the rest of his life.

The cottage was just how he remembered it: plain and weather-beaten, hidden among the blue canopy with a view of a glass pebble beach. At first it surprised him that nobody bought up this place for development, but on closer inspection, it seemed a terrible place to build. There was no space between the ocean and the main road to place a multi-story condo, not even one with a thick elevator pillar for its base. Plus, there was that massive refinery just out of view, so long as one didn't look to the right. The trees were necessary to retain any value for this humble shack.

Regardless, Sarsuk figured he'd squat in this place for the time being. The lock wasn't too hard to open. Inside, he found much less than he'd even expected. A single wood room, with whatever finish this place once had had stripped off by the weather. In one corner, a single bed covered with sand and the smell of mildew. In another corner, a mini fridge under a countertop about two hundred years out of date. Curtains lining the windows had long since faded of color, save for the bird droppings. The boards creaked under his steps.

Well, at least he'd have time. Maybe he'd go into town and buy a proper cleaning crew to staff this place. Or he could do it himself.

Heh.

Either way, this was it. It wouldn't be too bad of a life. He'd gotten so used to eating junk food that street vendors would be a lateral move. Maybe even better. Perhaps he'd put a business together here, take initiative with his life. Do something new.

Maybe Nyakkat would come back.

Sarsuk pulled his luggage off his shoulder and dropped it next to the bed. He was considering a nap, given how much sleep the company stole from him that morning—had he managed this in ten hours?—when he noticed something on the table opposite the kitchen counter.

A red envelope. Given how little weathering it had suffered, it couldn't have been there long.

Tilting his head, Sarsuk took up the envelope. It was a thick, well-sealed coated paper that took effort to open even by ripping the leading edge with a claw. Inside was a placard note.

Sarsuk,

If you made it this far, well, that's farther than I expected.

Don't take this message the wrong way. I don't hate you; I didn't know you enough to hate you. And I'm sorry I had to drug you on our only night alone together, but I've done this long enough to know it's better to leave the target wanting. It makes them more predictable.

Yes, you were targeted. I can't say by who, just that it's not a foreign power. I'm not a traitor. If you're smart, you'll realize at once who my employer is and what we wanted from you.

Still, don't let it taint the memories. I had fun; I hope you did too. Unfortunately, this is where it ends.

—Nyakkat

Just below that, a tiny, round, transparent sticker, only noticeable against the flat color of the sheet with thin lines of gold etched in the center.

A listening device.

Sarsuk stared at the note. He caught a scent of smoldering. The card erupted into flames in his claws. He didn't even bother dropping it. The note crumbled to ash, and he was still trying to make sense of what he'd read.

He remembered the night at the festival when she leaned in close and stroked him up the thigh. She could have planted a bug on him then, something thin and transparent and hard to notice even with the military security measures. No broadcast frequency to detect, just a recording chip taking in sound.

When did she take it off? In his bed? At the pier? The bug would have had *weeks* of planning and fleet details from the secure room!

Sarsuk blinked. *She checked my wrist. Did she bug it too, to track wrist movements and get the password to my mobile com? She had all night to dig through my confidential mail!*

He'd only suspected her once she had everything she wanted.

Sarsuk twitched, as he heard a hoverplane roar overhead. He peeked out the open window, but saw nothing.

He heard someone move on the glass pebbles outside.

"Sarsuk," announced a voice. "Police Authority! Remove all personal devices and step outside with your head lowered."

She would have had everything she needed the day she drugged me...it was only one more day to the pier, when she planted the idea that this was a safe house. The messages she sent after didn't even have to be her own words, just evidence to suggest she still existed.

"You have to the count of three until we enter with full force."

I wouldn't have to come here to complete her plan, but I did... I walked right in on the assumption I was safe, but it just reinforces the evidence against me.

"One..."

I'm the only one they know who was on the inside. I'm the only one who ran. The only one with a convenient escape house, its location leaked to the authorities...

"Two..."

But...who's her employer?

"Three!"

The wall exploded into splinters. Three burly krakun in MP masks took only a half second opening to tackle him to the ground. Manacles latched over his wrists, his ankles, his neck.

"Sarsuk of Vestacorneria," the commandant declared, "you have been charged with espionage against the War Authority, breach of oath to secrecy, embezzlement of property in relation to government contracts, and tax evasion. What is your defense?"

"It was her!" Sarsuk pleaded. "I did nothing! It was Nyakkat, the krakun who looked like a coal fire!"

The blue commandant stepped in, boards creaking under his weight. Sarsuk, face to the dust on the floor, pinned under three officers, caught sight of the commandant as he walked up and leaned down. The black mask made his cold demeanor colder.

"Is this going to be your defense?" the commandant asked. "That you were fooled by a third party into taking these actions?"

"The espionage, definitely," Sarsuk whimpered.

"When you receive your legal counsel, I suggest you take their advice and argue a different strategy," the commandant said. "Because accessory to espionage in this degree carries the same penalty."

"I can plea bargain!" Sarsuk cried. "I can give descriptions! Everything!"

"We already have everything. Pictures of your accomplice in particular. Your additional role in the investigation will be unnecessary."

Oh...she also recorded our rendezvous at the pier...but they'll never identify her...

"Anything else?"

Damn me.

"Take him in."

A cage clasped over Sarsuk's muzzle. The last thing he saw as the three hauled him away was the breached wall of the small cottage, now ruined, the roof barely standing on the open side, under a single remaining post. He had almost gotten to like it for the brief minutes he was there. He wondered if he could have made something of the place.

Casting his eyes at the shimmering sky, he wondered what he'd done to deserve any of this.

End.

Special thanks to the Hayven Celestia Discord server for their help in editing the second edition, especially to Gre7g Luterman, Ryan Desmond, and Conrad Clement.

Read more books and stories by Rick Griffin
www.rickgriffinstudios.com

The second book in Final Days of the White Flower II
The Captain's Oath

The Hayven Celestia Anthology
Tales of Hayven Celestia

Read other stories in the Hayven Celestia universe
by Gre7g Luterman
Skeleton Crew
Small World
Fair Trade
Reaper's Lottery
Long Way Home

The geroo will return!

Made in the USA
Monee, IL
12 February 2022